MEDICAL

Sometimes the Worst Complication is Standing Right in Front of You.

NECESSITY

J. WILLIS

A Novel By

MITCHELL

SnowPack
publishing

Medical Necessity

ISBN — 13: 978-0692569580

(SnowPack Public Relations LLC — Publishing)

Copyright © 2016

SnowPack Public Relations LLC — Publishing

This is a work of fiction. Names, characters, places, incidents are the product of the author's imagination or are used fictitiously. Any resemblance to actual events, locales, or persons, living or dead, is entirely coincidental. Any real places or products, such as Charlottesville or Mercedes, are used fictitiously and also a use of the author's imagination.

Cover design/art, book design and book and electronic publishing layout by Clark Peak Design, Fort Collins, Colorado.

To contact the author: john@snowpackpr.com

First Edition

1st printing February 2016

This novel is dedicated to all the good people who take care of patients in hospitals every day. You know who you are.

Also dedicated to my wife Paula. Without her love, I wouldn't have amounted to anything.

CHAPTER
Bicentennial Baby
ONE

Royce Wexler never imagined that one day his job would be to babysit grownups.

It was 7 a.m. and he, the hospital CEO, sat in a lavish conference room with 15 others at Ascend Medical Center in Charlottesville, VA, or, "Ass-End" Medical Center, as its very unengaged workforce called the place. Most in the room were doctors who comprised the Medical Executive Committee, the physician leaders of the medical staff. The purpose of the meeting was to conduct the business of the medical staff with the hospital. But, more often than not, the personal grudges, grievances, and financial interests of each of the physicians present set the agenda. It was the place where most of the quarrels in the hospital were seeded.

At the moment Wexler was listening to Denise DeLuca, MD a pulmonologist under contract as medical director of the hospital's Intensive Care Unit. She was working up a slow tantrum, the target of which was Kate Reynolds, RN. Kate was the hospital Quality Director, a recently promoted young, enthusiastic and capable nurse with a new master's degree in business. Dr. DeLuca was neither enthusiastic nor capable and she hated anyone who was.[1]

[1]For cast of characters list see page 289–290

"I can't believe you brought this form to this meeting for approval when you haven't even bothered to have it reviewed at the internal medicine department level," she droned softly. Dr. DeLuca cultivated a quiet, whispered demeanor to disguise a mean streak. It was no secret — she told anyone who would listen — she was bullied and scorned as a child by her family and schoolmates. At times, she was a very competent, good doctor. Dr. DeLuca took great care of her patients — at least the patients she liked. Patient, family, or doctor, she could be either your greatest friend or your worst enemy.

"Dr. DeLuca, this form was approved at the Internal Medicine Department meeting last month," Kate Reynolds explained patiently. She looked down at a list. "You were not in attendance."

Dr. DeLuca sat back in her chair and looked straight at Wexler. "That's because I was busy saving lives," she sniffed softly, her standard answer whenever she was not where she was supposed to be. Dr. DeLuca wrinkled her nose slightly, which pulled her top lip up, exposing her two front teeth. This was a sure sign, her "beaver sneer" Wexler thought of it, that she was preparing to be very unreasonable.

Medicare required the form as part of pilot study project, one of several quality measurements first conceived by the government. It was one of many newly proposed measurable goals, known as Core Measures instituted by the government. This was nothing but a pain in the ass, as far as Wexler was concerned. But part of his sizable annual bonus, per the hospital's corporate office, was dependent upon gathering data for the study.

He had anticipated Dr. DeLuca's pushback and right before the meeting had pulled Dr. Paul Forrest aside for a word. Dr. Forrest was the Chief of Cardiology and Dr. DeLuca's primary handler. Dr. Forrest, who bore a resemblance to a famous television doctor, always sat directly across from Dr. DeLuca at the Medical Executive meetings. Before DeLuca could launch into one of her indignant hushed tirades, Dr. Forrest cut her off.

"Dr. DeLuca, may I suggest that we approve this form — which I agree is another example of government interference in our independent medical judgment," he said with an offhand laugh. He spoke in an authoritative, deep voice that never failed to mesmerize Dr. DeLuca. She owed much to Dr. Forrest, who was the immediate past Chief of Staff. He had helped quash a disciplinary complaint filed by another physician stemming from the death of a patient. With Dr. Forrest's help, a nurse was blamed for Dr. DeLuca's medical mistake and fired.

"Very well Dr. Forrest — I trust your judgment," Dr. DeLuca smiled broadly, flaunting an ongoing conspiracy. It was not lost on anyone in the room that elderly patients in the hospital with pneumonia were a good source of consulting revenue for both doctors.

Wexler paid no attention to the rest of the meeting. Approval of the study form was the only agenda item in which he was interested. It had cost him $90,000 for a new echo machine the hospital did not need. Wexler would have to make it up somewhere else in his capital budget, which meant denying a department manager needed funds to improve care. But, such was the burden of leadership.

Forty miles away in Valley View, Leo Miller made the final turn into the parking lot of Valley View General Hospital, a 75-bed, community-owned facility in a bedroom town outside Charlottesville. It was Tuesday, the day the Unitarian Church across the street changed the message on the marquee in front of its very modest building. "Take care; the word once spoken, takes on a life of its own." Up the street the mega Christian Life Church had gone with "Evolution — the Greatest Hoax on Earth" on their flashy electronic pedestal sign.

Leo pondered the Unitarian posting for a few moments, deciding that it had direct applications to one of his first chores of the day, which was to address "disruptive behavior" with a doctor — healthcare talk for someone who was acting like a jerk. Once again Leo was reminded that he spent 80 percent of his time dealing with the 20 percent of people who were a problem. Working in hospitals for the past 15 years, ten as an administrator, Leo had learned that doctors' stick together. Even the occasionally crazy or medically incompetent physician has a cheering section right up until their medical license is suspended. Leo's position was even more precarious because he was new to Valley View, starting his job as CEO and Administrator just three months earlier.

Leo liked to get to the hospital early enough to visit on the patient floors before his day unwound. In addition to an average of four scheduled meetings a day, invariably at least one crisis erupted that required him to rearrange his priorities — often hourly. The first thing each morning he headed to the medical floors to see staff and to visit patients in their rooms.

Up on the second floor, Leo smiled to see the Martin sisters, Ethyl and Mary. They were an odd pair. In their mid-40's, Ethyl was 14 months older than Mary. They lived together, slept in twin beds in the same room, traveled to work together — in fact they went everywhere together. Devout Baptists, they were like a combination of missionaries and an old married couple. They could clean a room faster than any housekeepers he had ever seen. This meant that the hospital did not have to assign a third housekeeper to the floor, as would be required in any other hospital of similar size. It had actually been tried. But while not hostile, the two sisters did not know how to fit a third person into their perfectly choreographed work routine.

The sisters offered other competencies as well. It was a rare patient who did not feel better in their presence as they comforted and laughed their way through their chores. It was "honey" this and "sweetie that" and the old folks in the hospital just ate it up. The Martin sisters had their fans, as some of the patients from the area nursing homes insisted on being hospitalized at Valley View just to visit with the sisters. They had worked at the hospital since they graduated from high school. The one thing they were not used to was a hospital administrator on the floor every day. It was a habit for which they did not care; they viewed Leo's daily visits with suspicion.

"Good morning ladies," Leo greeted the sisters as they swarmed around their housekeeping cart, grabbing cleaning cloths and emptying trash cans.

"Morning," Ethyl replied gruffly, not making eye contact. She normally spoke for the two. "Is there anything wrong?"

Leo laughed. "Ethyl — you ask me that every morning when you see me — I'm beginning to think you don't like me. How are the patients doing today?"

"My sister and I are just housekeepers, you have to ask the nurses," Ethyl answered. Leo knew he would not get an answer out of the sisters.

"It smells really good up here, clean," Leo said, flattering. He noticed the faintest of smiles cross the sisters' faces.

Leo moved on to the nursing station to check in with the Nursing House Supervisor. Part house mother and part master sergeant, the capabilities of any House Sup (pronounced like soup) determined if a hospital CEO got called in the middle of the night once a week or once a year.

"Hi Linda — anything going on this morning that I should know about?" Linda Murphy was short and stout with gray hair and dimples like little smiles.

"Hi Leo. You'll want to know about Mr. Rigton in Room 234. I don't think they've been in since you started — probably vacationing at the hospitals in Arizona," she said; Leo laughed. "He's upset because we keep reducing his meals. He orders enough food for several family members, who all think they have won a free vacation when one of them is lucky enough to be admitted into the hospital." Linda handed Leo a copy of the patient's last two meal orders.

"Why is Mr. Rigton here?"

"Cellulitis — and he's upset because we won't take him outside to smoke."

Leo knocked on the door and asked if he could enter. A gruff voice replied "Sure — it's a free world." Mr. Rigton was rail thin and bearded with slicked back dark hair. Two overweight women sat with him, one his wife, the other his daughter.

"Who are you?" the wife demanded.

"I'm Leo Miller, the Administrator. I've come by to see if we are taking good care of Mr. Rigton today."

The daughter snorted. "This is the worst hospital we've ever been in."

Leo looked concerned. "Is this the first time a family member has been in our hospital?" he asked. Leo already knew the answer. The daughter did not respond.

"So, what seems to be the problem today?" Leo continued.

Mr. Rigton lurched into a sitting position. "For starters, I can't smoke. And second, I can't get anything to eat around here."

Leo made a show of flipping through the mostly blank pages on his clipboard.

"I'm confused Mr. Rigton. According to your chart you had a big breakfast of eggs, bacon and pancakes this morning and last night you had roast beef, mashed potatoes and chocolate cake for dessert. Are you hungry now? I can ask your nurse to bring you a snack."

The patient looked at his wife with a frown. It was not unusual for patients to complain that they were not receiving food, pain medications and baths, or nurse attention at the bedside. Often the patients were confused and simply did not remember their care. It is rare that such a complaint could not be gently refuted with what's written down in the patient's chart. Leo preferred to think of it as educating the patient — except in such cases of Mr. Rigton and family, who were clearly hustling the system. Such patients appeared a few times a month — poor people who rarely had their voice heard. These patients and their families used the interpersonal skills they knew — to be demanding, accusatory, insulting and suspicious.

"They won't bring him the food he wants," his wife said.

"Mrs. Rigton," Leo said gently, "the reason we don't want patients ordering extra food for their family to eat is that it is very important for a patient's recovery that we measure what they eat. When extra food is ordered for family members, it makes it difficult for the nurses and doctors to do their jobs."

She looked away.

"I can provide you a $5 meal ticket for the cafeteria for today if that would be helpful," Leo said.

"There's two of them — what good is one pass going to do?" Mr. Rigton answered, attempting to provide for his family the only way he knew how.

"Well, I'll leave it here on the bedside table if you change your mind," Leo said. "As far as the smoking Mr. Rigton, you are receiving IV antibiotics for a very serious flesh infection. If you start moving around in a non-sterile environment, your condition can get worse. Has the hospitalist offered you nicotine patches?"

"Do you smoke?" Mr. Rigton replied. "Because if you did, you would know it ain't the same."

"I understand it's hard work being a patient, Mr. Rigton," Leo offered. "You listen to your doctor and nurses and you'll be out of here soon. I'll stop by tomorrow to see how you're doing," Leo said cheerfully as he left.

Leo headed downstairs to find the Chief of Staff, Akil Massari, M.D. Dr. Massari was an internal medicine specialist, originally from Egypt, who had been practicing at the hospital for two years.

Dr. Massari was an excellent doctor much admired by his peers for his gentle nature. He had masterful clinical skills and maintained an absolute refusal to be intimidated by medical staff politics. The doctor had been hired away by the previous administrator from Ascend Medical Center where he had grown tired of the likes of Dr. DeLuca and her constant toxic trouble making. Dr. DeLuca told the administrator that patients could not understand Dr. Massari's English. She started this rumor because she was upset Dr. Massari removed a patient from her care.

Dr. Massari was now the Medical Director for Valley View's hospitalist program, his job to oversee the management and care of inpatients. While he had been apprehensive about the arrival of a new hospital CEO, Dr. Massari appreciated Leo Miller's willingness to deal with problems. The radiologist they were meeting with this morning was definitely a known problem.

Several times in the past year the staff had noted and documented worrisome behavior on the part of the radiologist. From what Leo could tell, this radiologist had traveled from one hospital to another and state-to-state over the last several years. Bad doctors could hide out for years by moving around. While the creation of a national data bank for physicians with proven and ruled upon problems — ranging from sexual harassment to addiction to criminal behavior — had been finally implemented, it was still a dicey business for a hospital administrator to hold a doctor accountable.

Under extraordinary circumstances, Leo could summarily suspend a physician's privileges, but this was a risky move for any CEO, especially for a new CEO. A hospital's medical staff resented any hospital administrator unduly meddling in their affairs. But ultimately, the hospital CEO was responsible for patient safety.

Every medical staff has at least a few problem doctors and everyone who works in the hospital knows who they are. For the average hospital CEO at any hospital, much of their discretionary time is spent dealing with this handful of doctors.

Dr. Massari greeted Leo in the lobby.

"Leo, how are you this morning?" This was a question Dr. Massari asked each day with the utmost sincerity.

"Better now for seeing you my friend," Leo answered, as always. Both men smiled; they liked each other. "You ready?" Leo asked. "He is not going to be a stand up guy about this. The smart, crazy ones never are."

Dr. Massari nodded solemnly. "I believe you, Leo."

———

Flip Jensen peaked early in life. He was the first baby born in the bicentennial year — 1976 — at Ascend Medical Center. An Internet search shows a photo of Flip in his mother's hospital bed swaddled in a red, white and blue blanket hand-knitted by a hospital volunteer, who was the widow of a Medal of Honor recipient.

Born James Jefferson Jensen, he had been lavished with gifts and awards in a gift basket designed to appear as a Minute Man hat. Among the freebies was a full "Thomas Jefferson Patriot Scholarship" to the nearby University of Virginia, paid for by the hospital's auxiliary. Of course, none of this made the parents of the second baby born at the hospital a few minutes later feel very special. But the purpose of the recognition was not really to make anyone feel special, but to garner nationwide publicity for the hospital. On this count, the effort was very successful. Every five years or so, the hospital would entice Flip's parents back for another celebration of their son's birth, yielding more newspaper photos of Flip in patriotic costumes and settings.

By the time he started high school Flip was getting quite a bit of crap over these events from friends. Finally, in his junior year he rebelled — much to the disappointment of his parents. They had come to enjoy this ongoing special recognition for having extraordinarily good timing, as well as the limo rides and dinners that had come their way over the years. Royce Wexler had become administrator when Flip was eleven years old. Twelve years later he was tired of seeing this kid who became more sullen every time Royce saw him. He could stay home if he wanted to be around a teenager with a bad attitude.

However, the ongoing effort was a pet project of the auxiliary, which raised hundreds of thousands in funds for the hospital every year. The auxiliary helped him compete for a share of community goodwill that had historically gone to the do-gooders at the university hospital down the street. Royce was required to be enthusiastic about this wretched kid every time he saw him. Flip's feeble-minded parents, who were not any better, thought their son was a prince of some sort.

But during the last staged event, Flip had refused to disconnect from his music or wear the red, white and blue tie with the Navy blue blazer provided by the auxiliary. Instead he wore a black T-shirt with the bold pronouncement printed on the front "I'm Already Against the Next War." He insisted on the nickname his skateboarding friends had bestowed — Flip. He sported a curly blonde afro. The photo that appeared in the morning paper of Flip smirking among aghast little old Charlottesville ladies was not what the Auxiliary had in mind. That was the end of that project, much to Royce's immense relief. The once patriotic kid was a traitor to the cause of Ascend Medical Center's carefully crafted image.

Royce was meeting with his Chief Nursing Officer Stella Cooper late in the afternoon. He was reviewing staffing ratios, the number of nurses and aides that were assigned per patient. Currently they were staffed at the national average — one nurse per five patients and one aide per seven patients. Royce wanted to change the ratio to six patients per nurse.

"Royce, if we do that our patients will complain, the staff is going to get pissed-off and start looking for jobs somewhere else and our turnover will go up," the Chief Nursing Officer told him. "Not to mention the people who don't leave will have even a worse attitude than they do now."

Royce was expecting that response. "Stella — do the math. If I can reduce payroll costs by two percent we'll hit the 110 percentile on our bonus measures. You and I both come out ahead in our bank accounts if we put fewer nurses on the floor." Royce sat back and smiled broadly. "I don't see a downside."

At that moment the overhead announcement system went off. "Code Blue, ER parking lot. Code Blue, ER parking lot."

"Let me go see what that's all about," Stella said, glad for a reason to leave before she lost her temper with Royce. Any staff member who, in their judgment, felt that a patient, or anyone for that matter, was in imminent danger of dying could call a Code Blue. In her career, Stella had seen a Code Blue called on everything from a visitor choking on food, to a patient who had a heart attack following a stress test, to an inpatient reacting poorly to a medication. Occasionally a visitor would display psychosomatic symptoms to satisfy a need to be the center of attention. Stella returned about 20 minutes later.

"A guy got hit by one of our ambulances near the ER," she told Royce.

"Oh sweet mother of Jesus," Royce hissed, "this is going to look really bad on the news."

"It's worse than you know Royce," she said quietly. "It's Flip Jensen. He's on a vent and headed to x-ray."

Minutes after Flip Jensen got run over by an ambulance in front of the hospital where he was born, Ethyl Martin's pager buzzed at Valley View Hospital. As the housekeeping staff was not allowed to make phone calls except during breaks and lunchtime, she closed the door to the room she was cleaning. Ethyl used the bedside phone to call her cousin Murphy who worked at Ascend Medical Center. "A man just got hit by an ambulance in front of the ER," Murphy whispered into the phone. "The suits are going berserk because the patient is some kind of celebrity."

Ethyl hung up and dialed Channel 14 Eyewitness News Team. When the receptionist answered Ethyl asked for Luann Zahn.

CHAPTER

The Wonderful World of Management

TWO

Confrontation was contrary to Dr. Massari's nature. In Egypt, it was quickly instilled in all boys that dissent resulted in prison time, death — or even worse — torture. He had overcome great obstacles in his life to educate himself. He graduated in the top five percent of high school seniors nationwide. He got into college and medical school and then made his way to America to graduate from an internal medicine residency program. Being a man without connections in Egypt prepared him well for being a Muslim in the United States. He had to be twice as good as any American-born doctor.

Leaving Leo's office after their meeting with Dr. Divinity, his pulse pounding, it occurred to him that none of his training had prepared him to be in charge. Evidently, leadership involved a great deal of strife. Leo had coached him on this truth, grooming Dr. Massari to help manage medical staff problems.

Leo explained to Dr. Massari that based on his experience working in hospitals and with medical staffs, about 25 percent of doctors go into medicine because they really want to help people; about 25 percent go into medicine for the money and/or prestige; and the other 50 percent fell somewhere in between.

"You my friend, are in medicine for the right reason," Leo told him.

Before the meeting, Dr. Massari had greeted Leo in the lobby. The doctor had already made rounds on half of the 14 patients for whom he was caring in the hospital that day.

Leo and Dr. Massari returned to Leo's office in administration where they found Dr. Neil Divinity, the radiologist, waiting. All three entered Leo's office and sat at a small conference table. Dr. Divinity slouched in his chair and looked bored. Dr. Massari noticed there was none of the small talk that Leo usually liked to make before getting to the point. Leo spoke.

"Dr. Divinity, in the short time that I have been here at Valley View, I've received two incident reports from staff about your behavior. I also came across two other complaints filed in the past year. This week, I also had a patient complaint about you."

"Complaints by whom?" Dr. Divinity replied. He began rocking on the back legs of his chair.

Dr. Massari noticed that Leo paused and frowned. Leo later told him that Dr. Divinity's answer was a red flag. The fact that the physician did not ask the nature of the complaints, but instead wanted to know who made the complaints, indicated he was possibly more interested in retaliation than taking ownership of his actions.

"Three hospital employees, one physician and a patient — that's all you need to know for now doctor," Leo replied. "The patient who complained is the family member of a woman on whom you performed a pain block."

"Oh, you're talking about the mother of patient Lamb — she threatened to punch me you know. What are you going to do about that?"

Leo also explained to Akil that over the years he had learned that asking a question was often a diversionary tactic — another red flag.

"What did you say to her?" Leo asked, careful not to respond to Dr. Divinity's question. Dr. Massari noticed Leo answering a question with a question, a counter measure.

"Nothing. I was talking to the patient when her mother threatened to assault me. I don't appreciate being threatened in the work-place — what are you going to do about it?" Dr. Divinity asked again.

Leo picked up a paper from his desk. "According to her statement, you told her daughter to quit whining about her back pain or you might have to use a square, dull, rusty needle."

"That's a lie," Dr. Divinity stated.

"Doctor, a staff member standing outside the room overheard the conversation and reported the same conversation almost word-for-word in her incident report."

"Her?" Dr. Divinity responded. He smiled and continued. "Look, I was just kidding. I was trying to get the patient to relax. She was tense and it was just going to make the stick more painful for her if she didn't loosen up. But you wouldn't know that — you're not a doctor. I'm not going to tolerate family members being present in the future when I perform pain blocks if this is what I have to put up with." He looked at Dr. Massari.

"It's a hostile work environment in the OR when I'm threatened with being punched. You're the Chief of Staff — what are you going to do about it?" Dr. Divinity almost snarled, suddenly popping his chair down on all four legs and glaring at Dr. Massari. Dr. Massari surprised himself by speaking in a firm, steady voice.

"Dr. Divinity — I am here as a courtesy. Leo tells me that he is giving you a heads-up about this problem. He also tells me the next step, if you do not modify your behavior, is that he will turn over what documentation he has to the credentials committee for review and possible disciplinary action."

Dr. Divinity exhaled sharply. "Look, I don't need some primary care doctor telling me what I should be doing. Are we done?" This was an especially pointed insult. Specialists, including radiologists, sometimes considered themselves superior to noninvasive, primary care doctors who make much less money.

"Dr. Divinity," Leo replied. "I need you to hear what I'm saying. The first thing is that you are not to make any attempt to find out who filed these incident reports. For the time being, these reports are not going anywhere except right here in my office. Second, you first claimed that the mother was lying and then you admitted you made the statement. That means you are not being truthful to me."

"I told you, I was just trying to get the patient to relax!" Dr. Divinity said, raising his voice.

"Yeah, I heard you say that," Leo answered. "Here's the problem doctor — it didn't work — you upset the patient. You don't recognize that you created this entire episode through your insensitivity. See the difference? The three other reports also cite examples of upsetting patients with callous remarks that run contrary to conveying to patients that you care about them. One of the incident reports also states that you often infer to employees that you will make sure they lose their job."

"Give me an example," Dr. Divinity demanded.

"Dr. Divinity I hope I don't have to do that. As Dr. Massari said, this is a courtesy meeting to let you know that you are now on my radar. If you cannot figure out the problem about your own behavior, I can refer you to a personal coach who might be able to help you."

"Sure," Dr. Divinity said. "As long as you pay for it."

"I don't think so," Leo replied. "You have to have some cash in the game or you won't take it seriously."

"Listen Mr. CEO," Dr. Divinity said. "I've been working at this hospital for four years. You're brand new. You really think this is a smart move on your part? How come no one has ever complained about me before if this is such a big problem?"

Leo was not surprised to hear Dr. Divinity's not so veiled threat. But he knew that critical conversations about behavior did not get any easier with time.

"Doctor, to answer your second question, I can't speak for what happened before I arrived. But in the short time I have been here, I am very concerned about five documented complaints. I don't tolerate disruptive behavior because it's a good way for a hospital to get sued by its own employees for a hostile work environment and a good way to do harm to a patient. As to your first question, which actually sounds like a threat, I hold everyone responsible for their actions regardless of how long they have been working here."

Dr. Massari looked at Dr. Divinity. "Listen Neil — Leo is trying to help you out here. Why don't you meet him half way?"

"There's something you should know about me," Dr. Divinity said almost as an after thought. "I don't do anything half way."

"All right, I'm going to go ahead and end this meeting right here — I think we've covered everything," Leo said. "You need to read your contract, doctor — which I can terminate for cause due to unprofessional behavior. Consider this a verbal warning. But I want to repeat myself — you are not to say anything to anyone about the incident reports or try to determine who turned in the reports. You and I are going to have a problem if you do."

"Oh — great more threats," Dr. Divinity sighed. He looked at Leo with eyes that were vacant — shark eyes — and said. "You say it was a she who reported me?" He smirked again and stood up to leave, but paused in the doorway.

"You really think you're going to get another radiologist as good as me to come to this shit hole hospital?" He made sure to slam the door on his way out.

Leo looked at Dr. Massari, who sat wide-eyed and stunned.

"Welcome to the wonderful world of management Akil," Leo said. "You hungry? I'm buying breakfast."

When Leo Miller returned to his office from breakfast with Dr. Massari, his Chief Financial Officer, Marianne Quarters, and Chief Nursing Officer Ben Stall sat in the waiting area drinking coffee and chatting with their Administrative Assistant Jayne Vargas-Smith. Vargas translated to "steep hill" in Spanish, an apt description of Jayne's journey early in her life. Jayne was a young 27 year-old woman of stunning beauty who, at age six, was hit in the face with a swing blade by a deaf uncle. Jayne had walked up to her beloved uncle in what she thought was his peripheral vision to let him know lunch was ready. The resulting accident had required Jayne to undergo numerous plastic surgeries. Starting at the temple, the scar passed the corner of her eye and ended at her chin, a thin, shocking white line on her olive complexion. In her senior year in high school, Jayne finally abandoned attempts to cover the scar with make-up after her future husband, a classmate, convinced her that the contrasting imperfection only served to heighten her natural born beauty. It was a mature point-of-view for a young man and Jayne deeply loved her husband for helping her to accept herself as she was. Leo found Jayne to be extremely poised and confident for such a young woman. When there was a problem she almost always offered a solution. She also did a great job of managing the many people who vied for Leo's attention every day.

Leo took pride in the fact that when he started a new position he was always able to work with the staff he inherited. However, his policy was being severely strained by Marianne Quarters, the CFO. Like most CFOs with whom Leo had worked, Marianne's view of a hospital is that it was an accounting firm that did healthcare. Decisions were to be made solely based on the financial numbers with little consideration to the human component of a problem or opportunity. A mentor had warned Leo early in his career about this tendency.

"Remember Leo," the veteran administrator cautioned, "lawyers and accountants are absolutely necessary in hospital management, but don't ever let them make decisions for you. That's your job." His new CFO was often sullen and uncommunicative, punctuated occasionally by angry outbursts of dissent any time Leo contemplated spending funds that in her opinion were not absolutely necessary or already budgeted. After three months, he was growing weary of her moodiness. At the moment, she was talking to Ben and Jayne enthusiastically about her grandchildren, the only subject which seemed to cheer her up.

Ben Stall was an affable, somewhat effeminate and pudgy young man. Ben was a very sensitive fellow, Leo had come to realize, which made him very popular and respected with a mostly female nursing staff. His nursing background was in intensive care. Ben had been the Chief Nursing Officer for two years.

The three administrators relocated to a small conference table in Leo's Office.

"How did the meeting go with Dr. Divinity this morning?" Ben asked.

"About like you would expect," Leo said.

"The guy is scary," Ben replied. "I've been working at this hospital for five years and the entire time I've kept an eye out for him. None of the nurses go to Radiology unless they have to. This results in quite the power struggle between the nurses and radiology staff about who is going to transport the patient. That guy is always looking to amuse himself at some else's expense."

"He brings in a lot of revenue from those image guided pain blocks," Marianne injected. "The referring doctors increased their referrals to him by about ten percent a year over the last three years ever since Dr. Divinity got trained in that procedure."

"Yeah, that's true," Ben answered. Leo noticed that Ben tended to work both sides of an issue. "Before Dr. Divinity got privileges to do pain blocks, we had to rely on the anesthesiologists. They treat any department outside the OR like an after thought. They were often late or not available, which really screwed up the CT and MRI schedules."

"Which reduces revenue," Marianne added. She began clicking her pen, something Leo noticed she did when she did not agree with the direction of the conversation.

"So it sounds like his behavior has been a known problem for some time," Leo said, "and no attempt has ever been made to get him to change because he makes a lot of money for the hospital — that's what I am hearing you both tell me?" Leo asked.

Ben looked away and Marianne clicked and clicked.

In the Ascend Medical Center ICU Dr. Denise DeLuca sat perched on a high stool at the nursing station. This was her favorite place in the world, her universe, where she was master. She had originally chosen this spot because it was adjacent to the chart rack. With a turn of

her head in either direction, Dr. DeLuca had visual contact with any
of the 10 ICU beds and their patients. She could also closely monitor
all conversations between the hospital staff, including phone calls.
Some staff wrote notes to each other until they figured out that Dr.
DeLuca could read upside down. The nurses and assistants switched
to emails but the administration put a stop to this practice when Dr.
DeLuca sanctimoniously complained that it was distracting the staff
from patient care. She herself, however, was free to continue emailing
her many contacts throughout the hospital. With the introduction of
electronic medical records, Dr. DeLuca could pull patient records up
on the computer monitor she had set up at the ICU desk. She missed
the old paper charts, which sometimes lent themselves to making
changes in the medical record after the fact — very handy for covering
up mistakes or shifting blame. Occasionally she would have a phan-
tom impulse to reach for the chart rack where the old records nested
like bullets in an ammo belt. There were also cameras in the patient
rooms with a zoom lens, so she could access patients on the computer
screen without leaving the ICU desk.

These technological advancements gave her more time and oppor-
tunity at the desk to keep up a running commentary with the staff.
Dr. DeLuca was always on the look out for a new convert or any dis-
loyalty among existing followers. Not surprisingly, the ICU at Ascend
Medical Center had a high turnover rate, which was blamed on the
ICU Nursing Manager Margret Stephenson. Each year, one-third of
Margret's performance pay was based on keeping ICU nursing turn
over below 15 percent, a measure she never met.

However she had been hand selected, after just two years out of
nursing school, for the manager position by Dr. DeLuca who coached
her in completing her master's degree program. Dr. DeLuca insisted
the hospital cover the costs. Margret had just completed her course
work and received her degree and now she was contemplating being
part of the turnover herself. However, if she left before four years, she
would have to repay the hospital for the cost of her degree. Even if
Margret transferred to another management position in the hospital,

Dr. DeLuca would still find a way to extract revenge for such disloyalty. The doctor's tentacles ran deep in the organization.

At the moment, Dr. DeLuca was reviewing Flip Jensen's medical records.

"This is the worst case of AP I've seen," Dr. DeLuca commented out loud. Angie Simms, a very pretty woman who had dreamed of a career in nursing her entire life, knew that she was expected to participate in the conversation.

"AP?" Angie asked.

"Ambulance poisoning," Dr. DeLuca deadpanned in response.

Dr. DeLuca was in a good mood. Flip Jensen, celebrity baby, was now all hers. He was in a coma and on a ventilator. This was a high profile patient and she knew it was only a matter of time before she would be issuing statements to the press in her crisp white lab coat with a stethoscope around her neck. She got little shivers just thinking about the coming media storm.

In the meantime, Flip's parents were in the adjoining waiting room, waiting on the arrival of Dr. DeLuca to brief them on their son's condition and allow them into his room. She had decided to allow only one parent at a time to visit — divide and conquer. She would cite infection control issues for this arbitrary policy — Flip was scraped up and at risk for bedsores. She had not forgotten their indifference when she attended Flip's last hospital sanctioned birthday celebration. They were going to have to earn her approval.

Her desk phone rang.

"Denise — it's Royce. Luann Zahn from the Eye Witless News Team is on her way. We need to huddle. Can you come down to my office?"

"Of course, Royce," Denise said airily. "This is no worry at all — we will wrestle this to the ground. Just give me a few minutes to speak to the patient's parents and I will be right down." She placed the phone back in the cradle and did a couple of spins in her chair, before dismounting like a little kid in gymnastics class. ICU manager Margret Stephenson walked into the unit just in time to witness these aerobics. Margret exchanged a brief glance of dread with Angie, who was caring for Flip. There was always a price to pay for Dr. DeLuca's euphoria, because it never lasted.

***

Brittany Sawyer, emergency room R.N., swore under her breath. The next patient chart was one Owen Gregor. Gregor was well known to the emergency room staff at Valley View Hospital. He came in several times a month.

"Sawyer, you sound like a sailor with a boil on his butt," said Rachael Diller, M.D. the emergency room doctor who had previously practiced eight years in the Navy.

"That's because Owen Gregor is the next patient up," Brittany answered.

"Fuck," exclaimed Dr. Diller.

'That's what I said," laughed Brittany.

"Son-of-a-bitch," Dr. Diller continued.

"I said that too," Brittany admitted.

Dr. Diller had encountered Owen Gregor on her very first shift at the hospital. He had presented himself at 1 a.m., two hours after she began work. Amazingly, he knew that it was her first night. He had presented with a severe toothache. She wrote a prescription for Percocet and referred him to an oral surgeon.

"Oh yeah, the Owen Gregors of the world know which doctors will likely give them the candy," Brittany had explained to her later. "I can guarantee that he also knows which car you drive too." Dr. Diller looked alarmed. After eight years of caring for sailors and military families, the likes of Owen Gregor — who seemed to have no other purpose in life than working the emergency room for pills, food and the occasional overnight stay — was a shock to her ordered system.

"Why would he know which car I drive?," Dr. Diller asked.

"Because that way he can cruise through the parking lot and see which doctor is on duty. He knows which doctors he can work for meds," Brittany had explained. "If he doesn't like what he sees, he drives to the next hospital. Remember — this is his job. He takes some of the pills himself, but he sells a lot of them to other slackers for money to pay his expenses and buy food."

Brittany entered the exam room. Owen was, at 24, already an expert medical malingerer. He was stocky and bearded with the words "Hell" and "Deth" tattooed on his fingers above the knuckles, one letter for each finger. He looked healthy. The nurses had learned a long time ago not to be the least bit sympathetic to Owen Gregor. He commenced moaning and grimacing when Brittany walked into the exam room.

"Good morning, Mr. Gregor, what seems to be the problem?" Brittany asked, starting the dance.

"Ahhh — I've got a real bad pain in my gut," he gasped. "I think it's my hereditary pancreatitis acting up." Brittany almost laughed out loud. His pulse was normal, his muscles relaxed and he was not perspiring.

"The doctor will be in to see you as soon as possible," she said. Owen stopped his writhing and moaning on the gurney where he lay. "It better not take an hour like last time," he growled. "I might fall down." Brittany turned around and stepped to his bedside where she reached across and put up the bedrails.

"We wouldn't want that to happen. Here's your call light," she said laying the wired control next to him. "Pushing it every five minutes will not get the doctor in here any faster," she advised and left.

Brittany found Dr. Diller at the physician station, making notes in another patient's chart. She laid Gregor's record on the desk.

"Let me guess," said Dr. Diller, "He's got a toothache?" Brittany shook her head.

"One of his favorite complaints, I agree — but nope."

"Back pain?"

"Not even close."

"Chest pain?"

"You're getting warmer."

Dr. Diller flipped open the chart and read Brittany's notes. She almost snorted the coffee she was drinking out of her nose. "Hereditary pancreatitis? Looks like someone got access to the Internet," she said.

"Yes, they have computers at the public library now," Brittany said.

"Let him wait," Dr. Diller instructed. "I've got sick people who need me."

"He's threatening to fall down," Brittany informed the doctor. After his fall, he would complain of arm or leg pain, which would require an unnecessary trip to Radiology and an x-ray for which the hospital would not get paid — Owen ignored all hospital bills. It would also mean another patient in actual need of an imaging scan would have to wait.

"My vote is go ahead and see him," Brittany advised the doctor. "He's either looking for pain meds or to get admitted for a few days — a cot and three hots. Just don't give him what he wants, and let's get him out the door. The worst thing that will happen is he'll be back the next time all the sooner."

"OK, but you're going in with me," Dr. Diller instructed.

About 10 minutes later the two women burst into the exam room. As expected, the patient was lying with his hands behind his head, watching the wall-mounted television. He momentarily appeared to be very comfortable and at ease, which instantly changed to moans of pain as he flipped over on his side and rolled up into the fetal position.

"Mr. Gregor, just so you know, I'm not prescribing any narcotic pain medications for you today," Dr. Diller said. Gregor's discomfort immediately intensified. "I think I needed to be admitted," he gasped. "They can control my pain better up on the floor with an IV drip."

"I need to examine your stomach," Dr. Diller responded, snapping on a pair of rubber gloves. The patient did his best to lie still, his convulsing legs rubbing out a rhythm on the gurney pad.

"So Mr. Gregor," the doctor asked while she felt around his abdomen, "why do you think you have pancreatitis?" she asked.

"Hereditary pancreatitis," he corrected. "My uncle had it."

"Hereditary pancreatitis is very unusual, as 90% of pancreatitis is caused by excessive alcohol consumption. The only way to confirm hereditary pancreatitis is be tested for it," Dr. Diller informed Owen. "Just because your uncle had it does not mean you have it."

"I was tested," Owen stated, his agitation increasing. "At the medical college."

Dr. Diller did not feel any rigidness or spasms in his abdomen.

"There is only one hospital in the country that tests for hereditary pancreatitis, Mr. Gregor and I'll give you a hint — it's not in Virginia," Dr. Diller advised as she stepped back from the gurney and opened his chart. "Mr. Gregor you've been in this emergency room approximately 55 times in the past twelve months. We've run blood work on you approximately 45 times and there is not any record of you ever reporting pancreatitis or any lab results indicating that you suffer from that condition — or any condition, for that matter. I also note that you have been prescribed pain pills about 30 times. I'm more worried that you may be addicted to pain pills, than have an alcohol problem."

Gregor became still and glared at the doctor. "You calling me a liar?"

Brittany took a few steps backwards, opened the exam room door and stood halfway in the hallway, ready to call for help.

"Mr. Gregor, I'm telling you what I know as a fact as a doctor. If that upsets you, that's your problem." Dr. Diller held Owen's bad-ass stare with indifference. Owen finally jumped off the cot and grabbed his jacket from the foot of the gurney.

"I want to see the administrator right now," he yelled, storming out the door and headed towards the lobby. "I'm going to sue both of you," he hollered back over his shoulder.

Brittany picked up the chart. "Do I chart this as a miracle cure or patient left against medical advice?"

"Against medical advice — with prejudice," Dr. Diller replied. She left the exam room to find a sick person.

CHAPTER

"Badside" Manner

THREE

Luann Zahn, a television reporter with the Channel 6 Eye Witness News Team, hung up the phone with Ethyl Martin, a housekeeper at Valley View hospital. When they had met the year before, Luann was sick, depressed and questioning every aspect of her life. Her work consisted of running down the details of car accidents (the holy grail of local news reporting), assaults, murders, missing people and badgering public officials all in the pursuit of a 25 to 40 second story in which she would present herself as an expert on the topic at hand.

She had learned all the reporter tricks — how to tilt her head just so, lift her eyebrows and open her hand in a grand presentation as she talked to the lens to convey sincerity. Her voice spoke a hard edge to give authority. After three years of grinding out five stories a week, she knew it was a stupid, dishonorable way to make a living. But the perks of being recognized were just too good to give up.

She was struggling through this loop of self-doubt, fed by her illness and desertion by her girlfriend, who was not interested in being supportive of a hospital stay into its third week. She had even dramatically considered suicide. But when she thought of her own death being fodder for the news beast that she fed every day, she just couldn't do it.

Ethyl and Mary Martin turned out to be just what she needed. They traipsed into her hospital room chattering away and laughing about someone in their church who had tried an online date without much success. Mary invited Luann into the conversation while she reached under her bed with a broom.

"Now why would anyone go to the worldwide inter-web to find someone for a date?" Mary asked Luann.

The question startled Luann. No one had asked her opinion about anything since she had fallen ill. Instead, her conversations had centered on answering questions from doctors who had many theories about why she needed to be in the hospital. There was endless speculation about white blood cell counts, reoccurring fevers and spots on her tongue. Specialists were summoned and more tests were run. The nurses were mostly nice, but very task oriented with many patients for whom to care.

Gradually, she began to improve. It was Dr. Massari, the hospitalist, and his gift for diagnostics that had helped her medically. Over the course of a few weeks, he was able to convince the gastroenterologist, the allergist, the pulmonologist and her family doctor to allow him to manage her care. He discontinued most of their therapies and added a combination of antibiotics and physical therapy. Dr. Massari understood a truth that all really good doctors admit only to themselves and few others: patients often get better for no apparent reason. A smart doctor tries to stay out of the way and get a patient out of the hospital as soon as possible before any harm can be done.

"I did — found someone through an Internet dating site," Luann answered. Ethyl stopped sweeping and leaned on her broom. Mary slowed as she carried the trash out of the bathroom. Everything the sisters knew about romance and relationships they had gleaned from an English version of a Spanish soap opera about a group of real estate agents. They had watched the program five days a week since they were 15, still depending upon their ancient VCR to record the program each day. It seems all those empty houses for sale full of neatly made beds, stocked bars and cozy sitting areas can be quite convenient. Deceit, moral turpitude, quarrels, dirty deals, betrayal and jealousy are all standard fare in the world of real estate. However, the characters in "By Appointment Only" never spent any time at a computer, just as the sisters themselves had no use for the Internet, email or cell phones.

"Why did you do that?" Ethyl asked.

"It saves time — I work a lot," Luann offered. "Also, I found some-one that was much like myself." Mary spoke up again.

"And how has that worked out — I mean dating someone like your-self?" Mary asked, genuinely interested.

Luann understood that Mary's question was not intended to be cruel. But there it was: a big, ugly, obvious truth. She first looked stunned and then began to softly cry. The Martin sisters each took a side of the bed and sat down to do something they did even better than cleaning rooms — saving patients from themselves.

Luann remembered all of this as she hung up the phone from speaking to Ethyl about the accident at Ascend Medical Center. The sisters were with her every day until she was discharged, even coming in on their days off to visit. Luann — who was chronically scheduled and overbooked in every aspect of her life — had weeks to think. Unplugged from her life, and feeling depressed and vulnerable, her misplaced priorities and moments of unkindness stood out above her professional accomplishments. No wonder her girlfriend — who was just like herself — bugged out.

"Call me when you're better," her girlfriend had said during her last visit. "I didn't sign on to be a caregiver."

Luann vowed improvement.

She made peace with the fact that local television news was the dumb jock of the news family. With her newfound insight she was able to convince the news director to allow her to start a nightly fea-ture titled "Ironically Speaking". Double standards, hypocrisy, dumb decisions and planned lunacy were the focus of the program. And she didn't care if the subject of her exposés were a station advertiser. Car dealers would keep a test driver's own car keys to pressure a sale;

banks were sloppy with old customer files that blew out of dumpsters; airport curbside luggage handlers who demanded tips up front; and environmentalist leaders who dumped their auto oil down the sewer were all fair game. Smart companies who were featured owned-up to their folly, admitted their mistake and came out looking better for the beating in the public eye. The defiant and arrogant could remain ensconced on the program for weeks, digging themselves in deeper. Within six months, "Ironically Speaking" boosted the station's evening news ratings from last place to first. In the TV news business, ratings equaled revenue.

While the old Luann would have demanded more of everything — airtime, her own news van, money — the new Luann presented a business case for expanding and syndicating "Ironically Speaking". The once a week program expanded from 60 seconds to three minutes Monday, Wednesday and Friday, and was promoted Tuesday and Thursday with 30-second teasers. Only national public television news regularly allowed its correspondents more airtime. Without asking, her salary was nicely bumped, she was named producer and editor, and she was assigned her own camera man.

Luann had called the public relations contact at Ascend Medical Center more as a courtesy to her friend Ethyl than any real sense that the story had potential. Virginia Stowe, spokeswoman at the hospital, confirmed that a visitor had been hit by one of the hospital's ambulances but the condition and identity of the patient was not yet being released.

"My contacts tell me that the patient is a known person, a celebrity," Luann said in response. There was a slight pause before the spokeswoman repeated the same information in a slightly higher pitch. It wasn't a long pause, but it was enough — a "tell" that something was up.

"You know what, Virginia? I'm coming over there with a news van — maybe I'll do a stand up in front of the ER for the 6 O'clock news," Luann answered.

"I'll call you back," Virginia answered immediately.

"OK, but make it soon before I find out what's really going on," Luann advised. "You know you won't like it if that happens."

Back in the administrative conference room for the second time that day, Dr. DeLuca munched on a piece of dark chocolate from the candy bowl in the middle of the table. She grabbed a handful and dropped these into her white lab coat with the hospital logo embroidered and her name stitched over the right pocket "Denise DeLuca, M.D. Chief of Intensive Care". She loved her lab coat and wore one everywhere, even grocery shopping.

Royce, Virginia Stowe, Stella Cooper, the CNO, and Harold Fellows, the Hospital's Manager of Security all filed into the room over the next few minutes. Royce linked the hospital's Board chairman, Jim Wallace and the hospital's attorney, Robert Wallace (the two were cousins) by speakerphone. Jim Wallace, a CPA, was the president of a large investment firm in Charlottesville and had been on the Board for eight years, the last two as chairman. Like all Board members, he was eligible to serve for 12 years. His cousin Robert had been appointed the hospital's attorney shortly after Jim had been named to the Board.

Royce convened the meeting. He started by filling in the Wallace cousins. Jim Wallace, the chairman, did not take the news well and when he did not take news well, he tended to get profane.

"Goddamnit, are you telling me that we ran over our own fucking walking billboard?" the Board Chair growled.

"Well," said Royce, "I think we may have some good news on that front. I'll ask Harold to explain."

Harold Fellows was not comfortable in meetings, especially with a room full of white people. Harold had forged a ten-year successful tenure at Ascend Medical Center with a two-year community college degree and a knack for not getting noticed. He was appointed Manager of Security, which supervised the housekeeping and security operations, when the former white director got caught running an after-hours custodial service using hospital equipment and supplies.

Harold headed off problems before they made it to his boss. He rode herd over his department employees, managing them with a mixture of fairness and discipline that kept his people fairly satisfied and in line. He trained his housekeepers to also act as unarmed security guards, equipping them with walkie-talkies. He would sometimes go weeks without a face-to-face encounter with anyone from Administration and he liked it that way. He did not like giving an opinion, as it ran contrary to his survival instincts.

Harold cleared his throat, and spoke slowly.

"I reviewed the security tapes from the ambulance bay," pointing a remote at the VCR player where he had loaded a copy of the file. He pushed the button. "While I know you gentlemen on the phone cannot see what were are watching — "

"I'll need a copy of that ASAP," said Robert Wallace, the attorney.

"Yes sir," said Harold, "I've got a courier on the way over to you counselor."

"Good, thank you," Robert replied, impressed.

"You can see on the recording that Mr. Jensen comes into the frame around a car at a stop sign and into the path of the ambulance," Harold explained.

Jim Williams seemed to cheer instantly. "What? He walked in front of the ambulance?"

"Ah — no sir, he is on a skateboard."

On the screen Flip Jensen, curly blonde hair tugging in breeze, flashes by the car in the hospital's parking lot and into the intersection. An instant later, the ambulance blurs into the frame from the right. Flip hits the side of the ambulance, bouncing hard to the pavement with a snap of his head.

"How old is the Boy Wonder?" asked Jim Wallace. Like Royce, his experience over the first bicentennial baby had not been inspiring.

"He is 23," answered his cousin, the attorney, doing the math.

"What in hell is a grown man doing riding a skateboard around?" exclaimed the Board Chair. Harold rewound the tape and set the remote down. He pushed back from the conference table slightly while everyone else leaned forward.

Dr. DeLuca was growing restless.

"Does anyone want to know how the patient is doing?" she breathed quietly.

"What was that?" Jim Wallace exclaimed, who had heard Dr. De-Luca perfectly well. "You have to speak up or sit closer to the phone, I can't hear you."

It amazed Jim Wallace that Denise DeLuca was able to get through medical school. It would probably not surprise him to learn that as a student she was a superior suck-up and when that did not work she was underhanded or whiney, whichever worked. Dr. DeLuca was not an unheard of brand of doctor, the type who got passed along at times when she had not performed well in her medical rotations. No attending or professor wanted to be left holding the bag on her when she melted down with a quiet vengeance. Denise made it her business to know who was taking amphetamines to stay awake, which of the faculty was copping a feel (never with her of course, but she was known to fabricate such a claim when needed) and, with her ability to read any document upside down, what medical mistakes were sitting on the desks of her attending instructors.

Dr. DeLuca had started out working as a teenage volunteer at her local fire and rescue squad. In her first week, a mother whose toddler had fallen down the basement stairs in a walker grabbed Marilyn's hand as the medics worked on the child. The mother was hysteri-cal with guilt, had sobbed on Denise's shoulder and then was reborn when the baby cried and came back to life. Denise, who was along as an observer, was hooked as the mother thanked her over and over again for saving her daughter's life. That's when Dr. DeLuca, who had no aptitude to be a doctor, decided to go into medicine for the wrong reason: what she could get out of it.

She remained a volunteer until she graduated from high school. To get her out of their station, the volunteer medics could not sign a letter of recommendation fast enough for her to be a volunteer at a nearby hospital. Dr. DeLuca now gave speeches to high school students about how they should follow their dream, although the students had a hard time hearing much of what she said. She always ended each speech with a quote she had seen in a candy wrapper, which she decided to attribute to Jackie Kennedy: "Those who bring sunshine to the lives of others cannot keep it from themselves."

For Jim Wallace, every encounter with Dr. DeLuca took twice as long as needed as she slow-talked to get her way. He noticed that when Dr. DeLuca was upset, which was often, she talked slower and softer to force others to lean-in closer and listen intently. He had also heard numerous and regular complaints about her bedside manner — that she was mean — from patients, families and other doctors over the years which he referred to Royce to handle as CEO. Royce always promised follow-up, but did nothing. He was never going to change Dr. DeLuca and he was never going to hold a doctor accountable.

In the grand scheme of things, the hospital made a lot of money for its corporate parent — mostly by virtue of its location in the affluent suburbs of Charlottesville. But Royce was considered to be a dynamic and top-performing CEO, so his boss left him alone. Royce found it a more efficient use of his time to manage Dr. DeLuca's dysfunction rather than change her.

Dr. DeLuca had worked for a number of years to get Jim Wallace to like her. She had personally gone to his office and given him and his staff complimentary flu shots. When she saw him leaving a board meeting one evening with a terrible head cold, she had offered him painkillers to ease his symptoms. She was disappointed with his continued hostility. She cleared her throat and paused for several seconds.

"I'm sorry Jim, I could not make that out, repeat back, please" she responded in her normal near whisper.

Royce intervened, as he often did in meetings with Dr. DeLuca.

"Dr. DeLuca has an update on the patient," Royce offered, pushing the speakerphone closer to the doctor.

Dr. DeLuca leaned back in her chair and cleared her throat.

"The patient is in a coma. He has a frontal lobe concussion that typically does not swell, so his primary injury is treatable here at Ascend Medical Center. He sustained several deep abrasions that are being monitored to ensure that the patient does not develop bedsores. His blood chemistry is normal and does not indicate any infection."

"Any signs of drugs or alcohol?" the Board Chair asked, sounding hopeful.

"Would that help?" replied Dr. DeLuca.

There was a long pause, the kind of silence when a group of people is considering possibilities.

"It's a yes-or-no question," Royce finally said after several seconds.

She shrugged. "The test is negative — but there are some other, more in-depth tests we could run." Dr. DeLuca offered.

Stella Cooper, the Chief Nursing Officer spoke. "Harold — please play the tape again."

The footage pictured Flip, in focus approaching from the left frame of the video and rolling past the stopped vehicle. She noticed for the first time that he had ear phones in, with a wire running into a back pocket. The ambulance entered from the right side of the frame, a blur. Flip ran into the ambulance.

"That's the reason he isn't dead, I think," Harold offered. "He struck the ambulance with the skateboard first — the head injury came from after the impact, when he hit the ground."

"How fast was the rig going?" Stella asked.

"Pretty damn fast," the public relations director observed.

"Yeah, that's what I was thinking too," said Stella. "The hospital and the rescue squad have an agreement that ambulances will slow to 10 mph when on the hospital campus. Isn't that correct Dr. DeLuca?"

Dr. DeLuca was the medical director for the West End Rescue Squad — the same squad for which she had once volunteered in her youth. Just as she had arrived back in the community as a newly graduated physician, a long time family practice doctor who had served for a couple of decades as an unpaid director, announced he was retiring. Dr. DeLuca had quickly filled the void and then convinced the former hospital CEO to create a $40,000 medical director stipend contribution to the squad. In exchange — with a wink and a nod — she ensured that 90 percent of the ambulance traffic was sent to Ascend Medical Center, a change from the equal split between Ascend and the university hospital. If anyone questioned the change in the usages pattern, Dr. DeLuca fabricated some grievance about the university related to quality of care, proximity or trauma call coverage.

The squad's management was now firmly handled by those in her control.

"Yes that is correct — the one exception being if the patient is in danger of coding," Dr. DeLuca said.

Stella picked up a copy of the policy. "That's not what the policy says, Dr. DeLuca. There is nothing in this policy that offers an exception based on the condition of the patient."

"Well, that's my verbal instruction to the squads," explained Dr. DeLuca. "They should travel as fast as they think is necessary if the patient is at risk."

Royce frowned. It was always a problem when a hospital did not follow its own policy.

"Dr. DeLuca, in theory all patients in an ambulance are at risk of coding — I mean that's why they are in an ambulance in the first place, correct?" he asked.

Virginia Stowe, who would soon be on the other end of Luann Zahn's microphone, was nervous.

"Listen folks, we need to figure out a statement to release pretty quick. So far we have a patient on a skateboard who was listening to music, crashing into an ambulance that was driving too fast."

"We don't know if the ambulance was driving too fast," Dr. DeLuca said very quietly. "I will review the medical record for the patient in the ambulance and get back to you on that."

Royce was in no mood to hear Dr. DeLuca's "we're busy saving lives here" speech.

"OK, here's what you are going to say, Ginny. A visitor riding a skateboard in our parking lot ran into an ambulance during an uncontrolled decent on a grade out of a parking lot. The patient is not being identified to protect family and patient privacy. Don't make any comment about the ambulance's speed, we can always make a statement later about that. You OK with that, Robert?" Royce asked the hospital attorney.

"You're not breaking any law," the attorney replied.

"Royce, I don't think this is a good idea," Virginia said. "It's better to get in front of this now rather than have it blow up in our face later," she said. "Let's disclose that we are reviewing if the ambulance was being operated in accordance with policy — we don't have to specify whether it's a written or verbal policy," she added, eyeing Dr. DeLuca. Virginia had heard the stories about Dr. DeLuca's "badside manner" and knew she was at risk by disagreeing with the doctor.

Royce could see Dr. DeLuca's upper lip rise into her beaver sneer. It was time to move on, to make a command and control decision.

"Let's do it my way, Ginny," Royce said.

"And what if Luann or any other reporter asks me about the ambulance speed?" Virginia said, not happy.

"Harold," Royce asked, "has anyone outside this meeting seen the recording of the accident?" he asked. Harold shook his head.

"No sir."

"Then it shouldn't be an issue," Royce said.

"Yeah, no problem," said Jim Wallace, the chairman, over the speakerphone.

"Yeah, but what if they do," Virginia persisted, her voice growing sterner. "I'm the one hanging out there in front of a television camera."

Dr. DeLuca stood up. Her upper lip was pulled so far back she looked as if she might bite through the table.

"I remind you that I am the Medical Director for the ambulance service. Any questions about the ambulance in this matter are to be referred to me," she hissed at the spokeswoman. "Do you hear me?"

Virginia stared back wide-eyed. Royce frowned and looked down at his hands.

Dr. DeLuca was quite pleased with the results of her tirade. It was time to make a grand exit.

"I'm leaving, I have a patient to save."

When she was gone, Royce spoke.

"Ginny, if you get any questions about the ambulance, you don't know anything about it — you'll have to get back to them. Then you come talk to me — not Dr. DeLuca. Understood?"

I understand all right, Virginia thought. *You'll never stand up to this crazy bitch doctor, which means I'll have to watch my back for the rest of the time I work at this hospital.* Virginia just nodded.

On the other end of the conference call, the board chair Jim Wallace had an unpleasant premonition, like a man who has caught the first glimpse of hair loss in the mirror. His firm managed half of the hospital's sizable portfolio, which grew nicely every year with the average seven percent earnings the hospital cranked out. He thought Dr. DeLuca was a turd in a swimming pool, which, when he thought about it, was an insult to turds.

Robert Wallace, his cousin, on the other hand, smiled to himself. Bad publicity was always good for an attorney's business.

CHAPTER

Specialist

FOUR

Dr. DeLuca returned to her office in an adjoining building connected to the hospital. She opened the door and stepped into the lobby where she, like everyone else who entered, was accosted with a three-foot by four-foot gold-gilded framed exhibition, featuring a full color photo of herself seated, holding a diploma (displayed in the frame below the photo) and wearing full blown academic gown and cap. Unknown to Dr. DeLuca, the photographer had done some retouching to thin her face. When Dr. DeLuca saw her svelte image staring back at herself she did not hesitate at the $800 price tag. It was an imposing presence in the room. As she always did, she took a moment to take herself in, to feel impressed. Her revelry was interrupted, however, when her cell phone buzzed — the call she had been expecting all morning.

"This is your fault," he growled in greeting. Denise chilled and then flashed hot.

"I'm going to take care of it Ace," she whispered.

"We'll talk about it tonight," he responded.

"Be sure to watch the local news — I'm probably going to be interviewed," she offered eagerly. There was a long pause.

"If I want to see your fat face, I don't need to watch television, now do I?" he said. "This better not come back on Randy."

"Ace — I told you — I'll take care of it," she pleaded, looking around to make sure none of her staff could overhear her conversation.

He hung up.

———

Other than the buzz of painkillers, there was nothing Owen Gregor enjoyed more than the glow of righteous indignation. Owen decided at a young age that lying was justified, especially when the other person did not believe what he was saying. More and more, the emergency room doctors at Valley View Hospital doubted him and this had to stop. If he said he had pain that was all they needed to know. He was tired of being the bad guy. It was time for a new strategy.

When he walked into the hospital administrative offices, the secretary was on the phone, so he sat down across from her in a row of chairs. He liked waiting in administrative offices as he often heard tidbits of information that came in useful later. Jayne was on the phone with a nurse in the emergency room who was calling to give her a heads-up about one Owen Gregor, a difficult patient who threatened to complain.

"He's got a very light, thin red beard and hair, is very fair skinned — almost red — and tattoos on his knuckles," Brittany Sawyer relayed to Jayne. "He can be very charming and when that doesn't work he starts yelling," she advised. Jayne looked at the man seated before her.

"I can see that," Jayne replied. There was a pause.

"He's already there?" Brittany asked, not surprised. "I'll bet a pay check that he is not flopping around like a crash test dummy in pain"

"That is correct," Jayne said. "OK, thank you for your help."

Owen smiled brightly at Jayne. "Well, Good Mooooorning," he said with much enthusiasm and a touch of sarcasm that made Jayne uneasy. "My name is Owen Gregor. Where's the Administrator?" Jayne reached for paper and pad.

"He's in a meeting right now. Why don't you tell me what you need so I can fill him in. He can call you when he gets out," she said.

"Oh no, not necessary," Owen said, continuing to speak in syrupy, exaggerated voice. "I'll just sit here until he comes back."

"That could be a couple of hours, sir," Jayne said. "You can wait down the hall in the lobby and I will find you when he is free. He's also good about answering emails if you want to try that."

"I'll wait," Owen repeated. Without pain medication, he could feel an undertow of agitation beginning to percolate.

At that moment, another man, middle-aged, walked into the office. He was bulky, wore an oversized white insulated vest and heavy rim glasses. His black hair was a tangle. The man looked tired and anxious, although not unkind.

"Excuse me, is the administrator in?"

This is the way of hospitals. Problems are not sequential, some days the unhappy stack up like refugees. When a hospital disappoints a patient — either through poor service, an error or just plain stupidity, the mistakes come one after another. Upset patients usually end up at an Administrator's desk after multiple sins, real or imagined, by the hospital staff.

Jayne had the identical conversation with the new visitor, who identified himself as Warren Harris.

"My wife is in the ICU and I'm concerned about how the doctors are taking care of her," he told Jayne.

Owen perked up. With another unhappy person his odds for getting what he wanted had just improved.

"Hey — you'll have to wait in line behind me buddy," Owen said, snarky. "This hospital has a lot of problems."

Warren turned, looked at Owen, none too happy. "Who are you?" he asked.

"Just another dissatisfied customer," Owen answered. "This hospital really sucks," he added for good measure.

"Mr. Gregor, you need to wait in the lobby," Jayne instructed calmly. "Mr. Harris and I need privacy to protect patient confidentiality. I will come find you when Mr. Miller returns and can see you."

Owen thought about it for a few beats. He did not like anyone telling him what to do and this was the second time this morning a woman had disrespected him. This tendency had been the cause of many troubles in Owen's life, a loner living with his elderly mother who still hoped that one day her son would get his life together. Despite two anger management classes, several short stints in jail and the public humiliation of being dragged into the back of a police car, when Owen felt slighted, he had poor impulse control. At that moment Jayne, who sensed Owen's turmoil, raised her eyebrows and added;

"Please?"

This gesture was enough to placate — that and the fact that the big dude Harris was now glaring at him. Owen did not fare well in fist-de-cuffs with other males, his natural inclination was to hide under the furniture. But one thing that Owen always got was the last word.

"Yeah, well, if I'm not in the lobby it means I had to go back to the emergency room because of my pain. Either that, or I've gone to call my lawyer," he added as he departed.

***

Leo settled into his chair.

The monthly Trauma Committee Meeting was never not interesting. The Trauma Committee was composed of the Surgery and Emergency Department (ED) medical staff. In a long standing point of contention, medical personnel called it the Emergency Department (ED), while the non-medical public called it the Emergency Room (ER). Staff who worked there answered by either name.

The current Trauma and Surgery Medical Department chairman was Palma Hauptman, M.D., a general surgeon who had no patience for chit-chat or fools. Dr. Hauptman was a tiny Filipino woman who started working as a hospital aid in her home country. She was smart, attending nursing school while working nights in the hospital laundry. In three years she was managing the operating room in the government hospital where she met her future husband, Maurice Hauptman, M.D. Dr. Hauptman was a plastic surgeon of bland features and proportions who worked with a medical charity to correct cleft palettes in children residing in third world countries. Behind his back there were many snide remarks about a plastic surgeon who could, himself, use some plastic surgery.

Maurice was an introverted scientist and a brilliant surgeon who was very appreciative when Palma began assisting him every day and acting as a translator. After their daily OR schedule, fixing horrific birth defects in little children, Palma escorted Dr. Hauptman in the afternoons and evenings through Manila where he indulged his other passion of photography. By the end of ten days, the two were engaged. It had occurred to Dr. Hauptman that his disorderly and lonely life could benefit immensely from this forceful woman who whipped his daily routine into shape and made him laugh with her directness; in drive and ferociousness, she reminded him of his late mother. While this truth would be a concern for many, Dr. Hauptman found it very reassuring.

"Dr. Hauptman, you need a woman to keep you straight. I want to become a great surgeon like you — we make a good team."

Both were surprised when they actually fell in love. It turned out that photography was not the only thing Maurice Hauptman could be passionate about. He had no problem submitting to the administrations of his smart and forceful wife. Much to the amazement of his family, friends and colleagues, the marriage was not a mistake and not a plot by a third world gold digger. Maurice became a much better man with Palma. He transformed from a dowdy middle-aged man to a dapper, outgoing fellow who rose every weekday morning with his wife at 5 a.m. to endure a rigorous workout in their home gym.

Nurse Palma gunned through an American undergraduate premed schedule in two and half years. This was in part due to her new husband's money and oversight, but mostly because she was brilliant, driven and born to practice medicine. She was accepted to medical school at the Medical College of Virginia where she mentored most of her fellow, younger first-year residents, who nicknamed her "Ty-phoon". A few would not have made it without her. She convinced two of her closest resident friends to join her in surgical training. Patients loved her dedication and would see no one else once under while her care.

She was direct with everyone — colleagues, patients, nurses — and hospital administrators. Leo had learned that she became terse when she was hearing something she did not like or if she felt there was not an honest effort to deal with her concerns.

"OK, who's not here?" Dr. Hauptman said, more than asked Flo Johnson, the medical staff coordinator. Dr. Hauptman took it as personal affront when one of her colleagues did not show up for her meeting. To not be excused ahead of time was asking for future displeasure. Flo, like most people in her position, was very detail oriented and a bit subservient, a not surprising trait in someone who was a high school graduate and found herself working every day with highly intelligent, highly trained and sometimes egotistical perfectionists. But it was fair trade-off; a medical staff coordinator made a good living.

"We're just waiting on Drs. Ziff and Maury," Flo answered. Dr. Ziff was an ER physician and Dr. Maury was a fellow surgeon.

Dr. Hauptman pursed her lips in disapproval. "Let's get started."

Leo had never seen a medical department meeting that was con-sistently so well attended. In Leo's experience, it was a struggle to get doctors to tend to governance, the quality and peer review chores conducted in medical department meetings. All doctors were time poor and often exhausted, especially primary care physicians who worked harder and longer to see more patients.

On one occasion Leo had found a family doctor asleep in his car at the main entrance when he arrived as the sun was rising on a sum-mer morning. The family doctor moonlighted as an ED physician in a community almost 100 miles away. The physician had retrieved records from the chart room, which were not allowed outside the hospital, before that department closed the evening before. He planned to return the completed charts first thing in the morning. He made the mistake of lying down for a few minutes in his car, sleeping for 10 hours before Leo woke him, tapping on the car window. Leo helped the doctor carry the medical records back into the secure area, unlocking the door with his master key. He then fetched coffee for the doctor and extracted a promise that never again would the physician take records out of the confines of the department. Within six months the physician closed his practice and went to work for a company that provided temporary physician staffing to rural emergency rooms. His departure left Leo with a shortage of primary doctors in his community.

Surgical specialists, on the other hand, were indifferent to demands on their time from the hospital, complaining that any time not devoted to seeing patients and operating was an imposition. In recent years, administrators at some large city hospitals had begun paying doctors up to $100 an hour to show up for routine medical department meetings. Leo thought this a bad precedent. Fortunately, in a small town, the medical staff and hospital needed each other to succeed.

The meeting proceeded quickly with a review of service statistics for both the operating room and emergency room. Surgical stats included on-time starts and operating room turnover times. ER stats included patients who left without being seen, wait time to triage, total time spent from registration to discharge and, for patients who were admitted, the amount of time it took from the ER to a bed on the floor.

Dr. Hauptman, working with the OR Nursing Director, had all but eliminated late starts for scheduled surgeries. Late starts annoyed patients and made every other surgeon behind the offending physician late for the day. Dr. Hauptman demanded the OR Director get the operating rooms cleaned, prepped and turned around ready to start the next case in the established hospital standard of less than 15 minutes.

Where Leo had seen many medical staffs dismiss such data points as being inaccurate, irrelevant, or an affront to independent physician judgment, Valley View's performance on national surgical benchmarks placed it in the top 15th percentile of hospitals nationwide. It made most of the medical staff feel proud.

Dr. Ziff, the Medical Director of the ER, entered and took a seat. He did not apologize for arriving late and did not look like a man who wanted to be there. He was dressed in shorts, a t-shirt and was wearing flip-flops.

"All right, now that Dr. Ziff has arrived, let's start case review. Everyone who is not a physician is excused, except for Mr. Miller, Flo and Ms. Maxwell," she announced. Sherri Maxwell, a nurse (RN) and MBA, was the Director of Quality Improvement and was responsible for bringing all cases of unexpected death to the appropriate medical department meeting for peer review. She also brought cases that fell out due to unnecessary harm or risk that may have been done to a patient.

The dismissed staff filed out.

"Sherri, please describe the first case," Dr. Hauptman instructed.

"Our first case is Heather Parker, a 17-year old female who presented in the ED July 12. Her parents are divorced and she was at her father's house over the weekend. He allowed her to have a party at which several dozen teenagers showed up. After a few hours, a ladder was raised up against the side of the house by some of the teens so they could climb up on the roof to do who knows what. Heather, the patient, fell off the ladder and on top of a sprinkler junction box. Her father drove her to the hospital when she began complaining of abdominal pain. On arrival she was in quite a bit of pain and very combative. Her father was not forthcoming with pertinent information but finally admitted that she, like all the other teens, had consumed alcohol," Monica said.

"Was a trauma alert called?" Dr. Hauptman asked.

"I was on that night and got involved with the case shortly after the patient arrived," said Dr. Ziff. "The patient reeked of alcohol and was vomiting. She was complaining of abdominal pain, but it appeared at first that this was related to the vomiting. She was also yelling and swearing quite a bit. And it took us a few minutes to get the facts out of the father, who had been drinking himself and was extremely distraught."

Dr. Hauptman leafed through the chart. "So according to the notes it looks like a trauma alert was called 28 minutes after the patient arrived," she said.

For patients who arrived by ambulance, the Paramedics have the training to call a trauma alert en route to the hospital. A trauma alert notifies and assembles staff — from blood bank to radiology to surgery — to immediately diagnose and take the patient to the operating room from the emergency room upon arrival if necessary. In the trauma field, the first 60 minutes is known as the "golden hour" — where good decisions and medical care can mean the difference between life and death.

For patients who arrived by private vehicle, the professional medical assessment is lost. Sometimes patients or family will not call an ambulance because of concern about the cost or due to the erroneous belief that the ER visit is not reportable to public authorities if they drive the patient in themselves.

"That's correct," replied Dr. Ziff. "The attending ER physician — Dr. Diller, ordered a drip to treat the dehydration and nausea due to the alcohol and a pain med injection. Both meds helped to get the patient calmed down so we could get her in the CT scanner. About that time the blood work came back and we were seeing an elevated white cell blood count. Dr. Diller and I were concerned about a ruptured bowel from the fall, so we activated the trauma alert."

Dr. Hauptman spent a minute reviewing the chart. "Shouldn't the trauma alert been activated as soon as you learned of the fall." she asked. "Based on the chart, you could have activated a full 20 minutes sooner — or more."

Dr. Ziff looked annoyed. "I remember that night. We had already had to deal with a couple of other disruptive drunk and drugged up patients. We also had a long-haul truck driver who had a vibrator — which was turned on — up his rectum. He was quite concerned about the refrigerated cargo he was carrying and had his rig idling in front, blocking in two ambulances."

"You should have referred that to a specialist," cracked one of the other doctors, who honked loudly at his own joke. A few others snickered as well. Dr. Ziff's mood did not improve as he continued.

"We saw nearly 15 patients in a two-hour stretch by the time this guy and his daughter walked in. We were doing the best we could," he stated. There was a pronounced silence as every physician in the room reflected and envisioned the ER that night. Most every doctor in the room had found themselves in a similar situation, where the sheer force of sick and injured patients sloshed in like a giant tide. ERs were set up to respond to their average patient volumes; peak surges at the average hospital gummed up the works.

"Yes, I remember this patient as well, Dr. Ziff," Dr. Hauptman answered. "As you know, I was on call and took the patient to the OR. She lost almost two feet of large bowel that I could have saved if we had opened sooner," Dr. Hauptman stared at Dr. Ziff, letting that fact sink in. "Given the other patients that you were seeing that night, is it possible that your value judgment of this patient and her father prevented you from recognizing a serious medical condition and delayed treatment? In other words, Dr. Ziff, did you see a drunk teenager and irresponsible parent first and a possible trauma injury second?" Dr. Hauptman asked.

Leo had seen this happen before, especially in ER doctors. It was a "blame the patient" mentality — which was often deserved, but could, on occasion, foster a dangerous lack of urgency. However, this was the first time he had seen the issues discussed among physicians in a case review. Leo did not think Dr. Ziff would react well and he was not disappointed. Dr. Ziff's face flushed red while his lips narrowed and whitened. Several seconds went by with silence.

One of Dr. Ziff's ED colleagues, Dr. Montoya spoke up. Dr. Montoya was long time Valley View ER physician with no interest in being in charge or participating in any quality or process improvement. He had a reputation for being quick to write prescriptions for pain pills — "giving the candy" — and in fact had been the doctor that the waiting Owen Gregor had been seeking on his ER visit earlier that day.

"Dr. Hauptman, you speak a totally unacceptable question in your premise. You do not work in the emergency room and as such, do not understand how important the value judgments are as we treat a patient. My experience is that surgeons want us to call a trauma alert for anything that could conceivably require surgery, which of course improves your outcomes. But it is also is quite expensive for the hospital when we call an unnecessary trauma alert, especially after hours when staff must be summoned." Dr. Montoya looked at Leo for support.

Valley View maintained a Level III Trauma Center ED, which meant the hospital was able to care for most of its trauma patients with in-house resuscitation, surgery and intensive care. More seriously injured or ill patients had to be transferred to Trauma Centers in Charlottesville or Richmond for such services as neurology, spine or heart surgery. Although there were on-call costs to keep nurses and other staff ready to go at a moments notice around the clock with maintaining a Level III ED, Leo said nothing. Leo had learned sitting in many case review meetings that one doctor running interference for another was common and this was often the first step on the way to a resolution. It was always best for an administrator not to say anything about a case review unless the chairmen invited him to speak.

While Dr. Hauptman was direct, she was not by nature vindictive — although she did not respond directly to Dr. Montoya.

"Dr. Ziff, I want to remind you and all of our colleagues in the room that the reason we conduct case review is to improve upon our outcomes. We are all better doctors when we learn from our experiences. What we discuss in this room is confidential and free from discovery in the event of a lawsuit. I believe I have asked you a reasonable question based on the medical record, your own statements and the outcome. If you do not wish to talk about this now, I can move on to the next case and return or we can continue this discussion next month at this meeting once you have had time to think about the issues raised today."

Dr. Ziff was a man who preferred his discontent to fester.

"Yes, let's do that Dr. Hauptman — discuss this next month."

"OK," Dr. Hauptman said. "What's next?"

"A bow hunter who fell out of a tree stand and shot his buddy in the thigh with an arrow," Sherri answered.

There were more snickers around the room.

CHAPTER

Fourth Estate

FIVE

Luann Zahn was all a-tingle. She could hear fear in a phone, like a shark smells traces of blood in the water at a great distance. The tension in a voice, respiration rate, or the barest of hesitation — all offered ready clues, especially from the evasive. She often marveled at the clumsy, blatant efforts to spin answers to her inquiries, to not answer her questions. Every day she spoke to someone trying to hide something. Luann treated a company that didn't return her calls especially harsh.

The press was America's fourth estate, the keeper of the public's right to know, defender of democracy. Luann took this responsibility seriously. Reporters kept politicians and business honest and exposed those who were not. In return advertisers bought commercials for all the anxious viewers who could not help themselves from tuning in to the death, mayhem and personal attacks that passed for news. The news shuffle had to be danced and Luann, like all reporters, appreciated good two-step partners.

This is why she was intrigued by Virginia Stowe's call back. Virginia was usually a good spokesperson. She understood the news cycle, that reporters needed good "B Roll" — video footage to compliment a story when the reporter was narrating and not on the screen. So when Virginia called back to tell her that the patient was in critical condition but did not offer to meet with her or otherwise help Luann cultivate a story, it was unusual. Virginia was a little too chipper — which was not like her at all. She also told Luann that an ambulance had not hit the patient, but the patient, while listening to music through headphones, had run into the ambulance while riding a skateboard. Virginia still had no name, sex or age of the patient to offer, citing next of kin and patient confidentiality. And she did not want to go on camera to give a statement. Virginia was queen of the sound bite, empress of the "all publicity is good, just spell our name right" school of media relations. She told Luann she had permission to do a stand-up at the ER entrance, but no one from the hospital would go on camera. This was very odd indeed.

Then Ethyl Martin, her housekeeping connection at Valley had called. She advised Luann that the patient was one Flip Jensen, the famous Ascend Medical Center Bicentennial Baby.

"How on earth do you know that Ethyl?" Luann asked after a few seconds of shocked silence. Luann's mind raced — this was rich, too good to be true.

"Luann — have I ever steered you wrong?" Ethyl said in her very pointed cadence. "I'm going to give you the address of that poor man's parents, who are in the ICU now with their baby boy. But one of them will be home soon."

"How do you know that?" Luann asked again in astonishment.

"Because my source," Ethyl said drawing out the word, "tells me that only one parent is being allowed in the ICU at a time and they are right aggravated about this policy," she conveyed. Ethyl was very careful not to describe her cousin by gender as she had seen the heroine do in her soap opera "By Appointment Only".

Unknown to Luann, Ethyl's cousin who worked at Ascend had acquired the medical records user name and password of Dr. Denise DeLuca. The doctor was in the habit of writing this information on the back of her business cards until she had a chance to transfer it into her phone. Her cousin, who had been secretly recruited as a union organizer, had a friend in housekeeping that made it his personal business to go through all gray boxes. These were a system of secure, locked trash bins distributed around the hospital to ensure the protection of patient records and other confidential information. The filled gray boxes were picked up by the maintenance department for storage in a room off the loading dock until the trash company sent around a specially equipped truck to shred the documents. As pickup was scheduled once a month, the housekeeping staff had plenty of time to go through the contents for evidence of administrative mischief to convince the unskilled work force to join the union.

They found many interesting gray box tidbits, including Dr. DeLuca's handwritten password. Access to the hospital's medical records system, especially through the account of the doctor caring for this patient, was an especially good stroke of luck. It all but guaranteed that they could monitor Flip Jensen's medical condition without detection.

"Thank you sweetheart, I owe you one," Luann cooed back to Ethyl.

"You bet honey, see you at lunch next week," the housekeeper replied. Luann devoted two lunch hours a week to eating on a rotating schedule with her many sources in Charlottesville.

Luann sat at her desk and considered her options. It was a luxurious feeling to bask in the warm glow of possibilities. Her cameraman Chuck Conley — nicknamed Dusty — was a tall, lanky fellow with a thick handlebar mustache and cowboy good looks. He sat across from her slowly rotating his head in slow, wide circles. An array of popping and grinding noises emanated from his neck.

"Dusty, it sounds like you have glass in there," Luann laughed. Dusty smiled slowly, but continued.

"We Conleys are wound tighter than a pack of prairie dogs at a riding lawn mower convention," he explained.

Dusty was a good cameraman. He didn't say much, but he was smart. So during an interview, if he occasionally whispered a question to Luann, she listened. He was also tall and solid, which tended to impress the people she was interviewing — especially the ones who got hostile. More than once, Dusty stepped in between Luann and an interviewee who did not like the questions she was asking.

"Need to protect the talent. Need that paycheck." He always said with a big grin when she tried to thank him for his muscle. Luann knew that Dusty was fond of her and enjoyed their work together. He spent a good part of his off time on a horse, chasing a girlfriend around who was a barrel racer and a weightlifter.

"So, you have a plan yet?" he asked Luann. But Luann did not seem to be listening any longer. She was gazing inward at the flow chart in her mind, probing for the weak link, the path of least resistance to the truth. After a few minutes she let out a soft "Ahhhhhhh."

Dusty smiled. The boss lady had just figured it out, had her "ah-ha" moment. Her face relaxed, a landscape of calm. It was go time.

Owen squirmed in his lobby seat. He had returned to the administrative office twice in an hour to advance his complaint with the pretty Hispanic woman behind the desk, which went nowhere.

Both times she chirped, "He's still not out of his meeting yet!"

He considered returning to the ER to try again for pain pills, but the shift change that would bring a different group of nurses and doctors on duty was not due for another few hours. The prospect of burning up gas in his truck to drive to Ascend Medical Center in Charlottesville or even further to the many hospitals an hour east in Richmond to make the rounds of those emergency rooms had Owen feeling very sorry for himself. Most of these hospitals were not-for-profit, living off their tax-exempt status and denying care to hurting people like himself.

Owen thought back to the first time he snuck pills from the medicine chest. His 16-year-old psyche, stressed with the normal hormonal and emotional tempests of teendom, went on vacation with the Valium and Percocet, courtesy of his hard working father who was wracked with back spasms from his auto body shop. When his father began hiding the pills several months later, Owen found a ready supply in the medicine chests and night stands at his friends' homes. It seemed every family he knew had a stash of pain killers.

Of course within two years Owen had worn out his welcome with both family and friends alike. It did not go unnoticed that when Owen was around, things disappeared. But by then Owen was 18 and as an adult he could visit the emergency room on his own. His nickel and dime days of hustling pills from other people were over — he hit the mother lode in that wonderful place known as the emergency room. His father was also dead by then. The old man, buzzed with painkillers, dropped a car on his chest one night in the shop. It was a lesson to Owen that working could kill you.

His cardinal rule was to work only enough to achieve unemployment. Owen was never late to work, never violated any policies and never had any performance issues. He was careful to have witnesses when his supervisor invariably lost patience with his passive-aggressive ways. He was always the first person laid-off in the "reorganization" that would follow, mostly designed to move him out the door. With standard benefits and extensions, his longest stretch receiving unemployment income had been nearly two years.

With some ambition on his part, he could make the rounds of regional hospitals and end up with half a dozen prescriptions netting about 100 assortments of painkillers and Valium. He sold half for a profit of $300. Between his unemployment check and having no expenses living with his mother, he did well enough. And he had not even tapped into the disability gravy train yet, the holy grail of all medical malingerers.

He was a master of working the system, which had served him well until recently. But lately he was having the worst run of luck. His mother was threatening to change the locks and all of a sudden the doctors in the emergency room wouldn't do their job. Now here he was wasting his time sitting in a hospital lobby waiting to talk to some suit about his medical needs. It was no wonder the American healthcare system was in the crapper.

An undistinguished middle-aged man wearing a shirt with the hospital logo above the pocket turned the corner into the lobby. A young woman carrying test tubes and in a lab coat smiled as she walked by and said "Hi, Leo". Owen scrambled to his feet.

"Are you the administrator?" he asked.

Leo stopped to size up the young man in front of him. Although he was not impressed by what he saw, he kept an open mind.

"I am — Leo Miller," he said holding out his hand. Owen was surprised and after a few beats, he loosely shook Leo's hand.

"You sure do have a nice hospital here," Owen continued, sounding sugar sweet. "But unfortunately, I was in your emergency room this morning and they refused to take care of me," Owen announced, louder than he needed. Several people in the lobby looked his way. Owen believed in the power of embarrassment. But Leo was a veteran of such behavior, from the homeless patient to the highest trained doctor. He smiled.

"What's your name?" Leo asked, ignoring his comment.

"Owen......Owen Gregor," he mumbled.

"OK, Owen, let's go to my office and I'll do my best to help you," Leo advised.

Jayne smiled brightly as they entered.

"Hi Leo. Murray is available to sit in on your meeting with Mr. Gregor." This is what made Jayne such a good administrative assistant. She was a step ahead, putting Murray Duff, the ER Director on notice about the waiting Owen Gregor. Owen, who knew most of the ER staff, including the guy who had told him no dozens of times, did not look pleased.

"Hey listen, I've talked to that guy Duff until my gums bleed, he don't listen or care," said Owen continuing his syrupy monologue. "I'd rather work this out with you, the boss man."

That's probably the only thing you haven't been in the ER for, bleeding gums, Leo thought.

"Mr. Gregor, if you want me to meet with you, I need Mr. Duff here. He's the ER manager; I don't know what happens in the ER because I don't work down there.

OK, Owen thought, it's show time. He took a step back, balling up his fists.

"This a bunch of crap. I've been waiting for two hours and now you're trying to screw me and you know it," Owen's face reddened as he worked up his anger, his voice rising. "I'm tired of the quacks and idiots you have working at this hospital —"

Leo held his hand up. "Stop — stop right now," Leo said firmly. Owen was not used to being interrupted, especially in the middle of a tirade. He looked surprised, but was silent.

"Mr. Gregor, you don't get to call anyone who works here names. Here's what we're going to do. You are going back out into the lobby to wait for another 10 minutes. I'll be happy to get you a cup of coffee or something else to drink to help you calm down. When Mr. Duff gets here, we'll be ready to sit down with you. Otherwise, we're done here — this meeting is over and I can't help you. What do you want to do?"

Owen was nothing if not adaptable. He changed tactics, biting his lower lip to work up a few tears. He dropped his head and cupped his hand up over his mouth. "I'm sorry," he said in small voice. "It's just that I take care of my mother and there are mornings I can hardly get out of bed because of my hereditary pancreatitis. I can't find anyone to help me. I'm sorry — I shouldn't have yelled."

Leo looked at Jayne, who was surprised. But this was a conversation that Leo had many times over the years with pain pill addicts. He had learned the tactic well from 2 a.m. phone calls from patients who were under the delusion that Leo could tell a doctor what medicine to prescribe. He also experienced this same trifecta of emotion — ingratiation, anger and self-pity — from many narcotic seeking patients.

Owen returned to the lobby to wait again. He had only been seated a few minutes when a woman sat down next to him. She was heavy, but young and really pretty with black hair. Owen noticed she was looking dreamily in his eyes with a slight smile. Owen knew that look.

"Hi, I'm Felicia," she said slowly. She had a great voice, low and husky.

"Owen," he said

"I really like your tattoos," she said covering his DETH knuckles with her hand. Owen was transfixed.

"You have any others?"

"No, but I could get some," he grinned. Owen had a great smile. His mother was a big believer in dental work, certain that a dazzling smile was the first step to full time employment.

Felicia's laugh started deep in her throat and worked up the scale like a meadowlark.

"Well, Owen," she said, leaning forward generously pressuring Owen's shoulder through her blouse, "you know anything about cars?"

"Hell yes — does the Pope live in the woods?" Owen smiled again.

Felicia arched her forehead, confusion making its way through her foggy mind.

"Are you Catholic?" she wondered out loud.

"No sweetheart, just forget about that." Owen smiled again and leaned into Felicia, turning on what he had that passed for charm.

"Yeah, I know a lot about cars. My old man ran a body shop and we rebuilt engines too," he explained. Felicia was not sure what Owen meant about a body shop, but never mind. She had pushed a few buttons and this fellow was responding — that was good enough for now. She explained slowly to Owen that her car was in the parking lot and would not start. She had a dog at home that needed medicine. Could he help?

Owen noticed that she had green flecks in her eyes. Owen's love life had consisted of a string of bad tempered, mean girlfriends. His last relationship had been with an angular, cranky little Italian girl who liked to punch — whether she was pleased or upset. Felicia was just plain voluptuous by comparison. She had a bright patterned skirt wrapped around her big hips, the kind he had seen African women wearing in a magazine. She had on low cut tank top with a shawl draped over her shoulders, which seemed to be slipping lower. She was a big enough girl and there was plenty to see.

"Yeah, I can, but," he leaned in again, her hair smelled like the air freshener in his truck, "I have an important meeting soon with the hospital CEO. I've got to get him straight about a few things. This lame place does not want to take care of my back pain," he said, playing a hunch. "I used to be a volunteer firefighter and got hurt saving an old lady's dog from a house fire." Owen looked down modestly with this pronouncement, recalling the time he accidently set a smoky fire in his bedroom. He had watched a volunteer firefighter do exactly as he claimed, pulling his mother's little mutt from their house.

Felicia laughed again, her trill really getting to Owen.

"Oh baby," she whispered, "you don't need to go to a meeting to get what you need. I can fix you up." She pulled the bag open on her lap for a quick peek at several prescription bottles. "After you get my car running, that is," she promised lazily.

When Leo returned to the lobby at the end of the agreed upon 10 minutes, Owen was nowhere to be found.

Jayne was surprised when Leo returned alone.

"I guess he got a better offer," Leo joked.

Jayne laughed, neither realizing how close Leo was to the truth.

"Oh, by the way, the husband of a patient came in this morning upset with his wife's care. He wanted to see you — it was about the same time Mr. Gregor was in the middle of his performance."

Leo had mixed emotions. He always preferred to address patient or family complaints while the patient was still in the hospital when he still had a chance to do something about it. But some days, even in a hospital where the CEO cared about such complaints, it could take hours. He was thinking about all the other work on his desk, including the 100 emails he received every day. But Jayne had good news for Leo.

"Ben convinced him that as Chief Nursing Officer he could help, so they went up to the ICU. Ben said the husband — a Mr. Harris — seemed to calm down after Ben spent some time explaining his wife's care."

Just then, the door to Administration opened and Mr. Harris himself walked in.

"You must be the Administrator," he said, offering his hand. Leo saw a bulky, middle-aged man, perhaps not yet 50, who wore very large, black glasses, which gave him an intense, but earnest air.

"I just wanted to tell you myself that you have a really wonderful staff at this hospital. Your Chief Nursing Officer — Ben — was very nice to spend time with me this morning. I know you are all very busy. I realized that I was just so stressed out about my wife being sick that I wasn't acting like myself — I was being unreasonable. He really helped calm me down."

Leo thanked Warren Harris for his compliment.

"It's a good reflection on you as the CEO, so you get some of the credit I think," Warren said. "And — the great news is — an hour after Ben was up in her room, she woke up — and she recognized me!"

Mr. Harris left to rejoin his wife at her bedside.

Jayne smiled behind him as he left.

"He's a really nice man. Ben told me that his wife is more than 20 years older than him, but you can tell by the way he talks that he really loves her."

Royce Wexler was listening to a group laugh on the other end of the speakerphone. It was his boss — the Division Vice President — and a few other corporate types he had summoned to be on the call. The VP, who had thoroughly enjoyed the tales of Flip Jensen and his exploits over the years, had Royce repeat the story about Flip's most recent mishap.

"Riding a skateboard into an ambulance — Jesus, you can't make this stuff up," the VP bellowed.

Royce chuckled a bit — it was always wise to share the VP's mirth — but he did so with a lack of his normal gusto. Virginia Stowe, the hospital spokeswoman and Stella Cooper, the Chief Nursing Officer, were in his office, unhappy with the locker room laugh fest. Royce held his hand up to Stella who looked on the verge of saying something she shouldn't.

"Yeah, it's ironic," Royce conceded. "But I want to give you a heads-up that this is going to hit the news in a big way. There is a local investigative reporter with a syndicated show who is covering his accident like a bad rash. She keeps calling because she wants to interview the attending doctor about his condition."

On the other end, the corporate Corporate Director of Public Relations — the head flack — saw his chance to make himself useful in front of the boss.

"Virginia, just do what I do when a reporter calls who I don't want to talk to; wait until 2 o'clock in the morning and then call them back. That way you can just leave a voice mail that you're sorry you missed them. It puts the ball back in their court."

What an idiot, Virginia thought, *no wonder our company's image is terrible.* Virginia gave a well-behaved answer.

"Take my word, if I call this reporter at two in the morning, she'll answer," Virginia said. "She's not going away, and she is brutal with any company that ducks her calls. I'm going to need call her back within the next hour."

"But," she said, changing the subject before she was ordered to do something she didn't want to, "We have a bit of a problem with this incident that is not common knowledge," she said.

It suddenly became very quiet on the other end of the phone.

Royce explained.

"It appears on the security tape that the ambulance was driving much faster than the posted on-campus speed limit."

"Aren't ambulances supposed to drive fast?" It was the Corporate Director of Public Relations again.

"That's a very insightful question," Royce answered. "The answer is: sometimes. If the patient is coding or in eminent danger of coding, it's the drivers decision on how fast is fast enough."

"So what was going on in the ambulance?" the VP asked.

"Another good question. Our medical director, who is also the medical director for the ambulance company…" Royce paused to let this happy coincidence sink in "…is reviewing the medical records now."

"OK, keep us posted," the Division VP intoned. "This shit always blows over any way. On another matter, let's talk about your planned outpatient surgery center in Valley View. I've reviewed your pro forma — the earnings look really good — and I got tentative approval for the project from corporate yesterday for $10 million. The only new condition is that you will need to rent out 70% of the second floor to physicians for office space before the project will be funded."

"That's great news," Royce replied. "I'll have docs lined up who want to be in the building, I guarantee it. I already have a couple of surgical specialists going to Valley View once a week for mostly out-patient cases, so they will be eager to have an office across the street."

He leaned across his desk to receive high fives from Stella and Virginia, who smiled at the news.

"Do you have a bead on property yet?" the VP asked. Royce had been quietly working with his Board chair, who was a boyhood friend with the pastor of the evangelical church which sat adjacent to Valley View General Hospital. They had already secured a handshake deal to buy the church property for market price plus a sizeable donation from the Ascend Hospital Foundation to the church to fund its community health education program. The terms of the donation allowed up to 75% of the donation to be used for discretionary purposes.

"Yeah, I have a real prime location — a church next door to Valley View Hospital. The pastor and his Board want to build a new mega church a few miles away off the interstate," Royce advised. The call ended. Royce sat back in his chair and grinned at his two managers.

"It's a fine day, ladies. After I finish taking their surgery market share, the hospital Board at Valley View will be begging us to buy their little hospital. Then all those referrals for specialty services will come here instead of the Medical College."

He looked at his watch.

"I have to go — I'm scheduled to play a round of golf with Dr. Forrest to discuss medical staff issues." As part of his CEO benefits, Royce received a membership to one of Charlottesville's most exclusive country clubs so that he could entertain physicians and community leaders. It cost $20,000 to join the club and $2,000 in membership dues a month. All paid by Ascend's corporate office.

"It's probably not a good idea for me to be here any way, what with that reporter creeping around," he added.

"What about Dr. DeLuca?" Virginia asked. "I may need help handling her."

"Just don't let that reporter anywhere near her and we'll be fine," Royce instructed.

"Royce — to the best of my knowledge I don't have any control over Dr. DeLuca," she replied in a worried tone.

Royce waved her off. "Ginny — you'll do fine. I'll call DeLuca before I leave and tell her the way it's going to be."

Both Virginia and Stella noticed he told that lie with absolute sincerity.

CHAPTER

$10 Aspirin

SIX

Dr. DeLuca skulked through the ER like a businessman on a porno shop lunch break. None of the ER staff, including her physician colleagues, gave her demeanor a second thought. Dr. DeLuca was just weird, treating everyone else as a bit player in the great saga that was her life.

She was looking for her ambulance crew. Two of them were across from the main nursing station, restocking their crash box from a supply the hospital provided. Raymond Hubiak — known as Shades because of the sunglasses he always wore, even when he was putting in an IV line in a thrashing patient — looked calm. Randy, a student volunteer and her boyfriend's son, was a wreck. He jumped when Dr. DeLuca said his name and looked wide-eyed upon an emergency room that was insanely loud.

A confused, demented elderly woman pleaded in a panic over and over again for her mother. A two-year old with an earache cried non-stop in great gasping shrieks. And a college student who had been drinking all day on a float trip down the nearby Rivanna River in celebration of reaching legal age was loudly rapping, "All I Want for My Birthday is A Big Booty".

The police had not yet arrived to investigate and take statements because Dr. DeLuca had made sure they were not notified until 10 minutes ago. She had spent a lifetime calculating response time to her daily drama to the point that managing authority was second nature. She grabbed the two men by a handful of shirt in the small of their back.

"Come on," she instructed, propelling them to an empty consultation room used to examine patients with eye, ear and nose complaints. A dentist-like examination chair was bolted down in the middle of the room. Dr. DeLuca drew the blind on the observation window and instructed Randy to get into the chair. She took a hand towel out of the cabinet, wet it down and then heated it briefly in a warmer. She then laid it across his eyes, leaving her hand resting on top.

"OK guys, I want you to take a deep breath, let's all calm down." She winked at Shades, who smiled in understanding. He was wise in the ways of Dr. DeLuca.

"Where's Burly?" she asked Shades. Burly was Shade's cousin; the two almost always rode together on the same shift.

"Where else? In the lounge chowing down," Shades said. The hospital maintained a lounge for the rescue squads well stocked with food and drink. The idea was to entice them into to delivering their patients to Ascend Medical Center where they would dine in style.

"I ran over that man," Randy said with a moan. "How am I supposed to explain this to my father?" Dr. DeLuca began massaging his forehead through the towel. She shared his apprehension about his father; Horace "Ace" Fury was terrifying when displeased.

"Randy, you didn't hit him. He ran into the rig — he was, I kid you not, riding a skateboard. It was recorded on the security camera," she told him. "And anyway — listen to me Randy, because this is important, — you were not driving. Shades was driving. Isn't that right Shades?"

"That's the way I remember it," Shades agreed.

"Do you know why you were not driving Randy?" she asked him.

"Because I'm not allowed to?" Randy guessed.

"Smart lad," Dr. DeLuca said. "You are correct, Randy," she exclaimed in her best game show host voice, "because ride-along volunteers are not licensed to drive ambulances, even though I know you are getting pretty good at it." Randy's breathing slowed and Dr. DeLuca felt his head drop as his neck muscles relaxed.

"Does Burley know this yet?" Randy asked hopefully.

"Don't worry about Burley, he does what Shades tells him," Dr. DeLuca assured him.

"Can you see the driver in the video?" Shades asked. Shades owed Dr. DeLuca for every minute of his good life. He first crossed paths with her at his high school after one of her rambling, inaudible motivational talks. Afterwards, he had waited until she was in the parking lot to ask her advice about an alarming discharge of a private nature. Dr. DeLuca, never one to miss the opportunity to have someone indebted to her, had instructed him to remove his sunglasses.

"Raymond — I'm going to take care of this for you," she said, seeing the relief and gratitude in his eyes — her personal drug of choice. She withdrew the ever-present prescription pad from her pocket — her magic wand, she liked to think of it — scribbled out a remedy and handed it to him.

From this initial meeting, Shades was recruited to cut her grass and do other chores around her house. He actually spent more time sitting with her on her patio, listening to her talk about her own high school days and the many injustices she had suffered. A few years later, while in a bar on his 21st birthday, he had overheard several locals discussing Dr. DeLuca, which seemed to confirm her version of events. But he also heard an interesting tidbit that verified a suspicion.

"Remember part of our 'unofficial' initiation into the Varsity Club was to convince a freshman to show up on Saturday morning for a non-existent pep rally?" someone said. They all laughed in memory. "After DeLuca fell for it, the varsity table mysteriously collapsed in the lunchroom on Monday — made a hell of a mess. We're all sitting there with pudding in our lap and DeLuca walks by and said "See you at the next pep rally". I mean it was brilliant. She was so much fun to screw with, but man, she would get back at you in ways that were evil scary."

"Did you just say you screwed her?" another of the group had asked in mock surprise. A roar of laughter followed, accompanied by much palm slapping on the bar that turned most heads in the place. The storyteller held his hand up for quiet and effect, taking a sip of his beer before declaring:

"My friend…I would not screw her even with your dick," as Shades took a sip of his own beer, most of which sprayed out his nose onto the other EMS trainees, who were celebrating with him. Dr. DeLuca had intimated to him that she was very experienced in the way of casual sex, but with her Shades could never be sure if this was true or another one of her self-delusions. She had never hit on Shades.

This memory unreeled in an instant as Dr. DeLuca answered his question.

"No — I have seen the video, Raymond, you don't need to worry about it. The only problem is how fast the rig was moving. But given that the patient was in acute myocardial infarction, the speed was appropriate." Dr. DeLuca gave a circular motion with the index on her other hand — go with it — and looked at Shades with arched eyebrows.

"What's that mean?" Randy asked from under his towel.

Shades smiled back at Dr. DeLuca. "It means the dude was having a heart attack, Randy," he said.

"I thought you said his chest pain was probably nothing," Randy said, sounding more and more relaxed as Dr. DeLuca continued to massage his temples.

"That's what makes medicine so interesting, Randy," Dr. DeLuca intoned, reaching into her pocket to take out an electro cardiogram printout, to hand to Shades. Shades studied the graph, looked at the name and was genuinely impressed — which pleased Dr. DeLuca.

"Every case is different and things are not always as they appear. Just remember Randy, you didn't see anything from the passenger side of the front seat. You let Shades do the talking when the police get here."

Early Jensen picked listlessly at the Chinese take-out that Luann had brought with her to the Jensen home on the east side of Charlottesville. It was a modest brick rancher in a modest neighborhood inhabited by modest owners. Luann and Dusty where sitting at the kitchen table with Early, Flip's father. Early was a man who did not like confrontation. When faced with a difficult person or a situation, he went sideways until he could get around the problem. Whatever the strain, it wasn't worth it. He and his wife had happy lives. But with their son wired up in an intensive care bed at the hospital, there was no "getting around" this problem.

"Thank you for bringing us food," Early said quietly, looking down at the table.

"Well, my station has been following your son for a long time Mr. Jensen — he's almost as important a part of Charlottesville as Mr. Jefferson himself," Luann explained, referring to Thomas Jefferson, who was one of the founders of the city and the University of Virginia. Nearly half a million people visited Monticello, the 2,700-acre home of the former President and signer of the Declaration of Independence. And in any given year, thousands of these visitors required emergency room care for everything from appendicitis to dehydration. Ascend Medical Center was the official medical sponsor for the historical site.

"When we heard he was in the hospital we wanted to do something to help," Luann soothed. Dusty had his camera sitting on the table with a wide-angle lens, rolling. He was really hungry, but ate very slowly so as not to give the impression that his focus and thoughts were not on the situation at hand.

"Yes, your station has always been very interested in Flip and his story — and very kind," Early offered before he choked up a little.

"How's your wife holding up?" Luann asked quietly.

"Well, it's her turn to be with Flip, and naturally she's very upset."

"What do you mean it's her turn?" Luann asked.

"The doctor told us that only one of us could be in the room at a time — and then only for 15 minutes an hour. My wife thought it would be better if I came home and tried to rest for a while.

She's not used to this kind of stress — I should be there with her,"
he said wearily.

Luann looked at Dusty with surprise. She had spent a lot of years
covering all kinds of hospital and medical stories: bus rollovers, a
quadruplet birth, domestic violence requiring hospitalization, freak
accidents (like this one), and first-in-the-state-surgical advancements
among many. Last year she had conducted an interview at Ascend
Medical Center in an ICU with an entire Hispanic family in the room
surrounding a comatose patient. Restricting family access by parents
was not standard operating procedure.

"Who told you that only one of you could be with Flip at a time?"
Luann asked.

"That lady doctor taking care of him — Dr. DeLuca," he said, with
just the barest trace of resentment. But for a man like Early, even
just a little bitterness was unusual. And Luann had a feeling about
Dr. DeLuca. Her name had come up a few times recently, fleeting
references to ego and dysfunction — just the kind of personality
rich for discovery.

"Mr. Jensen, if you want — and if you invite us — we can go back
to the hospital with you and ask why the hospital has such a policy to
keep a father and mother away from their child. You'll have to in-
sist — to be strong — that you have asked me to accompany you, but
I'll bet we can get you both into that room at the same time. Would
you like me to see if I can help?"

Early nodded and was suddenly very hungry.

───────────────

On his way to work the next morning, Leo Miller listened to yet
another news story on run-away healthcare costs. Leo had come to
understand that American healthcare was interwoven with strong
cords of capitalistic and entrepreneurial fibers. Medical advance-
ment, breakthroughs and contributions to a long life came with
great overhead costs as everyone who worked in medicine, including
himself, made a good living. Where there is money and power, there

is strong temptation for personal gain to trump even religious belief and common decency.

Media coverage of hospital costs stirs up patients. At times, a patient would show up in his office with an itemized bill complaining that the hospital charged too much. There wasn't much any administrator could do about such gripes as most insurance contracts, including Medicare, did not permit co-pays to be waived. The thinking is that when patients don't have to pay anything, it encourages use of services that further drives up expenditures — which in Leo's opinion and given human nature, was true. Leo had found that trying to explain a truth that people with insurance helped subsidize the cost of uninsured patients did not help at all. This news often rendered people speechless with new anger. Even though it took four people making combined salaries of close to $100 an hour to get an aspirin to a patient, charging $10 for it was a losing argument.

As he drove by, Leo noted that both churches had changed their marquees. The Unitarians proclaimed "The Difference Between the Right Word & the Wrong Word is the Diff Between Lightening & the Lightening Bug. — M Twain". The Christian Life Church simply announced "Special All Congregational Meeting Saturday 4 PM". This struck Leo as odd.

When he entered the Administrative Office, Ben Stall was already there, which was unusual.

"Did you see the news on Channel 6 this morning?" he asked Leo, already knowing the answer.

"No. I might if they actually reported news but most of it is just a review of the local police crime blotter," Leo laughed.

"True, but this morning our colleagues at Ascend Medical Center were bigger news than the latest car crash — well kind of," Ben said, laughing at his own joke. "I didn't catch it all, but apparently they ran down their famous first born bicentennial baby in the parking lot with an ambulance."

Leo drew a blank, not understanding.

"Oh yeah", Ben said, "That would have been before your time." He switched the television on in his office; the station was repeating the story every 30 minutes and they didn't need to wait long. The news report had featured footage from Luann Zahn's interview with Early Jensen in his kitchen. This was followed by hidden camera footage next to Flip Jensen's bed, shot from a remarkably crystal clear hidden camera attached to Dusty's shirtfront.

Luann was betting a lot on this undercover approach, a first for her. She was bolstered by the fact that Early Jensen, a detail-oriented man, was able to produce a living will document signed by his son Flip which stated that his parents had all decision making control if he were ever to become incapacitated. Early had forgotten he had it until Luann asked, on an off chance, if he had one. It was not as good as a Power of Attorney — which was rare — but Luann, after consulting with her editor and the station lawyer, decided it was enough. Surprise — known as "ambush reporting" in the television news business — was the means to this end. She had given the hospital their chance and they had stonewalled her.

An undercover video can make anything appear suspicious and dramatic. When they were seated in the room, Luann looked into Dusty's button camera to bring her loyal viewers up to date. The big news, of course, was that the public relations symbol of caring and good health the hospital had spent years launching into the media atmosphere had taken a nasty turn into a boomerang of bad publicity. Of course that's not the way Luann said it. In the grand tradition of television reporters everywhere, Luann used the tried and true method of body language and voice inflection to bias her audience.

"I'm sitting at the bedside of James Jefferson Jensen, better know as Flip Jensen to many of you *(establishes relationship with the viewer)*, the beloved bicentennial baby *(repeating a media label, a proven emotional igniter)* of Charlottesville. Traaaa-gically *(draws out the key word with a slow dropping of her chin to the chest and arch of her eyebrows)* young *(tie-back to the infant image of 23 years ago)* Flip was perhaps fatally *(play loose with the truth)* when he was injured by a speeding *(embellishment, but closer to the truth than she realizes)* while making his way *(key skateboard omission)* across the hospital parking lot." She pauses, and casts a worried look at Flip in the bed.

"Now *(a great word for creating doubt)* hospital spokeswomen Virginia Stowe *(I'm giving you notice honey that I'm holding you personally responsible if you bullshit me again)* released a statement *(weasel words)* that Flip caused the accident while riding a skateboard *(roll hand at the wrist palms up towards camera in dismissal)*. But so far, the hospital has not released any evidence to support that claim *(the ball is your court Mr. Hospital administrator)*. But even if that is not the case *(I've covered my bases here in the event that my insinuations are incorrect)*, this traaa-gic *(ohhh, love that word, good for the ratings)* turn of events *(screw-up)* has one of Charlottesville's first families of birth *(sure to bring a lump to the throat)* fighting against a hospital policy just to be with their gravely injured *(let the tears and outrage commence)* son."

Dusty then turned to Myrtle Jensen who was sitting to his left. The group had arrived at the hospital when the shift was changing at 10:45 p.m. while the nursing staff was in report. They were not challenged. Third shift nurses were composed of a mix of experienced nurses who do not want to deal with managers — who rarely come in on the off shifts any way — and new nurses who get their foot in the door working the night shift. They make their own rules. If a few family members want to visit a patient, they were not going to interrupt their report from the outgoing shift to make a fuss.

"Mrs. Jensen," Luann asked in a quiet, concerned voice. "How is your son *(image of little baby boy)* doing?" Myrtle sits holding a baby photo of Flip, widely publicized and even used in the hospital's own on-going advertising campaign. Luann had grabbed it on the way out of the house with Early's permission.

"Well", she said quietly, looking at the comatose Flip, "the doctors say his condition is very serious." Her eyes were fatigued; she looked tired.

"And how has the hospital care been?" Luann asked with her set-up question. She was all voice now, the camera on Myrtle. Myrtle looked hesitant to say anything.

"Go ahead Myrtle, many of our viewers have grown up with your son and feel like he is their son," Luann stated quietly.

"Well, his care has always been good at Ascend Medical Center, — I mean the nurses, they are great — but….." her voice trailed off. Luann and Myrtle had talked beforehand about what should be said to best get what they wanted — open access to Flip in the ICU — but Luann could tell that Myrtle, like her husband, was very reluctant to speak her mind. It was a common misperception among patients and family members that if they complained the care would not be as good.

This was rarely true — in fact usually a patient who complained received extra monitoring from everyone to head off problems. But at Ascend there was truth to this fear. Dr. DeLuca, whose compensation was not tied to patient satisfaction — and would be incapable of changing her behavior if it were — routinely treated patients rudely, abruptly and unkindly if they violated her complex rules. Despite their conversation, Luann realized that Myrtle was not going to be able to make the point without some steering. But, that was the very essence of being a reporter: the knack for asking the right question, and finely honing any key response with some careful editing.

"Now *(create doubt)* Myrtle, I understand that an uncommon *(creates credibility as an expert)* hospital policy has been very stressful *(lead the subject)* in this traaa-gic *(Luann might climax if she could use this word one more time)* turn of events *(hospital screw-up)*. Can you tell us *(she and her personal friends, each and every viewer)* more about this concern *(outrage)*?"

Luann could see the outburst coming from deep in the back of Myrtle's eyes, rushing forth, a blue slash of response to a lifetime of going along. Myrtle had never wanted to showcase her baby boy to the world — it was just the ladies of the hospital auxiliary those many years ago would not leave her alone. She finally relented, her husband Early did not want to seem ungrateful to Ascend Medical Center. Her stress and insomnia had given rise to a startling thought: that Flip being smacked by an ambulance in the parking lot of the hospital was part of a grand design — retribution for her spinelessness, a refusal for her to say no.

"Let…me….tell you….something," Myrtle spoke low and tense. "This hospital is keeping my husband and me from being with our son — together, at the same time. The nurses are wonderful and even they don't like this policy…that only allows one of us at his bedside for 15 minutes every hour…it's not right." Myrtle seemed surprise, as if her words had come from someone else.

Sometimes this was the lot of hospitals — to provide cover for doctors. Dr. DeLuca's troubles were rolled up under a shroud of faceless bricks and mortar. This problem that Dr. DeLuca handled was now Royce Wexler's problem and his alone. The only recourse for her dysfunction would be to appeal to her fellow colleagues the next time her medical privileges came up for review. But that was risky. It was Royce's bad luck to be in a position to try to change someone who would never change.

For Luann, it was just plain good luck for a reporter to be there when a public figure went out of character. Her next question was a set-up for her work the following day. A good investigative reporter was always thinking about the next story.

In a hushed voice, with a glance at the comatose Flip, Luann asked her golden standby question.

"Myrtle, what would you say to the hospital administrator if he were standing in front of you right now?" Even as Luann asked the question, she could see the fire retreat in Myrtle. Myrtle's eyes went wet, running to her cheeks. But it was all right — Luann had what she needed.

"Just take care of my boy, get him back on his feet," she almost whispered.

Luann conducted her standup — the closing to any news story which almost always features the reporter talking on camera — in front of the Emergency Room. She reviewed the salient points: hospital indifference; lack of details over the incident; and most of all — Flip Jensen himself, on the verge of accelerating Ascend Medical Center from hero to zero. Her 90-second story on the morning news would be a teaser for the full three-minute segment she planned to have ready for the following evening. The hospital would be begging to talk after the images ran of Early and Myrtle Jensen crying their eyes out. Reporters do always get the last word.

"The story will run again in a half hour if you want to see it again."

"No, I've got my hands full running one hospital," Leo answered. "From the little bit I've heard since I've been here, it sounds like this kind of problem has been due for Ascend Medical Center. Didn't you used to work over in Charlottesville?" he asked Ben.

"Yeah, but at the University Hospital. But man, I used to hear some stories about Dr. DeLuca. She wouldn't have made it six months working at University," Ben stated.

"Why is that?" Leo asked. Ben sensed that this was more than a casual conversation. He was beginning to see a side of Leo that was insightful in regards to ethics, in his experience a concern not fretted about too much among those in power. He considered his answer before speaking.

"Because she is more concerned about what she can get out of medicine than what she can give," Ben answered.

Leo smiled. "That's a really good answer, Ben." He picked up his shoulder bag from Ben's desk and turned down the hall to his office. It was not until he had powered up his computer that he looked down and saw large chips of the desk laminate splintered around the broken lock of his file drawer. He pulled the drawer open; it was empty. Leo immediately picked the phone up and dialed his Risk Manager. Jenny Rybold picked up on the second ring.

"Hi, Jenny, this is Leo. Do you still have the copy of that file on Dr. Divinity I gave you yesterday?"

"Hang on," Jenny said. Leo heard her rise from her chair, then keys jangling as she unlocked the fire proof file cabinet in her office. He looked up to see Ben standing in his doorway.

"Yeah, it's here," Jenny confirmed.

"OK, good," Leo said. "I want you to make two copies. Give me one and send one by confirmed courier to the hospital attorney as soon as possible." He hung up.

"Everything OK?" Ben asked. Leo showed Ben the file cabinet drawer.

"I can think of two people in my office yesterday who would have a reason to do this," Leo said. "Did you notice anything unusual with the main door to the office when you got here this morning?" Leo asked.

Ben rubbed his chin. "Yeah, the outside door was unlocked — I figured the housekeeper just forgot to lock up. I was going to say something to the supervisor about it when I saw her on my rounds this morning," Ben said. "I'll look at the security camera recording to see what happened. We had to put that camera up a few years ago because someone was peeing in front of the admin door after we had a few layoffs."

Leo sniffed a few times.

"Well, I don't smell anything, I guess that's the good news." Leo pulled open his center drawer. There was a pile of change, mostly silver and a few crumpled one-dollar bills.

"Who ever did this wasn't after money," Leo said, more to himself.

Leo emailed his Engineering Director to get a police report filed. He could find nothing else missing. Most of the contents of the drawer were materials he usually purged every six months — nothing he would miss or could not replace. He kept important backup documents either on his computer or took hard copies to his home.

The office door creaked open and Warren Harris walked in. He looked like a new man — rested, showered and with his hair neatly combed down on his head. He smiled broadly when he saw Leo.

"Great news, my wife is sitting up this morning and eating some breakfast, she is doing so much better. This is a great hospital, your nurses couldn't be taking any better care of her," he reported.

Leo smiled back. "Glad to hear the good news, Mr. Harris, you've made my day already. I was just headed upstairs to the units, let's walk up and you can introduce me."

They entered Mrs. Harris's room in the ICU and as Warren had reported, his wife was sitting up in bed. Dr. Massari was seated in a chair next to the bed writing in her chart.

"Hey handsome," she chirped happily at her husband. "Dr. M is punching my ticket out of here today, I'm headed to the general floor."

Akil smiled and continued his documentation. "That's correct Mrs. Harris, the ICU is only for sick people. We just need to keep an eye on your electrolytes for another day and then you should be on your way," he said.

Warren sat down on the bed, extending one arm around his wife's shoulders and holding her hand with his other arm. To Leo's eye, it looked strange, this much younger man and his senior citizen wife. There was nothing to distinguish her from the thousands of other old ladies Leo had visited with during his career, except the light in her eyes. Hers were young eyes, a sparkle of promise and enthusiasm that Leo realized he did not see often in the elderly, male or female. What he usually saw was a look of someone who was confused or no longer interested in life. He recalled the last time he had come face-to-face with such enthusiasm.

A few months ago he had stepped into a patient room where one of the case managers — a nurse who worked with patients to get the care needed when they left the hospital — was kneeling beside the bed. The old man in the bed held her hand.

"Leo," she said, "Meet Mr. Hopkins. He's 92 years old and this is only the second time he's ever been in the hospital."

Leo looked into a relaxed face with alert eyes and a huge smile.

"How do you do, Leo?" he said. "I'm a tough old rancher, I should never have retired last year — been sick ever since." Leo immediately liked him, a man who didn't think the problem was his being 92 years old, but rather not working any more.

"Mr. Hopkins was just getting ready to tell me a joke, you want to hear it too?" she asked.

Mr. Hopkins scooted his shoulders a little higher up in his bed, which was in the sitting position. He spread his hands wide to begin his story.

"It's a good one," he promised. "This 90-year old man dies and rises up to heaven." Leo laughed; this was already funny.

"There are two other old geezers who also died on the very same day. One of them looks at the other and says "How did you die?" He answers, "I have a very precise doctor. He said I had 3 months to live because I had cancer, and sure enough, three months to the day, I died and here I am." He then asks the other fellow how he ended up at the Pearly Gates. The other fella says "I also had a very precise doctor. He said I had a bad heart and I would be dead in six months. Sure enough, six months to the day, I died and here I am." They both looked at the 90-year old and said, "How about you?" The third man looked at them both and said, "I have a really precise doctor. He said I have "seen-you" and I had 15 seconds to live and he was right.

They look at him confused. "Seen-you?", one of them said. "Do you mean sinuses?" The old guy answered. "No. I was in bed with the doctor's wife when he come home and he said 'I seen you', and then he shot me."

Their laughter, both Leo's and the social worker's, was genuine. The old patient looked extremely pleased with himself, enjoying their pleasure.

Leo repeated the joke to Mr. and Mrs. Harris, telling them about the old rancher. Their laughter was genuine too, as if it were a long time coming. It was moments like these, when Leo saw a patient and their family return to well-being, in which he felt his work was truly honorable. He and Dr. Massari left the room together. Leo waited until they were outside the unit and asked his Chief of Staff to follow him into a consultation room. He told him of the break-in and the missing files.

"Do you think Dr. Divinity did this?" Akil asked quietly.

"Well, he's one of two people I dealt with yesterday who might have had a reason to steal files — and he would be my first pick," Leo answered. "But I don't know. Ben is checking the security camera recording to see if it caught anything. The good news is that the original files remain safely locked up with Jenny in risk management. I'm having more copies made."

Dr. Massari thought for a moment.

"You know Leo, as weird and scary as Dr. Divinity may be, he's not stupid — pathological, yes, but stupid, no. I mean all of the doctors know about the permanent files that administration keeps on doctors in their privileging chart."

It was true that any documented adverse incident, behavior or complaint was retained in the event a bad one needed to be denied privileges. But it was Leo's policy that this information was never a surprise to any doctor who had the opportunity to address the matter long before privileges came up for review. The files were also maintained by the Risk Manager to remain undiscoverable by outside attorneys.

"It doesn't feel to me like this is something he would do — it's weird, even for him."

"As always, I appreciate your insight, Akil. I guess we'll wait to see what the security recording tells us," Leo said.

The two agreed that they would not talk about the break-in, but they also would not deny if asked. They would watch Dr. Divinity for any signs of his involvement. If the radiologist had done it, he would soon let it be known.

CHAPTER
Freeway
SEVEN

Her name was Felicia Monahan and like Owen, she was hooked on prescription painkillers. But as far as Owen was concerned, her addiction was an outstanding quality. That she was obviously more intelligent was yet another point in her favor. Then there was the rest of her: voluptuous and striking. Owen decided he would walk a mile on his knees just to go through her trash.

Felicia did indeed have a little yappy dog. His name was Freeway and he did need medication every day to control a condition that left untreated, would cause his eyes to explode. Freeway was an old, blind pug with only a few front teeth left in his head. Felicia had recently found the dog wandering aimlessly around a strip mall parking lot. No one had claimed him at the pound. Her vet said that pugs often developed health problems and were sometimes abandoned by owners who could not afford treatment. The dog immediately took an intense dislike to Owen.

Felicia also had an old car with a cracked distributor cap and frayed spark plug wires, an easy fix for Owen. His auto know-how was definitely a point in his favor with Felicia.

She was a CNA, a Certified Nursing Assistant, working for a tem-

porary staffing agency. CNA's have much less training than a Regis-
tered Nurse (RN), who graduate from four-year college programs or a
Limited Practice Nurses, (LPN), who require two years of community
college study. Felicia too desired the pain pills, but unlike Owen, she
maintained her supply by flying under the radar. Being in hospitals
and nursing homes for short stretches at a time as a temporary worker, she picked up the occasional loose prescription pad (careful to use
these sparingly, as a flood of scripts from the same doctor would trigger an alert to area pharmacies) or helped herself to excess pills from
elderly or deceased patients. It was truly amazing the bounty of narcotic pain meds that sat around unused by old people in their homes,
assisted living and nursing homes. They were of the generation that
toughed it out rather than let a pill be the solution to their problem.
Even with a terminal condition, many feared becoming hooked on
painkillers. A common attitude among these old folks was that keeping a supply on hand, often left over from surgical procedures, was
enough to control their pain rather than actually taking the pill.

But one thing Felicia never, ever did was to divert pain medications from any patient who was hurting. Even in hospitals, this rare
and despicable practice had trusted caregivers stealing pain meds en
route to a patient, then replacing it with aspirin or dietary supple-
ments and recording the pain medication as given. The only way to
identify diversion was when enough patients complained of poor
pain control. This was a slow process given the tendency of some
bedside caregivers to suspect the intensity of patients about their
pain complaints. But when the pattern seemed excessive, managers
would begin reviewing staffing schedules and set distribution traps
for suspected diverters. New computer accessed pharmacy bins made
it tougher to divert as well. Felicia made sure there was never a reason
that she might be a suspect. And to be on the safe side, she actually
did have a few legitimate prescriptions for pain meds and Valium,
which she filled only occasionally.

Felicia knew that diversion was the quickest route to discovery,
and losing her license and her income. Despite her addiction, she
really cared about her patients and was a good CNA because of her

compassion. Even her confused patients responded to her gentle way. The staffing agency received nothing but good feedback about Felicia. But one quality that addicted bedside caregivers shared was that they were almost always nice. It was a poor strategy to be obnoxious while stealing narcotic pain medication at work. But Felicia enjoyed her job and the fact that she was a comfort to others. Like a smoker who would not light up except when in a bar, she did not use when she was working. At work in the company of others she was her happiest.

A few days after she and Owen met at the hospital, they were sitting in her living room, each digesting 10-milligrams of Valium. They sat on her couch watching television.

"How come you use the pills? What are you running away from?" Owen asked her as they watched a weatherman display graphics that were predictable and calming, the sound barely up. Owen watched Freeway out of the corner of his eye, where the mean little mutt was banished to his wicker dog bed. The dog sat up rigidly, glaring in his direction wearing a sweater embroidered with the admonishment "Love Me, Love My Dog." Freeway had initiated several loud, ferocious sounding charges in Owen's general direction over the past few days. The dog sounded like it was having an asthma attack when riled. But it's tough to be an attack dog without sight and a sense of smell. Owen found the little dog's blind attacks amusing and he assured Felicia that given enough time, they would become buddies. Felicia was not surprised by her pug's anti-social behavior, as she seldom had guests. Freeway seemed to be a one-person dog. She was also not yet sure how she felt about the prospect of Owen hanging around to change her dog's mind, although Owen seemed as disinterested in Felicia as Freeway was intent on biting him. She supposed it was a libido issue, a casualty of the pills. But she could use a boyfriend to do the heavy lifting in her life and Owen was nice enough. He was certainly not going to hassle her about her pill habit.

To answer his question, Felicia would have to tell Owen far more about herself than she was willing to share with anyone. After all, how do you explain to anyone that your own parents were the worst enemies you ever had in life? What does that say about you?

Felicia found her parents' disdain a demon that never really left — even now, when they were dead. For she and her four older siblings, childhood was like one long prison sentence with verbal abuse, solitary confinement, hard labor and the occasional beating for infractions of an extensive set of rules and regulations. No talking at the dinner table; wearing clothes in a set order to school; no extracurricular activities (unless the parents wanted the kids out of the house so they could have private time, in which case they herded the four kids to the library, church or occasionally a $1 movie theater); banishment outside for most of the day, no matter what the weather; and exclusions from any social activity or functions with the few friends they managed to keep.

And these were just a few of the circumstances enforced in their upbringing. Any dissent was treated harshly. It wasn't locked in the basement abuse, but her childhood had been no fun. Worst of all was a total lack of respect, not to mention love. She and the rest of the Monahan kids escaped from home as soon they could, the circumstances of each departure more and more tragic as the rage in each child had longer to fester. Felicia was the youngest and was the last one out the door at the age of 16, when she ran away. Her parents did not look for her. It would be decades for the term PTSD — Post Traumatic Stress Disorder — to emerge. But when it did, Felicia saw the symptoms in herself: trouble sleeping; anger management; hyper vigilance; and even trouble concentrating when reading. The medicine — the pain pills and the Valium — helped control her ever-present anxiety, although it did nothing to address the source of her fear. But irony is the bedrock of all addiction.

"I have a touch of arthritis," Felicia finally answered. Owen noticed the long pause between his question and her answer, which he did not attribute to the Valium.

On the screen a lady reporter appeared standing in front of the Emergency Room at Ascend Medical Center. A photo then morphed on screen to none other than Denise DeLuca, M.D.

"Hey I know her," Owen exclaimed, reaching for the remote to turn the sound up. "She used to be my doctor until she went all psycho on me. Man, she used to write some sweet scrips, I tell you."

"...and according to Flip Jensen's parents, they were denied ready access to their son, who traaaagicly, continues to lie in a coma at Ascend Medical Center. The details of the mishap are still unclear and hospital officials have declined to release any video footage that we are advised should be available. I will be reporting on this developing story throughout the day. I'm Luann Zahn, reporting for the Eyewitness Channel 6 News Team."

"I like her," Owen said. "She did a story a few months ago about pain pill addiction and how it was all the fault of the doctors and hospitals because they won't take care of people."

"Oh, Owen, sweetie," Felicia cooed. "You don't really believe that do you?"

Owen had to think about that for a minute. He didn't know what she was driving at and he said so.

"Well, Owen," she said sliding her arm along the back of the couch behind his head. "Did you know that a doctor can lose their license — even go to jail — for prescribing pain medications and Valium without a valid medical reason? You can't blame them for being careful. And I'll bet you do come on kind of strong," she said stroking the back of his red hair lightly.

Owen froze, unable to gather his thoughts. But when at loss for an idea, Owen had always been a man of action. He finally reached across her lap to hold her other hand, raising it to his lips. Freeway growled again, but Felicia smiled and turned the sound back down.

Denise DeLuca was by no means an athlete. But she liked to imagine herself as a player in a medieval movie, sword in hand as she fought off enemies, swinging from one castle rampart to another, narrowly avoiding defeat and destruction. The drama and deceit in her life that others found so exhausting was but the stage to which she was born.

Her next challenge in the Flip Jensen saga was placating her live-in boyfriend Ace. That Dr. DeLuca had daddy-issues was a forgone conclusion. Her father was an alcoholic, misogynistic, angry logger who made no exceptions for his daughter. Nothing she did was of interest to or impressed her old man. Her mother talked of his terrible experiences in Vietnam, but the truth was he had worked in the back lines in supply, well away from the fighting. Every photo Denise had ever seen of him from his time in the Army he looked terribly hungover. With the easily available prostitution during the war and his unwanted family waiting for his return, her father was in no hurry to return stateside. He was screwed-up before he went to Vietnam, Denise later realized. But that didn't make her want to please him any less, which meant she was screwed-up too.

Denise was not so much in love with Ace, as she had a deep need to please on a visceral level. The fact that Ace gave her the abuse she knew she so richly deserved — her only basis for intimacy — had not promoted her understanding of love one bit. Theirs was a dysfunctional relationship with a fair amount of sub-dominance element mixed in. Ace's abuse, of the hair pulling, finger squeezing and breast twisting variety, rarely left marks. But their relationship was predicated on approval for him, and a kind word for her. Ace — a wiry, mean guy who carried a gun — had liked the idea of his son Randy joining the rescue squad. They met when DeLuca hired him to build a safe room in her house. As she did whenever she was trying to garner approval, Denise had moved too fast and inappropriately, letting Randy drive the rig after his second volunteer ride with Shades.

In the end though, Randy had come through like a champ. He knew how to lie to his father. Denise's behind the scene work had him believing the altered version of the truth with no hesitation and complete credibility. At first Ace was suspicious. Randy and Denise had learned that was part of the trick to placating him. With his son not in the line of fire, Ace relaxed and enjoyed Denise's ribald account of Ascend Medical Center's Bicentennial baby, who was now the punch line in an absurd marketing joke gone wrong. Denise, who was not much of a drinker, had — at Ace's insistence — too much to drink as the evening drew to a close with a good Ace ravishing.

The next morning was not cheery. With a hangover, Denise was not in her usual self-delusional form. And Royce Wexler was not in any mood for her at all — in fact, he was working himself into a rage.

"God damn it Denise, don't even try to tell me that you restricted access to the patient because you were worried about infection control. No one is going to believe that — I don't believe it and I sure as hell know you don't. What about you Ginny, you believe that lame-ass excuse? God damn it!" he added one more time, just for good measure.

Virginia Stowe enjoyed these moments, watching her boss and Dr. DeLuca go at it. In the end, she knew she was going to be the one who would have to bail the hospital out of this mess with Luann Zahn — as well as with the rest of the press who had begun to call her this morning. Virginia had stopped in the ICU on her way into the hospital to find Mr. Jensen at his son's bedside. It would have made her job so much easier if Flip's parents had declined permission to comment to the news media about Flip's condition or accident. But given that Luann's story had already aired an hour earlier and would run throughout the morning, the hospital was forced to speak to its side of events.

This was the first rule of brand management — never let someone else tell your story. With mixed feelings, she was able to convince Mr. Jensen to sign a media release form authorizing her to talk to the media about his son.

"I think as long as there is a medical reason to support Dr. DeLuca's concern, that may actually be a good answer," Virginia said, noting a fleeting shadow of approval cross Dr. DeLuca's face. Denise spoke even more softly than usual.

"Well, I'm a doctor, I suppose I would know about medical necessity," she said.

"You'd better sell this Virginia, because it ain't dog food if dogs won't eat it," Royce warned. Virginia had come to understand that Royce was pretty much useless in a crisis. He became emotional and infantile, refusing to leave his office until the fury was past. He would rotate in several of his managers to sit with him through out the day while he ranted about the injustice of it all, mocking all the key players in the story except himself. Yesterday, Luann Zahn's interest in Flip Jensen was theoretical, but with the story breaking this morning, Royce was in a knot. This was the moment when he would finally listen to Virginia, because Royce saw it as his job to be upset and his staff's job to make him happy again. While he never had any ideas to that end, Virginia understood that it was on days like this that she earned her money.

"You tell that damn reporter we saved that slacker's life," Royce was waving his finger at her now. It was pointless to reason with Royce when he was in his panic mode.

It took a few minutes but it was finally decided that Janet Ippolito, the Medical Director for the emergency room, would speak to Luann Zahn about Flip Jensen. Dr. Ippolito was female, had an Italian sounding last name like Dr. DeLuca and was not a pathological liar. She had been called upon in the past to be the public face of the hospital and did well.

This morning, Denise wasn't disappointed not to be on television. Flip was going to be in the hospital for a while, she would get her chance to be the center of attention another day. Denise had the mixed feelings she always had about someone who she sensed was not her friend. She had been especially attentive to Dr. Ippolito so far without results. But today her hangover was a greater force than her insecurities.

"Fine," Denise whispered as she rose to leave. "I've got lives to save, I'll check in after lunch." All she really wanted to do was find an empty bed and lie down for a few hours. She headed to the ICU where there was plenty of staff to cover for her. Her patients could wait.

Royce waited until Dr. DeLuca was out of the room and motioned for Virginia to shut the door. Still, he spoke softly, as Dr. DeLuca was known to listen from the other side.

"Ginny, do not let her, under any circumstances, talk to the press. There is no telling what she would say," he pleaded. Virginia sighed.

"Royce — we've had this conversation. I understand your orders,

but I have no control over Dr. DeLuca — I'm not sure anyone does."
Royce knew this to be true and then he had an awful thought.

"I know someone who has control over her — that creepy little
boyfriend of hers," he said.

Virginia did not like where the conversation was going. "Royce,
she works for you. You have control over her. Tell her what you expect," Virginia pleaded.

Royce smiled. "You know she told me that once she made dinner
for him — Ace is his name, Horace "Ace" Fury, no kidding. She said
she worked 12 hours, came home and he insisted she cook him a four
course meal, which he then refused to eat. She was up until midnight
by the time she got the kitchen cleaned up." He smiled again.

Virginia felt her stomach churn. "That's awful Royce. Why on
earth did she tell you that story?"

"I'll tell you why, Virginia," Royce said hovering with his hand
over the phone. "Because Dr. DeLuca is a professional victim, she always wants us to feel sorry for her so that we won't hate her when she
acts like the sociopath we know her to be." Royce stabbed the inter-
com button to his assistant. "Grace — get me Ace Fury on the line."

"OK, Royce. Oh, and the house supervisor called down to let us
know that Mrs. Wallace is a patient again. She's in the Four South
VIP room." Missy Wallace was the Aunt of Board chairman Jim Wallace and the hospital attorney Robert Wallace. She was one of the last
of the Charlottesville old guard southern ladies — rich, unmarried
and a bit loony. She was a first class hypochondriac who was admitted on a regular basis by her cardiologist, Dr. Forrest. It was Royce's
duty to show up at her bedside to prime the pump for her next annual
donation to the hospital foundation.

"Crap," Royce exhaled. "I swear, its like there's a plot to ruin my
day. OK Grace. Call Ace Fury and ask him if he can have lunch with
me today at noon, in my office."

Grace, who was a nice person, winced to herself. The kitchen was
always cranky about last minute requests to serve lunch. Never one
to play the "I'm the CEO's Assistant" card to get what she wanted, she

would be forced through a 10-minute apology and flattery fest with the kitchen manager.

"Yes sir," she answered cheerily. Royce did not like to hear any discouragement, other than his own. She hung up and sighed. Before Grace came to work for Royce a few years ago, she had assumed hospitals to be great places of healing, where everyone worked together in the name of medicine. She knew now that the powerful — administrators and doctors — viewed hospital patients as nothing more than a commodity. It was enough to make her wish that she would never be a patient, but it was inevitable. Sooner or later everyone would be a patient. Grace sighed again and rang the kitchen.

All good reporters know when they are being handled. There was a reason public relations people like Virginia Stowe were called "flacks", a reference to the WWII aerial images of deadly black puffs of death surrounding incoming allied bombers. Luann felt like one of those fliers, skirting the little explosions of resistance, denial and interference when she was on a mission. It was clear that the interview set-up in the Ascend Medical Center ER was only peripherally related to the story of Flip Jensen colliding with an ambulance. There was something she was overlooking, Luann was certain. The call tree to Ethyl and Mary Martin at Valley View Hospital was in play, so hopefully new information, even just a hint, would offer some insight. But until she could figure it out, Luann would go along with Virginia Stowe's little sideshow. Flip was not getting better any time soon.

Dr. Janet Ippolito was extremely popular and well-liked. She was in medicine for the right reasons. Slender, with dark hair that she wore in a ponytail, she could get a central line in a dying patient, recognize an internal bleed or wade through pages of blood chemistry reports better than any of her ED colleagues. Cheerful, helpful and intensely interested in good patient care, she quickly became medical director within a few years of starting practice out of medical school just up the street at the University Hospital.

Her youthful demeanor sometimes caused problems with older patients who were anxious that she did not have enough experience to manage their medical emergency. Men, usually unmarried, sometimes formulated a fantasy that her careful administrations implied a romantic intention. She was an expert in handling patients, charming the old people and shutting down the young fools.

"I am not here for you to date," she told one young, smitten patient. "I am the doctor and you are the patient and doctors do not date their patients. Do you understand me?."

Dr. Ippolito had a soft Texan dialect to her voice that portended calm in the most frantic of circumstances. Female patients, especially those with babies, loved her. The fact that she seemed to dislike Royce Wexler and Dr. Denise DeLuca made her very popular with the ED staff. They had a pool going to see how long she would remain at Ascend Medical Center. She was clearly too good for the place.

Luann had interviewed Dr. Ippolito before, who looked fantastic on camera. Dr. Ippolito was authentic and believable, which meant that whatever the hospital was hiding, she probably didn't know about it.

She and Virginia were walking in the ambulance bay, Dusty trailing behind them, camera rolling. Virginia walked out from under the canopy to an intersection in the parking lot and stopped.

"The accident happened right about here," Virginia said, stopping. Dusty panned his camera down, looking for bloodstains that had quickly been bleached from sight by the Maintenance Department. Virginia walked up to the entrance of the ER parking lot to make sure it looked good for the camera. Spreading her arms, she said. "He came from this direction on his skateboard."

Luann stepped to the spot and looked back at the ER entrance. She noted there was a security camera mounted outside the ER door, which pointed at them.

"Why was he riding his skateboard on hospital property? I mean, has it been determined why he was at the hospital?" Luann asked. Both she and Virginia were tagged with wireless microphones feeding directly into Dusty's camera.

"We do not know why Mr. Jensen was on hospital property," Virginia said in a nice neat "sound bite" that she knew Dusty would edit and use in the final report.

They returned to the ER to interview Dr. Ippolito. She wore a freshly starched white lab coat embroidered on the upper left side with her name, followed by the all-powerful M.D. moniker. The hospital logo was prominent on the opposite side of the coat. Dusty affixed another wireless microphone to her lapel. Luann re-introduced herself and noticed that the doctor held her hand for an instant longer than necessary.

"Dr. Ippolito, thank you for taking time today to speak with me. You were the doctor on duty when Mr. Jensen was injured in the hospital parking lot, is that correct?"

Dr. Ippolito answered in the affirmative.

"Can you tell us about it please?"

"Mr. Jensen was unconscious. The ambulance driver who had summoned help told me that the patient had hit the side of the ambulance on a skateboard. He had a contusion to the front of his head that was consistent with a blunt force trauma injury. I immediately called a trauma alert, which mobilized imaging and surgical resources to quickly treat the patient's injuries and improve the chances for a good outcome," she stated.

"What about the patient who was already in the ambulance? That must have been a bit of challenge to go from having one emergency patient to two in an instant," Luann said. This was a common reporter's trick. She asked a question, then suggested an answer with her follow-up comment.

"We're used to that here in the emergency room, we prioritize patients by the severity of each patient's condition. We are capable of taking care of more than one patient at a time," Dr. Ippolito said. "The other patient was having a cardiac episode that we were able to get quieted down fairly quickly."

"The patient is something of a celebrity at Ascend Medical Center. Had you ever met him before?" Luann asked.

"No, I've only been at the hospital a few years and that was before my time," Dr. Ippolito said.

"Are you aware that Flip Jensen's parents were not allowed to stay by their son's bedside together? They could only go in his room one at a time for 15 minutes an hour. Is that normal?" Luann said.

The look on Dr. Ippolito's face was killer, just what Luann was after. The doctor turned her head sharply to the right, arched her eyebrows and dropped her chin slightly, a universal expression of disapproval. A flash of insight immediately followed this as she, just for an instant, slightly tightened her lips. What the doctor was thinking, was that the situation had Dr. DeLuca's grubby, paranoid fingerprints all over it. But she had to be mindful of how she answered the question.

"Well, you'd have to ask the ICU Medical Director about that. I'm an emergency medicine physician. My job is to find something that might kill a patient right away. After the patient leaves the emergency department, I transfer care to another doctor."

"And who is the Director of the Intensive Care Unit?" Luann asked, savoring the moment, the entire reason she had agreed to the interview with the emergency room doctor, which was clearly a smoke screen Virginia threw up in an attempt to placate Luann's ongoing interest in the Flip Jensen story.

"That would be Dr. Denise DeLuca," Dr. Ippolito replied evenly.

"And in your experience, does Dr. DeLuca restrict access of family members to patients in the ICU?" Luann continued.

"You know, you'll need to talk to Dr. DeLuca about that," Dr. Ippolito said, smiling brilliantly. Luann concluded the interview and offered her hand to Dr. Ippolito, who again, held it a few beats longer than necessary.

Virginia Stowe tensed up at the mention of Dr. DeLuca, which did not go unnoticed by Luann. When Luann asked her next question, Virginia's anxiety ratcheted up another notch, especially when Dusty, on cue from Luann, lifted his camera and began rolling tape again.

"Virginia, I assume there is a recording of the accident from the camera mounted outside the ER. I'd like a copy of it for the report." Virginia drew her lips into tight little white lines.

"I'll have to check on that and get back to you," she answered as neutrally as possible. Dusty took a couple of steps backwards and zoomed out to get the two women in the frame together with the camera. Luann crossed her arms, looked down at the ground for effect, and then raised her head to stare intently at Virginia.

"You haven't seen a recording of the accident, have you?" Luann asked and smiled slightly. Virginia knew better than to answer the question. She swam to one of her islands instead — safe talking points that a spokesperson formulated ahead of any interview. It was a tried and proven method of not answering a question, especially if it meant lying on the air.

"In order to protect patient privacy *(and also due to the fact that the hospital might get sued over this freak accident),* I can't answer or discuss that matter," Virginia stated. She knew that Luann would ask the question again in a different form.

"So it sounds like you are saying there is a recording, is that correct?" Luann asked. Virginia repeated back her answer word-for-word. This was to let Luann know that she could ask the question as many times as she wanted and the answer would not change. It was part of the dance and Luann smiled. She signaled to Dusty to cease filming.

"OK, Virginia, but we'll be looking at a Freedom of Information Act request to get that tape," Luann advised. Virginia maintained her neutral expression.

"Well, Luann, you should do whatever you think is right. But think how you would feel if you had to watch your loved one on the evening news get hit again and again by an ambulance."

"Well, the way to clear all that up is to let me at least view the tape, Virginia," Luann said, continuing her line of inquiry.

"Like I said, I'll have to check on that," Virginia repeated.

"I also want to interview Dr. DeLuca," Luann said.

Virginia smiled.

"Look, Luann, Dr. DeLuca is now allowing both parents open access to their son," Virginia said. "The medical concern she had about infection control has passed, so I don't really see why that's a relevant subject of discussion. Dr. DeLuca doesn't like being interviewed anyway."

Luann looked at her incredulously. "Come on Virginia, now I know you're hiding something. Dr. DeLuca calls me a couple of times a month with the lamest story ideas and every single one of them involves her being interviewed."

Virginia cast her eyes to the ground. "Luann, we're just a hospital trying to do the right thing here. Can you just let it alone? As a favor to me? I'll owe you one."

Well, Luann thought, *that's a first.* She looked back at the security camera under the ER awning. The first mention of a recording of the accident seemed to have ignited this anxiety fest Virginia was clearly experiencing.

"I'll tell you what Virginia, you let me have a copy of the accident tape and I'll skip the interview with Dr. DeLuca," she offered. "Check on it and let me know — you're going to have to pick your poison. Otherwise, I'm going to interview Dr. DeLuca, who I have a strong hunch will be a real good talker."

"I'll have to check on it," Virginia repeated weakly.

"I need to hear something by one," Luann said. Dusty had packed up the camera and his gear and rolled up in the Eyewitness News Van. A couple walking up to the ED stopped on the sidewalk to stare at Luann, looking excited. They both gave a little wave. Luann smiled and waved back. She looked at Virginia a final time before opening the passenger door.

"Isn't it amazing that so many people still watch the local news? And isn't most healthcare local? Are you sure you don't want to get out in front of this story before it's too late, Virginia?"

CHAPTER

Inspiration

EIGHT

The old man was not crying today. Leo noticed it was quiet as soon as he stepped out of the stairwell into the hall on the medical floor. For the past few days, an elderly patient had been franticly speaking the language of the confused and remorseful. Even with a blanket over his lap and his bare legs extended under a hospital gown, it was obvious that the tall and distinguished man had once been a person of position. But he was in the throes of old age now, a general malaise of disconnect between his mind and body. Not a cheerful man by nature, he had recently started to lose his balance, stumbling and falling. He was admitted for dizziness. Tests would be ordered — some expensive, such as the ever-popular head MRI — but his path was on autopilot. He was tired of living. Leo had first walked into his room a few days ago in response to his cries.

"Sir — is there something I can do for you?" he asked, genuinely troubled by the man's anguish.

"Yes — get out," he ordered, resuming his moans and yells.

Dr. Massari could find nothing urgently wrong with him; a little blood chemistry out of whack, imaging studies normal for someone his age. At first Leo thought he might have been transferred out to a nursing home. But as Leo walked up to his doorway, he discovered the reason for the calm. A nurse knelt in front of the old man, who was seated in a chair, holding his hand and quietly speaking to him. Her white uniform glowed angelic in a streak of sunlight slanting through the window. She looked the patient intently in the eye, speaking in a low voice. Even with her back to him, Leo could hear the love in her words. The transformation in the old man was remarkable. He had a slight smile and a missing light was reignited in his gaze. He looked relaxed for the first time since being admitted. Leo remained silent in place for nearly a minute, unable to hear what words the nurse spoke. The patient was so transfixed by her presence that he did not notice Leo standing just outside the doorway.

Leo moved on to find the veteran house supervisor at the nursing station.

"Good morning, Linda."

"Hi Leo, how are you today? Linda answered.

"At the moment, really good, in fact — I feel inspired." Leo shared what he had just seen. Linda looked up from the chart she was reviewing, staring at Leo over the top of her glasses. She had worked at Valley View for 23 years and had seen several administrators come and go, a few of whom remained in their office for their entire tenure. In her experience, it was unusual to see a hospital CEO on the floor at all, much less nearly every day.

At first, no one trusted Leo. An administrator walking the floors and checking with patients and doctors could only mean trouble for nurses. But eventually the staff did begin to talk to him. This was a valuable strategy for whoever was in charge — to hear what they needed to hear, rather than what front line staff thinks a boss wants to hear. Although Leo cultivated this trait, it was also a part of his nature. It made him an effective leader, someone who Linda was now comfortable in confiding.

"That's Renee, one of my best nurses. Did you know that she is going through breast cancer treatment?" This revelation struck Leo as profound. He asked for the nurse's full name so that he could send a handwritten note to her home thanking her for the great example.

Leo moved on to visit with other patients. When he stepped just around the corner from the nursing station, he saw the Martin sisters at their cleaning cart outside a patient room. The patient was asleep, so Leo took a business card from his pocket and placed it on her bedside tray. He was surprised when he returned to the hallway to see the sister housekeepers still there. Usually when they saw Leo they scurried into a room to avoid him.

"Good morning ladies, it's nice to see you," Leo greeted the two. Ethyl seemed coiled to speak.

"Did you see that news report this morning about the man who got run over by the ambulance at Ascend Medical Center?" she asked.

"He was the first baby born in Charlottesville in 1976 — the Bicentennial baby," her sister Mary added.

"Yeah I did catch that this morning. Let's hope he recovers soon," Leo said. "How are our patients today — anyone who you think I should spend some extra time with?"

The sisters were not ready to change the subject. They knew something he didn't. They, the cleaners of toilets, had acted with cunning for the greater good of Valley View Hospital. The media elbow thrown in the throat of Ascend Medical Center was their doing. Of course, they could not reveal themselves to Leo, this new man who would take years to learn their ways. But they could school him in the methods of small town politics.

"So Leo," Mary continued, "do you think this bad publicity will help us shut down the new outpatient surgery center that Ascend Medical Center plans to build across the street?"

Leo was not actively listening. He was thinking of the young nurse, finding inspiration from her own health crisis and the lesson in her actions — to look beyond ourselves in all situations. He was thinking of the next patient room he wanted to enter. He wished he had eaten breakfast. So it took a few seconds for him to actually hear what Mary Martin had said, this housekeeper who rarely spoke, much less looked him in the eye, as she was intently doing at that moment. As it often did, the warm glow of the humanity of being a hospital administrator fizzled out quickly, extinguished by the harsh realities of the job. But

Leo knew leaders must stay calm when every one around them was in a panic. He forced himself to be casual.

"This is the first I'm hearing about that plan, Mary," Leo said. "Where did you get that news?" Mary looked at her sister Ethyl. Insider information made them both giddy.

"From the best grapevine there is Leo — the housekeeping grapevine. We have a friend who works over at the church — they are selling out to Ascend," Ethyl enthusiastically explained.

Leo had to smile — she was right. It was a common mistake to dismiss the so-called "unskilled" workforce in a hospital. Early in his career as a department manager, Leo had often hung around on the loading dock where the smokers gathered, many of them housekeepers, maintenance workers and kitchen staff. More often than not, their rumors were accurate. At another hospital where he had served as assistant administrator, his CEO had learned of a new cardiac program being developed at a competing hospital when a disgruntled housekeeper — who did not offer an identity in a cover note — mailed sensitive documents she had found in the administrative trashcan. The CEO called his counterpart at the other hospital and returned the documents by courier. But the heads-up helped his hospital take actions to diminish the surprise element of a new competing program.

"Love your housekeepers, Leo," Mary chimed in. "You never know when you'll need them for something other than cleaning up."

Ace Fury yanked the necktie off as he walked out of the front door at Ascend Medical Center, flipping it in the back of his pick-up truck. His lunch with Royce Wexler had gone well. Something for something was a language Ace understood. Wexler had been cagey about what he was after.

"Dr. DeLuca is such a spirited person about her beliefs, but sometimes her passion gets the better of her," Wexler had said after 15 minutes of chit-chat about Ace's remodeling business.

Ace was a man easily offended, often irate and excitable. He had a hard time winning bids and often keeping jobs when he actually did get work. The gravy train he was on now as the live-in boyfriend of Denise DeLuca was his best gig in years. She paid all the living expenses and was happy to give Ace money when he was nice to her for a few minutes at a time. But a man needed his own work.

He shared all this with Wexler, probing about the planned outpatient surgery center construction project. Ace had learned about the project from DeLuca, who in turn had heard about it at a Board meeting a few months ago, although the location of the new facility was so far a well-guarded secret. Ace had been bugging Royce about working as the plumbing sub-contractor on the project. Now Royce shared confidentially with him that the hospital would soon break ground on the complex somewhere in the area. Wexler supposed there would be some work for a good man like Ace Fury.

"That's great, Royce," Ace had deadpanned. "Who do I have to kill to get in on the project?"

Wexler looked startled.

"Heh-heh, no, no Ace, I'm not asking for anything like that, please don't misunderstand me," Wexler said in alarm.

Ace felt satisfaction that Wexler thought he would kill someone. He sometimes felt a rage akin to murder, but as a man always on the edge, he had cultivated good impulse control.

"Jesus, relax Royce. I haven't killed anyone — yet," he said with a wry smile. This guy was seriously creeping Royce out — he honestly was unable to tell if Ace was kidding or not. A prudent person would have changed the subject. But the little warning blip that pinged the self-preservation portion of his brain did not deter Royce; he continued.

"I just need you to talk to Denise on my behalf so that she will understand how important it is for her not to give media interviews related to the Flip Jensen matter," Royce said. "She speaks so highly of you that I know she'll honor your wishes."

That's a good one, Ace thought — *honor my wishes.*

"Royce — don't give it another thought. Denise and I have a great relationship and I'll make sure she understands the plan," Ace replied with a wave of his hand, which was holding his steak knife. He then cut into his New York strip, hungry now that he knew why he had been summoned.

"That's great to hear Ace, just great. Please ask Denise to come talk to me if she has any questions," Royce added.

Ace chewed vigorously, and then pointed his knife at Wexler for emphasis.

"Count on me Royce — Denise will not have any questions."

After lunch Royce made his pilgrimage upstairs to see Miss Wallace in the VIP wing. The VIP wing was reserved for anyone who contributed more than $10,000 a year to the hospital foundation. The Foundation had paid all the costs of renovating the wing, which featured opulent accommodations, including Jefferson ceiling lighting, wainscoting, high-end early American reproduction furniture, oriental carpets, as well as custom menus prepared onsite by a local chef. The entire wing was leased to the Foundation to avoid any pesky entanglements with federal reimbursement laws.

He used the stairs to avoid being stuck in the elevators with visitors or staff. He exited at the fifth floor and walked by the nurse's station. On any other floor in the hospital his appearance would be cause for alarm. They were not used to seeing the CEO on patient floors. Royce did not like being around sick people and staff who complained. His job was making decisions, which he could do just fine at his desk. One Christmas Eve, in a fit of good will generated after watching "A Christmas Carol" at home with his family, he had come into the hospital to visit the staff working the night shift. Royce, as he usually did, forgot to wear his hospital ID badge. At every turn he was challenged by third shift staff who did not know who he was and then acted with suspicion when he was finally able to point to his photo on the wall or in the patient admission kit. He was not in the Christmas spirit when he finally abandoned the hospital an hour later.

But on the VIP wing the staff smiled and said hello. The vice president of the Hospital Foundation carefully selected staff on this floor. They were experienced, attractive and had outstanding interpersonal skills — only the best for their donors. He entered Miss Wallace's room. Dr. Paul Forrest, the cardiologist and the past Chief of the Medical Staff was sitting at her bedside. He winked at Royce.

"Miss Wallace, the CEO of the hospital himself has come to pay you a visit — do you remember Mr. Wexler?"

Missy Wallace smiled weakly at Royce. She seemed very comfortable and content. Royce was reminded that there are some people who enjoy being a patient a little too much. These people want be the center of attention with a highly educated and skilled staff hovering over every detail of their well being. Any experienced bedside caregiver could recognize these patients. Royce knew that clinical psychologists actually had a name for the condition — Munchausen Syndrome. Patients or family members — such as the mother of an ill child who may actually poison the child to require hospitalization — will exploit, exaggerate and feign symptoms or personal misfortune to get attention and sympathy.

Miss Wallace was very rich and very lonely. Her nephews, Jim Wallace, the Board chairman and Robert Wallace, the hospital attorney, barely had time for their own lives much less a spinster aunt. Unknown to either of the nephews or Royce however, was that Dr. Forrest had aided Miss Wallace in rewriting her will and estate plans, worth almost $10 million. Dr. Forrest had introduced Miss Wallace to a childhood friend who was a top estate lawyer. Her new will would supercede the one her nephews thought was in place, the one written by Robert Wallace some years ago.

"Good afternoon Miss Wallace, I'm glad to see that you are looking so well. It is such a pleasure to see you again. Is the staff taking good care of you?" Royce asked as he sat in a chair next to Dr. Forrest. Missy Wallace smiled wanly, so pleased to have two tall, handsome men sitting next to her bed. Missy had played the part of a southern belle her entire life.

"Thank you Mr. Wexler, your staff is most kind and attentive — as is Dr. Forrest here," she said in an old lady voice mirroring her 82 years. "My bowels are not looking too well though. When I picked through my stool after breakfast I think I saw blood," she said sweetly.

She reached out to hold Dr. Forrest's hand, who grimaced ever so slightly. The doctor looked longingly at the hand sanitizer dispenser on the opposite wall next to the door. Miss Wallace was obsessed with the workings of her digestive tract, especially the business end of her intestines. She would discuss frequency, color, consistency and oddities with anyone; it was her favorite topic and perhaps explained her nephews' reluctance to spend much time with her. As with moneyed people everywhere, she assumed that everyone wanted to hear whatever was on her mind. Body language and nonverbal cues were of no help in dissuading her.

Royce and Dr. Forrest heard the click of very high heels on the linoleum floor in the hallway, which foretold the imminent arrival of Camilla Bonfield, Vice President of the Ascend Medical Center Foundation. They both craned their necks high, watching the door like expectant puppies. Camilla entered the room in a shimmering white glow. She was pale — from her white blonde hair and eyebrows to her snowy, ethereal skin. She had one blue eye and one green eye. Her entire life, people had stared at her in wonder, which she found tiresome. Willowy, with the most elegant of hands and elongated neck, Camilla was dressed impeccably. She mesmerized people wherever she went. It was not surprising that she made her living convincing people — even those without much to spare — to give their money to the hospital. Her demeanor — angelic and surreal — made it very difficult to say no.

Miss Wallace brightened considerably when Camilla sat down in a third chair across the bed from Dr. Forrest and Royce. Camilla reached for Miss Wallace. Royce was more than happy for Camilla and Dr. Forest to do all the necessary handholding.

"Miss Wallace," Camilla said softly, leaning forward, "while I am always so pleased to see you, it distresses me that you are back in the hospital." Her melodic voice was as exceptional as her appearance. The pull of this woman, who seemed unaware of her sultry aura, was breathtaking. Although Camilla was a winner of the genetic lottery, she was an introvert by nature. All her life she had grown up in the spotlight cast upon the exceptionally attractive, a status she despised. She did not prescribe any special grace to herself and had always worked hard to earn her success. When she married, she more se-lected than fell in love with, a second-generation policeman of Persian decent with olive skin and jet-black hair. It was her most fervent hope that their children would not be born fair or with green eyes. Miss Wallace smiled brightly at Camilla and squeezed her hand.

"Well not too good, honey, I got the dire-rear," Miss Wallace re-ported. Camilla patted her hand.

"Let's not talk about that Miss Wallace, I think only the nurses need to hear about your bathroom problems," Camilla said sweetly. "Have you had a shower today and walked around a bit?"

Miss Wallace loved Camilla, who she viewed as a daughter. Camil-la did not cut the old matriarch any slack about her toilet talk, which the old lady didn't seem to mind. The Wallace nephews had laid down the law with Camilla as to the size of the annual donation she was allowed to extract — $50,000. Camilla could easily get more, but she was a local girl who knew that you did not cross the Wallace family.

The length of stay for Miss Wallace's reoccurring hospitalizations was getting longer with each admission. Dr. Forrest kept her as an inpatient without medical necessity, which meant that payment from Medicare was denied more often than not. Royce's Chief Financial Officer — who tracked length of stay daily and projected losses from patients for whom they would not be paid — became increasingly frantic about Miss Wallace's extended visits. Although old, she had the good health that money can bring to someone with no bad habits. Dr. Forrest also took good care of her. He was counting on money from her estate to build the hospital a new, state-of-the art cardiac catheterization laboratory.

"Royce, you are stepping over dollars to pick up dimes," Dr. Forrest told Royce when he broached the subject. "She needs to see the hospi-tal as her caregiver and not some nursing home," he continued.

"You let me worry about when to admit her and how long she stays. You'll like the pay-off for the hospital once she passes." Miss Wallace was not a difficult patient. She liked to sit in her regular room of the hospital VIP wing and look out the window upon the streets of downtown Charlottesville, using a pair of high-end opera glasses to see the detail on the street below. She often spotted people she knew who occasionally acted salaciously with other people she knew.

"Why can't I just live here?" Miss Wallace asked. She snuggled down under a quilt that had been handmade by hospital volunteers.

"I like it here, there is always someone to talk to me — and I get to see you Camilla," she said in a slow, raspy southern drawl. Camilla smiled and brushed the hair from the old lady's forehead.

"Well, bless your heart, Miss Wallace, you are just the sweetest thing." Royce was not from the south, but he had learned that any time someone said "bless your heart", it wasn't really a compliment. Dr. Forrest leaned over, removing the stethoscope he wore draped around his neck.

"Miss Wallace let me take a listen to your heart please," he said rubbing the end of the stethoscope to warm it up. "Unless something has changed in the last 10 minutes, I think you are going to be with us for a while."

"Well, I no longer have the explosive bowel sin-drome," she informed him.

Six floors down in the basement of Ascend Medical Center, Harold Fellows, the Director of Security, studied blueprint schematic maps of the entire facility, looking for a new office space. He had to get away from the dead people in the morgue next door. Harold heard the heavy slap of male heels on the floor in the hallway leading to his office. Mark Swingle, the hospital's patient representative who visited with each patient every day, stepped in carrying a plastic bag that hung heavy.

"Harold, my man," Mark exclaimed as usual. Mark was a perpetually cheerful, outgoing guy who got along well with everyone. The two were friendly and saw each other several times a day when they went to the designated smoking area near the hospital loading dock. They both had good contacts spread throughout the hospital. Between them, they had an excellent record for sorting through rumors to figure out what was going on in Administration and with the Medical Staff.

"What you want white boy?" Harold replied with his usual response.

"I need you to come down the hall and help me with something in the morgue," Mark said cheerily.

"Exactly what you want me to do in the morgue?" Harold asked suspiciously. "I ain't interested in doing nothing with no dead people. Besides, I was just getting ready to eat my lunch," he said indicating a brown bag on his desk. Mark heard the apprehension in Harold's voice.

"It's nothing Harold. The house sup and I need to go in to check a deceased patient for a personal belonging. I just need you to stand near the door and let me know if anyone from a funeral home comes down the hallway. It would be awkward to be interrupted. You don't have to go in the morgue," Mark said clapping him on the shoulder.

They walked down the hall where the house supervisor already had the morgue door partially open. She looked focused, all business, nodding at Harold whom she recognized from his twice a day security rounds in the hospital. She and Mark stepped in and closed the door to a crack. He heard rubber gloves snapping into place and the two of them talking in low voices.

"How about that?" Mark asked.

"No, that doesn't look right," the house sup said. "Too big." Harold heard them rustling through the plastic bag. Whatever they were doing, the house sup rejected his choice several more times. Harold looked nervously down the hall. The last thing he wanted to see was one of the funeral home guys in their spiffy suits wheeling a body cart down the hallway. Finally the house sup sounded satisfied.

"Yes, that looks very good, thanks Mark." They both returned to the hallway and Harold was relieved to see her lock the door to the morgue and hurry away to the elevator bank around the corner. Mark peeled off a pair of rubber gloves and dropped them into the bag that Harold realized was filled with false teeth.

"What was that all about?" Harold asked. Mark grinned.

"There was a guy in the ICU who has been comatose and dying for the past few days. The house sup says his family is just the worst. They have been sitting around arguing over his money and his stuff the whole time — imagine that. They say that hearing is the last of our senses that goes when we die, so he probably had to listen to them."

Mark shared this all as they walked back to Harold's office. Harold sat down again at his desk while Mark leaned against the open doorway.

"So the poor old guy finally dies today and his family claims he had a brand new set of dentures missing — that he had them made right before he came in the hospital, but they can't remember the name of the dentist or show us a receipt. They want us to write off almost $3,000 — which coincidently is how much his estate will owe after Medicare and his supplemental insurance pay off. Can you fucking believe some people?" Harold looked at his lunch bag.

"Where you get all those teeth?" he asked. He was beginning to understand.

"Man, old people leave their dentures in the hospital all the time. Housekeeping finds them in the laundry or they go down to the kitchen on dinner trays when patients take them out to eat. They get put in interoffice envelopes and sent to me. There was a drawer full of teeth in my desk when I started six years ago and the pile just keeps getting bigger." Mark said. "I also have a bunch of hearing aides."

"But they ain't his teeth," Harold pointed out.

"Well, Harold my man, he's not going to complain, now is he? I'll call that family to give 'em the good news that I found his dentures," he said and for good measure added, "The douche bags".

"But they're going to know you're lying," Harold pointed out.

"Takes one to know one," Mark said, happy again. "See you on the loading dock, my man." Harold looked at his lunch, no longer hungry. He had to find another office. Down the hallway he heard Mark greet Virginia Stowe. "Ms. Stowe, you look like a woman on a mission," Mark said.

"Hi, Mark — I hope your day is going better than mine," she said curtly. Harold heard Mark laugh.

"My day is going great now," he answered, his voice fading out down the hallway.

If Harold had thought to ask the patient rep why he bothered to save false teeth, he would have learned that one of his performance metrics to receive bonus pay was to reduce the amount the hospital paid out for lost patient belongings claims by 50%. Patients lost many items in the hospital moving from the emergency room to surgery to the floor, none more costly than dentures and hearing aids. Occasionally, valuables were stolen. Reducing these payouts was worth $2,500 of his year-end bonus to Mark Swingle.

"Hello, Harold," said Virginia as she stopped in the doorway. "You got a minute?"

Harold sighed. No good ever came out of white people lined up in the hallway.

"Well, I was just gonna eat lunch," he said waving his hand at his brown bag lunch.

"Me too," Virginia said brightly pulling a power bar from her suit-jacket pocket. Harold frowned. It was Harold's habit to eat lunch alone, as he relaxed to the rhythmic hum of a large air handler in the space next to his office. Because he worked a second job as a security guard three nights a week, he would grab a 30-minute catnap cranked back in his office chair. But he liked Virginia; she was one of the more reasonable people in charge at Ascend Medical Center.

"Sure have a seat," Harold said indicating a stool next to his desk. "Why you want to eat with me today?" he asked.

"I need to look at the security tape again. There's a reporter hounding me; I might need to show it to her," Virginia said as she peeled the wrapper off her "lunch".

"Can't give you a copy unless Mr. Wexler says," Harold said. He reached over and inserted a tape into the player. The ambulance entrance appeared on the screen.

"Play it as slow as it will go," Virginia asked. The ambulance appeared on screen in slow motion, the image sharper on the higher-end security playback machine than the unit they had used to watch the recording a few days ago in the Board Room. Harold was about to bite into his sandwich when he froze. He hit the rewind button and started the recording from the beginning. Again the ambulance moved into the screen in front of the glass windows of the hospital. He hit the pause button, stood up to lean inches away to peer at the monitor, still holding his uneaten sandwich. Virginia saw a bead of sweat break out above his lip as his eyes widened.

"What?" Virginia asked. Harold looked like a man who had just seen a dorsal fin at the beach.

"You don't see it?" he said to Virginia. Virginia joined him in front of the monitor, searching. Then she looked beyond the ambulance at the rest of the frame.

"Oh my," she whispered. "How did we miss that?" Harold put his sandwich down and pushed it away. Virginia reached out and pushed the office door closed.

"Remember, this was your idea. I ain't telling him," Harold pleaded, more than said. Virginia patted his arm then reached for the phone and dialed an extension.

"Mary — is Royce there?" she asked the administrative assistant. She listened for a moment.

"OK, find him and tell him to come down to the security office immediately — it's urgent. I'll wait for him down here. Don't mention this to anyone else Mary, and tell Royce not to say anything to whoever he happens to be with — not a word."

CHAPTER

Cameras

NINE

Dr. Neil Divinity sat in the physician lounge at Valley View Hospital, fingers poised over the computer keyboard. With a little bit of sleuthing he had figured out how to send an email to a dummy account at the Charlottesville Public Library, which would then automatically be forwarded to the hospital CEO's email address. He began typing.

"Arf, arf, Miller, it's the hounds of mediocrity hot on your trail. Too bad about your office break-in, but you're sniffing up the wrong tree, fool. In your short time at the hospital, you seem to have a knack for getting things wrong."

While he never forced his way through a door, Dr. Divinity was not above looking about an open and unattended office. Most people had something to hide. Several months ago, while walking through the far-flung perimeter of the hospital on a scouting trip to determine where security camera gaps existed, he had come across just such an open door. The nameplate on the door read "Director of Engineering". After a few minutes he had found a heavy-duty gym bag under the desk filled with bondage and sex toys. There were also a couple of videotapes in the bag. It seemed the Director of Engineering and a few of the female housekeepers he recognized in the recording were seriously into an alternative lifestyle. While kinky sex — some of it filmed in the hospital — was of no interest to Dr. Divinity, leverage on a guy with a master key to the hospital definitely got him excited.

"How do I know you didn't make a copy of the tapes?" the Director of Engineering asked. He was tall with a head of thick black hair that peaked like an arrow down on the front of his forehead.

"Because if I ever have to see you naked again it will be too soon," Dr. Divinity said. The doctor had spent an hour walking around the facility to make sure the copy of the master key he now possessed worked. He handed the bag back to the director, who took a quick inventory. He looked up to sneer at Dr. Divinity.

"Get off on all this? Did you know that in the Civil War doctors served as pimps at the Confederate hospital in Richmond?" Dr. Divinity's fixed smile grew a bit broader. It was a poor insult, but Dr. Divinity appreciated the effort.

"They also performed surgery without anesthesia and didn't wash their hands. Most of us evolve," the doctor said calmly. "Just out of curiosity, why would you keep something like that in your office?"

"If you were married, you would know the answer," the director, who had heard the rumors, answered. Dr. Divinity's smile tightened. His wife had left him long ago.

Part of blackmailing the Director of Engineering had been a lesson in how to work the hospital's security camera system, which sat in a small room adjacent to the director's office. Dr. Divinity had a special fascination with surveillance, recognizing that its preponderance in society was increasing. But he was also secure in his belief that anything designed by other people was flawed and subject to his disruption. With access to the security recording files, which were held for seven days in the system's memory, he was learning a lot about the comings and goings of the new Administrator.

His inbox — routed through from the library — pinged. It was from the CEO.

"Who is this?" Leo wrote back.

Divinity typed with relish. "Someone who is watching you."

He smiled, a sweep of pleasure tingling his backbone. Playing both ends against the middle was a longtime tactic he had perfected — such a sweet endeavor. He signed off and left the lounge, feeling well satisfied.

Stepping into the hallway, he nearly collided with Jenny Rybold, the Quality Director. She had a handful of gift cards from the hospital's coffee shop.

"Good morning — or I guess I should say afternoon at this point in the day," she said, a bit daft. Dr. Divinity made her nervous. His facial expression never changed from a vague half smile, like a person enjoying a private joke. The techs in the Radiology Department called him "Dr. Haw-Haw, the man with the plastic smile" behind his back.

"Are you coming to the quality presentation on hand washing protocols in the doctor's lounge tomorrow at lunch time? I'll be having a drawing for coffee gift cards," she said, waving the stack in her hand, raising and slowing her voice to sound tempting.

"I don't drink coffee," he said, stepping around her as he continued down the hallway. He in fact washed his hands compulsively, but always in secret and with his own specially prepared solution of hand sanitizer.

"We're having a special lunch — lobster," she called after him.

"I bring my own food," he called back, which was true. He ate only grains, fruit and vegetables, which he prepared after very carefully washing his hands.

Owen Gregor was sitting in an ER exam room in a hospital in Harrisonburg, VA, about an hour northwest of Charlottesville. It was his first visit to the community hospital. The staff was polite, but they ignored him. After the first hour, he feigned a fall off the gurney, roiling in imagined pain to his right arm. After 10 minutes, when no swelling appeared, the big male nurse with a trimmed beard had assured him he was fine. That was an hour ago. It was clear the strategy at this hospital was to wait him out. His cell phone chirped.

"Owen, you should come to dinner tonight," Felicia instructed, more than asked.

"Well, I'm not finished at the office yet," he joked. Felicia sighed, which sounded marvelous. Owen did not detect the slight slur and dullness in her voice indicating pain meds.

"Well, you do what you think best, sweetie," she offered. On the drive over to Harrisonburg, Owen noticed the first hint of fall, brightening the air with clarity. High up on the Blue Ridge Mountains a tinge of color was starting to streak the landscape orange and red against a blue sky that glowed. He could not ever recall an invitation to dinner in his entire life.

"I'm just teasing," he said into the phone. "I'm on my way. You need me to get anything other than flowers for you?" he asked.

"Ohhhh, a sweet talking man!" she laughed that great laugh; at this particular point in time everything was perfect.

Owen walked out of the exam room and towards the ambulance bay door. His nurse was standing at the central desk flipping through a chart.

"You're leaving us then?" the nurse asked. Owen waded through an emotional current and then it came to him; he felt safe — maybe for the first time in his life.

"Yeah, I got something better to do," Owen said, taking pleasure in the truth of his words.

"Well, good for you," his nurse answered. "You take care of yourself." The nurse sounded like he meant it.

<hr>

Leo's Board chairman called back a few hours later confirming the tip shared by the Martin sisters. Ascend Medical Center had made a deal with the fundamentalist church just across from the hospital to purchase the property and church building for almost $8 million. The purchase stipulated that the church had to vacate the premises in 60 days to temporary quarters, which according to the Board chairman's calculations, meant demolition would be immediate with construction beginning as soon as the church was out. Royce Wexler was eager to get the new revenue stream flowing for a return on investment as he had performance pay for the following year riding on the project.

The Board chairman was astonished.

"What a bunch of horseshit. This community does not need any more operating rooms," she fumed. "We're only using the ORs we have at 75% capacity."

"Can we get the project denied by the county commissioners?" Leo asked. The Board chairman scoffed.

"Hell no, those fuckers got themselves elected with a pro-growth platform, Leo. This will be their first big opportunity to show off," she said. "Doesn't Ascend have to have state approval to build it? Maybe we can stop the son-of-a-bitches there."

Stephanie Mora was a retired Army nurse who swore profusely and often without awareness. A local girl, she had been Board chairman for three years. In his first board meeting she had expressed concerns about short staffing in the ICU, stating: "You have to get us some fucking nurses, Leo." The rest of the Board members had looked pained, like their lunches were backing up on them. Leo had smiled and replied slowly, "I don't think I can find those kind of nurses, Stephanie." She had look confused for a few seconds and then looked sheepish. She had refrained from profanity for the rest of the meeting. Other than her potty mouth, she was so far a good Board chairman.

"Stephanie, what Ascend will do is announce some new service that we don't have — radiation oncology would be my bet — and counter that they will be improving the healthcare of the community by expanding services. We could tie them up for a while, but it would cost a lot in legal fees and in the end it's unlikely we would succeed," Leo answered. "The current state administration rubber stamps most entrepreneurial medical projects — the corporate sector were big contributors in the last election cycle." He paused. "There's something else you should know, Stephanie and you're really not going to like this," Leo added.

"What?" she asked.

"This is no doubt a joint venture project between Ascend Medical

Center and physicians. It means surgeons and others who do procedures such as imaging, might be approached to buy in as partners," Leo advised. "Some of our own medical staff will likely become competitors if they buy into the project."

Leo also explained that without emergency and inpatient services to maintain, the new facility would offer lower prices than what Valley View could charge for the same outpatient procedures. Setting up across the street from the hospital was a classic way for entrepreneurs to, in the parlance of cynical hospital administrators, skim the cream (privately insured and Medicare patients) and leave the crap (Medicaid, uninsured and charity cases).

Leo expected another profane outburst, but the Board chairman simply said softly. "Damn, this is really bad, Leo."

There was silence for a few seconds and then Stephanie got riled up again.

"We'll deny the fuckers inpatient medical staff privileges," she growled. "Let them get their privileges at Ascend Medical Center in Charlottesville, see how they like driving 90 minutes round trip every day to practice medicine."

"Restraint of trade, Stephanie, cue the lawyers," Leo offered.

"Well damn, Leo — what's our plan then?" she said, exasperated.

Leo was not a man prone to self-pity, but sometimes being in charge of a hospital was like paying for a beating. The truth was that Leo's hospital was going to lose market share to this shiny new, standalone outpatient surgery center and there wasn't much they could do about it. Valley View Community would be robbed of a good portion of a main revenue source it used to eek out a small profit, much of it to be hijacked by its own medical staff. This was a power play by a competing hospital, an especially insidious assault on the financial sovereignty of a non-profit community hospital.

However this same scenario had been played out in many communities across the country and no administrator had yet figured out how to stop it. The bones of the healthcare system fostered competition, which at times could improve patient satisfaction and outcomes, as well as introduce new services. But competition also duplicated services, diverted healthcare finance dollars away from preventative care in favor of specialty services that compensated at higher rates. Market competition also fostered over-utilization, and not infrequently, fraud, to recoup the cost of the new facility investment.

Down the hall Marianne Quarters, the CFO, could hear Leo talking to somebody on the phone, but couldn't discern the topic. She didn't like Leo. All of his blathering about an inspired culture and an engaged workforce was bunch of happy talk that did nothing to help the hospital. Fear in the workplace was essential to maintain order. People needed to do what they were told. Leo's insistence that the senior executives get out of their offices and walk around every day to see if the staff had "everything they needed to do their job" was nonsense, a waste of time. Now he was talking about conducting employee satisfaction surveys and rolling the results up by individual manager. She left the office for a late lunch, stepping into the hallway to find the Director of Engineering standing on a ladder.

"What are you doing?" she asked.

"Running a new cable for the security camera," he said, his gaze holding hers. He nodded at the camera next to his head. "The line got cut for the old one. Must have been an accident when we ran cable for the new pharmacy prescribing system" he answered. "The overheads in this older wing are tight, it's difficult every time we have to squeeze another cable in. So sometimes another line gets cut or rubbed and we don't find out about it until something stops working."

The Engineering Director climbed down from the ladder, leaning casually with his elbow on one of the steps. He smiled — the CFO was not a great looking woman but she had a nice big bottom, the kind he liked. She seemed to have only one emotion — a blank stare of sorts, but he was certain he could elicit a broader range of emotion if he tried.

The recording of the break-in, which he was not about to reveal to the CEO, was inconclusive, but there was a "tell" about the identity of the person who broke in. The hooded intruder had reached up with their opposite hand and pushed the door open with their wrist, just like he had watched the CFO do numerous times on camera. This was a behavior the CFO had developed to compensate for carpal tunnel, the results of years of pecking away on a keyboard for several hours a day.

"Yeah, well you should finish up and get this ladder out of the hallway," Marianne said, taking a step backwards. She did not care for his demeanor. He grinned again, more of a leer.

"I'm going to stop by later — I want to discuss that purchase order I put in for a new truck for the department."

"Don't bother, I can tell you right now that request went right to the bottom of the capital pile," she said. He watched her walk away, grinning. This was going to be fun.

Dr. DeLuca was in a foul mood, looking to bully or blame. Enthroned in her usual place at the far end of the nurses' station in the ICU, she had arrived much earlier than usual to avoid Ace at home. She was banned from speaking to Luann Zahn or any other reporter about Flip Jensen, whose inert figure in room six was now an annoyance to her. Being the attending physician for the boy wonder was turning out to be a dead end. Her chance at national fame — the story was getting legs on national news sites — was squashed by Royce Wexler with help from the heavy hand of her boyfriend. She could feel a bout of poor impulse control coming on.

The nurses huddled at the other end of the station like mice in a snake cage. One of them was going to get worked over; they could see Dr. DeLuca ramping up. In the medication room, two of the new nurses unwisely conspired among themselves, one whispering to the other, "I guess her boyfriend", (when she was in a good mood, DeLuca talked incessantly about her "boyfriend") "made her wear a bag on her head last night." They both stifled laughter, the buzz of which transmitted through the glass door. Dr. DeLuca's ear was attuned to the frequency of ridicule. She fixed a hateful stare on the two, who startled.

Margret Stephenson, the ICU Unit Manager, walked out of her

office and noted Dr. DeLuca's dangerous posture. DeLuca's demeanor, which was never to be trusted, had been flashing red since she started the shift. The doctor had roughly extubated an elderly patient earlier in the morning, yanking the breathing tube out without a word. The man had gasped, eyes wide in fear. Now the doctor was getting ready to jump the nurses. Her anger permeated the unit; Margret had already found two medication dosing errors since the shift began. She sat down next to Dr. DeLuca.

"Denise, how about we walk down to the lounge for a cup of coffee?" Margret said. "I'm worried about you this morning."

"You'd better be," Denise said. "I'm getting tired of the terrible job you do running this unit," she breathed softly. She flipped the keyboard out of her way, stood up and leaned into Margret. "I'm going to Royce right now — you're incompetent and I'm sick of it." The doctor spoke in her quiet, coarse hiss, but still loud enough for the nursing staff to hear. Margret had heard this threat many times before from Dr. DeLuca. What was different this time was that, at that precise moment, Royce walked into the unit along with Virginia Stowe. Even Dr. DeLuca looked surprised and went silent.

"Hi, Margret, how's the unit today?" asked Royce, who seethed through clenched teeth at the sight of Dr. DeLuca. The nurses at the desk suddenly remembered tasks in patient rooms and scattered. They could not recall the CEO ever visiting the ICU.

Not waiting for an answer, he spoke again to Margret. "May Dr. DeLuca, Virginia and I use your office for a minute?" Again, he didn't wait for an answer.

"Dr. DeLuca, I need to speak with you — now."

Luann Zahn was not surprised when Dr. Ippolito called to ask if they could meet. She got the vibe — that was easy. Still, Luann almost declined. The Flip Jensen story was stalled. Virginia Stowe had not called back since their last conversation a few days ago. Other reporters were circling. Flip's parents reported no change. The Martin Sisters had nothing new — at least about Flip. They were worked up about some construction project, but that was a conversation for another day.

Her story was losing its legs. The national reporters would lose interest, pack up their news vans and move on to some other human tragedy to boost ratings. Still, she was certain that Virginia was hiding something; all of her instincts buzzed and dinged a steady rhythm.

She was waiting at Arnie's, a rough-around-the edges place several blocks from the hospital. It was the type of establishment where the bartender made every effort to short your change, where you stood a passing chance of getting hit with a pool stick and where some of the clientele didn't speak English.

Dusty first brought Luann to Arnie's, its customers a mix of cowboys, students, construction workers, girlfriends, illegals and others on the prowl. No newscast appeared on the numerous televisions spread around the large horseshoe-shaped bar, this was strictly a sports crowd, although calling Arnie's a sports bar was a little too generous. Luann was rarely recognized. The only regular who seemed to know about her day job was a handsome CPA named Kenny who had been born with tiny, deformed, short arms and with a few fingers protruding just below his shoulders. He drank his beer with his knees, hoisting his mug with the grace of ballet dancer up to his waiting partial arms. At least one shapely, beautiful and demonstrative woman usually sat next to him at the bar, whispering in his ear and stroking his hair

"Listen," he had told her the first evening when they shared a barstool together, "I may not have any arms but I have a winning personality and a pile-driver ass." Kenny was good company — and he did her taxes with a borderline legality that netted her a bigger return.

Dr. Ippolito had called her cell phone number, which was on the business card Luann had slipped into her hand a few days ago. She would be there as soon as she could after her shift ended. Luann sent Dusty home for the day to ride his horse and chase his girlfriend around the corral. She promised to call if anything new developed.

"So sorry to be late," Dr. Ippolito said a few minutes later as she slid into their booth away from the bar. She still wore her green hospital scrubs. She looked around, amused. "I see a few patients every month from this place. I believe it's what's called a dive?"

"No need to apologize, Dr. Ippolito, I haven't been waiting long," said Luann smiling back at her. "I don't have to worry about the Junior League counting how many drinks I have at Arnie's — not that I drink that much anymore."

"Glad to hear that, because," she lowered her voice considerably, "if you have to drink to have fun, you're not old enough to drink." Dr. Ippolito returned her voice to normal register. "I give that advice to drunk college students a couple of times a week — right before I stuff a tube down their nose and pump enough activated charcoal into their stomach to filter the National Aquarium."

"Have a drink, Dr. Ippolito?" Luann said as the waitress dropped off two glasses stuffed with mint.

"Please call me Janet, and yes," she insisted. "What is that?"

"A Mojito — it's a good drink for people who don't drink much," Luann said.

"How do you know that I don't drink much?" the doctor asked, genuinely curious.

"My reporter's instinct," Luann said.

Janet sipped the Mojito.

"My, that is tasty."

She laid a folder on the table.

"So how's the reporting business going?" Dr. Ippolito asked. She was a few years younger than Luann; trim, perky with pretty dark hair, and glittering pupils that picked up ambient light.

"Well, compared to what you do every day, I can't complain. I don't have to worry about a source dying — at least, most days I don't," Luann smiled. They talked for a few minutes about their backgrounds. Dr. Ippolito was the daughter of a Navy doctor — a surgeon. She had grown up in Virginia, where her father had shuttled back and forth between their Virginia Beach home, working assignments aboard ships, the Portsmouth Naval Hospital and Bethesda Naval Hospital.

He could have made a lot more money in private practice, but he loved serving his country in the Navy.

Her father was a good doctor and a good man. She knew early in her life she also wanted to be a doctor and had devoted herself to the academic discipline necessary to spend most of her first 30 years in training. What she didn't tell Luann was she so consumed with her vocation as a doctor, she had not had the time until recently to consider that she was gay. With a semblance of a normal schedule since she had started working at the Ascend Medical Center, the matter of her sexuality, long buried in an impossible study and work schedule, emerged.

"So are you actively gay?" Luann asked, taking a guess. Dr. Ippolito sank back into the booth, shaking her head. This had never before been discussed, only contemplated. Janet certainly never envisioned talking about the matter for the first time with a reporter.

The waitress brought another round.

"That's not unusual, Janet," Luann advised. She squeezed the other woman's hand across the table. "What do you have for me today?"

Janet opened the folder. It held two medical documents that Luann recognized as EKG readouts.

"Before I explain about these readouts, I want to tell you something — it's important that you understand," the doctor said. "Something every doctor learns by the second year of medical school is that sometimes you can really help a patient by not being totally committed to the rules. It means occasionally deviating from protocols or policy and doing what's best for the patient, not the system — whether it's the insurance company or the hospital or even the family. Even doctors who don't exactly embrace such an outlook will look the other way when they see a colleague going down that path."

Luann nodded and sipped her drink. "Sure doctor, we all deal with those kinds of professional courtesies among our colleagues." Dr. Ippolito shook her head vigorously, looking down at her lap while Luann spoke. When she looked up she was intent and focused. She started on her second drink.

"No, you're not hearing what I'm saying, Luann. When a doctor uses their independent judgment that runs contrary to normal protocol, there's always the chance that they could be wrong. That can result in harm to a patient. And a doctor who has knowledge that such a course is being taken is at risk of going down too — of risking their reputation or even their license. But doctors don't rat each other out — unless it's really bad. The doctor has to be either incompetent or crazy. This," Dr. Ippolito said, tapping the papers in front of her vigorously "might just be both."

"Janet, I want to hear about this, I do. And you're even cuter when you explain it the way it is." The doctor smiled shyly. "But I'm still trying to wrestle the Flip Jensen story to the ground, so it might be a bit before I look into this," Luann said, also tapping the chart and hooking Dr. Ippolito's finger with her own.

"Oh great, now you're stealing my best move," Kenny said as he slipped into the seat next to Luann. Janet quickly withdrew her hand into her lap before she realized Luann was laughing, raising her glass to Kenny for a sip.

"Dr. Ippolito — this is Kenny, a friend of mine — he's a funny guy," Luann said. "Kenny, this is Janet, who is a new friend of mine — she's a doctor by the way." Kenny nodded.

"I know a lot of doctors — you ever fuck anybody's arms up?" Kenny said.

"No, but come to the ER over at Ascend some day and I'll see what I can do," she deadpanned. He was handsome. Her third Mojito arrived. "What do you do?" Janet asked casually. She occasionally treated patients with missing limbs, but this was her first social encounter.

"You mean when I'm not trying to pick up lesbians?" Kenny answered. Dr. Ippolito spit out her drink. Luann laughed and gave Kenny another sip from her glass.

"Kenny is a CPA, and a pretty good one," Luann said. "He helps his clients lie on their tax returns."

"It's not a lie if you believe it," Kenny said. "My clients don't get audited too much because a CPA with no arms really freaks out the IRS suits."

"Isn't that a bit manipulative, using a disability for personal gain?" the doctor teased.

"Hey, we all have to use our God-given talent the best way we can," Kenny said. "Even if God doesn't like you too much." Luann smiled at Dr. Ippolito.

"Well, my work is done here," Kenny kissed Luann on the cheek, and then slid out of the booth.

"Nice meeting you, doctor. You could do a lot worse than news girl here." Kenny walked back over to the bar, where a woman from the local university was saving him a seat.

"Kenny always help you out with the ladies?" Dr. Ippolito asked.

"He's worried about me," Luann said. "He says I work too much to compensate for the fact that I'm lonely."

Janet took another sip of her drink, thinking. She set her drink down. "Well, I guess we'll need to work on both of those problems," the good Dr. Ippolito said softly. Luann's eyes widened. They each reached across the table for a few moments. Then Janet then picked up the records on the table.

"But first I've got some more work for you. These are from the medical record of the patient who was in the same ambulance that whacked Flip Jensen." She watched Luann's eyes go from moist to dilated in a heartbeat.

"You haven't forgotten what I told you about doctors, have you?" Luann shook her head no. Dr. Ippolito flipped over the first EKG.

"This is the readout that was in his chart when I got to him that day he arrived in the ER. These irregularities here are ST elevations — it means he's having a heart attack. And that's how I treated him. He was treated with powerful drugs, received a cardiac cath, which showed nothing and was referred to a cardiologist." She paused and scowled.

"A week later the cardiologist calls me and said there's nothing wrong with his heart — he has a hiatal hernia. He wants to know where the hell I got my training — if I got any medical training at all — because obviously I don't know the difference between a hernia and a heart attack or how to read an EKG."

Dr. Ippolito declined the next round of drinks offered by the waitress.

"So I logged into medical records and the first thing I notice is that his chart is completed — that almost never happens in a week — in fact, I've never seen it happen in a week. I'm probably one of the most diligent doctors in that place about charting and my notes were still in the pending file — that's why I still had the original EKG. So, I track his paper chart down in the record scanning room and I find this," she said, switching to the second EKG again. "That," she said, "is a normal EKG taken which was on the ambulance. It was replaced in his chart."

Luann smacked her hand on the table. "I knew the hospital was hiding something."

"Luann, hospital administrators don't know anything about this kind of intrigue, they're not doctors. A doctor did all this — this is exactly what I was trying to explain to you. Doctors almost always commit this kind of sin to help patients. But that's not what this is. This is a doctor covering their ass."

"Why?" Luann queried

"Hell, I don't know Ms. Zahn. You're the reporter." Janet was feeling relaxed in a way she could never remember.

"What I know is that the ambulance this patient was in is the same one that hit Flip Jensen. You'll have to figure it out fast, because I'm getting drunk and I have to get home to sleep — I switch shifts in 24 hours."

Luann was all business now, holding her glass under her lower lip like a microphone, rubbing it back and forth while she thought. She again recalled Virginia, wound tight in the ambulance bay, trying hard not to reveal something important.

"Come on news girl, tick-tock," Dr. Ippolito teased. The "ah-ha moment" jumped her with claws out, scrambling up her spine, ferocious.

"How fast would an ambulance need to drive for a patient not having a heart attack?" Luann asked. She watched the smile on Janet's face transform into something malevolent. Her lips tightened liked a catapult.

"That bitch!" Dr. Ippolito said. "I will tear her head off and spit in her neck." Across the room, Kenny slowly turned in their direction, arching an eyebrow at Luann. Luann took another sip and smiled at Janet, who was looking wilder by the second.

"My, my doctor — you're quite the mean drunk," Kenny observed.

———

Up on the 5th floor of Ascend Medical Center, Missy Wallace was in her favorite seat by the window, opera glasses in hand, scanning the Charlottesville streets below. Camilla Bonfield was up for her usual end-of-the day visit, smoothing out the quilt on Miss Wallace's bed. Today, Miss Wallace had eaten a large meal of prime rib, potato, salad and rolls, all the while complaining of stomach pains and bloating. Her stay was extending into its second month, much to the increasing protests of the hospital's Chief Financial Officer Stewart Alexander. Royce finally had to get stern with the CFO, who had sent him an email detailing his concerns.

"Give it a rest Stu, she's a great benefactor to the hospital. Dr. Forrest said she needs to be admitted so we can take care of her," Royce groused. "She has dementia and she doesn't know who she is most of the time."

"Royce — I'm not even a doctor and I know she doesn't need to be here — we're not a nursing home. And if she wasn't worth a zillion dollars, she wouldn't be a permanent patient. Medicare denies all of our payments for lack of medical necessity," Stewart argued.

"Damn it, Stu. I don't want to hear this anymore. Just don't bill Medicare if you're so worried about it," Royce said.

"Royce it's illegal not to bill for services if we provide services to a Medicare patient," Stewart countered. "We're not running an assisted living home here. We're gonna get our asses caught in the ringer if you keep allowing this."

"Well they'll have to catch us now, won't they? The federal government is not worried about a hospital in little old Charlottesville, Stu," Royce said, his final word on the topic.

Stewart went to Camilla to make his case. She did not care for the CFO. A big, burly man, he thrust his lower lip out in between sentences while his eyes wandered about her luscious parts while he spoke. Camilla listened politely and then told Stewart he should discuss his concerns with Royce or Dr. Forrest. Her job was to make sure Miss Wallace was comfortable during her stay. Stewart stood up and sketched a box on the white board in her office, drawing several lines from top to bottom.

"Camilla, this is the view from a jail cell," the CFO said, tapping the white board. "Don't think you won't get splattered if this donation scheme blows up in our faces," Stewart said, turning and leaving her office.

The truth was, Camilla did have concerns about Dr. Forrest's effort to keep Miss Wallace in the hospital. But it was not Medicare she feared — it was Missy Wallace's nephews on the Board.

"Camilla," said Miss Wallace from her station at the window. "I do believe I see someone we both know, come take a look." She pointed to the street below. "See that neon sign that says "Arnie's"? That's one of our ER doctors, she's very nice to me whenever I come in." Camilla touched her hand to the old woman's shoulder, who handed over the opera glasses. Camilla located the sign and focused in on the petite dark haired woman in hospital scrubs. She was talking and gesturing vigorously to someone standing in the doorway of the bar.

Arnie's was indeed not at all the kind of establishment she or Miss Wallace would visit. Suddenly, another woman stepped out from the doorway of Arnie's and hooked an arm around Dr. Ippolito's waist while setting her other hand on her shoulder. The effect on Dr. Ippolito was immediate. Camilla saw her shoulders relax, her hands dropping to her side as the other woman spoke. When the other woman turned her head skyward from Dr. Ippolito for an instant, Camilla let out a soft gasp.

"What is she doing?" Miss Wallace asked. "Why would a doctor be in such a tacky place?" The two women kissed lightly on the lips and Dr. Ippolito turned quickly and walked around the corner. The other woman went back inside Arnie's. Camilla handed the glasses back to Miss Wallace, rubbing her shoulder in a way that always made Miss Wallace sigh.

"I'm sure she has her reasons," Camilla said lightly. "I don't think it's anything to concern ourselves about."

CHAPTER

So-Sammy

TEN

Owen's friend So-Sammy was in the middle of his fentanyl patch story, the one about the dog. Owen had heard it many times. It was So-Sammy's go-to story when he wanted to entertain and impress. So-Sammy's daughter, Cricket, was stretched out on the other end of the couch with Freeway resting in her lap. The Pug was seriously shedding on her black, bejeweled "Future Porn Star" t-shirt. Freeway let loose an occasional snarl in So-Sammy's general direction. The blind Pug had serious issues with men. But whatever had happened, it had not intimidated the pint-sized, bug-eyed freak. Freeway was one pissed off little beast.

"So I'm on this really shitty run of bad luck, I can't get a scrip out of an ER doctor anywheres. I swear it's like a bad run of cards. So I start to get all hinky. So I stop at my grandma's house and even she's out of the good pain pills left over from when my granddaddy had the cancer," So-Sammy said. Freeway's disapproval intensified, rumbling in his throat like a four-barreled carburetor. "So, she's a cute little fucker," So-Sammy said, absently-mindedly reaching over to pet the dog.

"Doooon't do that," Felicia instructed sweetly from her seat next to Owen, across the coffee table from their guests. "Freeway takes offense at being called a she and if you put that finger anywhere near he'll get a whiff of your man smell and bite the fool out of you. You'd be surprised how much it hurts. Just ask Owen."

"Fuckin'A," Owen confirmed, holding up a bandaged finger.

"Daddy, leave the little puppy alone," Cricket giggled, scratching Freeway's skull under his loose tawny skin. The Pug quieted and leaned into her fingers. Cricket was a shapely, cute young woman. She had an extensive wardrobe of "Future Porn Star" clothing, including a pair of sweatpants with the slogan embossed across the seat, a Christmas gift from her father. Cricket had been helping her father with his Oxycodone and Vicodin schemes since she was a little girl. She could fake abdominal pain or a migraine better than anyone Owen had ever seen. Doctors hated to see a kid in pain.

The "Future Porn Star" clothing was the bait, its promise validation of the idea that less is more. Doctors associated with her care cursed their bad luck, prevented by state and medical academy law from becoming involved with a patient. Word got around when Cricket was in the house, though. Soon, other medicine men showed up, their lust camouflaged by clipboards, files and stethoscopes. So-Sammy called them the second opinion brigade. There was always a new group of residents joining the rotation at the teaching hospitals in Charlottesville and Richmond. And of course, there were the middle-aged doctors lined up at the divorce starting gate feeling all sexy. Cricket had many frustrated suitors. Cricket was, in fact, the "good girl" her daddy proclaimed her to be.

"So, I find this box of Fentanyl patches in my grandma's kitchen cabinet. Her old chocolate lab is dying and she got a script from the vet for her dog. So, can you believe that shit? A dog can get a script but not me, a person. So, I'm thinking, I weigh about three times as much as that dog, so I figure about three of those patches ought to fix me up. I mean, it's been like four days — I'm feeling so-so, if you get you my drift. So, at that point heroin is probably going to be my next move if I don't get something going." So-Sammy paused for effect to sip his beer.

Owen and Felicia had been off pain meds for a week. There was no telling what could cause a person to turn their life around, to become someone better. For Owen and Felicia it turned out to be each other — it can be that simple. The world looked different to them — brilliant, but ragged. Alert and clear headed, they looked better and better to each other. So-Sammy's story made them antsy but as Owen was learning from Felicia, he was their guest, which required a level of hospitality and accommodation that Owen was trying to cultivate in his life.

Owen, Cricket and So-Sammy were long time friends. So-Sammy had been a year ahead of him in high school. He was an unremarkable longhair who went unnoticed until his junior year. That was the year the football team needed a place kicker. The coach went looking for one with tryouts in the lowly gym classes. So-Sammy was the youngest of four boys who kicked the football uphill in the backyard betting on everything from pink bellies, to chores, to stolen beers. The coach almost wept when he watched the boy jackleg a football 50 yards. He started out acting as if he were doing So-Sammy a favor and finished begging him to be the team's kicker. So-Sammy laid down the rules with the coach — no haircut and no running laps. He would spend his time drinking soda and practicing field goals — in that order. So-Sammy, in his own words, "could give a shit about being a football player" — he wanted to meet girls. And his plan was successful, Cricket being living proof.

About the same time he became a big man on campus as the school's kicker, Owen's father hired So-Sammy to help in the garage doing oil and tire changes on Saturdays. In the last game of the season So-Sammy, his hair streaming out of his helmet, became a target of special interest in a game against a military school. By that point, So-Sammy was the leading scorer on the team, banging field goals through the uprights from as far out as 47 yards. And by his own account, he "had more pussy than a witch on Halloween". The score was tied when So-Sammy followed through on a 37-yard field goal as the clock ran out. So-Sammy stood to admire the ball's perfect trajectory to another three points when one of the cadets speared him helmet-first and off center on his left side, breaking his collarbone and tearing a rotator cuff. It felt like getting pinged with a nail gun.

"Got you freak!" the linebacker screamed, bent over in So-Sammy's face as he writhed on the ground. So-Sammy had won another game — his fourth of the season at the whistle — but it would be his last. His injuries were his port of entry to the twilight world of narcotic pain pills. He began sharing his meds with Owen's dad to help with his back pain — and then with Owen after his father's funeral.

So-Sammy put his beer down and continued his story.

"So I'm feeling really good for awhile, my first buzz in nearly a week. Cricket was with her mother that weekend, so when my grandma asked if I wanted to stay for dinner and watch the game shows, I was very agreeable. So, we're watching "Jeopardy" and, I swear, the game board starts sending messages to me, like "A long sleep is the reward for a good life" and "The sun don't shine on the same dog's ass every day" — I remember those two. So, I'm sitting there trying to figure out what life lesson I'm supposed to be learning from "Jeopardy". So, in the distance I can hear my grandmother calling my name and her dog starts howling and I'm watching this light above me get smaller and smaller until it's a pinprick and then it blinks out. So, in hind sight all this was a warning, but at the time I had no concern."

Freeway commenced his low-key threats in the interlude. So-Sammy frowned at the Pug, annoyed, but amused. "So, that dawg has got some real hostility issues."

"Yeah," Owen said, "you don't think that little blind mutt is anything to worry about until he latches on."

So-Sammy laughed. "So, ain't that life brother — a bite on a soft spot when you least expect it! So, speaking of which, the next thing I know, three days later I'm waking up in the ICU at the University hospital. I'm hearing a lot of snide dog joke remarks, which would have probably been funny if I hadn't felt so bad. So, the hospital doctor is yapping at me about liver damage, which ain't happened — but could happen, like I got capacity to worry about what could happen. So, they got a substance abuse program but I ain't got no insurance so they lose interest in that course of action real fast.

So I tell the doc "Hey no problem, I'll see you soon in the ER". So, that pisses 'em off and I get discharged. I meet my grandmother out front and that Lab of hers is sitting in the back of the pick-up bouncing around like a pup. So, he lives for almost another two years — misdiagnosed by the vet. So it turns out I did that dawg a favor getting him off those fentanyl patches."

Until this week Owen had been in the habit of mistaking irony for humor. *I guess it's a thin line,* Owen thought to himself. So-Sammy was sitting there waiting for him to laugh, as he always did. Felicia smiled softly, as she had been doing most of the evening. So-Sammy, who did not do well with awkward silence, spoke again.

"So where you been Owen? Cricket and me ain't seen you at the office in a couple of weeks." Their code for any ER was "the office". Now Owen felt awkward. He could not find the words to tell his friends that their shared experience wasn't good enough any more. Especially when he wasn't sure he had the resolve to change. Felicia reached over and held his hand. Owen could feel tears.

"Owen — what's wrong buddy? You sick?" So-Sammy asked, rising and stepping over the coffee table to sit on the edge in front of his friend. Cricket followed to kneel beside her father and place her hand on Owen's knee. Freeway burrowed across the couch like a prairie dog stretched out in the sun. Felicia dropped Owen's hand to reach around and hold him. The narcotic lubricant he had relied on his entire adult life to manage his inner conflict was gone. It was his old self and his new self, meeting for the first time. And both were disappointed in him at the moment.

"Are you sick?" Cricket repeated her father's question. Owen shook his head.

"No more pills for me," Owen managed to say. "I'm going to miss you both," So-Sammy put his hand over his daughter's hand to squeeze Owen's knee.

"So, why?" So-Sammy asked. Owen looked at Felicia who reached up and stroked his cheek.

"I'm just going to try it for a while without the pills, see what I can do," Owen said. "Both of us want to see. That's what I wanted to tell you both tonight. I need to stay away from the pills — and you all for a while. I think that's the only way I can make this work." Owen sniffled a bit. "I'm thinking about opening my dad's garage back up. But I'm so worried about you both."

"No need to worry about me Owen, I'm going to marry a doctor," Cricket said, absolutely certain. This left only So-Sammy with no immediate new plan for the future.

"I'm thinking about playing football again," he said with a final slap on Owen's knee. "So, if that don't work out I still got my disability payments every month," So-Sammy advised. "So, you're just borrowing trouble worrying about us Owen."

Freeway yelped in his sleep as the fur on the back of his neck rippled in alarm.

The house supervisor was waiting for Leo when he walked on the floor.

"Mr. Rigton is back in — and he wants to see you," she told him.

"Why has he been admitted this time?"

"He's a noncompliant diabetic. His sugar runs wild, he turns into a crazy man and then complains bitterly when the ER doc hits him with a shot of Haldol with an Ativan chaser to get him under control," the house sup explained. Haldol was in the class of drugs known to those in hospitals as "chemical handcuffs". Combined with Ativan, most patients couldn't remember their name. But they tended to be cranky when the world jumped back in their face several hours later.

"Is his family in the room?" Leo asked.

"Just his daughter. His wife evidently is a taxpayer now, got herself a job down in the kitchen," the house sup said, looking over her glasses with a hard stare. Leo knew what that meant. As the hospital funded its own insurance plan, the cost of Mr. Rigton's frequent hospital stays were now paid for by the hospital itself.

Mr. Rigton was sitting up in bed with his hands clasped behind his head laughing at the television. He looked well. His daughter was in the chair beside the bed and looked decidedly unhappy.

"Good morning, Mr. Rigton, how's your stay so far?" Leo asked.

"Still can't smoke," he said, glaring.

"Well now that your wife is working here, you can use the smoking cessation plan," Leo advised. "Several dozen employees and families have been able to stop smoking — it's a really helpful program." Mr. Rigton's glare turned to disdain.

"I like to smoke."

Leo smiled at his daughter.

"My father is worried about his wallet. Someone took it from him last night in the emergency room," she told Leo. She was much friendlier than her last visit.

"There's $248 in that wallet," Mr. Rigton said. "My wife just got paid and someone stole it from me last night while I was sick."

"Mr. Rigton, there is a receipt in your medical record for the wallet with the cash amount stated at $248. I'm certain it's in the safe in the business office. How about if I go check for you?" Leo offered.

"You do that — and there better be $248 in that wallet."

After he finished rounding with patients, Leo stopped in the business office. It was the domain of his CFO. Out of loyalty to the CFO, the business office manager felt it proper to be ever so indifferent to Leo.

"A patient is worried about his wallet," Leo told her.

"You must be talking about Mr. Rigton. His wife has called twice wanting us to give it to her." She opened a safe and pulled out a thick, worn billfold with a chain attached. Leo flipped it open and pulled out a wad of cash, which he handed to the business office manager.

"Count that, please," Leo said. She organized the money by denominations, then thumbed through the cash twice.

"Still $248," she announced flatly. She handed the money back. Leo reached into his front pocket, pulled out his money clip and peeled off a twenty, which he added to the back of the cash.

"Correction, $268," Leo said. The manager's surprise overrode her forced, indifferent demeanor.

"There is a serious lack of faith in this hospital," Leo said.

━━━━━━━━━

Dr. Denise DeLuca had two rules she never violated. The first was that no matter what shit storm she left in her wake it was always someone else's fault. The second rule was to always deny, no matter what the evidence — even the video Royce was huffing about. With reasonable explanation, any proof could be explained away. After all, no one wanted to think poorly of a doctor.

"Denise, are you hearing what I am saying?" Royce growled, his back to the office door so the ICU staff would not overhear. "Shades was sitting in the passenger side of the ambulance, Denise, you can see his reflection in the God damn glass on the building — on the tape." Virginia sat in a chair in the corner, while Dr. DeLuca sat behind the desk looking a little bit cornered. Normally, Dr. DeLuca would have Dr. Forrest run interference in any meeting where others might be angry with her, which was precisely the reason Royce had surprised her down in the ICU. "The medical record shows that the other EMT was taking care of the patient. That means the kid was driving."

"Royce, I don't know what you think you're seeing in that security video, but I assure you Shades was driving the ambulance," she said in her near whisper. "I will speak to both of them about this matter just to confirm. I *am* the medical director for the ambulance service," she reminded him.

Virginia did not envy Royce at times like this. He looked truly distressed for man who made a half a million dollars a year. Royce sputtered momentarily.

"You're telling me that what I'm seeing with my own eyes isn't true? That's your story Denise?"

"This conversation is getting a bit redundant, Royce. If you are so concerned about the recording I suggest you erase it."

This was Virginia's first time witnessing the workings of Dr. DeLuca's parallel universe, where not only what she said was true regardless of all facts, physical proof and evidence, but where if she merely thought something, that was also reality. Royce had all but called her a liar, which in Dr. DeLuca's mind, now seemed to completely justify her fabrication. Virginia, who had also seen the tape, had assumed she would be humbled and contrite when confronted with proof of her deceit.

"I've got a better idea, Denise. Not only am I not going to erase the recording, how about if I turn the tape over to the police and let them sort things out?" Royce sneered, any pretense of toleration gone. Their history together had always been defined by his indifference for her dysfunctional behavior — but not today.

Dr. DeLuca's voice raised ever so slightly, the only indication she was concerned by Royce's threat. She even smiled as her eyes went vacant.

"You really think that's a good idea, Royce? If what's on the tape is taken the wrong way, Ascend Medical Center could be looking for a new CEO."

Royce seemed to forget that Virginia was in the room. He jabbed his finger in her face. "Let me tell you something doctor, you'll go down with me," he said. Dr. DeLuca was an old hand at this kind of verbal tussle, her experience stretching back to her recess days in elementary school.

"Gee, I wonder who will have a harder time finding a job Royce? A hospital administrator who is disgraced on national news or a doctor in a country where there is a shortage of physicians?" she said, her voice barely audible. "Are you sure you don't just want to leave this alone?"

"You let your boyfriend's son drive the ambulance, didn't you? Shades didn't make that decision on his own. We all know he's your toady," Royce said, mad. Out in the unit, a few nurses looked their way through the glass wall.

"You mean the same boyfriend you just had threaten me if I talked to reporters?" she retorted back at him. Royce did not miss a beat.

"Which of course has nothing to do with Flip Jensen getting hit by an ambulance driven by a teenage volunteer. Come on Denise, I know you understand the concept of cause and effect. As you like to point out, you are a doctor."

Dr. DeLuca rose and walked around the desk, stopping in front of Royce. "Excuse me, I have lives to save." Royce glared at her. For an instant it seemed to Virginia he might lay hands on the doctor. He finally stepped around her and sat on the desk, facing Virginia, staring at the floor.

"What a liar," Royce muttered, after Dr. DeLuca left the room.

"This goes beyond lying, Royce, she's pathological." Virginia said. "She feels entitled and that makes her really dangerous. You should suspend her privileges to practice here immediately — no kidding. If word gets out of what we've seen on that recording it's going to be too late to back peddle. I'm telling you, Royce — and this is my best advice to you — it's one thing to manage a bad decision, bad judgment, stupidity or even arrogance. But what we're talking about here is criminal. And there is no amount of spin control that's going to successfully manage breaking the law. The quickest way for her to be right about you being gone is to sit on that recording. We need to turn it over to the police today, Royce."

Royce continued to stare at the floor, the folly of too many years of placating Dr. DeLuca an ugly hindsight. It was arrogance to think he was ever going to change her. Neither friendship nor threats were a strong enough force. Royce, paralyzed, said nothing. He was thinking of going to his office, closing the door and not coming out until it was dark outside. Finally, Virginia spoke.

"As soon as I get back to my office, I might send you an email repeating what I just told you. We need to do the right thing here, and quite frankly, I'm not going to jail to protect Dr. DeLuca."

"How do we go about doing the right thing, Ginny?" Royce asked.

"The first thing after we meet with the police is to call Luann Zahn and give her an exclusive. She's already figured out that the security tape is worth seeing. We need to get her on our side," Virginia said.

Royce finally sat up.

"This is going to look bad to the rest of the medical staff, hanging Dr. DeLuca out like this," he said.

"Royce, she doesn't have any friends on the medical staff. She broke the law and it's about time she figured out the price for crazy."

Royce smiled wryly. "Ginny, God-bless you, but you do not understand a basic fact about doctors: they stick together and administrators are their natural enemy."

Neither Virginia nor Royce noticed the speaker light glowing on the desk phone. Twenty feet away in a physician dictation cubicle, Dr. DeLuca was listening on a party line. A few years ago, she had tempted a phone system grunt with a pain killer scrip in exchange for tapping the phone line into the department manager's phone, for just a day like today. The line was unmarked, her secret. Dr. DeLuca listened to these two hospital administrators plotting her ruin. She smiled to herself, pleased as she always was when she baffled and confused. She was way of ahead of them and, in fact, delighted when she thought of what would happen next.

───────

Shades and Burley were coming back after a late lunch at Mooch's Barbecue on the west side of Charlottesville. Mooch's was on the old Route 250 that originally ran between Sandusky, Ohio and Richmond, Virginia. It was the main route long before the interstate highway system ran an end run around the original road. Mooch's opened when America took to the roads in automobiles after World War II and its reputation had lasted long after I-64 had sucked most of the life out of the old road. The joint had survived and prospered, providing an excellent living for three generations of its founding family. Mooch's Barbecue did not advertise, relying instead on 50 years of word-of-mouth. Its legions of patrons — from salesmen to circuit judges to soldiers — would go out of their way for its perfect blend of vinegary bite and sweetness. The parking lot was always full at Mooch's.

Shades and Burley made it a point to stop at Mooch's Barbecue whenever they had a run out to Valley View Community Hospital. They were transporting an elderly woman from University Medical

Center who had tired of all modern medicine had to offer and wanted to die at home. Her transfer to Community for dialysis would keep her alive until her son, on leave from the Navy, could arrive to take her home for good. Burley chatted with the patient in the back as Shades drove. The old lady was in surprisingly good spirits, the last of life's difficult decisions finally made. Burley told the patient of their plans for lunch.

"Ohh, I love Mooch's Barbecue, I've been eating it my whole life," she said happily. "My husband, son and I used to go to there almost every Sunday after church. I like to put their slaw on the sandwich, — oohh, that's been one of the best things in my life." She smiled up at Burley, her mouth watering for the first time in years.

Burley appreciated anyone's company who liked to eat, especially barbecue. He flipped through the old lady's chart. She was circling the drain, no doubt. She had perked up quite a bit since they had loaded her into the rig at University Medical Center. Sometimes the old ones would do that. Sifting through their simplest pleasures seemed to cheer them up.

"Ma'am, how would you like some barbecue?" The old lady beamed and for an instant, looked 20 years younger.

Shades and Burley finished their Mooch's feast in the parking lot at Valley View Community. They were headed back to Charlottesville on the interstate, the window down on Burley's side as he finished his cigarette.

"That was a nice thing you did, Burley," Shades shouted over the wind noise. "She only took a few bites, but she looked like she could die happy."

Burley laughed. "I think the admitting nurse smelled barbecue on her breath," Burley said.

"Yeah, I noticed that, cousin, but how worked up is she going to get about a dying old lady's blood sugar? If she raises a ruckus, we'll just tell part of the truth: we picked up our lunch on the way and the old lady was having a flashback," Shades told him.

Burley flicked the butt out and raised the window. He dabbed a napkin in his water cup and worked at a spot of barbecue sauce on his shirtfront.

"You know, Shades, I've been thinking about that whole Flip Jensen deal. If Randy starts talking like teenagers do, I don't think your Dr. DeLuca is going to be stand-up about that whole deal. I think she'll rat you out faster than an arterial line blowing." Shades reached up and adjusted his sunglasses. Burley knew his cousin fiddled with his sunglasses when he was either absolutely sure of himself or had serious doubts. He waited to see which it would be.

"Cousin, I've been thinking about that topic for quite some time — years, in fact. You and I owe her a lot, but I think after Flip Jensen, we're even. The day is coming when we will be parting company with Dr. DeLuca. But, don't worry, when that day comes, I'll have a plan."

Ahead traffic was stopped. Burley reached forward and flipped on the emergency lights.

"Damn, dispatch is already going to notice we're running late after our Mooch's run," Shades said. "Hit the siren, cousin, I'll work us down the emergency lane and get around these civilians."

"Go slow, we don't need to hit anyone else — at least not this soon," Burley joked.

They had gone about 800 yards when Shades saw the smoke. Flames appeared in another 500 yards. Cars were blocking the way, flashers blinking, halted at sharp angles, doors open. Shades steered towards the median before the first body blocked the way. More dead and dying were sprawled on the ground, partially hidden in a carpet of blooming lavender crown vetch that swept ahead to a large twisted bus and other vehicles, one of them in flames.

"Burley get those cars out of the way now — take the radio with you, channel 10." Burly hurled his bulk out of the ambulance and rushed forward. Shades grabbed the dash mike. He forced himself to be calm.

"Dispatch, Rescue 7 — we're at I-64 approximately two miles east of route 250 interchange. We have encountered a huge MVA — send everything — all ground units and helos — we need choppers — everything you can get from Richmond, Blacksburg, even Norfolk. Multiple vehicles, I see a bus and at least one van. We have burns, we have bodies on the ground. Do you copy Dispatch?"

"Roger that Rescue 7. Please advise number of injured ASAP. Stand by."

The civilians were milling about, the men with their hands on their hips or in their pockets, the women with their hands pressed to their faces or crossed across their bosom. Civilians were useless in an emergency. They wanted to help, but they didn't know what to do with people who were bleeding, gasping, moaning, vomiting, writhing or dead. Scared people do not save lives.

Burly came running back, for as much as Burley could run. He had a trail of civilians behind him who began dispersing to their vehicles to make way for the ambulance.

Burley climbed back in, breathing hard. He was pale despite his exertion and he gasped in a false start for several seconds. Finally he spoke.

"We need a bigger ambulance," Burley said slowly. Every other bad wreck the cousins had worked was no worse than "Houston, we have a problem" — a two to three rig disaster. Most of their calls were of the "That's Gotta Hurt" variety, a single ambulance and two EMTs dealing with everything from lightheadedness to bike crashes to births. The upper end of the number of ambulances demanded for a "We need a bigger ambulance" call had never been defined. Burley just said it was a shitload. He climbed between the seats and disappeared in the rear of the ambulance. "Remember where you heard it first, Shades, those news fuckers are going to forget all about Flip Jensen when word of this wreck gets out."

Shades began inching through the tangle of cars.

"How many?" Shades asked. "We have to tell dispatch how many."

"More than I could count in a minute — I could see dozens — but more than a few of them are dead," Burley said, pulling together medic boxes with a rattle and bang of urgency. He hollered back over his shoulder to Shades.

"We're in a little bit of luck. There's a third year medical student who has just finished his ER and surgical rotation and a couple of nurses from University who were on their way back from a community training session in Harrisonburg. There's also an orthopedic surgeon from Richmond. They're already triaging."

Shades transmitted Burley's information to Dispatch.

The Radio crackled back in response. "Rescue 7, the first medevac unit will be in the air in ten minutes, all available ground units are en route."

When they finally arrived at the staging area, the triage doctors and nurses had several victims laid out in the road, the priority to control bleeding and restore airways. A beautiful Hispanic woman with a blood-soaked abdomen stared open-eyed into the blue sky. The back of her left arm pointed skyward, propped up by a blonde-haired boy about ten years old was rolled on his side. The metal arm of dropdown tray protruded from his back.

Behind them a bus was on its side, twisted and split open. A long 12-passenger van was bent in the middle, facing the wrong way 30 yards up the road. A second 12-passenger van was burning on the opposite side of the highway.

"Shades — there's kids," Burly said, stricken as he threw open the rear doors in front of the triage operation. Shades switched on his mobile radio, which was tied into to the main radio in the ambulance. Burley went forward to the bus to look for victims who could be saved while Shades went to the triage group. The two nurses followed him.

"Who's running the scene?" he asked, "What do you need right now?"

"Dr. Rajad is in charge," calmly answered a lean, handsome salt and pepper haired man in shorts and flip-flops who was squeezing a thigh above an exploded kneecap. Shades assumed he was the orthopedic surgeon. The ortho doc nodded his head towards a young intense looking doctor with blood splattered up the front of his white lab coat.

Dr. Rajad was sitting on top of the same patient, a long, tall bearded man with a leather vest adorned with Vietnam themed army and MIA patches. He was bleeding from a puncture in his chest, opposite his heart.

"Fuck, hurry up doc, I can't take this much longer," the patient hissed at Dr. Rajad.

"Clamp, I need a clamp and forceps," Dr. Rajad said through gritted teeth.

Shades rummaged though his medic box, found the items and helped the doctor stop the bleeding. The bone doc spoke quietly.

"And down south here, I need a tourniquet, gauze, a syringe of saline fluid, an IV bag and a roll of tape. And I suggest we give the patient a shot of ketamine."

Shades' radio clicked. "Rescue 6, Rescue 12 we're near mile marker 77 but traffic is jammed up. Gonna be about 15 minutes."

"That's not soon enough for a lot of these people," the orthopedic doctor said.

"Hey doc, I can hear you up here," the patient grunted, in pain. Dr. Rajad had moved on to another patient, leaving a clamp protruding from a gash in the Vietnam vet's chest. Shades reached up and wrapped a large patch around the clamp. The orthopedic surgeon patted his good leg.

"Not you soldier, I'm feeling good about your chances." Shades moved to an unconscious, heavyset woman with a head wound who was gasping for air.

The two nurses introduced themselves, but Burley had already forgotten their names. One was a blonde. They followed behind him as they intubated patients with the case full of airway tubes from the ambulance. Any victims with arterial bleeding were already dead unless another victim had the clarity to use a tourniquet. The head injury patients — and there were many riding unsecured in the large passenger vehicles — were in various stages of injury, from treat and release to critical condition. Some of the ambulatory were wandering about with a vague feeling there was something they should be doing. The effect was that of a zombie movie. Their triage evolved into convincing these people to sit down so that those who were bleeding, broken and prone could be located in and around the wreck.

A Hispanic girl, about ten years old, came running from behind the bus. She smelled of smoke and had bloodied hands. She grabbed the blonde nurse by the wrist and spoke rapidly in Spanish, gesturing back towards the smashed vehicles. She began tugging on the nurse's arm, wanting her to follow.

"Rescue," she said because she could not recall Burley's name either, "find someone who speaks Spanish and come find me — hurry." She grabbed the medical box and trotted after the girl into the haze spreading across the road. There was a group of civilians lined up in the opposite lane, in front of the stopped westbound lane of traffic. Burley jogged towards them, gesturing, hollering.

"Habla Española?" he yelled several times until he had to stop about 40 yards away, bent over on his knees, his lungs heaving. Several people, all Hispanic, jogged towards him looking eager to help.

"Habla Española — and English." Burley clarified. He wanted a cigarette but the pack was missing from his shirt pocket. All of the civilians stepped back except for two dark haired teenagers, a brother and sister.

"You two up for a big adventure?" Burley asked, still working to catch his breath. "You're gonna see some really messed up stuff — people hurt, bleeding. Some of them only speak Spanish — can you help us with that?"

"We help take care of our grandfather, he had a stroke," the girl offered. Her brother nodded vigorously.

"OK my dearies, you're now officially rescue translators. After today you're going to have something really interesting to write on your college applications." He handed his medic box to the brother and headed back to find Blondie, his teen assistants following.

"Either of you kids have a cigarette?" Burley asked as they approached the wreck.

"Ah, no sir — our parents don't allow us to smoke. It's bad for your health," the girl replied. Burley actually laughed out loud. It was an occupational hazard for many in healthcare to develop a fatalistic attitude about life span. Some of the most prolific smokers Burley encountered at the hospital were respiratory therapists.

"Hey Blondie, where are you?" Burley yelled as they approached the side of the twisted van. "Blondie, I've got help."

"Who are we looking for?" the girl asked. Burley held his hand up, listening in the haze from the burning vehicle.

"Blondie!" he hollered again. Suddenly, the little Hispanic girl came running from around the other side of the wreck, speaking rapidly. The teenage girl — Anna — knelt in front of her.

"She says her father is trapped in the wreckage and he's bleeding, the nurse is helping him," Anna said. Her brother, Pablo, looked jazzed up. "Yeah, that's the situation, her dad's in trouble," he said, jittery.

"Let's go," Burley said. He looked back at Anna's brother, who looked pale. "Don't you pass out on me Pablo, we've already got enough Mexicans down." Pablo's smile was grim.

On the other side of the van Blondie was bent over on her knees, one arm extended inside the van. Burley could make out the grimacing face of a middle-aged man. The legs from another victim, bright pink socks on the feet, extended from underneath the overturned vehicle next to Blondie.

"Find something to cushion my knees, I've got my hand holding a bad cut. How far out is help?" Burley realized that in the few minutes, which had passed since he and Shades had split up, he had heard nothing on his radio. He clicked the transmitter button and spoke into his collar. Pablo yanked a seat cushion out of the bus for Blondie. This unleashed a chorus of wails and prayers from inside the vehicle. Pablo jumped back while his sister leaned over and peered inside the twisted chassis. She began speaking in Spanish to the people inside.

"Shades, this is Burley, over." Burley had to call a few more times before Shades responded. He got down on his knees next to Anna and could see at least two new victims bloodied and panicked. The smoke was getting thicker.

"Sorry Burley, I'm up to my elbows in airways, over."

"When we getting help cousin? We got a bad bleeder on this end and some trapped people I can't even get to yet, over."

"It was 15 minutes a few minutes ago, traffic is stopped and the median approach is not optimal. Air unit about the same, I think. You got any idea yet how many casualties we're talking about, over?"

"No — I haven't even been able to get to the bus yet. How many at your location, over?" Burley snapped on some new rubber gloves.

"Pablo, get the flashlight out of the box, quick lad," he said.

"I've got six treated, four dead and we got another half dozen laid out. Some of the civilians and the veterans are transporting victims over to the ambulance, over."

"They said it's just the two of them, sir," Anna reported in. "They don't think they are hurt that bad."

The two people, a woman and a girl, were trapped between two seats, crimped on the floor of the vehicle. They did not appear to be in shock. Burley could not see anyone forward of them in the beam of his light. Given the frame compression caused at impact, this was for the best. He was guessing some of the dead he had seen in the median were ejected out of the front of this vehicle. The motor compartment was almost sheared away and was belching black smoke. If the engine caught fire the flames would probably not consume the rest of the wreck, but the smoke would likely kill anyone still inside.

"Damn, I ain't no firefighter," Burley mumbled to himself. He scooted out and grabbed Pablo by the arm. "Listen — I want you to run back around the other side of this wreck — go around the back, do not go near the front — and run as fast as you can to the ambulance — did you see it when we came over?" Pablo nodded intently. "You tell my partner Shades that you need the fire extinguisher. I'll call him while you're on your way. I need you back here in 60 seconds, you understand?" Pablo took off before Burley could finish speaking.

"Stay away from the front when you come back," he yelled again after the boy. Just past the rear of the vehicle a man in a green fatigue jacket was approaching. He was limping. Burley returned to his medic box looking for something he could give Blondie to pack the wound on which she had a life grip. He pulled out a wad of dressing packing. The man's daughter sat holding her father's hand, quiet.

"Blondie, see if this will work," he said. She reached back and grabbed the supplies. Blondie torqued her body into the van to get an angle to use both hands on the patient, who was semi-conscious. Burley heard a deep slow drawl.

"What the hell are you people doing over here?" Burley, on his knees, looked up. The man looked scruffy, long hair and beard. He reminded Burley of a guy he had seen walking along the side of the road when he and Shades were driving their commander to a division meeting. The commander, a Vietnam veteran, took a long look at the pedestrian as they passed and offered an observation.

"You know, when I was in Vietnam that is the exact kind of guy I wanted with me because I know he would cover my back or die trying. But when there's not a war on, I worry about what a guy like that is doing."

The man was bleeding from a gash on his leg and his right eye was dilated.

"Trying to get these people out of this van before it catches fire," Burley answered, reaching for his flashlight. The man didn't seem to like that answer.

"We got American citizens — veterans — over in that bus who need your help. Quit fucking with these illegals and get your sorry ass over there," he said, his speech slightly slurred. Burley noticed stripes on his sleeve.

"Sure thing, Sarge, as soon as we keep these people from burning to death," he answered. Pablo came careening around the end of the van with the fire extinguisher, his teenage feet flapping like a circus clown. He tripped, but quick-stepped his way towards Burley in a controlled fall, beautifully setting the big fire extinguisher in front of Burley. In the same instant, the confused vet pulled a pistol out of his pocket.

"I said NOW, get your butt in gear and help my friends," the Sarge bellowed as he fired into the air. This pissed Burley off to a degree that he found surprising. EMS people hate guns, and no good ever comes from some yahoo civilian waving one around at a scene. Everyone wants to be in charge.

Later, when the news reporters turned the accident into pop culture entertainment that was about them and not the victims, it was said that Burley acted with great heroism. The truth was that he had done nothing but improvise since arriving on the scene; he was not at all sure he had been making good decisions. But the bit with the fire extinguisher was pretty slick. Burley sprayed Sarge right in the face with the extinguisher which drove him back a few steps, and then wacked him on his injured leg with the nozzle, which brought him to the ground. Pablo actually caught the gun, a small 22 Beretta, as it flipped straight up into the air. Pablo looked at Burley like he had just scooped up some dog droppings.

"Burley, was that a gunshot, over?" Shades called over the radio, anxious. Burley gently took the gun out of Pablo's hand and released the clip, which Pablo also fielded. He aimed into the air and pulled the trigger to make sure the chamber was empty. In the distance he could hear multiple sirens and the chop of a helicopter. He picked up a couple of bottles of sterile water and handed them to Pablo.

"Here, wash that spray out of his face," he said pointing to the Sarge, who was clearly not going to be any further trouble. "He's in shock, so find something to put under his legs to raise his feet, Pablo. Remember, if a patient is red raise their head. If they're pale, raise their tail." He also instructed the teen to put on some rubber gloves and wrap the wound on Sarge's leg with bandages out of the first aid box.

Blondie and Anna were working the little's girl father out of the van, his bleeding halted. As Burley ran around the front of the wreck to spray the engine, he heard Blondie call after him.

"Nice work, Rescue." Burley had a good feeling about her compliment.

CHAPTER

Womens

ELEVEN

No fewer than three Eye Witness News Teams, four Action News Teams and two News First Teams in the state of Virginia anointed Shades and Burley as heroes. Even the Eye Witness News Station in Charleston, West Virginia got in on the story, as several of the veterans injured in the wreck were from the state — including the subdued Sarge. The Vietnam vet was not charged for his gunplay as he was deemed to be in shock. Truth be told, Sarge was notorious in his neighborhood for his propensity for waving guns around. But such are life's little ironies, often overlooked by the news media in the throes of hero worship. The third year resident and two nurses, as well as the orthopedic surgeon from Richmond got mentions, but they just didn't have the visual appeal of a big gleaming ambulance in front of which to conduct interviews. Shades and Burley got mentions — a few paragraphs — in both the daily and weekly Charlottesville papers. Thanks to their Division, they were profiled as the EMS Team of the Month story in the leading national EMS trade magazine, *The Siren*. Blondie also gave Burley her phone number.

It was the worst motor vehicle accident in the history of the state. The two 12-passenger vans were overloaded with 32 migrant farm

worker passengers between them. The charter bus held 67 people for
a total of 99 victims. When rescuers hoisted the bus up they found
a compact car underneath with another body to bring the total to
an even 100. The death toll was high with most of the fatalities being among the Mexican and South American pickers. Of the dead,
23 were in the two vans with another 13 aboard the bus and a college student in the compact car. A full third of the passengers were
dead at the scene.

The media hailed Shades, Burley, the two nurses and the two
physicians in preventing the death toll from going higher. Some 15
patients were saved with active timely airway and bleeding management. Most of the victims remained in ICUs in four area hospitals
along with another 28 admitted for less serious broken bones and
soft tissue injuries. Only 20 patients were treated and released. The
hospitals and their staff had performed admirably, utilizing a regional
disaster plan that had been practiced many times over the years.
Charlottesville had reason to be proud of their medical community.

The only person who was not happy was Dr. Denise DeLuca. She
introduced herself as the Rescue Squad's Medical Director to several reporters who showed up at the Rescue Squad Headquarters
and the hospital. Dr. DeLuca made it very clear that she was available for interviews. In phone messages to local reporters, she pitched
her insight about the incident and the squads, especially Shades and
Burley — whom she had handpicked to enter the emergency medical services field. But so far, in the first week following the accident,
nothing — she had not been interviewed on television even once. It
didn't help that neither Shades nor Burley had yet mentioned her in
any of their many interviews. She had dropped a few hints to the two
that it would help their story if she were part of it. When that didn't
work, she went with what she knew worked best: threats.

"I don't want to have to bring this up, but using those teenagers at the scene of the accident violated several standard operating procedures," she told Shades one day in an ER waiting room
where she had pulled him aside. Burley, per usual, was in the EMS
lounge eating lunch.

"They had no medical terminology training, which is required for patient translation services. And what was Burley thinking having that kid patch up that crazy guy?" The story of how Burley had subdued the armed, addle-minded Vietnam War veteran but had declined to press charges was getting big news legs. Calls to Burley came in every day from around the country for interviews.

Shades was not in the mood, and in fact doubted he ever would be again. He held her gaze several seconds, thinking about what he was about to say. Then he took his sunglasses off.

"Was it any more against standard operating procedure than letting your boyfriend's son drive an ambulance?" Shades asked. And for good measure he added, "Denise." It was the first time Shades had ever called her by her first name.

Dr. DeLuca sneered quietly in response.

"Listen Raymond," she said. "We can do this easy, or we can do this hard," she whispered, curling her lip back, her eyes going out of focus on the wall behind him. Shades wasn't sure what she meant.

"Do you know none of the other squad members like you?" she added for good measure. Shades smiled.

"I know how the other people on the squad feel about me, Denise, because I talk to them every day. Do you know how they feel about you?" She looked startled.

"They love me."

"No, Denise, they are afraid of you," Shades said quietly, hoping to see some hint of insight. He realized at that moment that the doctor did not know the difference between love and fear. He then made the mistake of feeling sorry for her.

"Denise," he said, again, not unkindly. "I appreciate everything that you have done for me and I know Burley feels the same way. Neither of us would be an EMT today if it weren't for you. But let's be honest — your interest in the two of us has always been what you could get out of the relationship, and for a long time that seemed like a fair trade-off, but no more. You don't own us, those days are over." Shades put his sunglasses back on, a little convinced that in that moment he could change Dr. Denise DeLuca.

Dr. DeLuca had never been capable of discriminating and weighing her options. She wanted what she wanted.

"See, Raymond," she growled low. "You think that just because you got yourself famous things have changed between us. That's a big mistake you're making." She paused, then added her hallmark dig.

"You forget, I know about you." It was Dr. DeLuca's go to threat, the one she grew up hearing from her mother. It terrified her because Denise always had much to hide. But Shades had heard this line often enough to know she was just fishing.

Shades said nothing. He knew it was best to let Dr. DeLuca have the last word, so he stepped around her to leave just as Burley walked up, all smiles.

"Hey doc, how you doing? Long time no see," he said to Dr. DeLuca. "That was some accident, huh?"

Shades grabbed his arm and pulled him towards the door. Burley stumbled backwards, looking between Shades and Dr. DeLuca. She followed, glaring at him. "You better decide real quick, Burley, whose side you're on," she warned. Denise looked up to see Dr. Janet Ippolito watching from the nursing station. Dr. Ippolito snapped shut the chart she was working on, stood up and quickly moved towards Dr. DeLuca.

"Dr. DeLuca, could I have a word?" she said flatly. Dr. DeLuca halted as Burley, who glanced back nervously, followed Shades out of the ambulance bay door and back to their rig.

"Janet, I have to get up to the ICU but I promise I'll come back before your shift is over," Dr. DeLuca said.

Dr. Ippolito trailed Dr. DeLuca to the rear elevator in the ER that ran directly to the ICU.

"Denise, you have been doing nothing but ducking me for the past week. You and I can either talk or I can take my concerns to the emergency and trauma department meeting next week and we can talk there," Dr. Ippolito warned. "Something was not right about a certain EKG read out."

Dr. DeLuca stabbed the elevator button.

"You really think that's a good idea Janet?" Dr. DeLuca said, staring straight ahead.

"You threatening me doctor?" Dr. Ippolito asked incredulously.

"I know about you," Dr. DeLuca mumbled automatically, stalling for time until the elevator arrived. She just needed to get back the ICU, her domain where people did what she told them. It was several moments before Dr. DeLuca realized Dr. Ippolito had gone quiet. She glanced sideways to see an expression of alarm, fear and anger on the ER doctor's face. Dr. DeLuca had scored a direct hit, but about what was a mystery. The elevator door opened. Dr. DeLuca stepped in and left the ER doctor speechless, but angry. It was just another day at the office for Dr. DeLuca.

On Tuesday the Unitarian Church marquee advised: "Everything will be all right in the end. If it's not yet all right it is not yet the end." This counsel gave Leo patience with the cast of characters parading through his office over the past few days. All had demands.

The wanna-be cowboy showed up first. He was "all hat, no cattle" as an old uncle who was actually a cowboy sometimes said of such imposters. Cowboy Hat was upset because there was no proper parking for his extra long, chrome trimmed, diesel pickup truck. He expected line-of-site from the lobby to his steel steed. His "rig", he explained, was fundamental to his happiness and identity, although what he said was "No one fucks with my truck." He threatened to take his business to a Charlottesville hospital 40 miles away if Leo did not have the parking situation remedied before his mother's next pain injection treatment.

Next came two retired elderly gents inquiring about the hospital's accommodation for the deaf. The conversation was punctuated by a lot of confused looks and "What?" as neither of the men could hear very well. They seemed like a couple of nice fellows with too much time on their hands. They referred frequently to the Americans with Disabilities Act. Neither, however, was familiar with the Telephone

Relay Service offered by the National Association of the Deaf or used sign language or used hearing aides. They did not lip read.

This was followed by a repeat visit from a middle-aged woman with vague complaints about the care she had received on the floor almost a year ago. She seemed to enjoy taking up Leo's time in 30-minute blocks and Leo got the distinct feeling she was lonely. As she spoke without much point, Leo stared at the empty New Life Christian Church building from the window in his office. The electronic marquee was gone, dismounted from its pedestal and already moved to storage to reappear in front of the new church out by the interstate.

The complaint she and the others bore all related to the tear-down of the empty church to make way for the new Ascend Outpatient Surgery Center and Medical Clinic. He had been renting the parking lot from the church for staff parking during the week to open up spaces for patients and visitors. That ended with the sale of the building to Ascend. The phone cable to the deaf interpretation service had been cut as the construction crew moved an office trailer onto the church property. The grievous lady patient was a member of a church volunteer group that disbanded while the new site was under construction.

Leo knew from experience that the only thing for certain is that things change. He had always accepted this condition of professional life and had always adapted. But in the face of this change, there was a fear to which he was unaccustomed. He could think of no good response and others would notice soon that he had no plan. Leaders kept their heads when everyone else around them went into a panic. Leo knew a scared leader was halfway to failure.

<hr />

Burley called it: a pile-up that killed and injured 100 people had reporters forgetting their own name, much less that of Flip Jensen. The press swarmed the hospitals, interviewing anyone they could get to stand still, with the exception of Denise DeLuca, M.D. Dr. DeLuca was a known media hound of the first order, an ingratiating interview who could not be brief to save her life. She rambled in a long whisper that made it impossible to edit down to the eight to twelve-second sound bite essential to television newscasts. Even the out-of-market reporters who put her in front of the camera quickly realized their mistake, stopping the interview with an abrupt "cut" and dropping their microphones in frustration.

Luann Zahn had done her share of stories on the disaster to appease her editor, who had her camped out at University Medical Center where the worst of the crash victims had been admitted. She had even coined the go-to tagline for the event — "The Great Charlottesville Crash." Most of the other television reporters paid her the ultimate professional compliment and swiped it from her, growling into the camera like lounge lizards — "The Greaaaaat Charrrrlottesville Cra-ashhhhh." She was sick of reporting on it and wanted to be back at Ascend Medical Center. There was a bigger story there, even bigger than The Great Charlottesville Crash. Luann had a faked EKG on the patient in the ambulance and a gut feeling from the very start that Virginia Stowe was not telling her everything about the first skateboarding baby's sudden delivery to the ICU.

Luann did not differentiate between an omission of fact and outright lying; to a reporter, it was the same thing. She also knew that media spokespeople did not lie for their own benefit, but rather under orders. Since the crash, she had learned from Flip's parents, Early and Myrtle Jensen, that Flip had suffered a prefrontal cortex brain injury to the front of his head. There had been no brain swelling. This was the reason Flip was still at Ascend Medical Center rather then being transferred to the University Medical Center across town. What she didn't know was the fact that Flip also had really good medical insurance was another reason to hang onto him. If he had been uninsured, Royce Wexler would have strongly suggested that Dr. DeLuca ship him out.

Another sign that there was more to the story was that none of the three neurologists in the same practice based at Ascend would agree to an interview about Flip Jensen or even about pre-frontal cortex brain injuries in general. They cited patient confidentiality. She instead had to get a neurologist at University for the interview, which had not yet aired. Most of the available airtime on the news report was mandated for back-story coverage of the "The Great Charlottesville Crash".

Their sponsors loved this story and all of the available advertising spots had been sold. The sales manager had the production crew working over time to cut one to two minutes out of reruns so that extra commercial time could be added to boost news profits. A good local disaster did not come along very often. The same ad revenue could occasionally be reaped from a national or world disaster that kept people nervous and in front of the television, such as an earthquake during the World Series or an airline crash. Such calamity upped viewership, and more eyeballs in front of TV screens was always good for business, both for the station and sponsors alike. It was a core local television rule: if a story bleeds, it leads.

Luann was sitting in one of the station's editing suites with Dusty, viewing the first interview with Virginia Stowe, the one where she got all twitchy about Dr. DeLuca. Her editor passed by walking briskly, throwing on the brakes when he saw the two sitting in the darkened room with only the glow of the monitor screen illuminating the their faces. He stepped backwards like a cartoon character into the doorway.

"What are you still doing here?" he asked, exasperated. "You're supposed to be over at University rustling up some interviews with the survivors' family members. I need tears and fears for the newscast tonight, we've got Russell Sanitation coming on as a new client and I promised Hank in sales a good show," the editor said. Luann began to slowly tap her nail on the console, drumming out her irritation. Dusty made himself busy rewinding tape, surprised when she stayed calm.

"Tommy," she finally said to the editor, "how would you like an interview with the Medical Director of the ambulance service of the first responders? No one's aired that story yet."

The editor's face went awash with conflict as he weighed the benefits of sobbing family members against an exclusive. Luann gave him a nudge in the right direction.

"You can send Mandy over to talk to the survivors. She's got a face like an angel — sad people just eat her up. That story she's trying to work about the safety record of subcompact cars is not going to be ready today any way," Luann suggested. The editor thought about it; Dusty was betting he wasn't going to go for the change in plans.

"Good idea, Zahn. You keep thinking like that and you can take my job when I move up to a bigger market," he said as he moved on down the hall into what he knew was a brighter future.

Dusty looked at her and smiled.

"That was slick girl, nice work. I was not looking forward to taping a bunch of Hispanic families about their comatose loved ones. Hispanic grief is very powerful," he observed.

"Yeah, well, Dr. DeLuca has not been returning my calls, which is very odd considering that she's been jumping every reporter within 100 miles trying to get interviewed. While we're talking to the doctor about the crash, it will be a good time to slip in a few questions about Flip Jensen," Luann said. "I'm going to get that story wrestled to the ground one way or another."

Flip Jensen was having his reoccurring-dream in which he was a jet pilot aboard an aircraft carrier. As his aircraft rolled up to the catapult, he banged on the inside of the canopy to get the attention of the flight deck crew. He wasn't a pilot, he had talked his way into the cockpit; he was a fraud. The harder and more frantically he gestured to those below, the bigger they smiled and signaled back with salutes and thumbs up. The aircraft bucked and shuddered and then exploded forward as the big ship's huge steam catapults hurled it down the deck and off the bow. The huge fighter plane powered forward in a long silent arch and then dropped into the ocean with a surprisingly gentle splash. The seawater parted up and over the canopy as the plane followed a gentle glide path to the bottom of the ocean, trailing a soft curtain of bubbles. It was beautiful and peaceful, but still Flip pulled furiously at the canopy to escape, but with no response.

Myrtle Jensen noted the tiny tremors firing off through her son's body. It was a hopeful sign, she thought. The Tunisian neurologist, recently graduated from an American medical school, said only "Maybe, we'll see". The dreadful Dr. DeLuca was also dismissive, as usual.

"Don't get your hopes up, he's been in a Level I coma since he got here, those muscle twitches are not in response to any stimuli," she sniffed. "That neurologist is new and I don't know him. And, he's foreign."

"His name is James," Myrtle replied. Dr. DeLuca looked confused.

"The neurologist?" she asked.

"No my son, his name is James. You never call him by his name," Myrtle said.

Dr. DeLuca pretended to be involved making notes in Flip's chart, annoyed again by his mother's delusional expectations for her son. Since Royce Wexler and her boyfriend Ace had colluded to deny her the recognition she wanted from the media, she was working ruthlessly behind the scenes to get Flip Jensen transferred out of the hospital and over to University. Dr. DeLuca was an early adopter of the Internet. She just needed a starting point, an anointment by the media. The right television footage to share on the growing Internet would be just the thing to help her create her own fame. But if she could not get interviewed on television no one else would either, including that perky Dr. Ippolito in the ER.

Now that Dr. DeLuca knew the ER doctor had a secret, she was working her contacts to find out what Dr. Ippolito might be hiding. Denise loved secrets, including her own. Secrets were currency to be used in barter, to achieve ends that could not be accomplished in any other way. She turned and left Flip's room without any further comment to his mother. On the way back to the ICU nursing station her phone chirped. She recognized Luann Zahn's number. For an instant Dr. DeLuca thought of Ace's fist wrapped in her hair, pulling her face close as he threatened her with the humiliation and pain that awaited her if she spoke to any reporters about Flip Jensen. Normally, Ace's domination was arousing, but this time he had successfully conveyed to her that this threat was different. It was the first time that she knew that he would hurt her for something other than pleasure. Since the Flip Jensen incident, Dr. DeLuca had not been returning Luann's calls. Dr. DeLuca reasoned it would not hurt to listen.

"Hello, Luann."

"Hi, Dr. DeLuca." There was no mistaking that voice, ghostlike and passive. "I've noticed that no one has interviewed you about the crash. Would you have a few minutes to talk to me today about the first responders?" Denise stared into the manager's office, thinking about the conversation she had overheard between the hospital spokesperson and Royce Wexler. She was going to need to create her own good public image.

"Dr. DeLuca, are you still there?"

"Oh, sorry, Luann, I was signing an order. So you said you want to talk about the crash?"

Luann could hear it, the under tone of hesitation with a twist of deception. "That's correct Dr. DeLuca, you know it's the big story at the moment and I can't believe that no one has thought to get your views on the work of the first responders. After all, you are the Medical Director for the ambulance service," Luann said, fairly certain that flattery would grease the skids. Dr. DeLuca agreed to meet the next morning in her office at 8 a.m. That was very early for a television news reporter whose work day generally did not start until mid-morning.

She called Janet who was working day shift and would be off soon. Janet sounded terse and upset.

"What's wrong, sweetness?" Luann asked. The two had continued to spend time together at Arnie's, drinking and talking.

"I'll tell you later, it's our favorite doctor," said Dr. Ippolito.

"You mean Dr. DeLuca, of course. I finally got an interview with her for tomorrow," said Luann.

"Really?" said Janet who suddenly sounded cheerful. "I'll see you at Arnie's in an hour," Dr. Ippolito said.

Several blocks west of Arnie's, Jim and Robert Wallace sat in the first floor of the Central Building, sipping scotch and eating pistachios. The building had been in their family for three generations. It was a view they liked, especially as the day got along into the late afternoon. The sun blinded anyone who tried to look into his office. They were both wealthy, family money having started them on their way. The two worked their contacts in Charlottesville, mostly other families with old money and ties. After all, no one wanted a lawyer and CPA who needed a lot of explanation about embarrassing transgressions.

Even in the 1990s' Charlottesville was a place where the Revolutionary and Civil Wars still, in part, defined who you were and what entitlements you could expect. The local joke was it took 10 Charlottesville blue bloods to change a light bulb: one to turn the bulb and nine to talk about how good the old one was. Jim and Robert — named respectively after James Monroe and Robert E. Lee, were cousins, but brothers in all ways. They sported thick, silver hair anchored by low healthy hairlines that capped expensive custom made suits, ties and shirts. Their dark, polished dress shoes had tassels.

They were talking about their favorite subject — women.

"That Camilla is a fine girl," Robert drawled. "If she would divorce that Mexican, I'd marry her in a minute." He looked down and brushed pistachio crumbs off his blue button down oxford shirt. He swirled the ice cubes around lazily in his glass.

"You need another wife like Elvis needed more sleeping pills," Jim said. Robert was divorced three times, none of his ex-wives received any alimony. Such was the advantage of being an attorney. "What's wrong with that little sporting girl you got holed up across town?"

Robert frowned and cocked his head in concession. "Holed up is about the size of it, I reckon," he snorted. "She is pretty and agreeable, but has no breeding," he said, a little drunk. "I can't take that woman anywhere without my mother finding out about it," Robert said. "What I need is to find a woman who will fuck like my little trollop but knows how to dress up to play bridge with my mother and the rest of the old ladies."

The door opened as Robert's secretary came in to see if they needed anything before she left for the day.

Jim poured another finger of scotch and shook his jowly head. "Damn cousin, you keep making the same mistake. You seek out the company of the classiest woman you can find and then you act all surprised when they don't like getting naked. Camilla don't seem like the fucking kind to me," he offered.

"You are some bad, evil men, talking about southern women like common trash," Miss Shirley told them as she set a pitcher of ice water between them. "You be sure to drink some of that water before you leave and call a taxi if you drink much more of that Scotch," she reminded them. She had been giving them the same advice every Thursday night for 20 years. And it worked. So far, there was not a DUI between them.

"Oh we don't mean anything by it, Miss Shirley," Robert assured. "We're just a couple a old horn dogs — we're all bark."

"Hmmm, I doubt that, but you are sweet gentleman," she said, patting Robert on the shoulder. "I'll see you all tomorrow," she said as she left.

They sat quiet for a moment, thinking.

"You should marry Miss Shirley," Jim offered. "She would know what she was getting."

"Naw, cousin, I learned a long time ago to never put your dick on the payroll. That never turns out well — we got plenty of clients that learned that expensive lesson."

They sipped and munched for a while longer, watching the common folk outside.

"So what's Marvin come up with?" Jim asked. Marvin Wallace was his cousin's investigator. Marvin, black and unassuming, did well in bars, hotels, and restaurants — anywhere he could get work as a janitor or pose as a drinking man. Marvin's family had been working for the Wallace family in one capacity or another back to the days of slavery; they had assumed their master's name when freed, a common custom. Jim Wallace stretched his legs out in front of him, slouching in his chair as he shut his eyes and tilted his head back.

"That lady reporter Luann Zahn is queer as the Women's National Basketball Association and she's got eyes for that lady emergency room doctor. They've been meeting every few days at Arnie's and seem to be warming up to each other, so it sounds like that lady doctor is thinking about being queer too," he sighed. "Why would a nice looking, smart lady like that not be interested in men, like us for instance?" he wondered.

"Reckon she just needs a good poke," Jim said. They both laughed. It was an old joke between them, their sure cure for lesbianism.

"So what are those two women so keen on meeting for any way?" Jim asked. He leaned forward to watch two women in short skirts walk by.

"From what Marvin can tell, they're talking about something that happened at the hospital," he answered.

"Must be the crash," Jim supposed.

"That's what I thought," Robert said, his eyes still closed. His voice was getting softer, slower — he felt sleepy. "But he heard the name Dr. DeLuca mentioned several times."

"Aww Christ, why don't that surprise me?" Jim exclaimed. He took a sip. "I wonder if it has anything to do with the boy genius getting knocked over by the ambulance in front of the emergency room." They both paused once again to consider the irony and odds of such an event and not for the first time snickered a little.

"Well, DeKooka's the least of our problems right now, Jimmy," Robert said. "The hospital CFO is giving Camilla a hard time about Aunt Missy staying at the hospital. That boy needs to be educated. You understand what I'm saying?"

"I do, cousin," Robert answered. "I'll yank Royce's leash up hard, get his attention." They were quiet for a bit.

"We needs some womens. You know Jimmy, that little dolly of mine has a friend who is real agreeable. We ought to take a ride over there right now before I fall asleep," Robert offered.

"Come on Bobby, we're not all divorced like you," Jim answered.

"Well, not yet, that is, cousin," Robert drawled. They stared out the window for some more lady watching. Every once in a while one of them would mutter "yes sir". After a few minutes Jim spoke.

"She really got a friend, huh?" Jim asked.

"Yes sir, who do you think cuts my hair?" Robert murmured. "She's a hairdresser......great hands......smells nice." His head went back and he dozed off, echoing his cousin's soft snores.

There were two things Owen Gregor always swore that he would never do. The first was get a job and the second was clean a bathroom. But here he was, chasing a ring around the toilet after a shift working at a downtown parking garage. Every day life looked a lot clearer now and it was more boring than he remembered. He was wiping little figure eights around the bowl with a pink toilet brush, the likes of which he had never seen before. It looked like something that might be used to groom a unicorn.

For years he thought it was figuring out the hard stuff that made him lie, cheat and bully to get the pills. But he was beginning to understand the hard stuff of life was the mundane. He scrubbed harder.

"This has got to be love," he muttered.

"I'll say baby. There's nothing hotter than a man on his knees in front of a commode," Felicia cooed, "especially when he's not barfing." Owen felt awkward and a bit irritated, a combination that in the past had often not served him well. Owen sighed and turned on his knees. Felicia had on the same low-cut blouse and shawl as the day he met her in the lobby at Valley View hospital. Her cheeks were flushed, always a hint of how she felt about him. There were times when he wanted to go back to the pills. And then moments like these were the antidote to the haze he had lived in for so long. He wondered when the pull between the two universes would end and his path would once and for all be clear. He smiled at her, the right thing to do it turned out. She let the shawl slip off.

Luann was the first to arrive, as usual. Kenny hopped down from the bar, his girlfriend of late carrying his beer over to Luann's table. He whispered something in the young thing's ear. She giggled and walked slowly to a table of other young pretty things. Both Kenny and Luann admired the sway of her backside.

"That's enough to make me wish I had hands," Kenny offered.

"I'll drink to that," Luann said. She held Kenny's beer up for him with one hand and sipped her own with the other.

"See those two guys over at the end of the bar, one of them has on a BB King t-shirt?" Kenny signaled for another sip. "They come in a few times a week and share naked Polaroid's of their girlfriends," Kenny revealed. "I'm going broke buying them drinks, because I really want a look."

"Why don't you just offer them some photos of your own lovely?" Luann asked. Kenny stopped in mid-sip.

"Damn, Zahn, that would be a good idea — if I had hands to hold a camera," Kenny said. Luann bumped him shoulder-to-shoulder and laughed.

"What's a good idea?" Dr. Ippolito said sitting down across the table. Kenny slid out.

"I gotta go," he said, signaling his girlfriend from among her friends.

"That guy gets more action than I do," Luann said in true amazement as Kenny's pretty girlfriend draped her arm around his shoulders and led "his handsomeness" — Luann's nickname for Kenny — out the door.

Janet was distracted. Dr. DeLuca was not going to define who she was, that was for damn sure. She re-seated herself next to Luann, found her thigh, which surprised Luann. She gave a nice profile smile to the doctor, looking into her drink.

"Let's take a ride to your apartment and on the way I'll tell you the questions you want to ask Dr. DeLuca when you see her tomorrow," Janet said. A lifetime of denial flushed through her with a drop in her stomach that felt like a carnival ride. Luann returned her caress and for a moment, it looked like a bit of a wrestling match in the confines of the booth. The waitress approached and set two Mojitos down on the table as the two rose to leave.

"Kenny ordered these for you before he left," she smiled, happy for the two.

"We'll take them with us," Dr. Ippolito said. She was in her doctor take-charge mode, directing protocols and setting the timetable.

"Well, I hope you're not going too far," the waitress advised, worried about open alcohol containers in a car. She had lost some good regulars to poor judgment of the jailing or dying kind over the years, and she liked these two.

"Far enough," Janet said, "in fact all the way." Luann giggled like Kenny's girlfriend.

———

Some hours later, the phone on Royce Wexler's bedside table buzzed like a hive of bees. He came awake excited, groping for the receiver like a man stretching for a handhold on a cliff face.

"Wexler," he croaked into the phone.

"Royce, it's Stella."

Royce recalled the last time his Chief Nursing Officer had awakened him with a blast from the phone in the middle of the night — his Chief of Staff had collapsed from a heart attack.

"Someone better be dead," Royce warned.

"I wish Royce. It's worse. Flip Jensen is gone." Royce thought Stella sounded uncharacteristically rattled until he heard beyond her tone to what she had just said.

"Dead?" Royce said, stuck on the subject.

"No gone, like not in his bed, Royce, vamoosed, disappeared," Stella said tersely.

"He's in a coma for Christ sake, how can he be gone?" Royce paused, certain that stating the obvious was unhelpful. He sat up and turned on the lamp. His wife stirred, reaching for her sleeping mask.

"Royce, I have been at the hospital for 90 minutes since the house sup called me. Flip Jensen is nowhere to be found." Royce's grip on the phone was murderous and his hand began to ache.

"Tell me where you've looked," he said. Stella almost growled.

"Royce, I've been through this building myself — I even checked the physician sleep rooms — where I had the distinctly unpleasant experience of waking up Dr. DeLuca," she told him. Royce felt his mouth go dry.

"Why is DeLuca spending the night in the hospital? She never does that," Royce said.

"I don't know Royce, I didn't have time for chit chat," Stella said. "All I can tell you is that Flip wasn't in her room — he isn't any where in the hospital."

"I'm on my way," Royce said, standing and pulling off his pajamas as he hung up.

"Fucking DeLuca," he mumbled. His wife had heard this many times before. Reassured that nothing was too much out of order, she rolled over and went back to sleep.

CHAPTER
Security
TWELVE

Denise DeLuca had almost no experience at not being guilty. When suspected, she had always found it prudent to deny responsibility, but to ever so slightly imply that she knew more than she admitted. It was a handy tactic to make her appear part of the solution, plus to create the aggravation that was her stock and trade.

She had spent the night in the hospital to avoid Ace. It was the only way to hide her plans and to keep him from knowing about her interview with Luann Zahn in the morning. If she thought it, Ace figured it out. It was a trait that first attracted her to him, because no one ever "got" Denise DeLuca. But now he knew her too well. She reached under the bed and pulled out a file of the x-rays of her breasts. She put both films on the light board mounted on the wall. She studied the lesions again, satisfying her medical judgment one more time.

A commotion in the hallway alerted her to Royce's arrival. She could hear the low rumble of his baritone voice, followed by the feet scurrying in his wake. Denise was already dressed, anticipating the uproar, thinking over the details one more time. She had succeeded in life, risen to a position far beyond her family and class because she would do what others would not. The few people who learned that about her and who could not be won over very quickly learned to go about their business, back down or leave. She had become a doctor living by this code and she would remain a doctor by sticking to the plan.

Royce, passing by in the hall, heard the freaky little hissing chuckle that only emanated from the depths of Dr. Denise DeLuca. He rapped on the door.

"Denise, open it," Royce insisted, his voice low. He waited, Stella beside him, trying her best not to be offended by Royce's curtness that was bordering on rudeness. He had arrived 15 minutes ago and proceeded to treat them all like morons. Royce had even looked under the bed, like Flip would be hugging the bottom staring back like a grinning cartoon character.

"Denise, we need to find your patient. Come out here and talk to me." Royce tried his best to sound friendly but he sounded deranged. It was clear that rising in the middle of the night did not agree with him. Not so clear was what he would do if Dr. DeLuca did open the door. Stella leaned in close to Royce.

"Royce, the security guards are meeting at the ICU desk, you should sit in on their briefing. I've initiated the emergency preparedness protocols, so we're going to need an incident commander," she said, trying to reason with him. Royce stopped tapping on the door.

"Why the in the hell did you initiate the emergency plan?" he asked. "We need to keep this quiet — the whole town is going to know about this now," Royce told her.

Virginia Stowe came clicking down the hallway like a card in the spokes of a bike tire.

"Thanks for not calling me," she said to Stella. The two were normally amicable, but it was late — or early — Royce wasn't sure which.

"I was trying not to roust anyone out of bed I didn't need to Ginny, I was sure we would have found him by now," she said.

"For future reference Stella, the second person you call after Royce is me," Ginny said pulling a brush violently through her hair while she groped around in her purse for make-up. "You don't think word is going to leak out about this? It doesn't matter if you activate the emergency plan or drop a cone of silence on the ICU, word is going to get out." The brush in her hair sounded like a flag snapping in the wind. "There are no secrets in a hospital. One of the nurses or the security guards has probably already called and talked to someone outside."

"Excuse me for interrupting the hen party, but if we want to find Flip we need to talk to Dr. DeLuca, which is what I was trying to do before you interrupted me." He jiggled the door handle. The heavy institutional door rattled as if in the wind. There was still no reply.

Mark Swingle, the patient rep, rounded the corner. He was wearing slippers.

"Hey, who called this meeting?" he smiled. Royce stared at his feet.

"Oh don't worry, boss, I got a pair of shoes and shirt and tie in my office," Swingle offered. "I thought I better dress down in case we had to start digging for a body." Normally Royce enjoyed Swingle, who always had funny patient stories.

"Mark, I'm not in the mood," Royce warned. He leaned forward to beat his fist on the sleep room door. "Denise — open the fucking door." Mark stepped up close to the door. "Is Dr. DeLuca in there?"

"Yes, Mark, and I need to talk to her about what happened to Flip Jensen, *her* patient," he said, then he raised his voice again, "who has disappeared on the same night she decides to stay in the hospital." Swingle leaned forward to whisper in Royce's ear. Royce cocked his head and looked at Swingle in surprise.

"All right. Stella and Ginny, let's go to your security briefing," Royce said. He walked backwards pointing at Swingle with both hands. "You better be right," he said. Royce turned abruptly just before reaching the ICU swinging doors, gave the doors a hard push and disappeared. Mark turned, knocked and spoke softly.

"Denise, open up, it's me. He's gone." The door opened and Mark Swingle slipped in.

***

Janet Ippolito was in a deep sleep rendered by deep satisfaction. An arm and a leg were hooked over Luann's backside, like bow and stern anchors. It had been nothing like she had imagined. That she had feared this warmth seemed so foolish. How she had suppressed the clarity offered by passion for so long would take some sorting out. It made her wonder what else she had gotten wrong in her life.

Janet heard her cell phone vibrating, the ringer off. She was not on call and her brain was in a state of relaxation the likes of which she had never known before. She urged her body to answer but fell back asleep. A minute later, her pager woke them both.

"That's it doctor, we're breaking up," Luann groaned.

"Cheer up, news lady, the last time I got paged when I wasn't on call it was for the Great Charlottesville Crash," Janet said, laying on top of her, not quite ready to focus on her pager. Luann was taller and curvier than Janet, who felt as if she was lying in warm sand.

"Throw that in my face," Luann mumbled. "That damn crash pulled me off the Flip Jensen story, which was the story I should have been working the last three weeks." Luann sighed. "Hmmm, that feels nice."

"Anatomy class," Janet explained. She finally read the text message on her pager with one hand and gave a final squeeze with the other. She silently handed the pager to Luann who struggled to brush the hair out of her face and read the message. She felt Luann sway and buck like a diving board beneath her as she searched for her own cell phone beneath the bed. Janet heard her punch a few buttons and a ring on the other end. Janet held on; Luann reached backwards with her other hand and stroked her bottom. A voice answered, gruff and low.

"Dusty, wake up we need to roll. The hospital has lost Flip Jensen," she said. "Yeah, lost — as in missing, gone, can't find him. Royce Wexler himself is on the scene." Luann rolled over on her side, facing Janet. "No, I'm not fucking with you and yes, I have this info from a good source — in fact a great source," she said, smiling into Janet's face. Her phone buzzed, indicating another incoming call. Luann, who normally wore contacts, held the phone close to see the call waiting.

"Dusty — hold on — I can't believe this, it's Myrtle Jensen on the other line. Damn, this is one hell of a night," Luann said. "Sit tight, I'll call you right back."

Royce was wondering where this fool had found a whiteboard in the middle of the night. One of the two security guards hired to patrol the hospital at night — Sergeant Casey as he identified himself — was drawing an outline of the hospital. Harold Fellows, the Director of Engineering and Security, was on his way in. He lived in Stanardsville, about 40 minutes north from the hospital. Sergeant Casey considered Fellows to be unqualified for the job of keeping the hospital secure. In his mind, Fellows was a maintenance man who treated security as collateral duty. Casey had a two-year security management degree going to waste. This was his big chance to make his case for a separate security department reporting directly to the CEO, whom Casey had never met before tonight.

The rent-a-cop had on a wide brim state trooper style hat, a big black belt with a radio, mace and handcuffs hanging down. *Thank God this guy did not have a gun,* thought Royce, *he'd probably be waving it around.*

"Once we were alerted that the patient was missing, my squad *(the other officer, Royce thought)* and I immediately secured the perimeter," Sergeant Casey said. "I personally took command of this operation." He put down the black felt marker and picked up the red marker. He made a little wavy line around the borders of the hospital campus he had drawn on the white board.

"What does that red line mean?" Royce asked, immediately regretting his question.

"That sir, is me securing the perimeter," Sergeant Casey answered, pleased that the CEO was taking an interest in his operation. Royce looked at Stella, who despite the calamity in their midst, was trying hard not to laugh.

"And while you were securing the perimeter, did you find Flip Jensen?" Royce said.

"Ahh, that's a negative sir, we did not," Sergeant Casey advised. "But we will." He picked up a green marker and began drawing arrows from the red line into the center of the white board. Stella began laughing out loud. Sergeant Casey did not seem the least bit concerned by her reaction, so focused was he on Royce Wexler.

"So our operative plan now is to redirect our security resources, such as they are," he said with just a tinge of reproach in his voice. He tapped the white board in the center with the plastic end of the marker. "Flip Jensen has wandered off somewhere into the bowels of this hospital, probably in a delusional and confused state."

Stella, who was probably laughing as much from the stress of the last few hours managed to ask her own question.

"Is that your professional medical opinion?" she managed to say. Virginia Stowe, seated next to her, stared at Sergeant Casey with a mixture of disbelief and horror. She glanced at Royce and realized he was bored. When Royce was bored, he looked to be amused.

"Royce, I think we need to call the police and get some help on this," Virginia said. Sergeant Casey was not about to let his big opportunity get hijacked.

"Well, I'm not a doctor," Sergeant Casey allowed to Stella, addressing her question as he hooked his thumbs into his security belt, "but I do know a thing or two about human nature. That boy wanted his mamma. You can tell by the way his subconscious twitched his body around in the bed when she would sit in there with him. I've seen this with my own eyes. You all don't come in at night, so I'm just sharing this with you for your own benefit." Royce was smiling broadly, something he did when he was getting annoyed.

"Sergeant Casey, don't you think you should get out there," he said pointing to the white board, "and redirect your resources?" The security officer leaned his elbow on the nursing station and crossed his legs at the ankles, not an easy move for a big man. There was still no sign of Harold Fellows.

"Mr. Wexler, I know this is probably not the best time to bring this up. Well, actually, maybe this is a really good time. This hospital needs its own security department with professional management. This incident would never have happened with better security." Sergeant Casey had the air of a fellow who was extremely pleased with himself.

"And how, exactly, would you have kept Flip Jensen from disappearing, Sergeant Casey?" Stella queried. Sergeant Casey smiled, feeling confident.

"Well, I noticed up in the nursery you put tracking beacons on the newborns, so that they can be found if anyone kidnaps them," he said. "I would do the same thing for every patient in the hospital. That way if a patient goes missing, we switch on the computer program and we go find them," he explained. "But there's a lot of other things we could be doing, too. For example, there are no security cameras in this ICU wing. So there's no way to keep an eye on things in real time or to even go back and rewind a recording to see what happened," he said. Royce thought about the capital requests that Harold Fellows had made for the past three years for money to do just what Sergeant Casey had proposed.

"You know, you're right," Royce said, waiting for it. Sergeant Casey pulled away from the desk, stood tall and looked serious. "This isn't the time to talk about it." Virginia almost felt sorry for the guy. The phone rang at the nursing station. The nurse who answered listened for a few moments.

"Mr. Wexler," she called over, "it's for you."

"Not now," he snapped. She listened some more and covered the mouthpiece.

"It's Flip Jensen's mother," she said urgently. Royce's foot slipped off the rail of the stool and he lunged forward. Stella noticed that Sergeant Casey smiled ever so slightly. Royce violently waved his arm.

"Tell her I'm not here," he snarled. He looked at Ginny and Stella.

"How does she know I'm here at 2 o'clock in the morning Ginny?" he demanded.

"The only secret that exists is the one you keep to yourself. And, Royce, I'm telling you, no one I know does that," Virginia said. "Someone always talks." She smiled, but it was a hard smile, even now when she was right.

The nurse relayed the message to Myrtle Jensen and then listened for an extended period, staring at Royce shaking her head. Now she pointed at him, doing a wave of her own, motioning him over. She covered the receiver again.

"Mr. Wexler, she said she knows you are here and if need be she can get in the car and drive over with Luann Zahn," the nurse informed him. Royce froze; Virginia strode to the desk and took the phone.

"Hello, Mrs. Jensen, it's Virginia Stowe. Mr. Wexler is tied up at the moment, but he can call you back shortly. Or if you'd like, he can meet you in his office in the morning, say about nine? It's very late and I know you would probably like go back to bed," she said, looking down at the floor. She slowly looked up, listening, her eyes focused inward.

"Yes, we are missing something," Virginia said. "We've been looking everywhere...yes, I know...of course, wait — we'll come to your house — right now if you'd like," she said, continuing to listen and then quietly placed the receiver back in the cradle. Royce cleared is throat.

"So, you think she suspects anything?" he asked her.

"Yes, Royce, I think she suspects something," Ginny said, her voice tight. "Myrtle's son is at home right now, sitting on her couch drinking a beer."

"Wait," Stella said. "I don't understand, I thought Flip was an only child. He has a brother?" Royce looked between Stella and Virginia, clearly bewildered.

"No, Stella," Virginia said. "Flip is at home. He walked home — from the hospital."

"That's impossible," Stella stated, not for the first time that evening.

"And it's clearly against medical advice," Royce added. At that moment the swinging doors of the ICU burst open with the scurrying form of Mark Swingle. He hurried up to the group.

"Royce, good news," he said. "Dr. DeLuca doesn't know anything about the whereabouts of Flip Jensen. The bad news is, now we have to find him."

Sargent Casey scratched his nose to hide the smile on his face.

———

"I don't remember shit," Flip said again. It seemed to Luann that he was telling the truth. His mother had persuaded him to stop drinking beer. Flip was now guzzling orange juice out of a gallon jug. He was a bit wild-eyed and his white blonde curls were matted and greasy from weeks of lying in the ICU bed. Flip shook his head sharply.

"Man, I feel jacked up," he complained.

"That doesn't bother your head when you do that, honey?" Myrtle asked, rubbing the back of his neck. She had been touching and patting her son since she first heard him on the front porch steps. Ever since he was a boy, Flip had a way of hitting the front porch boards so the nails made a squeaky announcement of his return home. Tonight, she had imagined that the sound was part of the ragged dreams she experienced in the brief sleep she had managed since Flip's accident. When she awoke and went to the front room, there he was, sitting on the couch — like a ghost. It gave her a start before she realized it really was Flip. Early Jensen sat in stunned silence on the other side of his son, shadows of joy and bewilderment playing out across his face.

Luann had the interview she needed with footage of Flip talking to his parents. Flip only had recollection of waking up in a panic, incredibly thirsty, pulling lines out of his arms and chest and fleeing down a back stairwell to exit the hospital. He was very talkative and friendly, not at all like the Flip to whom she was accustomed. She had interviewed Flip and his parents several times over the years. In the past 20 minutes, however, he had become increasingly twitchy.

"Maybe we ought to get you to a hospital," Luann suggested. "To University," she added. Flip stopped in mid-gulp slamming the jug to the table. A geyser of orange juice sloshed up the front of his hospital gown.

"Screw those doctors sideways, I'm done with hospitals," Flip growled.

"What I'm thinking is that we find you some new doctors and a different hospital to be pissed off at," she suggested. "You're acting like maybe you don't feel so well."

Early reached his arm around his son's shoulder. Early had mostly been silent.

"Son, I think that's a good idea. Let's get in the car and go to University Hospital. If you start feeling bad it could add another 20 minutes by the time an ambulance gets here."

Flip started to say something and then stared intently at his father. He was silent, his blonde eyebrow furrowed in concentration. Luann motioned to Dusty to start the camera up again; she sensed something good was coming.

"Damn, you should have seen his face," he finally said. Myrtle looked at her husband, then at Luann and Dusty. This sounded like nonsense.

"Whose face, honey?" she asked, rubbing his shoulders.

"The kid driving the ambulance," Flip said. "He wasn't expecting me. I misjudged the distance. He was driving faster than the ambulances usually go — I just remembered that."

"Why were you at the hospital?" Luann asked. Flip exhaled in contempt.

"Because when I ride my skateboard on hospital property it pisses off the tight-ass who runs the place," he admitted. "That guy doesn't like me. He musta figured I didn't notice that all the times I had to go to the hospital, him standing around like he had better things to do," he said looking at his parents. "Him not even talking to my mom and dad."

That was it! It had never occurred to Luann to ask who was driving the ambulance and Virginia Stowe certainly didn't feel obligated to tell her. It was the sin of omission. This explained why Virginia was still stalling the release of the security tape from the camera outside of the ER. Well, she knew now. Then she remembered the faked EKG Janet had given to her weeks ago that was stuffed in her desk somewhere...the EKG of the patient in the ambulance that hit Flip... driven by...a kid?

Luann smiled as she pulled her phone out, indicated she had to make a phone call and ducked into the kitchen.

"Janet, listen, just listen…" Luann whispered urgently into the phone. A few minutes later when she returned to the living room, Flip's mother was helping him on with his coat while his father pulled the car out of the garage. And now, Luann had things figured out.

———

A week later, the Martin sisters were cleaning the room of Naomi Purdue, a sweet lady from the Garden of Grace nursing home who was recovering from a nasty bladder infection. Naomi had been confused when she was admitted three days ago, but she was coming around. For the first two days she had thought her hospitalist, Dr. Massari, was the janitor and got agitated when he wouldn't empty the trashcan. She was slowly coming out of the infection-induced fog she had been in for over a week. She had apologized to Dr. Massari this morning when she figured out her mistake.

"He was real nice about it," Naomi told the sisters, who worked the room with their heads down, but their ears alert.

"He's a nice man," Ethyl said. "And a really good doctor. I'd want him to take care of me if I was in the hospital."

"Either of you girls ever been in the hospital?" Naomi asked.

"Just Mary when she got her tonsils out when she was ten," Ethyl answered. Mary nodded. The television was on, no sound. Dr. Denise DeLuca appeared on the screen.

"I like it better here than at the nursing home," Naomi said. "At least here the nurses come when you want something." She looked at the television.

"Is this the hospital where the baby boy got hit by the am-bew-lance?" Naomi asked. "I swear, I've been so confused the last week or so I can't hardly figure who is who. I tried to watch my show last night, but I couldn't figure what was going on and turned it off. Did I hear right — that boy got his self up and walked out of the hospital in the middle of the night?" Ethyl stopped sweeping and Mary peaked out from the bathroom door, her hands in rubber gloves.

"Naw, not this hospital. It's that big one over in Charlottes-ville — Ascend. And yeah, the boy did walk out in the middle of the night, went right home to his mother. That doctor right there," she said pointing at the television where Dr. DeLuca was talking, "gave him a shot of some new medicine that woke him up like Jesus at the resurrection. She also let her boyfriend's teenage son drive the am-bew-lance which caused the accident in the first place." Ethyl sat down on the edge of the bed, settling in. Mary shut the door to the room.

"But get this — it turns out she was getting beat up by her boy-friend — he made her put his son behind the wheel, something about getting credit to get into college," Ethyl said, incredulous.

"Can you imagine?" Mary added. "A lady doctor getting beat up by her boyfriend. I guess her book sense don't really help when it comes down to a man." Mary pointed her still gloved hand at the television screen. "Lookie, there he is." On the screen Ace Fury was getting out of his truck at a construction site, looking none too happy about a television camera being stuck in his face. "He's got mean eyes," Mary announced.

"Wait, wait — slow down," Naomi said. "I can't hardly keep this all straight." Ethyl and Mary both gave a little hoot.

"Honey, the suits can't hardly figure this one out. That lady doc-tor says she got cancer, which makes you feel sorry for her a little. But then she's also in trouble for faking another patient's medical record."

Mary chimed in.

"And she's checked herself into one of those homes for beat up women!"

"They called those shelters," Ethyl clarified.

"I used to get my cats at the shelter," Naomi said.

Luann Zahn came on screen.

"See that lady reporter?" Ethyl asked Naomi.

"Oh yes, I do recognize her," said Naomi. "I like her."

Ethyl smiled a bit.

"She's our friend. We helped her out a little on this am-bew-lance story — and that's all I'm saying about that. We took care of her when she was in this hospital — in fact, she was in this same room as you."

Naomi looked around the room and then at her bed. "Are you telling me I am sitting in the same bed that a celebrity slept in?"

"Yes ma'am," Ethyl said and patted Naomi's leg. "Kind of makes you think about what a small world it is, don't it?" Outside the roar of heavy equipment was a muted but constant background din through the heavily insulated window.

"What's all that racket outside?" Naomi asked. Ethyl rose off the bed and took a peak out of the window through the blinds. Clouds of dust roiled up where an earthmover was scraping the site level.

"That might be our jobs going up in dust," she murmured. Mary took the lead.

"Well, that same hospital where that boy walked away is building itself some operating rooms right across the street," she explained.

"What on earth for?" Naomi asked. "We got a perfectly good hospital here with operating rooms and doctors. We don't need those people from Charlottesville coming over to our town to take care of us."

"Amen, sister," said Ethyl. "But the state said it's OK, gave them permission to do it — they call it "certificate indeed". Said it would expand new services into the community. Sometimes it seems those bureaucrats ain't got the common sense God gave geese," she said.

Leo Miller walked in, making his daily rounds. Without missing a beat, Ethyl reached up to wipe down the blinds. Mary, in an equally smooth move, pulled the mop out of the wringer and stepped back into the bathroom.

"Good morning ladies," he said cheerfully.

"Who are you?" asked Naomi.

"I'm the administrator, Mrs. Purdue. I wanted to stop in to see how you're doing today and if everyone is being nice to you," Leo answered.

"Oh my, yes," she said. "Especially Ethyl and Mary here. We've just been having the nicest talk," she said, and then, because she had spent her years working in poultry plants, cafeterias and laundries under the watchful eye of a boss man, she added, "while they clean my room."

Leo smiled. "Well that's a nice compliment for the sisters here. I don't ever worry about whether Ethyl and Mary are working hard, they know what needs to be done." Mary smiled to herself in the bathroom. She liked this administrator.

"Why's that other hospital building across the street?" Naomi asked. "It don't hardly make no sense at all. Seems like they are just picking a fight," she said. "We don't need some big fancy pants hospital from Charlottesville coming over to our town taking our jobs and money. What was the Governor thinking, allowing such foolishness?"

"Well, Mrs. Purdue, you summed that up very nicely. I couldn't agree more. But it is what it is," he said.

"I'll tell all of my friends not to go to that place," Naomi said. "I've lived here in Valley View my entire life, so I know everybody," she offered. "Well, at least any friends and neighbors who are still alive. But I got eight grandchil'ren and three great grandchil'ren, so I'll make sure they know how evil that place is," she added, getting worked up.

"My husband Arnie worked at Mooch's Barbecue for almost 30 years. Then one of those chain barbecue places — what was it called..." She stopped for a moment trying to remember.

"World's Best Barbecue," Ethyl said. "They had terrible coleslaw — nothing but mayonnaise slop."

"Yes, that's the place," Naomi said, excited. She couldn't get anyone at the nursing home to have any kind of serious conversations with her. "They closed after six months. No one in the community would go there. They got some outsiders off the highway who didn't know any better — didn't know about Mooch's — but locals did not spend their money there. We'll do the same thing to that Charlottesville hospital when they open that place," she said, waving her hand at the window where a dust cloud was boiling up from the construction site.

"I certainly appreciate your support," Leo replied. Ethyl and Mary continued their work, but they were still listening. Leo knew what he said would be spread around the hospital within an hour, so he chose his words carefully.

"It's a little more complicated than that, though," Leo told Naomi. "Most patients, such as yourself, you go where your doctor sends you, right?"

Naomi nodded in agreement.

"Well, if your doctor owns a facility that treats you, you probably won't know that unless you ask. The hospital from Charlottesville that is building that building across the street will probably try to get doctors here in Valley View to be owners. After all, doctors who have their own practice are basically small business owners — and doctors are smart people. So if the surgeons, radiologists and other doctors own part of that building, they will want to take their patients there so they can collect the insurance payments — and the money from patients. They will need to pay for their investment," Leo explained.

"I'll tell my family doctor not to send me to those doctors," fumed Naomi.

"That might mean you have to drive to Charlottesville to get out-patient treatment," Leo told her. Mary could not contain herself.

"That's not right, Leo," she exclaimed, stepping out of the bath-room. She swished her mop around in the bucket in aggravation. It was the first time either of the sisters had ever called Leo by his first name.

"That's capitalism in healthcare, Mary. The reasoning is that com-petition improves care and lowers costs," Leo said.

"What nonsense," said Mary. "It's just people who already make a lot of money getting greedy. They don't think we can figure that out?"

Ethyl piped in. "Every patient they take from this hospital just makes it harder for this hospital to stay open." Leo smiled again.

"I think maybe you two ladies ought to be running the hospital and I should be cleaning the rooms," he observed.

"No thanks," Ethyl said as her sister shook her head in agreement. "We are fine right up here. And we need to mop that floor you're standing on. Why don't you go down to your office and figure out what we're going to do about that place those Charlottesville pirates are building?" she stated. Naomi whooped a little.

Dr. Denise DeLuca allowed herself a little shiver. At long last, she was the victim she had always imagined herself to be. She was awash in sympathy and empathy — twin goals that had long eluded her. National and cable news networks had all showed up to talk to her and now she was getting calls from national talk show hosts — Olivia and Beatrice Waters were leaving her messages! Mark Swingle, the patient rep who had loved her since middle school, had helped her come up with the plan once she had shared with him what she had done. Mark's passion for her had always made her suspicious, but after all these years she could still count on him. He was married to a Polish woman he met online. But he still pined away for Denise. She had always manipulated his affection, presenting herself as a tragic figure — which now, with his help, she was. It had been his idea to goad Ace into hitting her when she returned home early the morning after Flip Jensen walked away from the hospital.

Poor Ace. He was so predictable and now he was taking the blame. Ace was ducking in and out of cars with his hands over his face, totally bewildered at the sudden turn of events. She was going to miss him and his penchant for doling out the abuse she knew she richly deserved, but then again, she could probably get him back. There was plenty of time and a glorious future ahead to figure that out.

For months Dr. DeLuca had been reading with fascination about the emerging cases of comatose patients waking up after being injected with Ambien. It was absolutely counter intuitive that a drug intended to help people sleep would bring people out of a coma. It was her idea to add a bit of adrenalin to the dose. She smiled; *that sure had worked.* Flip Jensen had lit out of the hospital like a dog loose on a highway.

Her eye, where Ace had hit her after she provoked him, had blackened into a perfect hue of deep midnight blues and mottled purples just in time for her early morning interview with Luan Zahn. Denise had her talking points ready: she was a battered woman who had been abused and forced into allowing her boyfriend's son to drive an ambulance. Yes, she had switched out the EKG films — under further threats. She was so ashamed — a professional, intelligent woman like herself in an abusive relationship. She felt so guilty that she, on her own, took the chance of trying a new, unapproved protocol with her patient. But the gamble had paid off. Flip Jensen was up and walking around — a tribute to her skill, daring and compassion as a physician. She would say she was just a humble doctor trying to do the right thing for her patient.

And on top of all this adversity, she was dealing with lesions in her breasts that appeared suspicious — possibly breast cancer. These lesions had been present for a few years and had not changed in size, which meant they were most likely benign. But only Denise had the past x-rays, as she went into the system and deleted the electronic versions. She would not announce she was "cancer free" until she had worked through the state investigation into her medical license that was surely to be conducted. She had called Dr. Forrest just before her interview with Luann Zahn and asked him to be her primary care doctor. She was healthy and had never had any interest in asking another colleague about her own care. Dr. Forrest pointed out the obvious.

"Denise, I'm a cardiologist — you need an oncologist," he said patiently.

"I don't know any oncologists," she told him. "I can't trust myself right now, I'm too upset, Paul. I do trust you to find the right specialist for me," she said.

"Very well, Denise," he said, happy to reinforce her dependency upon him. "Send the films over and I'll get on the phone today. I have a medical school buddy in the oncology program at the medical college in Richmond," he assured her.

The interview had not gone at all as Luann thought it would. She had the inside scoop on Dr. DeLuca from Janet, who confirmed the sociopathic rumors that Luann had been hearing for years working in the Charlottesville television market. She now also knew of De-Luca's threat to out Janet as gay. But this was a really good story, the black eye standing out nicely against the crisp white lab coat that Dr. DeLuca wore, her stethoscope draped around her neck in tradition-al doctor style.

Luann was pretty sure she knew what was going on, but for now she decided to go with Dr. DeLuca's version of the story. Picking it apart would be work for another day. She had the added bonus of making an end run around Virginia Stowe, who was not informed of the interview. Luann would make sure Ascend Medical Center would regret the day they jerked her around. Dr. DeLuca was expecting an interview on the Great Charlottesville Crash, but she was about to launch what was known as an "ambush interview".

"Thank you for agreeing to speak with me this morning Dr. DeLuca," Luann said. She smiled — the calm before the ass-kicking. She had tried to put make-up on her battered eye, but Dr. DeLu-ca had declined.

"It's been quuuite a night. A little less than 10 hours ago your pa-tient Flip Jensen, who was hit by an ambulance heeere at the hospital a month ago, woooke up from a coma and essscaped from the hospi-tal to walk home to his parents' house," she said. Dr. DeLuca's calm expression did not change, and in fact, she began nodding her head in agreement half way through Luann's opening statement, to set the stage (outrage). Luann was not expecting this reaction.

"Actually Luann, as his personal *(attending)* physician I adminis-tered an unapproved *(illegal)* treatment to Flip — which worked much better than I had anticipated because he's up and walking around today, returned safely *(with memory problems)* to his family. I did this because I felt partly responsible for the accident which caused him to end up in the hospital," said Dr. DeLuca. Now it was time for Luann to look surprised, which she struggled to keep from showing.

"How are you responsible?" asked Luann, in a voice lacking any drama at all. Out of the corner of her eye she could see Dusty, stand-ing behind the tripod-mounted camera. He looked puzzled too. This was not the way they had envisioned the interview. In their discussion in the news van from the station to the hospital, they had agreed that it was very possible that Dr. DeLuca would walk out of the interview when she realized they were not talking about her role as the ambulance medical director, but rather the Flip Jensen accident.

"Well, I am a doctor — but even doctors are human —" she paused, choking up. She reached up and wiped tears from her eyes. Denise had learned as a child to cry on demand. She just thought how unfair the world was to her, which never failed to make her feel very emotional, and, as always, she was quickly buying into her own version of the story. "I've been in an abusive relationship and I'm afraid that brought about some very poor judgment on my part, something that I now very much regret."

She went on to explain how Ace's son had been forced to drive the ambulance by his father, her boyfriend — to get community service for his college applications. She carefully added that Randy did not want to drive the ambulance either. This had actually been her idea in her never-ending quest to get Ace's approval. But no one would believe Ace by the time she finished telling the story. After all, she was a doctor.

As she was being interviewed, Ace was being served with an eviction notice from Dr. DeLuca's home. Something Dr. DeLuca did not skimp on was good legal muscle. Randy was invited to stay, because it would look good if he did.

Luann had very mixed emotions. Dr. DeLuca had just spoiled a great story she had dogged and uncovered over several weeks. But on the other hand, she was getting an exclusive story that she quickly realized would have national and international exposure. This story could very well be her ticket to a bigger television market; more money, more prestige and access to bigger stories.

Dr. DeLuca could tell that Luann Zahn liked what she was hearing. She was taking her chances with the media, betting that her colleagues in medicine might spank her, probably even suspend her license for her use of an unapproved protocol. But the long-term image gain would be worth the beating and she would eventually get her license back. Dr. DeLuca had been interviewed by the country's most well known right wing radio host who, on the air, asked her to be his personal doctor.

"This country needs more doctors like you who will stand up to the federal government's bloated bureaucracy and regulations," he told her on the air. "I'm going to put my money where my mouth is and ask you, Dr. Denise DeLuca, if you will accept me as your patient," he boomed. The host was a notorious doctor shopper, hooked on narcotic pain medications. He had a good feeling about his prospects with Dr. DeLuca.

"Is there anything else you would like to add?" Luann asked.

"Just pray for me," Dr. DeLuca whispered.

CHAPTER
Under the Bus
THIRTEEN

Camilla Bonfield picked up Jim and Robert Wallace at their building downtown. They were on their way to a meeting with Royce Wexler. Camilla had picked sides and she was going with the Wallace family. Even if this decision was the wrong choice, she was betting that they would find something for her to do making the same salary. Her income was higher than her husband's, a police officer, and they needed the money.

Jim won the race to the car and got to sit in the front seat with Camilla. This meant that Robert would get to ride shotgun on the way back from the meeting. Camilla looked mighty fine today, more so than usual he thought. He liked women in tight, short clothes, but Camilla made long and tailored look better. Jim admired Camilla's profile and legs. For the hundredth time he wished he could see her naked just once before he died.

"Pull in here, I want to get some coffee," Robert barked from the backseat.

"Robert, we're already late," Camilla advised.

"Royce can wait," Robert growled. "I need some caffeine to sit through a meeting with him and that pack of corporate bandits."

Camilla pulled into the convenience store and followed Robert inside while Jim stayed in the car, eager for a view of her in full stride. Robert stepped up to the coffee machine. That pot was nearly empty, while the one next to it was dripping a fresh pot. In mid-reach, he guided his hand to the right for the brewing pot and poured himself what was the fresher pot of coffee. With the pot gone, coffee from the percolator dripped down on the burner making a loud, rhythmic sizzling heard throughout the store. He slurped the cup loudly, and exited, leaving Camilla to pay.

"I'm really sorry," Camilla said to the young woman behind the counter. "He made a mess on your burner. If you have something to wipe it down, I'll be glad to do that for you." The young woman looked surprised, but laughed.

"Oh, don't worry about it. He does that every morning," she replied. She had a dazzling smile, her white teeth against cocoa skin. Camilla tipped five dollars. As she reached the door, Owen Gregor, who was finishing his night shift at in the University Hospital parking garage, held the door open for her and smiled warmly.

"Good morning," he greeted her, smiling and looking her comfortably in the eyes. Men did not often smile at Camilla — or look her in the eye. They usually stared at her with a combination of insecurity and lust. She rewarded him with a smile of her own.

"Thank you," she said. Jim, watching from the car, wondered what he could do to get such genuine smile of appreciation from Camilla. It was truly something to see.

Owen got his coffee and chatted with Devine Brown, the clerk, for a few minutes. They had gone to high school together.

"That's a pretty lady, O-win," she said, her southern dialect bending his name in a shape he never tired of hearing. They both watched her get into her car with two older white men in suits. One of the men in the back seat threw a wad of coffee soaked napkins out the window.

"I'm gonna have to pick that up," she said calmly. "She pretty as Miss Felicia Monahan who you always going on about?" Owen smiled, relaxed.

"Felicia is plenty pretty — and, I'm learning, beautiful on the inside," Owen offered. It was Devine who had got him thinking about opening his father's garage again. On that mental cue she crossed her arms.

"So you think some about your daddy's garage, O-win," she said. "Say yes, and I'll buy you a cup of coffee."

"You're really sold on this idea, aren't you?" Owen asked. She looked at him, serious.

"I just been waiting for you to grow up, O-win. If you're really off them pain pills, yes."

"Well, I believe I am," Owen said. Devine smiled.

"Well, that's good. A little faith — and love — is a powerful thing." She reached under the counter to her bag and pulled out a paper. She had calculated the start up costs for opening the doors.

"There ain't no back taxes on your daddy's building — how come O-win?"

He pictured his mother, ever patient and hopeful that he would re-open the business. She had finally settled for just getting him out of her house.

"My father left a trust fund, enough to support my mother and keep up with the taxes," he said.

"Well, God bless daddy." She did some more figuring.

"I'll come to work with you, get all the black people to bring they cars in. We ain't got anybody we can trust since Mr. Johnson retired. If I'm working there, they know you won't be cheating. All you gotta do is be the mechanic," she said, not for the first time. "We be partners."

Owen was thinking about it. His visits with Devine lingered a bit longer every morning. He studied the figures on the sheet. He still knew some parts distributors who would float him credit.

"It'll take a few months for me to save up half this amount. You come up with the other half, and we'll do it," he decided. Devine stuck her hand out.

"Let's shake on it before you change your mind," she instructed. Now it was Owen's turn to smile; he was starting to get used to the idea that people might count on him. Devine made a few notes on her copy of the financials.

"I'll get my church to help clean the place up, slap some paint on. We can take it out in trade, servicing the church bus and the reverend's car," she said. She paused, staring at him intently.

"One thing, though, O-win. Your girlfriend can't work there, I'm telling you that right now. I can't compete with that," she insisted. "It'll only be trouble."

"No problem, partner," Owen said. "She has a good job — and the patients love her. But the same goes for your boyfriend." Devine scowled.

"I ain't got no time for a boyfriend. They more trouble than they worth," she stated with conviction.

"Yeah, well, when you're a successful business owner, you'll be a very eligible woman about town," Owen told her.

"I really like the sounds of that — an eligible woman," Devine said with a laugh.

Owen yawned.

"I gotta get some sleep, which I think I'll be doing much better now," Owen said. "Don't forget you owe me a cup of coffee, I'll be back to collect tomorrow," he added as he yanked the door open to leave.

"Make sure you throw that cup in the trash, I got my eye on you," she warned in mock concern. Owen made a show of slam dunking the coffee cup into the trash, saluted and climbed into his car.

The three of them were on the phone with corporate. Royce liked to amuse the Wallace cousins, who composed his Board executive committee, by making large mocking gestures in response to what they were hearing from the other end of the line. A financial analyst was going over the projections for the outpatient surgery center they were building in Valley View. Royce rolled his eyes, made a loose fist and rapidly flicked it at his wrist towards the speakerphone, the universal symbol for jerk-off. Robert especially enjoyed these displays and muffled a laugh; Jim smiled slightly and shook his head in tolerance for his cousin. Unlike the other two, he was listening.

"Say that again please," Jim instructed.

"The office will need a 70 percent pre-construction lease commitment before the final sign-off on the project," the analyst said. Royce leaned back in his chair, spreading his hands and frowning at Jim: you doubt me?

"Not a problem," Royce assured. "I'm working on that and will have a medical director signed from the Valley View medical staff in the next week. He'll buy a share and recruit others from the medical staff to do likewise," Royce announced, pushing off from his desk to give himself a spin in his chair. He then stood up and bowed at the speakerphone.

"You know you can't make the medical directorship contingent on him buying a share," said one of the corporate attorneys on the other end of the line. Royce extended his middle finger at the speakerphone.

"Understood," Royce answered. "I'll have the terms of the agreement to you soon. I'm going to need a faster turn around on the contract than the last one," Royce added, taking a dig at the attorney in front of the corporate CEO.

"I'll get it to you as soon as I can," the attorney said tersely. "We've got 14 other hospitals, you know Royce," she added.

"Perhaps you could hire more lawyers then," Royce said in mock concern. "When I am negotiating with a doctor, they don't want to wait a month to see a contract — that's all I'm saying." Royce bent over at the speakerphone. Robert laughed some more.

"OK, folks, that's enough," the corporate CEO barked. "Royce you'll get your contract. You just be sure your revenue projections are good — I'm losing patience with executive teams that blue sky their numbers. The earnings better be there."

Royce sat down, tired of performing.

"Understood boss. Don't worry; every case is going to be coming right out of Pleasant Valley Hospital. I predict that after a year — at the most — they will be ready to be purchased. All those referrals going to University will be coming our way in the next 24 months," he said again. He had been repeating this elevator speech for a year now and the financials the CFO had pieced together backed the claim.

"OK, let's move along to the last agenda item. Hank, I believe this is yours?" the CEO said. Over the speakerphone, the VP for Corporate Media Relations could be heard clearing his throat and shuffling paper. He spoke very slowly.

"I'm concerned about Dr. DeLuca and the ongoing attention she is generating. What is being done to get her off the front page?" he asked, a question with no real answer — his specialty.

"You'll have to talk to Ginny about that, Hank," Royce answered. He hated this guy. He was full of advice that had no practical application on site in the local market. "But I can tell you what steps the Credential Committee is taking, as well as the state of Virginia," Royce said, shaking his fist at the phone. "I mean, I'm not an expert like you Hank, but it seems to me as long as outside entities continue to dick around with Dr. DeLuca, she'll be in the news. It doesn't seem there's anything we can do about that — unless I'm missing something." Robert snickered; Royce was putting on a good show today.

The corporate CEO spoke again.

"OK, enough with the pissing match. Answer the question Royce," he said, annoyed.

"Well, the first thing you have to understand about Dr. DeLuca is that she always wants to be the center of attention and she'll act badly to get it. Look at what she's engineered, a regular Fellini film. And brothers, I am here to tell you, she is making a meal out of it. If our own credentials committee doesn't suspend her privileges — and I'm not so sure they will — the State will probably yank her license. She's already got a lawyer to rattle cages for her, so she'll fight it — especially if this creates more attention," Royce said.

"Right wing radio and television think she's a hero, taking matters into her own hands. You know, standing up to the FDA and federal government — cutting through the red tape to save a comatose patient," the VP chimed in again. Royce looked incredulous and scowled at the phone, hands spread apart.

"Hey, Hank, you mind if I finish the story?" Royce said. There was muffled laughing on the other end of the phone, but the VP persisted.

"Look Royce, this story is bigger than Ascend Medical Center and Charlottesville. We have 14 other hospitals that could get dragged into this mess if it's not handled right," the VP said very slowly and pointedly.

Royce was ready for that line of reasoning.

"Oh really? How many other hospitals does she have privileges at? The last time I checked, it was only my hospital," said Royce, letting that sink in. "I know it's a problem, you don't have to tell me every time we're on the phone. Ginny knows how to handle the press," he added, slapping his cheeks as a look of mock surprise swept his face to the further amusement of the Wallace boys. Hank was a power-hungry toad who tried to seize control of the local hospital public relations and marketing staff to strengthen his position at the corporate office.

"How can your own credentials committee not suspend her privileges? If they don't, you'll have to do it," the big boss instructed. Royce squirmed a bit.

"Boss, you know how a medical staff feels about a hospital CEO telling them what to do," Royce answered.

"Royce, Hank is right — she's poison. She was on the cover of *Popular* magazine last week. We can't risk market share in the other markets because some gonzo doctor with a personality disorder wants to do whatever she feels like. You suspend her privileges if you have to Royce. But don't tell your Chief of Staff yet; who knows, your credentials committee might still do the right thing," the CEO said. The call ended.

"Can you believe we pay those guys a million and a half dollars a year in corporate overhead? I don't know what they do all day," Royce said. He began scrolling through the emails on his desktop.

"I thought Camilla was coming to this meeting?" Royce said.

"We decided she didn't need to be here after all," Jim said. "She's just the driver today." He changed the subject.

"So who are you meeting from Valley View about the project?" Jim asked. Royce answered without looking from his screen.

"Dr. Neil Divinity," Royce said, starting to type. "He's the guy we've been looking for. A radiologist — hates Leo Miller, the new administrator — and he's scary smart. He'll be here tomorrow — perhaps you two can stop by, talk him up, make him feel important."

Robert laughed. "You really stuck it to them today, Royce." He stood and stretched his neck. He walked to the office door, flexing his arms and rolling his shoulders, and then stopped and locked it. He retraced his steps, reached down and grabbed his chair, which he heaved over the desk, hitting Royce with a glancing blow to the face. Royce fell to the floor, his glasses askew, blood beginning to seep from a split above the brow of his left eye. The chair rattled into his monitor and swept it to the floor in a cascade of splintering glass and plastic. Royce sat stunned on the floor, his hand cupped to his gashed forehead. Robert settled on the edge of the desk, looking down at Royce. Jim had not moved.

"You know, Royce, a lot of people look at Jim and me and they just see a couple of fat white guys in nice suits," Robert said calmly. Royce started to get up. Robert picked up a large brass nameplate inscribed with "Royce Wexler, MBA, FACHE" in two inch letters; it was heavy. He looked it over like it was fine piece of art.

"Naw, you stay there on the floor, Royce. Jim and I need to talk to you about a serious matter now and if I don't like what I hear, I'm gonna throw this at you too," he said — and then he smiled, a big genuine, satisfied grin, like a man who had been wanting to throw a chair for a long time.

"Anyway, as I was saying, people look at us and figure we got where we are because of our family money and expensive higher education. And all that is mighty fine, Royce, I'm here to tell you. But what gets you what you want in this life is being willing to put a hurt on someone. You know what I'm saying, Royce?"

"Yeah, believe me, I follow you," Royce managed to say. Blood was dripping from the bottom of his balled up fist and onto his pant leg; he felt faint. Royce was not really surprised. He had made a career associating with people who eventually turned on him, although this was the first time he had been bloodied.

It was Jim's turn to speak.

"Now Royce, do you have any idea why we're having this meeting?" he asked. The only sound was of Robert tapping the brass nameplate in his hand.

Royce knew.

"I was going to tell you about the new will Dr. Forrest managed to arrange with your aunt as soon as we had the Dr. DeLuca problem under control," Royce said. "I need Dr. Forrest for that first. You heard what my boss said."

"Our dear old aunt is nearly 90 years old, Royce. That's a pretty big decision for you to be making on your own," Robert growled. "I'm having a hard time with that story — you've known about this for at least a month." He raised the brass nameplate high. He really wanted to bash Royce again.

"Put it down, Robert," Jim said. "Royce may still be able to help. You do want to help, right Royce?" Royce ran the pecking order through his head, something he did often during the day. Right now the Wallace cousins were the apex predators.

"Of course," Royce answered.

"Good, good," Jim said, standing up, buttoning his suit jacket. "The first thing you need to remember is that we're your bosses — not those fellows at corporate."

He stepped over the wrecked computer monitor to look at his reflection in the window. He straightened his tie.

"We'll be delivering Dr. Forrest to you for a disciplinary and privileging decision that even you can't fuck up, Royce. Camilla will take care of Aunt Missy."

"Camilla ought to be running this place," Robert said, flipping Royce's nameplate on the desk with a clatter as he followed his cousin. He turned a final time to Royce.

"That's going to need stitches, and I hope it hurts like a dog passing a razor blade."

Jim offered a final observation.

"You know Royce, all those telephone conference calls we've had over the years, it makes me wonder if you were performing your little monkey show while I was talking to you on speaker. It really does. Do try to get back into our good graces — you might even get to keep this job. Lucky you, huh?"

Marvin Wallace had spent two hours coaching the woman about what she needed to do per Mr. Jim's instructions. He didn't like this assignment — even with the large up front money and more money if she stayed quiet. It was risky. But as always, Mr. Jim had a nice twist laid out, a plan that would have the Charlottesville police thinking they had stumbled onto a big time plot. Marvin comforted himself, knowing he was the last of the black Wallaces to work for the white Wallaces. It had taken some covert maneuvering of his own, but his kids and his nieces and nephews were all in college or graduated, out in the world — clear. Mr. Jim had two sons who were unambitious, stupid and on the way to amounting to nothing. Mr. Robert had no children — at least none he recognized. A 100-year-old tradition was getting ready to end and it couldn't come fast enough for Marvin. He was tired of these fools.

But they were dangerous fools; this he had seen with his own eyes.

Today the marquee in front of the Unitarian church read like a fortune cookie: "Luck always favors the prepared mind." Marianne Quarters, the CFO at Valley View Hospital, had started noticing the church postings when she had heard Leo Miller babbling on about it one day to Jayne Smith, their administrative assistant. Of all the things she didn't like about Leo Miller, his enthusiasm was at the top of her list. She had good company — Dr. Divinity. Stealing the files out of Leo's office and turning them over to Dr. Divinity had forged a useful alliance.

Quarters was doing her part too. For the past few months she had been hiding money. This was an old CFO trick, more infamously used to save money in a good month for a bad month. Both were strategies used by senior executives so they could take credit for meeting earnings, which meant bigger bonuses. By performing the inverse accounting and making the bottom line look worse, it would force the CEO to focus every day on finances, rather than the market growth and cultural changes that he had pledged to the Board of Directors. Dealing with a failing hospital bottom line was an all-consuming task that upset employees and medical staff since rapid cost control was necessary. It was the exact kind of turmoil that got a new CEO terminated.

The Director of Engineering was a problem. He had continued to pester her about the evidence he felt he had implicating her in the break-in. Quarters had declined to view the security camera recording he constantly spoke about. She dismissed his overtures with scorn and sternness, but he did not seem dissuaded. Quarters had approved the truck he had been trying to buy for his department, but still he persisted. Recently his talk had been suggestive and spiced with double meaning. She had heard the rumors about him, which was surprising. Quarters was not very well connected in the hospital, even though she had been CFO for several years. She kept to herself and rarely went up on the floors to visit the staff.

Ironically, she could only meet with Dr. Divinity in the basement, near the Engineering Department. Dr. Divinity explained that only this section of the hospital did not have security camera coverage — and she should not approve any capital requests to alter that fact. He did not mentioned that he had taken the liberty of adding a few covert cameras to complete the coverage, cameras which automatically switched off just before he passed within the range of view. This was possible with a sensor he had attached to the back of his hospital ID badge — which he now gladly wore without reminder from the hospital's rent-a-cops who guarded access to the facility at night.

The secret footage was sent wirelessly to a recording unit hidden in his locker. Dr. Divinity had to review the tapes within 48 hours to keep the old footage from being recorded over, but he found the process surprisingly relaxing. For a man who did not sleep more the four hours a night, anything that calmed his mind was useful.

The CFO was also useful, he had decided. She had sought him out a few months ago to hand over the file Leo Miller had so smugly used to intimidate him.

"So why are you helping me?" he had asked, the obvious question. She had smiled, which looked as spooky on her as on him.

"I have a proposition," she answered. It was Quarters who had recruited him for Royce Wexler and Ascend Hospital Incorporated. With a long time member of the medical staff at Valley View investing in Ascend Medical's building, as well as serving as the medical director, other specialists would follow. For Quarters, it was her ticket to a new position at the bigger hospital in Charlottesville. It seemed the CFO now at Ascend was sideways politically; Wexler was on the hunt for a replacement and offered the position to her — if she could deliver the sale of ownership shares among Valley View Medical staff to the new Ascend Medical Outpatient Center to be built across from her office.

But all of this was in jeopardy. The circumstantial evidence of the recording in possession of the lecherous Director of Engineering was enough to taint her prospects at Ascend — or any place else, for that matter. But it seemed to her that her relationship with Dr. Divinity was also the solution to her problem. He obviously had leverage, because how else would he have set up what appeared to be a command center in the department? She had to be vague with Dr. Divinity about her motivation for stealing files and setting up the pending meeting with Royce Wexler. It was enough for him that he despised Leo Miller as much as she did.

She could generally figure out when he would be in his lair in the video security room by looking at the OR schedule. She worked to time these visits in order to minimize the risk of running into the Director of Engineering, who always took his lunch promptly at noon. He sat with a group of housekeepers and kitchen employees — always female — on the look out for another submissive conquest. When possible, she waited until Leo Miller was on the phone or out of his office before leaving for lunch. She did not care to bid him good-bye or for him to know what time she left.

When she opened the door with her master key, Dr. Divinity was at his desk, eating what looked like cooked grain from a plastic dish.

"You should knock," he said without looking up. They both sat silently for a minute, neither uncomfortable.

"When is your meeting with Wexler?" she asked.

"Tomorrow. They changed the location. We're meeting with a couple of people from his Board in their office," he said.

"That would be the Wallace cousins — Jim and Robert. They seem to be running that hospital," she offered. "Be sure to ask for top dollar, they can't get the building leased without you."

"And what's top dollar?" he said, still not looking up.

"Ask for 12 thousand a month, you should be able to get 10 thousand," she said.

They went quiet again. Dr. Divinity was scanning through the hospital's camera footage, without much purpose, it seemed to Quarters. She was not much of a conversationalist, but compared to Dr. Divinity, she was down right chatty.

"I need your opinion," she finally said. He did not respond, so she proceeded.

"You seem to know your way around the camera system. I need to find the recording of the night the CEO's office was broken into." The half smile always on his lips widened just a bit. He tapped the keyboard a few times and the scene changed.

"You mean this recording?" he said. On the screen she saw herself approach the door concealed in a sweatshirt, but the telltale turn of her wrist evident. He made a few more keystrokes and read a few lines of code. "Looks like there has been one copy burned from the master. Now who do you suppose would have done that?"

The silence returned. Finally, he spoke again.

"He told the CEO that the camera wasn't working that night — cut cable," Dr. Divinity pointed out. "He can't share that recording without implicating himself," he speculated further.

"I can't take that chance," she said, perhaps too eagerly. He turned back towards the monitor and snapped the power button. On screen, she disappeared into a little white dot as he turned the monitor off.

"I'll tell you what," he said with more cheer than she had ever observed in the man. "Let's see how my meeting goes tomorrow. If it goes like you say it will, I'm sure things will work out you. It'll be our secret." His eyes slid sideways to hers. Then that smile again. It sent a shiver through her.

Up on the main floor, Jesús Vargas sat in the Valley View Hospital cafeteria. He was waiting for his niece Jayne Vargas-Smith to join him for lunch. Jayne was the oldest and favorite of his many nieces and nephews and their time together was always the highlight of his week. For many years he felt only guilt when he saw her, the scar on her face a reminder of the horrible accident so many years ago that might have killed her at his hand. But she was compassionate and forgiving. In fact, she begged him to forgive himself — she even learned sign language to urge him to just be her uncle, not the one who blamed himself for unintentionally hurting her. Now, days would go by and he would not think of the accident. With her love and support, he had stopped drinking. But still, every time he saw her he remembered just a little bit.

Jayne came through the door talking to a few of her co-workers. As always, when she spotted him waiting she lit up with a smile so lovely it turned heads.

"Hello Uncle," she greeted him, leading with a kiss to his forehead. When she spoke, it was like a gentle tide ebbing.

"Hola, carina," he answered in return, squeezing her hand. She settled down and reached for the salad he had bought her. He unwrapped the tuna sandwich.

Although Jesús was deaf, he got by with help from others on his work crew and, at times, by pretending he didn't understand English. Jesús was a good, fast carpenter, from framing to finish work, and a whiz with blueprints. He had a good reputation among the contractors in the area.

They caught up on their week and the Spanish soap opera, "By Appointment Only", they both watched every day. Jayne more listened to the program to kept her Spanish fresh, but Jesús believed these people lived just over in the next town. The rest of the family thought the program was silly and he certainly didn't talk about it on the job. But their discussions over the years about the plot and characters were an important device in forging a bond with Jayne. While he was glad for an absence of that kind of drama in his life, he often thought about what he would do if he were one of the characters in the program.

"Your boss seems like a nice guy," Jesús said. Leo was sitting at a nearby table with some of the admissions staff and a few nurses. Jayne followed his gaze and smiled.

"He is, Uncle. There are some people around here who see that as a weakness, which makes me sad," she said. "So do you know where your next job is yet?" Suddenly Jesús seemed apprehensive.

"Yes…across the street — at the new medical building. I thought about not taking the job, but there is nothing else being offered right now and probably not for some time," he explained, feeling guilty. Jayne continued to eat slowly and thoughtfully, looking at her salad and then back up at him.

"It's OK — you have to work. That building will get built just the same even if someone else is getting the paycheck," she assured him.

"Thank you, carina. I know that building is bad for the hospital. Perhaps people will not go there," he speculated, "if they knew that too."

Jayne sighed.

"People will go where their doctors send them, Uncle. From what I have heard, some of the doctors here will become owners in the building. Doctors are just like anyone else — they watch out for their own wallets first," she explained. After a few bites, Jesús saw Leo rise from his table. He spotted Jayne and walked over to their table. Jesús watched his lips closely.

"Hello, Jayne — is this your uncle I hear so many good things about?" he asked. Jesús brushed his hands off and stood.

"Jesús Vargas," he said. He bowed his head as Leo was using both hands to hold his tray. Leo nodded back.

"Jayne tells me you're an excellent carpenter," Leo offered.

"Yes — and I do a little plumbing — just enough to be dangerous, Mr. Miller," Jesús joked.

"Please call me Leo. It was nice to meet you, Jesús, your niece does really good work at the hospital helping to take care of patients." This was something Leo made sure to tell all family members of his employees.

After Leo left, Jesús noticed he continued to greet employees and visitors.

"He seems to like his job," Jesús said.

"I've never worked for a good boss before," she said, sounding forlorn. She realized he was staring at her, concerned.

"There's just some politics going on. This project is stressing everyone out," she added. Jesús nodded, watching her while he chewed. He swallowed, wiping his mouth with a napkin.

"Well, that Charlottesville hospital is certainly in a big hurry — we've already been told overtime will be approved every day and on Saturdays," Jesús told her. "I'll be working on both the framing and plumbing crews."

Jayne smiled again. "Well, at least you'll be just across the street. We can eat lunch together more often," she said. Jesús felt loved, once again marveling that a person so sweet of nature could be related to him. He wished he could do something to make her worries go away.

———

Kenny sat waiting for Luann at the bar in Arnie's. He was going to miss her when she was gone. Her good work on the Charlottesville crash and the Flip Jensen story was attracting a lot interest from television news departments in larger markets. He had called her earlier and told her he had a present for her. It was actually a present for himself, as it would keep her in town a little longer. Kenny knew a lot of people, but he didn't have a lot of friends.

When presented to his mother at birth, she had named him Ken because, she asserted, he was as handsome as a Ken doll. Her prophecy turned out to be true — he was an exceedingly good-looking man, just without arms. Kenny had a set of prosthetic arms of the wire, pulley and hook type that he used at work to bang away at a keyboard, but they were useless for drinking beer. The fake arms also scared the women away, who were drawn to him through maternal instinct and delivered to his bed through his charm and a good "word-of-mouth" reputation, as it were. He could also kick box with devastating efficiency, which he'd had to do a few times to prove a point with the local yahoos. But they were all buddies now, on "equal footing", as Kenny liked to say. He and the yahoos were one big huddle, competing for the college ladies who migrated to Arnie's like swallows to a watering hole.

Luann, as usual, arrived first before Dr. Girlfriend, as Kenny had dubbed Janet Ippolito. Luann entered a room like a plane full of passengers de-boarding in an airport terminal; a low rumble followed by an explosion of movement and purpose. She spotted Kenny at the bar and took the stool next to him. Kenny preferred the bar as he could — with a practiced and graceful maneuver — slide his glass to the edge of the bar, raise it with his knee and guide it to his mouth with the grace of a Japanese kabuki dancer

"Hi, handsome. No lovelies tonight?" she greeted. He put his beer down and served up his best Kenny smile.

"You're the first one," he said, giving her an up and down.

"If I were straight I'd do you right here," she said.

"Even a lesbian goes straight once she's been in my arms," Kenny countered. Arnie himself, back from two months in Florida, set a Mojito down in front of her.

"I wish you were straight so I didn't have to listen to this routine one more time," Arnie lamented. He leaned on his hands, speaking to Luann.

"So that DeLuca is a real piece of work," he observed. "She seems real pleased with herself, if you ask me."

"As always Arnie, you have great insight," Luann said between a few sips of her drink. "The woman has no shame. She would adopt a baby from China if she thought it would get her public approval."

"Has anyone ever bothered to find out if she's a good doctor?" Kenny asked.

"I followed this story on CNN at my condo in Ft. Meyer," Arnie said. "According to the Chief of Staff at her hospital — that Forrest guy — she's the best." Kenny reached down and hooked the strap on his office bag on his foot, hauling it up to the bar. He shook out a sizable envelope that he dropped in front of Luann.

"Take a look at that. We're doing a project for a national client using what's called MedPar data from the Federal government. Feds started issuing this data about eight years ago, but not too many hospitals — or anyone else for that matter — have paid much attention to it. It's collected directly from all Medicare admission patient records and let me tell you, it speaks the truth. Since we had the data set already, I spent a couple of lunch hours slicing and dicing the data for the Charlottesville area hospitals," Kenny explained.

He hoisted his beer a few times while Luann reviewed the executive summary. Arnie reached down under the bar, turned the volume up on the stereo and shut off the speakers at the end of the bar where they were gathered. He had configured the sound system so that conversations just such as this could be held privately, without anyone overhearing. Luann's eyes widened.

"Am I reading this right?" she asked, flipping to the next page.

"Reading what right?" Dr. Ippolito stepped up behind them, draping her arms around Luann and Kenny. As usual, she was dressed in hospital scrubs.

"Some info Kenny scammed on local hospitals. Ascend doesn't look too good," Luann told her. Janet pushed in closer to read over Luann's shoulder.

"It's a study of inpatient stays for Medicare — which is the largest patient population in most hospitals. I ran several fields — charges, outcomes, and why the patients were in the hospital," Kenny said, eyeing a curvy young thing who had just walked in. Janet reached down, running her finger down a column.

"We have the highest charges and the worst outcomes?" she said incredulously.

"What's outcome mean?" Arnie asked. Janet slipped onto the bar stool with Luann, who slid over to let her read the report. She flipped to the next page.

"The number of days the average patient stays in and if they live to get discharged. The joke is that the best outcome is if you come out," Janet murmured. "Damn — the patients who do the worst are the pulmonary patients — that's mostly ICU patients," she added.

"Dr. DeLuca it would seem," Kenny said, working his best smile across the room to the young woman, who glanced up several times and laughed nervously with the other women at her table.

"That's a good assumption, but not conclusive," Dr. Ippolito said.

"Look on page 12," Kenny said absent-mindedly. "We bought the entire database set back to the first year. In the first two years patients were identified by doctor. The state medical society raised hell and got the law changed so the data could not be sorted by the doctor," he said. "But I figured out how to unlock that field. You'll see data for every pulmonologist in the service area. Look at her outcomes — she's a fucking menace."

"How did you figure this out?" Luann asked, listening.

"My good looks are not the only devastating personal quality I possess ladies — I'm also very clever," he said as he got to his feet and headed towards Miss Curvy's table. "I'll be back in a minute, don't lose that data set." They had learned long ago that Kenny was seldom "back in a minute" once he had made his selection. "The three of you can figure out the rest," he said kissing Luann on the cheek.

Indeed they could. The data told a story that no amount of bluster or excuses could explain away. Arnie was appalled.

"Improving these scores is the job of whoever is in charge," he sputtered, reading the data with growing agitation.

"But how?" Dr. Ippolito asked. Arnie held his hand up and rubbed his thumb and forefinger together.

"You make part of their income dependent upon it," Arnie said. "I do it here in the bar. The shift manager measures all the bottles and the kegs after each shift and reconciles it with the receipts. If the alcohol usage falls within certain parameters, the bartender gets a bonus. It's the best way I have found to keep the employees from giving away free drinks to get a bigger tip — they make more money and for me and it's cheaper in the long run. You pay for the performance you want to achieve," he growled in typical Arnie fashion. "If I can figure out how to run a bar more efficiently using data, a hospital sure as hell ought to be able to do it."

Janet was stunned. She did the math in her head, calculating how many patients she was sending to their deaths at the hands of Dr. DeLuca. DeLuca's mortality rate was almost twice that of any other pulmonology specialist — even those who served the ICU at University Medical Center, which cared for sicker patients. With about a third of her admitted patients going directly to the ICU, it worked out to about one patient a month being mismanaged to death by DeLuca. She could see some of their faces, patients she had stabilized in the emergency room before being sent to the ICU. Luann watched her, growing concerned. She stood and slipped her arm around the doctor's waist, who was leaning on the counter, her finger boring in on the data line for Dr. DeLuca.

"It's not your fault, Janet," Luann said quietly. Janet stood up and fingered the stethoscope she realized was still around her neck from her shift in the ER. She looked to be all business

"I know — thanks," Dr. Ippolito said. "I'm just thinking about the excuses she is going to give when she see these numbers."

"Such as?" Luann asked, pulling a reporter's notebook from her bag. Dr. Ippolito held up her fingers on her left hand.

"One — The data is flawed — not true, it comes right from the ICD9 admission form," she said flicking her forefinger down.

"Two — Our patients are sicker — not true," she said looking down at the spreadsheet. "Ascend has the third lowest patient intensity level ratio — a measure of how ill the patients are on admission — in the city." Her ring finger went down, three to go. Luann scribbled away.

"Three — We take care of more indigent patients, who have more chronic medical conditions," she said as a third finger ticked under. With her other hand, she skimmed across another column of data. "Look at the payer mix — we have the highest commercial mix in the city — so — I don't think so." Her pinkie and thumb were left. She thought for a minute, smiled.

"Four — Dr. DeLuca will say she was trained to have independent medical judgment to do what she thinks is best for the patient. Then she'll talk excessively about her miracle patient Flip Jensen," she said, looking at Luann. "That's going to be your toughest talking point because she got lucky on that count."

Her pinkie disappeared, leaving the thumb extended. Janet stood with her thumb extended, searching for a final justification that Dr. DeLuca would cite.

"Think, Janet — we are talking about Dr. DeLuca," Luann hinted, "You know what she does when she's cornered."

"Ah — I've got it," Dr. Ippolito exalted. "It's the hospital's fault for the high turnover rate in the ICU — which, because she runs the place, is unfortunately true."

"That statement makes the hospital look bad," Arnie observed. Luann and Janet both scoffed in unison. "We're talking about a world class sociopath here," Luann said. "That thought will not enter her consciousness. She will have no problem throwing the hospital under the bus." Luann read back through the notes. Arnie started laughing out loud, pounding the bar.

"Under the bus, Zahn — that's a good one. Buses have been good copy for you lately. You'll figure out something," he laughed, moving to the other end of the bar to take an order.

"You're hilarious Arnie," Luann called after him, but laughing. She snuggled up to her girlfriend. "This story just keeps getting better and better, thank you doctor."

CHAPTER

Outcomes

FOURTEEN

Dr. Divinity was not the sort to make a mistake — at least outside the realm of social skills. He had a keen mind for the workings of technology and mechanics, as well as spatial mischief in general. His rapid mastery of the hospital security system had required little of his 140 IQ capacity. So when the heat activated car bomb he attached to the exhaust system under the Engineering Director's truck had smoked and hissed like a second rate firework — instead of blowing him straight up as calculated — it was not without a sense of disappointment in himself. He had carefully researched the makings of such a device and added a few modifications of his own. He should have done better. It was rare for him to feel obligated, but he had made a deal with the CFO, and he might need her again.

The meeting with Royce Wexler had gone exactly as the CFO predicted. The two Wallace cousins were there, mostly silent as Royce did all the talking. Wexler seemed a nervous fellow, constantly glancing over at the Wallaces, who sat on a couch across from Dr. Divinity. He did not ask Wexler about the line of stitches along the left side of his face. When he stated his demand for $12,000 a month, the immediate counter was $10,000, just as the CFO had predicted.

Royce handed him two contracts written by Robert Wallace rather than wait on corporate. This would mightily piss off the corporate CEO. But that was a problem for another day. Wexler was more afraid of the Wallace boys than his CEO. Besides, the Wallace cousins had decided to invest in the outpatient center project and they were not going to let some corporate lawyer handle the legalities.

One of the contracts was for the purchase of an ownership share in the outpatient building. It would be signed within 10 days with the investment — $400,000 — due over the first two years of the operation. The bylaws in the contract stated that the newly formed Board of the said outpatient center would select the Medical Director from among the physician shareholders. Jim Wallace was designated as the acting chairman until owner elections could be held. The second contract was for the Medical Directorship, which would be signed 24 hours after the first contract.

"How do I know you won't withdraw the Medical Director contract after I buy in?" Dr. Divinity asked Wexler. Wexler started to speak, but Robert Wallace cut him off with his slow drawl.

"Well, aside from the fact that I don't think I want you for an enemy," he said, pausing to wait for Dr. Divinity's acknowledgement of this little joke. But there was no reaction from Dr. Divinity. Robert Wallace continued.

"You'll find in section 12.8 that you have 72 hours after signing the ownership contract to cancel the agreement." Dr. Divinity flipped to that page and scanned the language. He said nothing.

"Both of those contracts state that the building has to be 70 percent sold within two months before the contracts go into effect. We're counting on you to help us with that. You sure you have the connections to pull that off? You don't seem like a social kind of guy," said Robert.

Dr. Divinity slightly increased the stretch in his lips — his version of a smile. To his colleagues, he was an excellent radiologist, who often espoused his work goals, which were to maximize his income and his time off. If Dr. Divinity said taking outpatient business away from the hospital was a sure thing, they would believe him. He already had three physicians lined up to buy into the project; others would follow. As doctors, they felt entitled to take their share of the hospital's cash flow.

"Yes, I do," Dr. Divinity, said. "So exactly how are you cousins related to the project?"

"We own one share between us," Robert answered. "We're obviously not doctors, so think of us as silent partners."

"Really?" Dr. Divinity mused. "Are silent partners ever really silent?"

Royce watched Robert flush red where his neck rose out of his starched shirt and boldly colored tie. Dr. Divinity's smile transformed — every so slightly — into a smirk.

"I understand that you will no doubt want your attorney to review the contracts," Royce offered.

"Not necessary. I don't need a lawyer — it's not that hard to understand the law," he said as he stood and stuffed the contracts into his shoulder bag. "I'm leaving now."

After he left, Robert Wallace, who could still hardly contain himself from further assault on Royce Wexler, snarled. "You picked him to be your medical director? Good luck with that guy."

Royce looked like a man ready to start throwing chairs himself.

"Gents, what all hospital-based doctors want in their heart of hearts is a nice fat contract from a hospital — they all think hospitals have plenty of money to give doctors. Even the weirdos like that guy want their money. If he gives me any trouble, I'll dock his pay for non-performance — his duties are laid out in a vague sort of way and are open to interpretation."

"At $10,000 a month, what's his hourly rate?" Jim asked.

"I have no idea," said Wexler. "But what I do know is that we're going to take about a $250,000 a month right off Valley View's bottom line once we are up and rolling. There will be plenty of money to go around. And remember, the pay-off for us is when we buy Valley View. The referrals they are sending over to University will be worth millions more a month. Whatever we pay Divinity will be chump change. Hell, we'll probably upgrade to a Level 1 Trauma Center, so the next time Flip Jensen gets run over we'll figure out how to keep him in the damn bed."

Robert laughed — he couldn't help himself, that was funny. "Well, all you have to do is be right, Royce," Robert finally conceded. At last, the CEO seemed to be getting some backbone.

The Director of Engineering could think of several people who would want to blow him up. He had a knack for convincing unhappy, married women to join him for the most extreme and improper of sex acts, which he recorded in the industrial spaces of the Valley View Hospital. Some even did it for free, no payment requested or expected. Even though he made sure that all of his women wore leather head covers — in addition to other leather and chain accessories it was entirely possible a husband had stumbled upon his spouse's infidelity.

He was ready for this day. His adult bondage and domination site on the new and emerging website — by paid subscription only and established under a false identity — was starting to turn a profit. The month before, without informing his wife, he had established an equity line of credit on his home in the amount of $75,000, which he immediately withdrew. It was time to pack up his truck and disappear to the golden land of California, where producing dirty movies was legal.

The Director of Engineering had a sense his near death experience was a stroke of good luck. He did not stop by the hospital. He put his resignation and the paperwork to cash out his retirement and vacation in the mail. He did not report the matter to the police. Instead, he simply drove away.

Dr. DeLuca was not going to let the technicality of being suspended — albeit with full pay — as Medical Director and rising Chief of Staff, keep her out of the ICU. She was ensconced as usual at the unit desk, riding herd over patients, families (most of whom recognized her) and nurses. She was a celebrity now. Those questioning her actions and her decisions — her destiny — were now the bad guys.

Virginia Stowe knew right where to find her — everyone in the hospital did. The ICU was DeLuca's bully pulpit, her control center. Virginia clicked her way through the swinging doors, a sheave of papers fluttering in her clenched hand like a trapped rabbit trying to kick loose. Notoriety seem to agree with Dr. DeLuca; she had cut, lightened and styled her hair and was noticeably thinner. She had new make-up too. Virginia had to admit, she looked good.

"Ginny!" Dr. DeLuca greeted her effusively. "I don't think I've seen you since the story broke," she said. Virginia started to speak, but DeLuca grabbed both of her hands, knocking the MedPar data to the floor, and pulled her onto the stool next to her. She kept talking in a conspiratorial voice, but made sure she was loud enough to be overheard. She seemed to have lost her whisper.

"Do you know that talk show host Olivia is as nice as she seems?" Denise gushed. "She said I was an inspiration to millions of women. I mean, I always thought that, but it's really something to hear Olivia say it — she knows, right?" Virginia was losing her train of thought — this new made-over Dr. DeLuca was so much less...loathsome. The doctor prattled on as Margret Stephenson, the Unit Manager, walked over and rescued Virginia's data sheets from the floor. She shuffled them into a neat stack and handed the pile to Virginia.

"She wants me back on the show for an update on my breast cancer," Dr. DeLuca continued, breathlessly.

"How are you doing?" asked Virginia. The word around the hospital was that she was not in chemo or radiation therapy, nor was she missing office hours to go to her doctor at the Medical College hospital in Richmond. In fact, her private practice patients were lined up deeper than a congregation at a potluck. The consensus seemed to be that anyone this famous must be a good doctor. Now it was Virginia's unfortunate job to dispel that premise.

Luann Zahn was on the story. She had provided Virginia the copy of the MedPar data as a courtesy, making it clear that it was more than she and Ascend Medical Center deserved.

"Don't duck me again, Virginia," Luann warned.

Dr. DeLuca became very solemn, but still loud enough to be overheard.

"We hope to know more about my cancer soon," she intoned. She immediately cheered.

"But enough about me. Let's talk about how the hospital is doing in the public eye since I raised Flip Jensen from the dead." Virginia reached in close, lowering her voice.

"I'm glad you asked me about that. I hate to be the bearer of bad news, but you and I need to go some place private. I really need to review this information with you," she said, tapping on the stack of paper under her hand. "This is not good news, Dr. DeLuca."

Dr. DeLuca flipped to the highlighted pages and studied the info. Virginia watched her face pinch down as she transformed herself into the Denise DeLuca of old. She slid off her chair and walked around the corner to the physician dictation room.

"Where did you get this?" she hissed, true to form. "I thought you were my friend, Virginia," she added for good measure.

"I got this from Luann Zahn. She advised me that she is part-nering with the *Charlottesville Journal* to joint report the story," Virginia told her.

"This data is bullshit," DeLuca almost whispered.

"It comes right off the ICD9 form for each patient — that answer is not going to cut it doctor." Virginia had expected that response.

"Has Royce seen this?" Dr. DeLuca asked. She had not seen much of Royce since that night in the ICU when Flip Jensen had taken off. But she had been busy making the rounds to talk shows and giving interviews. Virginia also had not seen much of Royce. He seemed very distracted on the few occasions they had met. When her calls to his long suffering administrative assistant Grace went unreturned, Virginia had sent him an urgent email about the MedPar data and the problem it posed. Royce had given a vague reply and instructed her to handle the situation using her best judgment. She had replied again, summarizing that the data compared death rate data by hospital and that Ascend had the worst scores of any hospital in the city. She also reiterated that Dr. DeLuca had the worst scores of any pulmonologist not only in Charlottesville, but in the entire region.

"I'm keeping him posted," was all Virginia could say.

"Why is she doing this to me?" Dr. DeLuca demanded. "I thought she was my friend." Virginia got stern.

"Luann Zahn is not your friend Denise. She is a reporter and she's doing her job."

"But she was so nice when I told her about being abused and my breast cancer," Dr. DeLuca whined. Her upper lip began to slowly pull back into a sneer; now she was really getting mad.

"I'm not talking to her anymore. If she's too stupid to know this information is a waste of time, then she's on her own. You shouldn't talk to her either."

"Dr. DeLuca, that's not a very good strategy. A reporter always gets the last word."

"What the hospital should do is sue her and her station to stop such slander. You tell Royce that's my recommendation. Data," she said with disdain, "does not take care of patients, doctors do." Dr. DeLuca headed for the door back to the ICU. "I have patients to save," she whispered back over her shoulder.

Virginia returned to her office and sent an email describing her planned course of action to Royce. "Dr. DeLuca was no help in responding with the latest media story i.e. MedPar mortality data. In the morning I will issue the following statement unless I hear otherwise from you: 'The recently released MedPar data files are a new, untested tool in improving patient care. Ascend Medical Center supports any efforts to improve patient care. The newly available MedPar data will be reviewed and shared with the medical staff in support of our ongoing mission to provide the best medical care in Charlottesville. Because the data is new, it is not appropriate for Ascend Medical Center to comment on any specific doctor identified in the files.' I do not recommend any interviews or comments beyond this statement."

She hit send, hoping Royce was still checking his email.

Burley had to hand it to his cousin; Shades was slicker than cat shit on linoleum. Right after the The Great Charlottesville Crash he had written out a statement about the Flip Jensen accident and had Burley sign it. It was the testimony of the two EMS crew that they had been under direct orders from Dr. DeLuca to allow the junior volunteer to drive the rig. This action was part of a "community integration program to encourage high school students to consider the medical field as a career path". It was also their testimony that Flip had been the one who ran into the ambulance. Upon reviewing the document, their Squad Commander got on the phone with his contacts at *The Siren*, the major trade publication for the EMS field. He got his boys on as the cover story. Good publicity never hurt when doing the public relations shuffle. The squad commander also detested Dr. DeLuca, whom he had the misfortune of working with for the past several years in her role as medical director.

"We'll just put this in the file and let it simmer," he told Shades. "With any luck, we won't need it." It all seemed to be a moot point, with Dr. DeLuca taking the blame for Randy driving that day. No one had come around asking about why a 16-year old had been driving the ambulance. That was until Flip Jensen filed a $25 million lawsuit against the hospital, the ambulance service and Dr. Denise DeLuca. It would take years to sort it out. If the spectacle of the Bicentennial Baby getting run down by an ambulance and then a few months later sprinting out of the hospital in an adrenaline fueled medical experiment — both the doings of the same doctor — wasn't bad enough for the brand of Ascend Medical Center, the prospect of lawyers coming between the patient-doctor relationship was just down right seedy. Virginia's newest PR nightmare had just started.

Dr. Forrest was reading through his new patient's chart, trying not to stare.

"Mary Ellen Baynor, age 27, five feet five inches, 127 pounds-"

"Ah, that's one hundred twenty four pounds doctor, your scale is a just a little bit heavy," she said, lowering her voice and whispering. "Plus, I had all my clothes on." Dr. Forrest felt a flutter in his stomach. He didn't see too many young women in his practice. She was pretty and had a spiked hairstyle that looked surprisingly good. The "The Future Porn Star" lettering that glittered on her t-shirt was very distracting.

"All right, I'll just make a note of that Mary Ellen," he offered. "Scale is heavy," he wrote and then felt foolish.

"Cricket," she said. Seeing his confusion, she repeated herself. "That' my nickname — my daddy gave it to me." She smiled, cocking her head.

"OK...Cricket," he said, looking quickly back to his notes. "So Dr. Leonard in the ER referred you according to the notes. You were having some unexplained heart palpitations. Has it happened again since you were in the ER two days ago?" he asked.

She smiled sweetly, placing a hand between her round breasts, fanning them a few times. "Whew — not until just now. Aww, that's cute," Cricket chirped. "I made you blush."

Cricket had gotten this con assignment through her aunt, who owned a beauty parlor in Charlottesville. One of her boyfriends was a big shot who had enough pull to get an ER doctor make a referral to Dr. Forrest. True, she had been to the ER many times and she had complained about heart palpitations — as well as toothaches, abdominal pains, headaches and several other assorted symptoms. Based on what his hired man told her, that lawyer had a major feud of some sort with Dr. Forrest.

"But that's not your concern," Marvin stressed. Her assignment — which had paid her $500 upfront — was to get a script for narcotic pain meds.

"You gonna tell the police that you had sex with that doctor for them pills," Marvin Wallace had told her. "Whether you actually do or not is your business, so long as you get him to write out the prescription." For her successful effort she would be paid another $2,500.

Cricket offered up another of her terrific smiles.

"Seriously doctor, no, it hasn't been a problem since that night. I think I was just upset because I found out my boyfriend was cheating on me that day — and I broke up with him."

The alarm bells were buzzing and the red flags were waving. There were pulses of blinding light, a dull roar. The warnings were loud and clear. "No, no, no...don't do it" Dr. Forrest said to himself.

"Well...Cricket, you were probably just upset, correct?" he asked, stalling.

"Turns out, more than I should have been," she said. "I really need to stop wasting my time with man-children," she said with a hint of frustration. "They really stress me out," she added.

Dr. Forrest closed her chart.

"Ms. Baynor, I'm going to save you some time and a bill to your insurance company. I'm not accepting you as a patient and I'll note that in your chart. You pretty much diagnosed your own problem and I'm glad this little talk helped," Dr. Forrest told her. "I can refer you to one of our junior partners if you still think you'd like to talk to a heart doctor."

He was a handsome man — Melvin was right — he looked like that doctor on television.

"You married doctor?" Cricket said with some shyness. "I mean, since you're not my doctor it seems like it's OK to ask."

"Not for a long time," he answered.

The only thing Royce could count on any more was that every time he drove over to Valley View, the outpatient building was rising up out of the ground higher and in more detail. Here, walking around the construction site with his hardhat, safety vest and steel tipped boots, he didn't have to think about Dr. DeLuca and her latest media extravaganza, homicidal board members, lawsuits, reporters, an unreasonable corporate office, sociopathic medical directors, demanding female senior executives and patients who seemed more and more determined to get into his office to complain about their care. It was a hospital, for fuck's sake, what did they expect? Club Med? He liked it here — it gave him time to think. Royce spent more and more time visiting the site, "supervising" the project. The downside was that until the plumbing stage of the project was complete, he had to see Ace Fury, who was in the middle of the plumbing rough out.

The only thing worse than dealing with Fury when he was the live-in boyfriend of Dr. Denise DeLuca, was dealing with him now that he was the spurned bad player in a media freak show. The reporters had finally stopped showing up at the construction site to get candid photos of him barking, scowling or holstering his pistol in an open carry as he prepared for his day on the job site.

"Royce," Ace greeted in his lethargic way. "You're slumming it today, visiting us common folk." Since Royce had honored his agreement to allow Ace to provide the subcontracting on the project, Ace had adopted a familiar demeanor. He assumed that since Royce had kept his end of the bargain that meant they were friends. Being Ace's friend might be more distasteful than being his enemy.

"How's the crazy bitch doing?" Ace inquired. "If she gives you a hard time, just grab her hair and slap her ass — she loves it." Royce would probably have not been as offended as he was if had known this was actually true.

"Ace, you shouldn't be talking like that, even joking around. Most of the reporters covering this story are female. They would love to get you on tape talking like that."

"Aw fuck 'em if they can't take a joke," Ace said. "Interesting news lately — turns out she isn't even that good a doctor. But then, you probably already knew that," he said, laughing enormously, enjoying himself. "Even her star patient, Master Flip, is suing her."

"Hey Ace, I can stay in the office and be aggravated," Royce groused. Fury pounded him on the back.

"Don't take it so hard Royce, I'm just screwing with you."

"So how's the project coming along?" Royce asked, changing

the subject. He took a step backwards to get out of Ace's reach. Ace nodded his head in the direction of a group of workers in a ditch on the outside wall.

"It's going great Royce, these Hispanic crews are God's gift to construction. I hardly hire a white guy any more," he said. "Mexicans all have families to support, their Catholic guilt makes them work like indentured servants, they don't do drugs and they never call off. See the guy in the yellow helmet? He's deaf, so I'm getting a double bagger by hiring the handicapped."

"Jeez Fury, lower your voice," Royce cautioned.

"Why? He's deaf—he can't hear me," Ace said, immensely pleased with himself. "Watch this." He gave a big wave over his head and the foreman and crew, including Jesús, waved back.

"We joke around like that all the time Royce, they're just happy to have a job."

Ace continued on his tour, leaving the annoying — and slightly scary — Ace Fury behind. The truth was that he was afraid to renege on his offer to allow Ace to subcontract the job. The Wallace cousins might throw chairs at him, but Ace Fury might throw a couple of shots his way.

Royce took the fire stairwell to the second floor. From behind a chiller retaining wall lined with latticework, he could look through to Valley View Community Hospital. He had visited several years ago and knew that the administrator's office was to the east of the main entrance on the same side of the building. Royce tried to look in, to see if he could somehow sense the fear, frustration and hate emanating from that room. Surely that's what Leo Miller, the administrator, would be feeling every time he had to look out the window and see Royce's doomsday building going up across the street.

"Ahh well, better you than me, Miller," Royce said softly. When Ascend Medical Corporation bought the hospital, Royce would move Marianne Quarters, his soon to be new CFO — formally of Valley View Community Hospital — back over as the new CEO at Valley View. She would be there long enough to fire Leo Miller — that was part of their deal, which was shaping up nicely. That spook Dr. Divinity had actually met the minimum quota inside of 6 weeks: the ownership shares were 70 percent sold. He was amazed; he didn't think Divinity had the social skills to get through the baggage check line at the airport, much less sell this deal to a group of other doctors.

He picked up a metal washer and skimmed it over the edge of the building, watching it plunk into a mud puddle below. DeLuca had turned her latest troubles into further evidence that she was the victim. It was a life strategy that had served her well time after time. Royce now understood that it was foolish to think he could change her. Not camaraderie, threats, punishment, reassurance or reason had ever made any difference. Luann Zahn and the reporter from the Charlottesville newspaper were breaking new ground with the patient mortality data set. Royce sensed it was a new era.

"Data, facts and figures," Royce said to the skyline. "That's going to take all the fun out of being in charge."

Fortunately, it was a very confusing concept to most patients. He knew that most people didn't trust data and there was always a new study being released to contradict the old data. Patients certainly were not going to challenge their doctor over something they didn't understand.

DeLuca would trot some of her favorite patients out to testify to her medical razzmatazz. Royce knew she would talk her way out of this latest disparagement on her "good name" alone.

Flip Jensen would be tougher. Even though she had him walking around, awake out of a coma, it looked bad to have their world famous patient bringing a lawsuit. DeLuca's idea was to claim his injury had changed his personality, which was actually true of frontal lobe injuries. The lawsuit was a manifestation of his symptoms. After giving it some thought, Royce had to agree with this strategy. They would express nothing but sympathy and support for Flip Jensen — "genuinely" distressed that a patient who had meant so much could turn on them like this. Then they would settle quietly out of court. Ascend was only responsible for the first $50,000 of the deductible under their liability policy, so whatever was paid in settlement would come down to a business decision for the insurance company.

As part of the settlement, the hospital would require that the suit against Dr. DeLuca and the ambulance company be dropped.

He didn't like getting her off the hook, but public sentiment seemed to be with her. And frankly, Royce didn't really give a damn either way — he was not going to the mat to be right. Besides, the ambulance company would be very appreciative, sending more patients with insurance their way when it was a toss up between Ascend or another hospital. Such an appreciation would also mean fewer uninsured, or charity, patients arriving in Ascend's ER by ambulance.

The more he thought about it, the more he actually felt sorry for Leo Miller, who was screwed.

"Too bad for you, Leo," he announced, peering across the way again into what he was sure was the window of Leo Miller's private hell.

Leo was indeed looking out the window in his office. The Ascend outpatient building was but one of his troubles. He had a CFO who was becoming more insubordinate very day. At least half a dozen doctors on his medical staff were rumored to be owners in the Ascend Medical Center. Most amazingly, Dr. Divinity was rumored to be the medical director. When he heard this bit of news, he finally understood the element of ruthlessness in play against Valley View Hospital. Leo was not ruthless. He believed in fair play and transparency, which at the moment, was not feeling like a good strategy. Then he saw a glint of light reflected in the sun, streaking off the roof of the Ascend building. He traced the arc back to the roof to see a man in a hardhat and Day-Glo vest leaning against a partial wall on the roof. Leo had seen this guy before, who sometimes spent up to an hour staring across at Leo's hospital. The man seemed to be...waiting.

His phone rang.

"Leo — it's Rebecca, in the ER. Glad you're still here. I was leaving for the day and made a walk-through in the ED on my way out. We've got a situation that I think would benefit from your deft touch," she said. In the background Leo could hear what sounded like a choir warming up in an airplane hanger.

"What is that ruckus I hear?" Leo asked.

"That would be the Rigton Clan," Linda explained. "It seems they are upset because Dr. Roosevelt will not admit their mother into the hospital," Linda said. "One of the patient's granddaughters suggested we get you down here, she told me you've done a good job of managing her father in the past."

Leo walked into the ED less than a minute later. Dr. Roosevelt was a good doctor and a reasonable guy, but he absolutely avoided confrontation. The second a patient or family member acted up, Dr. Roosevelt would leave the room. The nurse was left to deal with the unhappy party and enforce the decision, which Dr. Roosevelt never altered no matter how loud the protest. The din Leo encountered suggested a mob action. Nearly a dozen people were wedged into a small ER examining room, which was abuzz with indignity. The doughy older woman in the bed had a face which rested in a nest of long gray hair. She looked from one family member's face to another, in slow rotation, immensely pleased to be the center of attention and the subject of such lively debate. She was relaxed — much more so than her family.

"Hi Leo, thanks for coming down," Rebecca, the ED nurse said, irritated. "Can you get these people out of here before I lose it?" she said tersely. Leo stepped to the doorway and flicked the lights on and off until the group went quiet.

"Folks, I need all but one of you to follow me down the hall," he instructed.

"Are you the Godda... — the administrator?" one of the men said, controlling his anger. One thing all Rigtons knew was that the sure path to being escorted off the property was profanity.

"Yes, I am. This way please and we'll sort all this out."

Leo led the group out of the ED through a back hallway and into a vaulted ceiling room that looked like a mini chapel. It was normally used to comfort families when a loved one died. He could hear shuffling steps and muttering voices behind him, the group sounded like a flock of enraged pigeons. There was a small refrigerator in the room with soft drinks and water, which Leo began passing out. Free stuff was the lifeblood for all Rigtons; several family members took two drinks until the stock was depleted, stuffing the extras into purses and jackets. When they left, the boxes of tissue and even the light bulbs from the lamps would go with them.

"Folks, I'm Leo Miller, the administrator. How can I help you today?" Leo asked. All of the women and girls were seated, including Harold Rigton's daughter, whom Leo recalled meeting several months ago in her father's room. Several of the Rigton men began speaking at the same time. Leo held up both hands.

"Please, one at a time," Leo said. This seemed to surprise the Rigtons, who never spoke one at a time. Leo could see their confusion.

"Perhaps one of you could be the spokesman," he said, which triggered more baffled looks. "You know, one person speaks for the group, does all the talking." Everyone looked to Jerry Rigton, who was the first in his family to go to technical school. He had slicked back hair that was bravely out of fashion for the times.

"Well, Leo, this is real simple. We want our grandmother admitted to the hospital. Your Dr. Roosevelt won't do it. What kind of hospital are you running here?"

"What is your name please?" Leo asked.

"Jerry," said the young man, who acted as if he were handing over money in sharing his name.

"Jerry — only a doctor can admit a patient to the hospital. And there has to be a medical reason," Leo explained. The Rigtons all reacted as one as a little ripple of disapproval coursed through their collective. This was too much for Harold Rigton to observe the established protocol.

"Well, she's very nervous and is about to worry us to death. She tells us her nerves are too stove up to get out of bed. We got things to do during the day, like some of us have to work," Harold said, as most of his family nodded in agreement. In the Rigton world, this was an outrage. In a family of slackers, the head slacker was pulling rank.

"To be admitted to a hospital, a patient has to meet what is called medical necessity. What you described are social reasons, which are complicated, for sure — but are not grounds to be admitted to a hospital," Leo said patiently. The Rigtons response was immediate and loud, the sound of a quarrel. They all began speaking at once. Leo held up his hands again.

"Folks, please, one at a time. I can only listen to one person at a time," he repeated.

"That's a bunch of crap," Jerry said as the buzz died down. This got the Rigtons' attention. At last, someone was finally speaking in a language they could understand. "If that doctor won't admit her, you do it then," he said, which the Rigtons obviously thought was a fine idea as the multiple sided conversations renewed. Leo held up his hands again, staying in this position until the chatter again died down.

"Folks, please listen to me. The hospital is not here to take care of your elderly grandmother because she is feeling nervous or wants to stay in bed. That's a personal problem that, if it gets serious enough, can be addressed by a psychiatric hospital. Or you can put Mrs. Rigton in an assisted living or nursing home facility. Hospitals are for people who have medical problems. We are not a social agency," he said firmly. Harold glared at Leo.

"So you're saying you just don't give a good-God damn about my mother?" Harold said. "I don't know what's happening in this country. We used to be able to bring my mother in the emergency room and leave her and the doctors would admit her for a week or two to run tests and give us a break." The Rigtons nodded their approval at this fine idea.

"I remember those days too, Mr. Rigton. But we're not allowed to do that anymore. Now, there has to be a medical reason, or we don't get compensated."

"What's compensated mean?" Harold growled.

"It means paid, Uncle Harold. What Leo is saying is that they won't get paid if they admit Grandma into the hospital," Jerry said, translating. The Rigtons recoiled, clearly agitated. Harold reached in his pocket and pulled out a $10 bill, which he dropped in the baseball cap he yanked off his head.

"If it's money, we'll pass the hat and pay for it ourselves," he said handing the hat to Jerry. The Rigton clan made a show of going through their pockets and purses. Leo sighed.

"Listen to me — please. Your mother is a Medicare patient. It is illegal for us to bill any Medicare patients any charges through Medicare without a medical reason. That means we can't take your money, either. Your mother cannot be admitted to a hospital unless the doctor can find a medical reason for doing so. That's what a hospital is for. Again, to repeat, what you need is an assisted living or nursing home facility."

Harold scoffed. "Hey, we're working people, we're not a hospital CEO who has that kind of money," he countered. He cocked his head, and a slow sneer slinked across his face like a cat that had piddled on the carpet.

"Maybe we'll just all leave. Then what are you going to do with my mother?" He looked immensely pleased with himself. Leo was not about to tell him that they regularly held patients in the ED who were not sick enough to be admitted, but were not able to be discharged to leave under their own power, because they were confused or were not lucid. In these cases, his staff of social workers would sometimes spend days on the phone to find psychiatric or nursing home facilities with an open bed for an indigent patient. Until then patient remained in the ED, it was Leo's policy not to admit them. Once word got out to the likes of the Rigtons they would see this as yet another service afforded to them by the hospital. But such patients placed a great burden on the ED staff, who were not organized to care for long-term patients.

"Well, in such cases where a patient is abandoned by their family —" these words had an immediate impact on the Rigton clan. They may not be in the highest of socio-economic classes, but they had each other "— we can discharge them to the waiting room to wait for a ride. If they are out there long enough, we'll send them home in a cab."

Harold, who maintained the menace in his face, raised his eyebrow and cocked his head for added affect. "Oh yeah? What happens if she falls in the waiting room or has a fit in the cab?"

"We follow our protocol and take her back to the ED and do another assessment." Leo knew at that point the ED doctor, even Dr.

Roosevelt, would likely grow weary of dealing with the patient and would find a reason to admit them. Then Leo would have a patient in a bed for which reimbursement would probably be denied.

"If there is a medical reason to admit her, the doctor will do it. If not, she'll be discharged." Harold Rigton laughed.

"Hey, we got nothing but time to figure this out, Leo. See you soon," he said, heading for the door. The rest of Rigton crowd followed him like some weird conga line.

Leo returned to the ED desk. Dr. Roosevelt, the only physician on duty for another two hours, was charting and waiting for lab and x-ray results to return for half a dozen patients.

"How'd it go with Ernest T?" Dr. Roosevelt asked, not looking up from his chart.

"Well, doc, I think they all left, confident in the knowledge that the matron of the family is now our problem," Leo told him. Dr. Roosevelt pushed some charts around, pulled out one from the bottom, flipped it open and pointed to the top sheet.

"Good news, Leo, she's got blood in her stool, internal bleeding. I'm admitting her," Dr. Roosevelt said. "You'll have to have your showdown with the 'forces of Rigton' another day," he advised.

Leo looked at the elder Rigton's medical chart. "That is some really illegible handwriting, Doc. You pat your kid's head with that hand?" Leo joked. Bad handwriting caused problems, confused staff, and sent the wrong medication to the wrong patient at the wrong time. Regulatory agencies hated bad handwriting; it was Leo's goal to get through one inspection without getting dinged for someone's scrawl.

"For you Leo, I'll try to put a shine on it since you're the only hospital administrator I ever met who actually gets anything done," Dr. Roosevelt said. "How's that look?"

Leo looked down at the immaculately written order in the chart: NPO, clear liquids only, colonoscopy STAT.

"No food. She's not going to be in a very good mood when I make rounds tomorrow, Harry," Leo speculated.

Dr. Roosevelt shrugged. "I'll bet you my next paycheck she goes AMA when she finds out she can't eat," Dr. Roosevelt offered, not looking up from the next patient's chart. "No need to thank me, I do what I can."

CHAPTER
Alarms
FIFTEEN

Royce went through the end of month financial report with the growing realization that bad press was good for business. Ascend Medical Center had a great month, exceeding budget by almost a million dollars for the third time in a row. In his CFO's (who was not long in the job) words it was "an embarrassment of riches". His year-end bonus was now assured as the hospital had exceeded its earning goals for the year. If the trend continued, Royce would be adding about $20,000 a month in each of the final three months of the year into his pocket on top of his already generous salary. It seemed that Dr. DeLuca's craziness did not keep patients away. She was now a genuine national celebrity; the sick, infirm and the dependent were flooding in as new patients to be divvied-up among a host of specialist colleagues, all loyal to Ascend Medical Center. This newfound business silenced the corporate Public Relations VP and his concerns about the negative press.

"All publicity is good publicity, even bad publicity," he mumbled to himself. "Just spell our name right."

Surely these results would also get the psycho Wallace cousins off his back. He absently reached up to stroke the stitches on the side of his face, which itched like a son-of-a-bitch. It had taken a plastic surgeon to patch him up. He told his wife he was injured when he had to help wrestle a patient in the psych unit to the floor. She seemed impressed.

Stella Cooper, his Chief Nursing Officer, stuck her head in the door.

"You busy Royce?" she asked.

"Stella!" he said cheerfully, "Come in. I was just looking at preliminary close for the month — we slayed it," he proclaimed.

"We should have — our staffing ratios dropped 12 percent," Stella answered. She did not look happy.

"Come on Stella, you're killing me here. Can't you be happy for a few minutes? We had another great month!" Stella recognized that Royce was in a manic phase, which was a bad time to discuss any concern. But she was really determined. It worried her that the only lesson learned from the madness of recent months seemed to be that dysfunction was profitable.

"Well, it is very surprising that we continue to do so well — really remarkable," Stella conceded. "And as we are doing so well, perhaps we could add some employees." Royce's smile faded.

"What — are you on crack, Cooper?" Royce bellowed. "Why do you think our numbers are so good? I don't wanna hear anyone complaining."

"Royce, you don't go up on the floors. Our turnover rate for nurses has been climbing for six months and this month we went over 20 percent on the year," she said. "I know you know what it costs to train new nurses."

"Yeah, and they always get trained, don't they?" Royce said propping his feet up on the desk. "Why are you here Cooper — besides to kill my buzz?" he asked.

"Well Royce, I'm not going to do it alone. I need to talk to you about Dr. DeLuca."

"No! Really, Stella — I feel good right now, just don't. I really don't want to hear any more about Denise DeLuca," Royce said, dropping his feet back to the floor and lunging forward to grab a letter opener off his desk, which he spun in his hands nervously.

"Royce, she's sitting up in the ICU, harassing the staff. The other doctors — who are pissed off that you suspended her privileges — are getting her to take care of their patients," Stella said. "Do you know she's got a physician assistant now, Royce? A PA who is seeing all of those new patients that saw her on TV so she can spend most of her time parked in the ICU practicing without privileges and making my staff miserable. She's a bigger problem now than before Flip Jensen, if that's possible. You have to get her out of the hospital, Royce," she pleaded.

"I'll talk to her," Royce said.

"When has that ever worked? Royce — listen to me. We've been lucky so far. She turned the Flip Jensen debacle around on both ends. She flew under the radar with this latest investigative story Luann Zahn did, mostly because no one understands mortality outcomes data. She thinks she's golden now Royce, which makes her dangerous."

Royce got angry. "Stella, you said it yourself — the medical staff is already upset with me. If I put more pressure on DeLuca, they'll revolt," he said loudly, almost whining. "It's me out front with my hind end exposed, not you."

Stella rose to leave, looked at Royce and snapped her fingers together high in the air. "Those finances you love so much will be gone faster than that ambulance that hit Flip Jensen. You need to get her under control Royce."

"I said I'll talk to her," he answered tersely.

It occurred to Owen Gregor, as he looked around the old man's garage where he had spent so much of his youth, that he was under the guidance of some good women. It was a realization a long time coming. His mother, although very discouraged at times, had never given up on him. Felicia, his girlfriend, saw something in him that he didn't know he possessed. And Devine Brown — well she was just a force, propelling him forward and into business with all the subtlety of two weasels in a sack. She had arranged for his refresher mechanic courses at the community college, hired contractors to get the place operational and negotiated with vendors to get the equipment they needed to start up. Devine had a customer service vision to create a hotel lobby-like atmosphere, rather than the grungy, cold garage waiting rooms of Owen's childhood. She'd even had internet outlets installed so the laptop computers people seemed more and more willing to carry around could be used while they were waiting.

It was the first day Gregor Garage was open for business.

A big, old pick-up truck pulled in out front and a woman in scrubs climbed out. A second vehicle pulled up in the lot and waited, engine running; her ride to work. Owen had the garage doors open, sweeping the repair bays out. He had a do-rag tied over his head, and with the bright morning sun in her eyes, she didn't recognize Owen at first. But he knew who she was immediately. He smiled.

"Gooood morning," he said enthusiastically. She stopped in her tracks and raised a hand to her eyes to look at him.

"Owen?" she said in surprise. "This is your shop?"

"Hi, Brittany. Yeah, this is our first day back open. And you're my first customer," he said, trying hard to make it sound like her good luck.

"I haven't seen you in a while, Owen," Brittany said, leaning her weight on one hip and crossing her arms. Her nametag for Valley View Hospital glinted in the sunlight when she shifted her weight.

"You won't be seeing me in the ER any more," he offered.

"You go through a program?" she asked.

"Kind of, I met a woman who straightened me out," he said. Devine walked out of the office into the sun.

"Two women actually. This is Devine Brown, my business partner. Devine, this is Brittany Sawyer. She's an ER nurse over at Valley View Hospital. She was one of the first women who got tired of my shit," he said, smiling.

"It freaks me out that you know my last name, Owen," Brittany said, frowning.

"I was good at what I did, Brittany. But I'm an even better mechanic — give me a chance," he told her. Devine reached into a bag she was holding and pulled out a small bouquet of flowers.

"These are for you, Ms. Sawyer, for being our first lady customer. And you don't have to worry none about being freaked out by Owe-in. When he not at home with that good woman Felicia of his, I keep him focused," Devine said. "Really, we known each other a long time and he's all good now," she said gently.

Brittany, was thinking. The window rolled down in the waiting car and Dr. Diller, the former Navy physician, stuck her head out.

"Brittany we need to go, we're going to be late for our shift," she warned. "And I still have to drop Jake off at daycare."

"Come on in, Ms. Sawyer and I'll write your ticket up. What you doing working all the way over there in Valley View any way?" she asked. As Owen had learned, it was difficult to say no to Devine Brown.

"It's a nice place to work. I used to work at Ascend Medical Center, which is not a very nice place to work," she said, following Devine into the office.

"Well, you be sure to tell everyone at Valley View that they get 20 percent off their first visit," Devine said.

Leo searched out the Unitarian signboard, squinting expectantly in the brilliance of the morning sun. Its prophecy glowed in the clean morning air: "Ambitious people climb, faithful people build". He continued, driving past the shadow of the Ascend Medical Center Outpatient Surgery Center. In a week the patients would begin arriving early in the morning at the surgery center — patients who would have once been cared for at his hospital. He had chosen to feel optimistic this morning, certain this was the best path in the absence of absolutely any credible reason to do so.

As he pulled in he saw Dr. Divinity enter the hospital. The radiologist had behaved since their talk several months ago. Leo did not attribute this at all to his power of persuasion, but rather to the doctor's involvement in the Ascend Surgery Center. Leo knew he was the medical director who had persuaded several others on the medical staff to buy in to the project. Dr. Divinity also remained his leading suspect in his office break-in. The copy of his disciplinary file was the only item of high interest to disappear.

Leo immediately went upstairs to make rounds. Dr. Massari was at the nurse's station, early as was his habit, reviewing morning blood chemistry work on the inpatients. He offered Leo an open and sincere smile without looking up, which Leo always appreciated.

"You look pretty intent there, Akil," Leo said in greeting.

"Yeah, I'm trying to get this patient out of here before we kill her," he said softly. "She was re-admitted for heart failure for a third time. Her immune system is shot, and if she stays much longer she'll pick up an infection, or we'll forget to give her a med or give her the wrong or too much med, or give her the wrong food tray with salt." he said. "She'd be safer at home with her husband, where she wants to be anyway, rather than sitting here waiting for us to make a mistake." He saw Leo's surprise.

"This is a good hospital, Leo. But this patient has old people problems that we can easily turn into a critical problem — even too many doctors taking care of her can do that. It would be better for her to get the care she needs from someone who knows her." Leo did not realize it was Mr. Harris' wife until he lumbered down the hall, wearing the same puffy white vest as when they had first met. Mr. Harris was clearly tired and worried.

"Good morning, Mr. Harris. I'm certainly sorry to see that your wife is back in the hospital," Leo offered. Mr. Harris only nodded in response. Dr. Massari reached up and gave Mr. Harris' shoulder a squeeze and looked him in the eye.

"Mr. Harris, I have a proposal," he said in his very precise English. "Congestive heart failure can mean many things — from simple high blood pressure to an enlarged heart to fluid buildup in the capillary ends — or all of those things. A patient in your wife's condition can live a long time — especially if she is happy and content. I think we can manage your wife's condition at home if I arrange for a nursing home care visit every day and you are willing to help manage her care. Would you be interested in trying that?"

He looked a bit alarmed. "I don't understand, I thought the best place for her was in the hospital."

"There are many caring people on this floor looking after patients," Dr. Massari said. "But think about what we have to do to render that care. We wake patients up late and early to check their vitals and draw blood, so they don't rest well. We make them wear funny gowns that don't cover their backside. We ask very personal questions, tell them what they can eat, what they need to do in the bathroom — even when their loved ones can visit. These are very intrusive processes that may very well contribute to their illness. Let me ask you something Mr. Harris: is your wife ever happy about coming to the hospital?"

"No doctor," he said.

"So let's get her out of here and see if we can improve her condition at home — what do you think?"

The haze of despair on Mr. Harris' face immediately lifted.

"Yes, of course. We want to be together, it makes us both happy," he said earnestly.

"I'll need you to sign a waiver because the established protocol is to keep her in the hospital. But I've read a couple of recent articles in the medical literature where this type of management therapy is getting good results," Dr. Massari explained.

"Yes, yes, of course I'll do whatever you need to get my wife home again," Mr. Harris assured.

"Get her to her doctors' appointments, make sure she takes her meds, take her for a walk and prepare a low salt diet?" Dr. Massari continued, smiling.

"Anything, doctor, I'll take care of it," Mr. Harris promised, beaming.

"OK, Mr. Harris — you and your wife are going be my first patients I've tried on this therapy, can I count on you to follow my instructions? And there are no guarantees — her heart failure will always be there, but I believe she'll be better off out of the hospital," Dr. Massari said. Mr. Harris nodded and grinned over his shoulder as he hurried back down the hall to his wife's bedside to share the good news.

Leo and Dr. Massari watched him go.

"Dr. Massari, it's truly a pleasure to see you work," Leo said. "Well done. Why don't you bring this new therapy to the quality committee and work it up into a protocol the medical staff can review and approve? I'll bet there are is a national study out there in progress in which we can participate."

"Leo, it is you who are the pleasure. I've never worked with a hospital administrator who actually got anything useful accomplished," Dr. Massari said.

When Leo got back downstairs to his office he felt good. But he also knew that the sense of accomplishment would be short lived as he re-entered the world of paper pushing and time management. He had no sooner sat down when Marianne Quarters, his CFO, walked in and shut the door. She laid an envelope on his desk.

"That's my month's notice and resignation," she said, still standing. She looked very satisfied. Leo felt enormous relief.

"I think you know that I'm not going to try to talk you out of it," Leo stated. "You and I have not been a good match since the first day." She shrugged and turned to leave.

"You can clear your office out now. I'll pay you out the month," he said. He could tell, even looking at her as she walked away, that she was surprised. He opened the envelope. She was going to Ascend Medical Center in Charlottesville as the CFO. He felt a flash of hot anger. She had waited until the week Ascend's surgery center was opening across the street to give her notice. There was a light knock on his door. Ben Stall, his Chief Nursing Officer, stepped in.

"Leo, can I talk to you for a minute?" Ben asked, sitting. It was times like these when Leo had to clear his mind and listen.

"Umm, Leo, I really like you. But I don't think I like being an administrator. It's just too mean of a job," he said.

"What do you want to do, Ben?" Leo asked gently.

"I want to go back on the floors, I'm good at being a unit manager — that's what I did before I took this position a few years ago when I was at University. In fact, they have a position open that they have offered me," Ben said, dropping focus from Leo and looking at the floor.

"So you are tendering your resignation?" Leo asked quietly. Ben nodded, reached inside his suit jacket and pulled out an envelope, which he handed to Leo.

"I'm sorry, Leo. But with the surgery center opening up across the street, you need someone in this position who is up for it — and I'm not," Ben said.

"Ben — I understand. Can you stay on for the month while I recruit a new CNO?"

"Of course." Leo held up the CFO's resignation. "I am assuming you didn't know that the CFO has also resigned this morning?" Ben went speechless. "It's OK, Ben, this will all work out. I wish you much success."

After Ben left, Leo shut his door and dialed his board chairman.

"Jesus, Leo," was all she could say.

"It's OK, Stephanie. The CFO leaving is a good thing, I'll find someone else I can work with, someone who shares my values. Ascend can have her," Leo said. "And I had already come to the same conclusion as Ben — he's not cut out for administration. In fact, I've been discussing the position with someone, so now I don't have to ask Ben for his resignation. We can both save face now — and he'll be happier."

The line was quiet. "Stephanie, you still there?"

"Yes, I was just thinking. This is going to be bad news to the medical staff, especially on top of the Ascend Surgery Center opening up." There was another pause. "I wonder if Quarters had anything to do with getting some of our doctors to buy in?" she proposed.

"You know Stephanie, that doesn't matter — she's history now. We can only worry about what we can control. We need to stick to our new plan," Leo answered. "Besides," he laughed, "she didn't know about this. I never told her — I didn't trust her."

"Leo — you big swinging dick," she kidded. "Oops, did I say that out loud? Fuck, I have such a mouth — damn Army." Leo had his first good laugh in months.

"We're going to launch the new plan the same day they open?" the Board Chair asked once they both stopped laughing.

"Yes. The campaign is ready to go in local newspapers and on the radio and we've got some news coverage lined up. The Chief of Staff is on Board. While Dr. Hauptman thinks the mortality data is too new to be completely credible, she thinks having a discussion about patient outcomes is long overdue," Leo said. "Besides, she's ready to take privileges away from the doctors who bought into the center. But I think we can avoid that for now."

"And tell me again how the nurse visits will work." Stephanie asked.

"We're going to send a nurse for a home visit to every discharged patient to make sure they understand their discharge instructions and to see how they are doing," he said. "This will keep patients from being re-admitted."

"Hmmm, not to put too fine a point on it Leo, but don't we like re-admissions? We get paid for them," she said.

"True, but remember we're trying to reinvent ourselves. If we want to convince patients to come to our hospital from Charlottesville and insurance companies to cut us preferred contracts, we have to reassure them that we're looking out for their best interest. Besides, I'm telling you, sooner or later, Medicare is going to start cracking down on re-admissions. That's why they're collecting the data. This will get us ahead of the curve," Leo explained.

"God damn, I like it, Leo. It's fucking brilliant," Stephanie exclaimed.

"We'll see," Leo said. "Thanks for your time Stephanie, it's always a pleasure."

Denise DeLuca was speaking with her agent again. She could hardly believe it — she had an agent. There was no doubt of her success now. She had listened in on the snide conversations in Margret Stephenson's office, where more and more she and her staff retreated to be out of earshot of Dr. DeLuca's hypersensitive hearing. She thought again, hunched down over the speaker in the doctor's dictation area, how clever it was of her to bug the one place in the unit where others thought they could speak in private. This was true vision, something none of them would ever have.

Sure, their remarks were hurtful. She thought with self-pity, and then anger, of the criticisms, ridicule and taunts she had endured.

"She's a legend in her own mind," Margret had quipped to the titters of her staff when they were in her office that morning. After all she had done for Margret Stephenson, Dr. DeLuca fumed, and this is how she treats me. While, according to her agent, she was not going to be around long enough to make sure Margret lost her job, she could sure make every day unpleasant.

Her agent — a fast-talking and very enthusiastic young man, was telling her about a medical correspondent opportunity at one of the major news cable networks. The position paid more than she could ever think of making as a doctor.

"You would be covering all the major medical news stories of the day, Denise — with social commentary!" he told her excitedly. "You name it — everything from AIDS to when the President of the United States gets hemorrhoids. I heard the other day that even Ebola is staged for a big comeback — can you believe it? That disease scared the fool out of the entire free world last time it showed up. The nation will be hanging on your every word. The point is, Denise, you would be on the air just about every day — a trusted household name," he said excitedly. He would get 15 percent of her earnings and with her name recognition, he would gather other rising stars as new clients. He was already counting the money.

In the background, an alarm screeched. Hospitals, especially ICUs, are full of equipment designed by companies that seemed intent on covering any product liability with alarms that sound at any hint of malfunction on either the patient's or the equipment's part. The hospital staff learned to ignore, doubt and despise alarms. They were quickly conditioned to simply hit the reset button to end the nuisance. Dr. DeLuca, with her keen hearing, especially hated alarms. If the staff were slow to get into a room to turn the damn thing off, it was one of the few times when she would actually raise her voice.

"What is that awful noise?" her agent asked.

"That's the sound of lives being saved," she said airily. "Hold on." Denise covered the receiver with her hand.

"People — will someone please turn that alarm off?" she yelled. "I'm on the phone with my agent!" A few seconds later, the noise stopped.

"Sorry about that, nothing gets done right around here unless I do it myself," she said, loudly enough for the staff to hear.

"Well, soon they're going to have to figure it out without you, because you'll be long gone with bigger things to do," the agent said, giddy. The alarm went off again in Room 6.

"Dr. DeLuca, I don't see how you can stand that," the agent said. "I'll let you go. As you say, sounds like you've got lives to save."

Denise had never mentioned to him that her admitting privileges had been suspended at the hospital, and she didn't see any reason to tell him now.

She slammed the phone down and stomped into Room 6. The patient, a nondescript old person in his late 70's, who was receiving dialysis for his failing kidneys, did not look alert. But DeLuca thought, *do they ever?* The nurse was fussing with the dialysis machine, which sounded its shrill alarm a third time just as Denise went to speak. She jerked the nurse back by the shoulder, stepped up and hit the reset button. She was a new nurse, just graduated — the kind DeLuca enjoyed most.

"Are you trying to kill this patient?" she demanded. The patient rolled his head towards DeLuca, alarm managing to rise in his lethargic eyes.

"Of course not, doctor — but I can't get this alarm to stop sounding, I'm concerned..."

"Listen to the new nursing graduate — she's concerned. We're not in training any more, missy, you're in the real world now. You probably haven't even taken your Boards yet, have you?" The nurse blinked back tears.

"I would not be here if I had not passed my Boards," she managed to say. The patient dropped his head as though he were trying to hear the conversation better. Margret Stephenson, the unit manager, stepped into the room followed by Royce Wexler.

"Listen to me because I'm only going to tell you this once. The alarms on these machines ring false 99 out of a 100 times. You can't get your panties in a knot over it. Just hit the reset — especially when I put the line in myself. You don't know who I am, do you?"

"Dr. DeLuca, Mr. Wexler is here to see you," Margret said. She looked at the nurse. "Go ahead, Amber, you can leave.

"I didn't do anything wrong," the nurse said, now crying.

"I know you didn't honey, go on into the break room and I'll be there in a minute," Margret said gently. After the nurse left, Denise hissed lowly at Margret, her voice a coiled whisper.

"You do not interfere when I am disciplining a nurse," she said. "Do you understand me?"

"Dr. DeLuca, it's my job to discipline nurses, not yours." Margret looked at Royce."You better get her out of here," she said, no longer able to hide her contempt for the doctor. Margret left the room to find her upset nurse. Dr. DeLuca turned to Royce, whom she had not seen in months. When he suspended her admitting privileges, he had done so by certified mail.

"What are you doing here?" she said to Royce. "You hate being up on the floor." It was true — Royce did not care to be around sick people. "What — did someone drop a twenty-dollar bill under a bed?" Dr. DeLuca added, laughing at her own insult. She could give as good as she got, and she certainly didn't need to be nice to him any more.

"That's very funny, Denise, I suppose humor is a real comfort to you these days," Royce said sarcastically.

"Why are you up here, Mr. Wexler?" she said. "I'm busy saving lives at the moment."

"Ahhh, so it's Mr. Wexler now. Why the formality?"

"And it's Dr. DeLuca to you, Mr. Wexler. It took me a while but, I finally realized that you are not my friend," she said. Her upper lip quivered slightly.

"Well, Denise, you're done saving lives here. As you might recall, you do not have admitting privileges and you are no longer the medical director of this unit. So, I'm telling you again, I need you to pack up your stuff, leave the unit and don't come back until you have privileges. I hope I don't have to call security to work this out."

Denise thought about it; the sight of her being forcibly removed from the ICU was a mixed bag. While it was just the kind of drama she liked, with her pending television deal set to launch, she just managed to realize such attention might dim her prospects.

Royce's eyes went big as he looked past Dr. DeLuca. Then he leaned over at the waist to vomit. Dr. DeLuca spun around to see the patient flopped over the side rail of his bed. The mattress behind him as well as the pillows used to prop him up in the elevated bed were saturated a bright red, the sheets and mattress soaked in blood. Behind them, Margret, who had just walked back into the unit after attending to her traumatized nurse, yelled for a Code Blue. She ran into the room, pushing by Dr. DeLuca, not even stopping to put on protective gloves.

"I told you," Dr. DeLuca stated, instantly in blame mode. "That nurse did not know what she was doing. This is you fault, Margret." Margret grabbed the dialysis line and frantically traced it back to the patient's body. The line pulled free from the beneath the patient, and spun in her hand. Without a return connection, all of the patient's blood was pumped out of one side of his body and onto the bed where it was absorbed into the mattress, all the while the pump alarm warning of the failure. The pillows used to prop the patient up in the bed had concealed the growing bloodstain until the patient passed out and fell over. Margret screwed the connection back in tight and pulled the unconscious man up into the bed. But the only sound was of air pumping through the unit — the patient had no blood left to lose. A steady red drip began from the bottom of the mattress onto the floor.

Dr. DeLuca walked out as Dr. Ippolito from the ER rushed in, responding to the Code Blue. A growing pool of blood began to spread on the floor.

"Denise — what happened?" Dr. Ippolito demanded as she slammed her stethoscope onto the patient's chest, which was as white as the sheet had once been. "CPR now, stand by the defibrillator." she said, calm.

"That's it, I'm done," said Dr. DeLuca, holding her balled hands up high. "I am tired of dealing with the incompetence of this unit. If you don't want me to take care of patients, Royce, fine — you figure it out," said Dr. DeLuca. She looked at Dr. Ippolito. "You be the doctor." She turned and charged out of the unit, narrowly missing the crash cart. Royce staggered out of the unit dry heaving, his tie stained wet.

"Someone get him before he falls down and cracks his head," Margret yelled. She then spoke to Dr. Ippolito who was listening intently to the man's chest. More people rushed in.

"The line wasn't screwed into the catheter," Margret concluded, devastated. Dr. Ippolito stood straight, looked at her watch. "We can't bring a patient back who has no blood. I'm a doctor, not God almighty. This man is dead, time 2:06."

Kenny liked bars. He had always been partial to being a regular, finding that his drinking friends did not find his lack of limbs to be especially notable. His mother still tried to protect him by advocating isolation, even after all these years, campaigning for Kenny to move back in with her.

"The world is a ghastly, mean place Kenny. You'll be better off here with me," she managed to work into every phone call home. He had put himself through graduate school, had a great job and was never lonely — yet his mother still thought the world was not ready for a man without arms.

He found that death and mayhem were easier to digest in the glow of beer signs and the giggling symphony of young nurturing ladies. Despite his reputation, he actually did not drink that much, one beer a night and a lot of club soda. Arnie, a client whom Kenny was making secure for retirement, kept his non-drinking secret.

Kenny was waiting, knowing Luann would be in sooner or later. The local news was lit up with the story of Dr. DeLuca killing a patient — even CNN. Arnie had broken his no news policy to keep track of the breaking story. There was outrage of the "shit-hitting-the-fan" type that Dr. DeLuca, who had been awarded media darling status, had the temerity to prove them wrong. Luann had scooped the story — complete with photos supplied by an unnamed source. Janet Ippolito was next to him, drinking another Mojito and hoisting Kenny's beer up for him.

"Where'd Luann get those pictures doc?" Kenny asked as the blood soaked shots from room 6 in Ascend Medical Center rolled across the screen once again — almost continuously for the past five hours. Only parts of the patient were revealed — a pale white hand hanging over the side of the bed against an out-of-focus field of red, a sheet pulled over a lifeless body, a peak of pale white forehead made even whiter against white hair.

"Isn't that some kind of violation of patient privacy?" he added. There was footage of the dead patient's sons — two big beefy fellows with hard twisted faces — bellowing that Dr. DeLuca had killed their father. Luann also had footage of Dr. DeLuca "no commenting" her way out of the hospital to her car. Luann knew what Janet had shared with her on the phone, but she was not going to reveal that source. Janet meanwhile, was acclimating well to Mojitos, which she had been drinking steadily for the past few hours. She was off the next two days.

"I don't know where she got the photos," Janet said. "The Chief Nursing Officer called a root cause analysis meeting within the hour. I left the unit and went directly to the debriefing," she said.

"What's a root cause analysis?" Kenny asked.

"It's where everyone shows up and immediately reviews what happened to determine what went wrong. Honesty is expected and there is no punishment, no matter what mistakes were made — well, at least no internal punishment. We can't do much about regulatory agencies," Janet said. "Arnie, can we turn that off?" she added. "I'm tired of looking at DeLuca." There she was on the screen again, looking irritated and put out.

"She show up to the root cause analysis?" Kenny asked. Janet made a snorting sound.

"She was too busy being on the way to her next television interview to blame that patient's death on the hospital," Janet said. "But it's not going to work this time. Three people heard her say that she set that dialysis line up herself. She didn't screw the line in properly."

"So where'd the photos come from?" Kenny asked again. "Somebody took those pictures with the intent of getting them to Luann. They must have used one of those new digital cameras," Kenny said. He leaned over and whispered. "Probably ought to give up on those Mojitos doc, they got you thinking it was your fault."

"It is my fault," Janet said. "And everyone else's fault who for all of these years made excuses for Dr. DeLuca," she said with a sigh. "I get that now."

"Surely this will be the end of her," Kenny said, thinking out loud.

"I don't know, Kenny, she seems to have a knack for getting around her problems. We'll see."

CHAPTER
Grand Opening
SIXTEEN

Today Dr. Divinity's enjoyment was intense, palpable. He was a patient man and had waited a very long time for this grand opening. It was the beginning of the end for Mr. CEO at Valley View Hospital.

He had not talked to Leo Miller much since their sit-down where the CEO had scolded him. He had seen him on the hospital cameras quite a bit, though. The idea of a paper pusher trying to tell a doctor what to do for the sake of such a flawed principle as patient satisfaction was absurd. Patients were not in a hospital to be satisfied, only healed. With the opening of the new Ascend Medical Center Outpatient Surgery Center, of which he was now the medical director and one-eighth owner, the universe would be set to rights. Leo Miller was a goner and Dr. Divinity was pretty sure that the hospital administrator knew it. Money and power would prevail as is the right order of the universe.

Since the Engineering Director had disappeared, Dr. Divinity expanded his covert camera network throughout the hospital. It was more difficult as he now had to access the control room in the middle of the night, but the results were worth the inconvenience. Among the secrets of the hospital he had discovered, was a married physician who was having an affair with a nurse. He also found a manager stealing supplies from his department, probably for resale. All of this activity was recorded on videotape and the unit carefully hidden in the overhead 100 yards away in a janitor's closet. The cheating doctor had vowed not to make referrals to the other doctors who were owners in the new competing surgery center.

"We'll see about that," Dr. Divinity thought, anticipating the look on his colleague's face at the moment his good principles were jettisoned by his lust and blackmail.

To commemorate the day, he pinned a small, pink breast cancer ribbon to his white lab coat. The female staff had asked him several times to make this gesture in support of the tiresome cause, one that he thought overwrought. He was a radiologist doing his part, using his expertise to spot the cancer on breast x-rays. But he was in a good mood today. He didn't often act impulsively; he was surprised at how liberating it felt.

Leo had to concede it was a beautiful day for a grand opening. Every week he watched the construction rise up and out like a runaway tumor. That was followed by truck after truck pulling around to the loading dock in the rear to deliver the latest state-of-the art operating room equipment, computers, and office furniture.

Word was that the building owners had also splurged, designing an art gallery into the lobby featuring modern art. Two of the physician partners and their wives were art collectors and had convinced the rest of the group that the gallery would offer a unique healthcare experience for patients and their families. And because they were purchasing work by promising new artists, the cost would be relatively low compared to well known artists. If a piece in the collection did escalate in value, it would be sold and the profits divided. Then there was the media coverage. This would be the first outpatient surgery center/art gallery anywhere in the country.

Today was message change day on the marquee at the Unitarian Church. The autumn sun was bright in his eyes, so Leo slowed down and squinted.

"The best solutions are often simple, yet unexpected."

He felt disappointed. This pronouncement seemed of the banal Chinese fortune cookie advice. He didn't realized how hopeful he was for an answer to his problems. But when he thought about it, none of the confidence he placed in the marquee predictions had really panned out.

Leo's plan to compete against Ascend would take time, but there was no other way. He was fortunate enough to have a Board that did not panic and understood that any short-term measures would be ineffective. Leo thought about walking across to the open house to meet Royce Wexler face-to-face. He was certain the Ascend CEO would be at the open house. Wexler was not content to take away a good part of this operating room business, but he had also robbed away his CFO. Even though Leo was glad to see her go, Wexler had made the move to further demoralize everyone at Valley View Hospital. Taking care of sick people could be a mean business.

Royce Wexler pointed his new Mercedes SL down I-64 west at 90 mph with nary a shake. He had taken delivery of the car the day before. His hands — and crotch — tingled, but that's what the machine was designed to do. This was offset by tightness in his shoulders that set in any time he was with the Wallace cousins. Robert Wallace gave no indication of a pending repeat of his chair-throwing tantrum, but he had taken the backseat behind Royce, while cousin Jim sat up front.

"Damn, Royce, this car will flat out shit and get. I might have to get me one of these," Robert said.

Royce had spent his entire bonus — almost $100,000 — on the car. But he was not about to tell the cousins that detail, as only his corporate bosses knew the specifics of his compensation. There would be plenty more money where that came from; by this time next year he calculated that the Board at Valley View would be desperate for a savior. His new CFO assured him that Leo Miller didn't have a clue.

"Got a lot of room in this backseat," Jim said, craning his neck around. He was recently separated from his wife and his cousin was acting as his divorce attorney.

"Lot of room for the ladies," Robert laughed. They joked a lot about such matters lately. "Maybe you'll let me borrow this car, try it out one weekend? I been praying every night for God to send me a sign if I should buy a Mercedes or a Cadillac. Maybe this is it."

"Sure, Robert, as long as you don't throw any more chairs at me," Royce answered, deciding that joking was the way to go, just one of those misunderstandings that happens between men from time to time.

"Maybe — but I ain't making no promises. You shouldn't have been fooling with my aunt's estate like you did — that was dumber than a two-dollar dog," Robert said. "Just don't fuck up no more and I'll think about it."

"I should have come to you when I found out what Dr. Forrest was doing," Royce agreed. He saw a look pass between the cousins in the rear view mirror and wondered what that was about. Robert cracked his knuckles.

"How come that new CFO of yours is not going to the party to-day?" Jim asked. "She seems like a mean old gal, like she would enjoy rubbing Leo Miller's face in that big old stink pile."

"She's not very social or very talkative, likes to work with her num-bers," Royce said.

"Well, at least Denise DeLuca's not a pain in our behinds any more," Robert announced. Royce jumped on the change of subject like a man escaping on horseback.

"Yeah, she'll be lucky if she can get a job reviewing medical charts for an insurance company," Royce offered. He knew on the matter of Dr. DeLuca that all he needed to do was keep the conversation flow-ing. The Wallace cousins hated her and not because she was dysfunc-tional and manipulative. They were the same way, but they resented anyone else who dabbled in the genre. The Wallace cousins considered deceit and misuse of power their exclusive domain — at least in Charlottesville, Virginia.

"Ain't it funny how those wing nuts on the right have dropped her faster than a queer going to his knees in a steam bath?" Jim laughed. "But I hear she's gonna sue the hospital," he added.

The car swerved to the right a tad as Royce looked at Robert, who reached out with two fingers and steered the Mercedes back to the left.

"Keep your eyes on the road there, son."

"Where'd you hear that?" Royce asked. "And what's she going to sue us for?"

Jim laughed from the back seat. "Royce I keep telling you, stop asking us how we know about things — just assume we know. You should call the yahoos at corporate tomorrow so they can pee their pants. But does it really matter why she's suing? She isn't taking the blame for bleeding that guy to death. Her lawyers are happy to take her money — ain't that right, cousin?"

"I resent the implication," Robert said. "But that said — hell yes."

Jim continued. "She's also going to sue the company that makes the dialysis machine, the company that makes the bed, and you."

"Nothing surprises me about that woman," Royce said.

"He ain't told you the best part," Robert said tilting his head back and raising his voice. "Tell him, cousin."

Jim giggled. "She's going to sue the dead patient's estate too," he said. "She claims he knew he was dying and fiddled with the line himself so that his family could sue her and the hospital — which they are doing, by the way."

"She's going to sue the guy she killed through her own negligence?" Royce said more than asked, incredulous.

"That ain't the way she sees it," Robert intoned with a yawn. He slipped his sunglasses on and laid his head back on the leather seat.

None of them noticed the numerous memorials posted on the ground at the site of the Great Charlottesville Car Wreck as they zipped by on their way up the road to greatness.

Jesús Sanchez parked his old battered pick-up truck at the far end
of the hospital parking lot in front of Valley View Hospital. This gave
him a good line of sight across the road to the main entrance of the
Ascend Medical Center Outpatient Surgery Center. He had been
working to convince his niece Jayne that things would work out, to
believe that God had a plan. She agreed, but with little enthusiasm.
Over the months, as the Ascend building progressed, her distress
increased. She had cried at their lunch meeting the day before. It was
tempting to tell her, but then she would be part of it.

To anyone looking at him, he was just another bubba sitting in his
pick-up with a hunting rifle racked in the rear window. It was deer
season in the Appalachian Mountains. Jesús was not a hunter, but he
might be parked awhile, so he needed to look and act the part of just
another family member waiting for a patient to be discharged from
the hospital. The open house would begin in about an hour, but his
plan would all depend on how many people showed up and when.
Two catering trucks were parked at the main entrance. Jesús watched
as the crew unloaded tray after tray of food and three rolling bars
with tubs of beer and wine. It was bigger and finer than anything he
had ever seen, even at the weddings of his many nieces and nephews.
He reckoned that the many guests who showed up would get full and
sluggish with free food and alcohol.

He tried to do the calculation in his head based on other construction projects at which he had labored. A few of those openings had
included a separate grand opening for the construction crews, but not
Ascend. He figured maybe 300 people would come through during
the six-hour reception. He asked Jayne if anyone from Valley View
would be in the building.

"Just the doctors who are the owners," she said.

"How many?" Jesús asked.

"Six, and one of them is the medical director — Dr. Divinity," she told him. "Dr. Divinity — he's been difficult for Leo." A thought occurred to Jesús.

"Is Leo going to the open house?"

"I don't know Uncle. That bas-," she stopped herself. Jayne never swore. "That administrator Mr. Wexler at Ascend sent him an invitation — I threw it away rather than give it to Leo. It had a handwritten note from Mr. Wexler — I remember what it said: 'Leo — Perhaps we'll finally have the chance to meet. Cheers — Royce Wexler.' But Leo knows it's today." That's when she started to cry.

He patted her hand. "Things will work out niece, I'm sure of it."

He picked up the copy of the Charlottesville Observer on the bench seat and folded it back to the crossword puzzle. There was no sense dwelling on the plan, it was in God's hands now — with a little help from Jesús.

Luann had been trying to get at Royce Wexler for months. Virginia Stowe, his flack, told her repeatedly that he was not giving interviews — especially to Luann. Virginia was no longer returning her calls. Luann had not been able to get an interview from anyone at Ascend Medical Center since the "Death in the ICU" case, as she had dubbed the death in her many reports on the incident. Luann had the family of the deceased man on video — they were talking up a storm every time Dusty turned on his camera. She had countless experts who were more than pleased to talk to the reporter who broke "The Great Charlottesville Crash" and the saga of Flip Jensen.

But most of it all, she had a lot of unused footage of the confessional interview with Dr. DeLuca. The doctor had disappeared. After the state had suspended her medical license, she was not to be found at her house, her cell phone was out of service and her office was closed. In the absence of an actual interview with Dr. DeLuca, Luann was editing outtakes from the footage so that a line-up of eager "experts" could analyze and speculate on the psyche of Dr. DeLuca. Intermixed with interviews of local contacts — patients, neighbors, co-workers, former employees in her medical practice (there were many former employees, she liked to fire people) — this approach had allowed Luann to keep the coverage going. But the story was fading. She needed a new angle and fresh footage.

"Let's take your truck, they'll see us coming in the news van," she said to Dusty. Her plan was to find Royce Wexler at the open house, stick the camera in his face and start asking questions. He would have two choices in the face of an ambush interview: stop and deal with it, which might mean giving unrehearsed answers, but, with the right uncomfortable, squirmy body language, that worked. Or refuse to talk to her and leave, which looked guilty. Either way, she would have what she needed for another few weeks of stories on her bi-weekly news program. Her station was making a small fortune in ad revenues, so the news director wanted all the chum she could churn up about Ascend Medical Center.

Janet had been a huge help in advising her about what questions to ask, especially the medical issues, but Luann would not put her girlfriend on the air. Luann had located several retired nursing managers and hospital administrators to interview — people who had already made their careers and money and had nothing to lose by speaking up.

Luann and Dr. Ippolito had recently moved in together, renting one of several houses that Kenny owned. They were month-to-month as, per Kenny's prediction, Luann was being intensely recruited by news operations in bigger markets than Charlottesville. But Luann was not going anywhere until this story played out. Dusty loaded the gear into his truck and they headed out to Valley View.

"You know the only way Royce Wexler is going to stop long enough to talk to you is if you show him your tits," Dusty drawled. He was steering with one hand, a cup of coffee and a cigarette in the other. The open vent window sucked the smoke out, away from Luann.

"Either that, or I get his chestnuts in my pocket," she said, rifling through a folder in her lap. She pulled out two pieces of paper and held them up side by side.

"And it looks like it's curtain B, Dusty," she said.

Dusty took a sip of coffee, then rotated his hand to take a puff. He exhaled out the side of his mouth, juicing the truck as he turned onto the ramp of the interstate.

"That's too bad, I always wanted to see your tits." She slapped him with the folder.

"Just drive, horndog," she said. "The only tits you should be looking at are your cowgirl's."

"We are no longer acquainted," Dusty said, looking straight ahead. "So even some lesbian jugs would look pretty good about now."

"See — I knew you were going to miss me when I'm gone, so I'm taking you with me," Luann told him, looking out her window. "I'm going to make it a package deal."

"I could use a change of venue.," Dusty admitted, a faint smile on the corner of his mouth. "You got a plan to get to Wexler yet?

"Don't I always have a plan, Dusty?"

Ethyl and her sister Mary stood in their slips, staring into the bedroom closet.

"Maybe we ought to wear one of Momma's dresses," Mary said. "They don't make material like that any more."

"One of her hats too?" Ethyl offered.

"Yeah, that'll class the place up," Mary said. "I hope they have shrimp."

"This ain't a social occasion," Ethyl reminded her. "We're going there to scope the place out. There must be something we can do to shut that place down."

"I think they'll have shrimp — I'm bringing a couple of freezer bags in my purse." Mary chewed on her lower lip, a habit since childhood. "Maybe we shouldn't wear the hats, we might be too noticeable." She picked up a peach colored number with white feathers from the top shelf, spinning it slowly around in both hands.

"Sister, there ain't no one going to be paying attention to a couple of old gals like us. Besides, all dressed up with our war paint on, I'll bet even Leo won't recognize us," Ethyl told her. "And, we work there now, we got the right to attend."

The practice manager knew the sisters from the hospital and had offered them the contract for cleaning the facility. Starting next week, they would walk across the street after their 7-3 at the hospital and spend two hours cleaning the Ascend Outpatient Surgery Center — at 30 percent more than their hospital hourly wage. Ethyl had reasoned to her sister that they would be on the inside working to find a way to shut the place down. The extra money would be nice too.

"I wonder why that invitation was in the trashcan?" Mary speculated for the hundredth time. "I know you keep saying it's because he doesn't want to dignify the open house with his presence, but ain't that what big wigs do? Get in each others faces and make a scene? That's what would happen on our soap opera."

"Guess we'll find out," Ethyl said, pulling out a red sequined jacket. "Momma used to wear this at Christmas, remember? Wonder who they got cleaning the floors with us Martin sisters on vacation for the day?" She held the jacket up to her sister's chest.

"I called Luann, she's coming. We ain't seen in her in a while," Ethyl added. "She wants us to do her another favor."

"Anything for Luann, sister. The old ladies are going to be upset we ain't there today — we're always working and there to greet them," Mary said. "But some things are more important — like saving the hospital."

"Amen to that, sister."

⸻

Dr. Akil Massari stood in a hallway window on the medical floor, two stories up. He fingered the stethoscope hanging around his neck like worry beads. Being the only Muslim on the medical staff, in fact no doubt, the only Muslim in the 40-miles between Valley View and Charlottesville, it seemed at times that his only protection was being a doctor. Otherwise, he was the first person to be noticed anywhere he went. He even kept his stethoscope on when he drove. He had been pulled over many times by state and local cops who patrolled the area roads. Dr. Massari always dressed better than anyone else and imparted perfect manners in order to be as nonthreatening as possible.

Invariably, the police officer, after running his license and keeping him sitting in his car for 10 or 15 minutes would ask, "So you're a doctor, huh?" — their idea of a compliment.

That would be followed by a free consult.

"So doc, I've been having this problem with a pain in my chest, what do you think it might be?" Dr. Massari found it best to act concerned, ask several background questions and then use his stethoscope as much as possible, which ironically put him within easy reach of the cop's gun. He would then ask who the policeman's doctor might be and urge that an appointment be sought immediately. He had come to know many of the region's law enforcement at traffic stops. Never once had he been ticketed.

The Ascend Medical Center Outpatient Center was pulsating, no longer an abstract notion. Leo had asked Dr. Massari to go with him to the open house in the middle of the afternoon. Akil was concerned for Leo. A doctor always had a job, even the bad ones. But hospital administrators came and went — the average tenure was less than five years. Time and time again, Dr. Massari watched Leo do what was right, in the face of corrupt intent and actions.

The doctor had long operated successfully under the pay-to-play cronyism in his own country before he could make his escape to America to complete his medical fellowship training. He knew the consequences when someone bucked the system, even someone like Leo. It was refreshing to see a leader put the mission of the organization first, but he knew that the most aggressive competitors in the hospital food chain would see anyone who was transparent like Leo as weak. It was often said of Leo he was a nice guy — too nice to be in charge. Akil had seen some mean people in charge in his time, both in Egypt and in America. He did not see it as an advantage, but then, what did he know? He was a man of the world who was not from around Valley View.

"What you doing, doc? Checking out the competition?" It was Linda Murphy, the house supervisor. She stood next to him, arms folded.

"I was thinking that they have a lot of cameras on that building," Dr. Akil said. "Why does a building that's not open 24/7 need so many cameras? Count them for yourself," he told her. Linda pointed with her finger.

"One, two, three, four, five…and that's only in the front of the building," she said

"Why so many?" he asked again.

"I don't know, doc — maybe they want a lot of pictures of us crying our eyes out," she said, bumping him shoulder to shoulder. He smiled.

"Well, they won't need a camera for that, Leo and I will be dropping by in a little while."

"My best advice, doctor, is to fake it until you make it," advised Linda.

"I've never had that luxury," Akil said, not unkindly. "The only choice for me is to always to make it, Linda." She turned, looking up at him.

"I'm really glad you're here," she said to him. "I think we're going to be good as long as people like you and Leo are here. For the first time in a long while I look forward to coming to work. That's got to be worth something, right?"

"I would like to think so, Linda, but we'll see," Dr. Massari said, still looking at the cameras.

The open house was scheduled from 2-6 p.m., with the official ribbon cutting scheduled for 5:00. The owners were circulating in the crowd. They would pay special attention to the referring doctors who attended the open house. Each would be offered wine or beer and then be given a tour of the new operating rooms and radiology department. They would end up in the art gallery with a vast spread of food and more drinks. A few wives of the physician-owners would be on hand to talk about the art hanging on the walls in another tour around the lobby. The building looked great, exactly the kind of place where a patient would want to be cut, injected or x-rayed.

Royce stood with Dr. Divinity, munching on a plate of expensive food; buffalo burger sliders, mushroom caps, and caviar were heaped on his small appetizer plate. Dr. Divinity was not eating and not talking. He stood staring straight ahead at the entrance with his usual sleepy half grin, waiting to see if Leo Miller would show. Virginia Stowe was also at the front entrance, pacing back and forth in front of the doors. She had already greeted a radio reporter from the local station and another reporter from the Charlottesville newspaper. It was not lost on her that Luann Zahn was likely to show up. If she did, Royce was to retreat through a nearby secure door upon her signal.

Outside, the Martin sisters pulled into the parking lot and slowed.

"Wow, I don't see any parking places," Mary said. They could see men and women in business suits streaming across the street from the Valley View Hospital parking lot.

"That don't hardly seem right," Mary said, getting upset. "That's not right at all — using the hospital parking lot to visit the enemy — them people ought to know better."

"They know sister, they just don't care," Ethyl told her. "Remember, we're parking around back any way — these people won't park there." She was right — they pulled into a space right next to the loading dock. The sisters entered the back door using their new employee cards. Before it closed down, Ethyl pulled a small stone out of her purse and stuck it in the bottom corner of the doorway.

The lobby was packed, but Royce could still see Virginia in the foyer, checking the crowd. She was so focused looking for Luann Zahn that she didn't notice Ace Fury and Dr. Denise DeLuca walk past her and disappear into the crowd.

The Ascend Medical Center Outpatient Surgery Center breathed great gulps of guests in and out for hours. A low hum intensified though the afternoon from guests arriving and leaving. Jayne had buzzed Leo twice but this time she walked down the hall and tapped on his door before she opened it.

"Leo, Dr. Massari has called down three times asking when you want to go over to the open house," she said. Leo was standing in front of his window. "It's getting late Leo, they'll be closing up in another hour," she added gently.

"Thank you, Jayne. Ask Dr. Massari to come down in 20 minutes and we'll go over."

The sisters stood in a corner, behind the serving table, nibbling and watching. No one looked their way, much less spoke to them. Per Mary's prediction, shrimp was on the menu. She was slowly filling up the plastic bag, slipping the shrimp in on the ice pack in the bottom of her large purse.

"These are the biggest shrimp I've ever seen," Mary said to her sister, leaning in close to be heard over the roar of the place. Mary elbowed her sister frantically.

"Look, look," she whispered. Ethyl stopped in mid-bite, the shrimp hanging in mid-air like a pink flare. In the center of the room Royce Wexler was greeting a long line of guests balancing food and cocktails. Two round men in nice suits with flashes of bright silver hair stood slightly behind him, looking bored and checking their watches. And behind them was the anti-Christ herself, Dr. Denise DeLuca. Her hair was longer and highlighted. She was smiling broadly behind sunglasses. Ethyl continued to stand with the shrimp held aloft, her mouth open. Dr. DeLuca arched her eyebrows and gave a little wave to the sisters.

"Look sister — it's that mean boyfriend of hers," Ethyl said, finally dropping her shrimp into the purse. They looked at each other, scarcely breathing.

"This is going to be good," Ethyl predicted.

"Look at her boobies!" exclaimed her sister.

Ace Fury was enjoying himself, talking at the Wallace cousins who were becoming increasingly annoyed with his prattle.

"I was a manager on this project," he said. "I handled the plumbing and dry wall work — I'm the guy who covered up all the mistakes," he said chuckling, nudging Jim Wallace. "If you need something covered up, I'm your man."

Ace had made a lot of money off the project, padding his charges with impunity. He was in a good mood.

"Who are you?" Jim Wallace demanded. "And why in the hell are you yacking at me?" His eyes widened at the transformation that swept over Ace Fury's face, from buffoon to menace.

"I'm also the guy that made your biggest problem go away — Dr. Denise DeLuca," he said glaring now. "So show some respect."

Ace and Denise had made-up, as they both knew they were destined. Co-dependence offers so much wiggle room for rationalization. They had traveled to Mexico for her extensive cosmetic surgery. This effectively kept her out of sight for a few months, frustrating everyone from the state of Virginia to the half dozen lawyers surrounding the ICU bleeder death. They had attended the grand opening uninvited to present the new and improved Denise DeLuca and to begin lobbying for her good referral from the hospital for her next job in medicine.

Royce Wexler moved up, grabbed Ace at the elbow, using his height to easily drape his arm over Ace's shoulder and clamped on.

"Jim Wallace, meet Ace Fury. He was the dry wall contractor on the project," Royce said.

"And plumbing," Ace added.

"Yeah, so I heard," Jim Wallace growled, still not impressed. "Why the fuck are you talking about DeLuca disappearing?" he said. Royce involuntarily let loose of Ace. "What?" he managed to say. Ace smirked.

"Well Royce, you told me to get rid of her, remember?"

"I remember you," Wallace said. "You're her boyfriend.

Shiiiit — you two deserve each other." Robert stepped into
the conversation.

"You guys are making a bit of a ruckus, and you shouldn't be doing
that," he said, looking around.

"What's he mean you told him to get rid of DeLuca?" Jim said.
Royce smiled broadly, his eyes in a panic.

"No, no — ha, that was a misunderstanding," he said, waving his
hands in front of him. "Ace, we discussed this. I did not tell you to
do any harm to Dr. DeLuca," he protested. Ace snarled at the three of
them and held that look for effect. Then he started laughing.

"Ha — I'm just fucking with you, she's OK," Ace said, enormously
pleased with himself. He reached through a few people standing off
to his side and pulled on an arm and presented Denise DeLuca: fifty
pounds lighter, lots of make-up, new hair style and more curves. She
looked like someone else. Robert squinted — she seemed to have had
breast implants, which peaked out over the top of a blouse with the
three top buttons undone. Royce was so relieved to see her alive, he
reached out and gave her a hug. Denise whispered in his ear.

"Did you really try to get Ace to kill me?" she asked for fun. Royce
felt her bosom boring into him and was flustered that he noticed. He
pushed her back at arms length.

"You and Ace are such kidders," he said laughing to show the Wallace cousins it was all a good joke.

Ten feet away behind the locked access door with tinted glass,
Luann spoke to Dusty in a hushed, excited voice.

"Are you getting all this?"

"In living color, boss," he grunted. "Man, she looks good."

"First you're hitting on me and now Denise DeLuca — we need to
find you a girlfriend," Luann said, loving the day and blessing the
Martin sisters for propping the back door open.

At the buffet table, the Martin sisters were in a trance, watching
the scene unfold. They were both working on the shrimp bowl, pausing for long moments in mid-bite. They continued to put every other
shrimp into the purse, being careful not to dip into the cocktail sauce.
Ethyl realized that they had drawn the attention of the catering man-

ager, who had already cast a few looks their way. The event crashers always went for the shrimp — it was a well-known fact in the catering world. Ethyl nudged her sister.

"Come-on, we got a boss headed our way," she said as they ske-daddled arm-in-arm to the far end of the serving table and around the corner to the restrooms. There was a long line at both the women's and men's restrooms, so they kept walking to the end of the hallway. The catering manager called to them.

"Excuse me," he called to the sisters. "Excuse me. I need a word please."

They came to the staff bathroom, stepped in and locked the door.

"Give me the purse sister, we got to get rid of the evidence," Ethyl said. Mary didn't argue. They should have left sooner, but it was worth it to see Dr. DeLuca.

"Didn't she look good — so different," Mary whispered as Ethyl dug out handfuls of boiled shrimp and flushed them down the com-mode. After a few flushes there was a loud knock at the door; Eth-yl worker faster.

"Did you see her boobies?" Mary repeated. This was turning into the most exciting day in years for the sisters.

"I know. She looks like she could be on our soap opera. And not as one of the good girls either," Ethyl replied. The knocking continued.

Ethyl threw the plastic bag in the trashcan and washed her hands.

"Are you ready?" she said. Mary nodded. They opened the door to the catering manager who looked upset.

"Young man — this is the ladies room. I think you are confused," Ethyl said calmly.

"You both wait," he commanded. He stepped in to find one lone shrimp floating in the toilet bowl, which he plucked out. The catering manager flipped through the trashcan and found the salty, fragrant storage bag, which he held over his head in triumph. He stepped into the hallway again. But by then the Martin sisters, who could move fast for a couple of old gals, were long gone.

In the lobby, Ace was satisfied that the Wallace cousins were now suitably concerned. Royce was damn near terrified, babbling and sweating profusely as many of the guests stopped to congratulate him on the opening of the building.

Meanwhile, Royce kept his back to Dr. DeLuca, using his large frame to block her line of sight while he frantically tried to get Virginia Stowe's attention, who was with a reporter from the Richmond newspaper. He needed a security guard to escort these misfits from the premises before the entire occasion blew up in his face. But he couldn't recall if they had hired security guards. Dr. DeLuca was chatting up the cousins, explaining things — many things — none of which were her fault. The conversation was animated between the Wallace cousins leaning in to lecture DeLuca, and Ace circling to keep things stirred up.

This weird dysfunctional Kabuki dance had been going on for 10 minutes — Dusty had already had to switch out the videotape.

"Damn, I wish we had some audio on them," Dusty said. Luann patted him between the shoulders.

"Just keep shooting, Dusty. The Martin sisters were close enough to hear what was going on. Between them and our keen instincts, we'll figure it out."

Then, pretty close to the timeline Jesús Sanchez had calculated, it happened. At that moment everyone in the viewfinder seemed to freeze. A collective gasp echoed through the lobby. It gave Dusty pause. He dropped the camera to peer through the glass.

"What's wrong?" Luann asked.

"I don't know — look," Dusty said, as she stepped in beside him to look into the Lobby. Every single person was in mid-grimace, stock still, swiveling at the neck and looking around in a panic.

"Roll, roll," Luann said, pushing the camera back up. People in the lobby began surging towards the front door. "What the hell is going on?" Luann asked, cracking the door open to get a better view.

The smell assaulted her, rolled over her like a disaster movie. She started to gag. She had been in porta-potties deep into a weekend music festival that smelled better.

Dusty tried to breathe only through his nose. The stench entered his pores and throttled his body.

"Keep rolling, keep rolling," Luann said, holding the door open for Dusty. No one was paying attention to a camera on the premises. The guests were pushing and shoving to get out. Royce stood bewildered, a napkin clamped over his nose. When he tried to talk, he wretched.

"Go, go Dusty, follow them out front," she said, turning back into the hallway. She held the door open.

"Where are you going?" he managed to ask, still filming.

"I'll meet you out front," she yelled, pulling the door shut behind her. She moved down the hall into a small room she had noted when they arrived. It was a room filled with small television monitors, each hooked to a videotape machine hanging from the ceiling. She hit the eject buttons on the machines labeled "Main Entrance High" and "Main Entrance Low" and replaced each with a blank tape from a new box. She pulled off the record tab protector on each VCR tape before she jammed them into the machine. She flipped open her cell phone and dialed the station as she headed for the back door, stuffing the tapes into her bag.

"It's Luann. I need 10 minutes tonight. Don't worry, it'll be good."

It took Ace a few moments to figure out what was going on. He had no sense of smell, which accounted for the fact that he'd never been interested in food. He ate when his stomach growled. Denise on the other hand, had a hyper sense of smell. One moment she was looking like her new beautiful self and the next her face collapsed in the middle. For a moment, the two Wallace cousins each thought the other had farted and were momentarily amused — and then stunned by the mounting, overpowering odor.

Something was seriously wrong — the smell was horrendous. They started to demand answers but the sewer smell reached in and grabbed the back of their throats. Speech was impossible. Ace grabbed each of the cousins in his strong grip, dragging them towards the door with Denise trailing behind, gripping the tail of his suit jacket. He turned to see Dusty and his camera trailing them.

"Don't you guys ever take a day off?" he asked. Dusty and Luann had dogged them for a couple of weeks after Dr. DeLuca's dramatic confession.

"Covering the grand opening," the cameraman barely managed to say, holding his camera straight down in his arm, tilted up to get a dramatic angle.

"It's not so grand, is it?" Fury responded, laughing mightily at his joke. They were finally through the doors and out front where it still reeked. Hundreds of guests stumbled away. Only Ace appeared untroubled, immune to the odor.

The Wallace cousins had pulled the decorative silk handkerchiefs from their suit pockets to cover their mouths and noses. They had menace in their hearts looking for Royce, who was standing at the curb on the other side of the street in front of Valley View Hospital. He waved tentatively as the Wallace cousins stormed towards him. Jim Wallace took up a position next to Royce and slid his arm around Royce's waist, who flinched. Robert stopped in front of Royce.

"My cousin and I have each invested $200,000 in this project Royce," he said slowly, waving his arm back towards the main entrance of the outpatient center. "What is this?"

"Hello — are you Royce Wexler?" It was Leo Miller and Dr. Massari. Jim Wallace dropped his arm and stepped back. Royce turned, relieved, and put his hand out.

"Yes, yes — how are you?" he said stepping towards Leo.

"I'm Leo Miller, the administrator here at Valley View," he said. "And I believe you know Dr. Akil Massari, our Chief of Staff and Medical Director for our hospitalist program."

"Of course, nice to see you again, Akil. Leo, these are two of my board members, Robert and Jim Wallace." The Wallace cousins grunted and looked impatient. Royce positioned himself as best he could between Leo and the outpatient surgery center, where dozens of people were pulling out of the parking lot en masse in a roar of automotive displeasure.

"I see you got my invitation," he said, the only thing he could think of to say.

"Well, no, I don't recall seeing an invitation. But Dr. Massari and I thought we would walk over for a tour any way." Leo and Akil had seen the mass, panicked exodus from the building. The rotten smell of sewer gas was strong in the air.

"Oh yes", Royce said a little too loudly. "We just finished up and my Board members and I are headed out. Perhaps I could give you a tour another day?"

"What is that smell?" Dr. Massari asked.

Royce gave a sniff. "Wow — someone has a sewer odor problem," he said.

"Have you checked with your engineering department, Royce?" Leo smiled broadly.

"No, but I'll be sure to do that."

"Well, nice meeting you, Leo," Royce said, ignoring Dr. Massari. He and the Wallace cousins headed back across the street to the out-patient parking lot where Royce's Mercedes was the only car left in the parking lot. The Wallace cousins covered their noses again.

Leo and Akil made sure to watch them until they pulled out of the parking lot, waving as they drove by.

"I don't understand." Dr. Massari said. "Does he not know that terrible smell is emanating from his building?"

"Yeah, he knows my friend. He is in serious denial, I think."

"There is no denying that smell," Dr. Massari said, waving his hand in front of his face. Leo suddenly felt cheerful.

"Smells like his new building has a problem," he said, unable to stop the smile blossoming across his face.

"Hola, Mr. Miller." Leo and Akil turned. Jesús Sanchez was sitting in his truck, the window down. There was something about his demeanor that was different — an aura of satisfaction.

"Dr. Massari, I'd like you to meet Jesús Sanchez, who is the uncle of my administrative assistant Jayne. He worked on the building. He's deaf, so be sure to look at him when you speak."

"How do you do," Dr. Massari said, offering a handshake, which was accepted. "What kind of work do you do?"

"Drywall," said Jesús, smiling. At that moment, Leo had a shocking epiphany.

"And he knows enough about plumbing to be dangerous," said Leo as their conversation of several months ago came into sharp replay. Jesús smiled slightly, waving a finger from the top of the steering wheel vaguely in the direction of the outpatient surgery center.

"You remember I said that, good, Leo," said Jesús. "This seems a very serious problem. They will need to know where to look to fix it."

"I understand what you are saying," Leo said. "We'll talk again soon."

As he and Dr. Massari walked back to the hospital, Dr. Massari spoke.

"I feel as though Mr. Sanchez and you were having a conversation I didn't quite understand. Is this another management lesson of which I need to be aware?"

Leo clamped the doctor around the shoulders. "Yes, Akil," Leo answered. "Your life is an open book and you never know who is reading. So be respectful to everyone."

CHAPTER
Conclusion
SEVENTEEN

Luann's report that evening on the six o'clock news was, as she promised her news director, a good one. There was just something about people running in a panic from a building that spiced up any television news report. The video featured the footage Dusty had shot from ground level of the open house, and showed guests fleeing from the rancid smell as if it had hide and teeth, nipping at their behinds. But the video tapes Luann had pulled from the surgery center's extensive video surveillance system showed a river of panicked people spilling through the front doors, a flash flood of humanity with their noses wrinkled up and twitching, some actually sick to their stomachs, which were full from the good food and drink of the grand opening.

But that wasn't even the best part. The images of Royce Wexler — in what seemed intimate discussion with Denise DeLuca and Ace Fury — jumped the entire wretched saga of the rogue doctor back into national news. Speculation about her long disappearance — only to resurface at the grand opening with a new figure, bigger lips and higher cheek bones, being escorted by her bad guy boyfriend — created a whole new audience from the Hollywood news programs.

Dr. DeLuca was now an even bigger celebrity than when Flip Jensen ran away from the hospital. The usual cast of characters lined up to condemn or support her. A conspiracy theory emerged that the once dowdy physician was a victim of a corporate medicine plot to discredit her bravery in standing up to the Federal Food and Drug Administration and their unreasonable approval requirements for new drug therapies. The fact that she was a sociopath who just happened to hold a medical degree was just too scary to contemplate by almost everyone except for those who knew her best.

Luann would remain at the Charlottesville Eyewitness Action News station for another three months before making her move with Dr. Ippolito and Dusty to the much bigger San Francisco market.

At the surgery center, every time the owners tried to open the building for patients, the foul smell emerged from its lair deep inside the sewage pipes to smite any remedy attempts. For months, the engineers hired by the construction company tried to find the problem. They drilled holes, rerouted vent pipes, ran robot scopes down the main lines to look around and yelled at the town engineer, claiming his inspection on the tap-in to the municipal junction box was flawed. The city dug up the line, found everything in order and sent Royce the bill. After 90 days and no income to service the loans they had taken to finance their buy-ins as owners, the six physician owners and the two Wallace cousins sued Ascend Medical Corporation for breach of contract. The corporate CEO at Ascend asked the Wallace cousins to resign from the Board. They refused, so Ascend had its sizable legal department remove the two. In true Wallace family form, they then sued Ascend Medical Corporation for defamation. There was no revenge better than making everyone involved pay for lawyers.

Leo waited several months before he put in a bid to buy the empty outpatient surgery building from Ascend Medical Center — for pennies on the dollar — before he spoke to Jesús Sanchez again. He found Jesús at his niece's desk one day after their weekly lunch when Leo asked if he had a minute. They sat down at the table in Leo's office.

"Jesús, I have put in a bid to buy the building from Ascend Medical Center. If they agree — and I think they will — I have two choices.

Tear the building down or try to succeed in locating the source of the odor, which of course, no experts hired by Ascend have been able to figure out." Leo looked directly at Jesús and spoke slowly, "You worked on the building — what do you think?"

"I think it would be a shame to tear down such a beautiful building Leo," Jesús said.

"When you were working on the building did you see anything that might explain the problem?" Leo queried.

"I don't hear at all Leo, which makes some people — especially employers — think I am stupid. But I see just fine and I always know what's going on. I know what this problem is, Leo." Jesús recalled in detail the hidden sewer loop line he had run from a few of the vent pipes into the duct work for the central cooling and heating system. He had carefully disguised the evidence when he dry walled the area. "I'll fix it for you and it won't take long or much renovation," Jesús assured.

There are no secrets in a hospital. A few days later the Martin sisters, in a bit of panic after so many months had passed, pulled Leo into an empty patient room while he was up on the floor making his rounds. They closed the door and motioned Leo to the corner by the window. Mary switched on the television set in the room, turning it up loud.

"Leo — we know what's wrong with the building," Ethyl said quietly, standing close to Leo so she could speak directly into his ear.

"That's cause we broke it," Mary added in the other ear. Leo suppressed a smile.

"What happened?" he asked.

"We got an invitation to the open house on account of we were hired to do the cleaning," Ethyl said, leaving out the part about finding the invite in Leo's assistant's trash can. She went on to give the details of their stake-out at the buffet table and her sister's love of shrimp.

"We don't buy shrimp much," Ethyl said, "cause it's so expensive." Leo made a mental note to review the pay scale for the housekeepers.

"So we stood in the corner, watching all the fancy people and packing some leftovers to take home," she added.

"The only problem is we got so caught up watching Dr. DeLuca and that boyfriend of hers, we lost track of how much shrimp I was putting in my purse," Mary said.

"Yeah, we panicked when the guy in charge of the food started giving us the stink eye — you can tell a lot about people from their eyes — and we had to make a fast get away to the lady's room," Ethyl explained. "It took us a few minutes to flush all that shrimp down the toilet to get rid of the evidence."

"How much shrimp was in that purse?" Leo asked.

"It's a big purse Leo," Mary answered. "We got two little dogs and I've use it to carry them around in."

Now Leo laughed. "So how much do those pups weigh?"

This reference point gave the sisters pause.

"Oh my gosh, Leo, we never looked at it that way. Our pugs weigh about 40 pounds between them," Ethyl said. "And that purse was about half full."

Leo laughed some more. "You ladies flushed 20 pounds of shrimp down the toilet?"

"Yeah, I guess we did. We didn't know it would make such a stink for so long," Mary said. "We're really sorry. But we've been too scared to tell anyone."

"Well, this is good to know — very good to know. I'm glad you told me this," Leo said. "Let's keep this to ourselves, OK? No one else needs to know."

"So we ain't fired?" Ethyl asked.

"Only if you don't turn that TV down," Leo said.

When he returned to his office, he asked Jayne to arrange to have fresh shrimp delivered to the Martin's home.

"You don't want to know," Leo assured her in response to her raised eyebrows.

Evil plots sometimes work out for the best.

Cricket got her wish — she married a doctor. After he declined to accept Cricket as a patient and she was established with a new doctor for six months, Dr. Forrest — who had thought of her every day — asked her out for reasons he didn't understand. Cricket, with great insight, accepted his calls after six months, especially as the doctor was careful to explain to her the rules governing such doctor-patient liaisons. It had been so long since he had been with a woman — he had buried himself in work since his last marriage — it was he who cried on their wedding night from such surprising and powerful emotions, even though Cricket was the virgin. She found this very endearing, a good way to start off a marriage. He was good-looking and a good man who paid to get her daddy, So-Sammy, through rehab. After a few months, she finally told "the doctor", as she called him, about the Wallace cousins arranging that first visit to him.

"That was a lot of money they wanted to give you to get into my trousers," he teased her.

"Don't flatter yourself, Doctor Forrest," she said. "My assignment was just to get you to act inappropriately. I was never that kind of girl until I got married." She smiled looking down at him, brushing her breasts across his face.

"That aunt refused to sign the new will they brought her. They thought they had her figured out, she told me. Turns out she didn't much like those boys either. Spoiled and mean their whole lives — oh my, that's very nice," he groaned a little bit. His hair was mussed and he was wearing only his white lab coat, his name spelled out across the right breast pocket.

"That old aunt wasn't as helpless as she let on. She ended up hiring Camilla Bonfield as her personal assistant and I think that lovely woman is going to do very fine in the aunt's will — I made sure of it with those new lawyers I found for her in Richmond. And I'm — I mean the hospital — is still going to get a new cardiac cath lab."

The look Cricket gave her new husband made his stomach zing. "Am I hearing you right — you're talking about some other woman — now?" She scooted higher; pillow talk aroused her. "OK, doctor, get busy," she ordered.

So-Sammy, cleaned up, went back to Gregor's to work for Owen. He had always believed in Cricket's plan to marry a doctor, but even he was surprised when she landed a specialist. It had taken nearly six months to get free of the pills, along with help from a neurologist and a surgeon to clean out scar tissue from his old football kicking injury. It felt good to get back in a garage, the smell of grease triggering powerful and fine memories. But he hadn't figured on Devine Brown, Owen's partner. There was no time for slacking off on a whim or booting a football around out back like the old days.

While Devine kept the vehicles rolling through the bays, Owen made them repeat customers. He always was a great mechanic — even before all the new diagnostic testing equipment began appearing in repair shops. But he could also fix older cars, so his reputation grew. Devine made sure that their charges were 20 percent lower than anyone else in town, and as a result they were booked out weeks in advance. There was plenty of time to gradually raise rates. And the customers liked the hotel-like waiting room. Devine's vision was definitely paying off.

Something wonderful clicked between Owen and Felicia, now his wife, just in the nick of time. They were two sun flares together — each the other's missing element. If they would ever be tempted to disappoint each other, they certainly now would never want to disappoint Devine.

Devine knew she had three former pill poppers in her charge and she kept an eye out. She got all three of them to join her predominantly black Baptist church, which was slowly integrating. It was one thing to disappoint yourself or your spouse, it was another to disappoint your church. It was a strategy that did not work for everyone, but looking down at the bottom of an empty Percocet bottle was a moment ripe for religious insight. Clear-headed for the first time in years, So-Sammy, Felicia and Owen found they could rise to the occasion every day.

———

Warren Harris kept his wife alive for almost four more years. The two were featured in a newspaper article about May-December romances that inspired several young women to make open marriage proposals to Warren, good when his wife passed. She helped Warren sort through the proposals, helping him rank the best matches. It was her idea, she actually insisted.

"Warren, darling, you've been a good husband and I love you — you know that," his wife told him. "But there is nothing gained by you being lonely. Besides, you have become accustomed to a certain level of physical intimacy. You're too young to give that up," she said giving his bottom a squeeze. After she passed, he went on to marry to a younger woman who made him happy for another 22 years. On his deathbed, he would give her the same directive — marry again.

Warren so successfully carried out Dr. Massari's care instructions, that Valley View Hospital eventually became a national model for its home care program. When new government hospital payment standards, laws governing hospital physician financial arrangements, and the Affordable Care Act were established over the next 15 years, it unwound the country club atmosphere between hospital administrators and physicians. Valley View was well ahead of the curve. When their colleagues at the University of Virginia Medical Center asked for their advice, Leo and Dr. Massari formed their own consulting company to help other hospitals implement the new world of population health management and value based purchasing.

———

It took the new Director of Engineering that Leo hired about a week to find Dr. Divinity's network of hidden cameras. The new man installed his own set of cameras to record the coming and goings of

Dr. Divinity. The new director was of the breed who grew up on computers and he was able to hack into the computer where Dr. Divinity stored files of particular interest. Among these files was the missing footage of the break-in to the administrative offices. Leo was surprise to realize it was his former CFO who broke into his office, not Dr. Divinity. But it was too late for that truth. Leo called Dr. Divinity to his office, once again with Dr. Massari as a witness. Dr. Divinity arrived with his irreverent attitude.

"I believe these are yours," Leo said, dumping out a boxful of fish-eye cameras on his conference table.

"No, I've never seen those," Dr. Divinity replied, all grins. "What are they?" Leo reached into the pile of cameras and pulled out a videotape.

"We have a new engineering director, a clever fellow who's even smarter than you, Dr. Divinity. He tapped into your own cameras and put up a few of his own," Leo said. "He's got some very fine images of you operating your spy network."

Even when alone, Leo could not help noticing the always-present smile, as if Dr. Divinity was reveling in how much smarter he was than the rest of the world. Leo stepped over to his desk, picked up a folder, and set it in front of Dr. Divinity.

"That's your resignation from the medical staff and your surrender of your medical privileges. Sign both please, one for you and one for me."

"I'm not signing anything," Dr. Divinity said.

"Then I'll be turning over this evidence to the state police for violation of state wiretapping laws," Leo said calmly. Dr. Divinity snorted.

"Wiretapping only applies to audio recordings, Mr. CEO, those are video cameras." Now it was Leo's turn to smile.

"Those cameras also have an audio track, doctor. I'm surprised you didn't know that, I mean you being such a smart guy and everything." Leo couldn't resist rubbing it in a bit. Dr. Massari lifted his hand to scratch his face — and concealed a small laugh. Dr. Divinity's smirk retreated.

"Doctor, what would be smart is for you to resign, think about what you learned from all of this and start over at another hospital that needs a good radiologist," Leo offered. Despite his criminal tendencies, Leo had to admit that Dr. Divinity was a good radiologist.

"I hear that you are looking to buy the outpatient building across the street," Dr. Divinity said. "How about if you make me whole on my investment — we sign an agreement about that — and then I'll resign my privileges," Dr. Divinity offered. Leo leaned back in his chair, stretching his legs out in front of him. He really wanted this guy gone.

"I hear that you and the other owners are suing Ascend Hospital Corporation for breach of contract related to the outpatient surgery center. I think that's a good plan, doctor. My prediction is that you'll probably do better sticking with that plan, rather than asking me to fix the problem for you."

Dr. Divinity looked at Leo as though he was seeing him for the first time.

"I suppose it's better to live to fight another day," he replied. The doctor leaned forward and signed his resignation letters.

Leo was right-on with his prediction. The corporate masters at Ascend Healthcare knew a losing hand when they saw one — it was not the first time the optimism of numbers predicting profit for a new service had failed to deliver. The settlement with the owners, led by Robert Wallace, netted back the original investment plus 20 percent of the projected three-year profits. Combined with the money it also paid to settle the lawsuit for the wrongful bleeding death in the ICU, Ascend paid out a sum equal to all the profits Royce Wexler had made in his entire tenure as CEO of the hospital. All the scheming, backbiting, abuse and failure to hold people accountable for their actions amounted, in the end, to zero of the financial success that was so prevalent in the company's values.

In the decade to follow, Ascend's reputation would plummet, leaving all of its hospitals unprepared for the coming of the Affordable Care Act and its merciless focus on quality, outcomes and patient satisfaction. When finance is the tail that wags the dog, a hospital achieves neither profits nor clinical competency. The company only managed to survive with the hiring of an entirely new executive team.

Of course by then, Royce Wexler was long gone. He and his then
new CFO Marianne Quarters, formerly of Valley View, were dismissed three months after she started at Ascend Medical Center.
With no good references, Quarters was finally able find a position as
a comptroller in an assisted living facility after 18 months of being
unemployed. She made a third of her former salary.

———

Stella Cooper, the CNO at Ascend, resigned right after the failure
of the outpatient surgery center opening to become the new Chief
Nursing Officer at Valley View Hospital, working for Leo Miller.
Royce Wexler, wrapped up in all his intrigue, did not see that one
coming. Throughout his career, many of the senior executives who reported to him had expressed frustration over compromising their values, but none had ever actually done anything about it. Just about the
time their personal doubts were reaching a crisis, they would receive
their performance bonus checks for tens of thousands of dollars. This
would keep them going for another year. Stella had taken her check,
resigned and gone to work for Leo Miller — who could not offer her
as much money. But he welcomed her into a work place culture where
she felt inspired about what she was doing every day.

Royce was reflecting about this turn of events while seated in a
doctor's waiting room. He was also thinking about his new Mercedes,
which he had sold to Jim Wallace for a third less than he paid for it.
But he needed the money. His wife had filed for divorce.

A nurse escorted him into the doctor's office, a doctor who Royce
had helped through several delicate difficulties in the past. This
guy owed Royce.

Once they were both settled, the doctor squirmed in a way familiar
to Royce — a prelude to a conversation that the doctor did not want
to have. Royce Wexler stared in astonishment as the words "advanced
prostate cancer" came out of the doctor's mouth. His best — and
only hope, really — was radioactive seed implant therapy. "What
type of medical insurance do you have?" the doctor asked. "The

better programs are out of state but I can get you in immediately." Royce heard no more.

He was 63 — two years shy of being eligible for Medicare. For the first time in his life, Royce had no health insurance. If he waited until he was eligible for Medicare, the cancer would surely kill him. He had a pre-existing condition and no insurance company would give him coverage for any amount of premium. Royce was also divorced, broke, and under investigation for Stark law violations. He had, in effect, become the exact patient he had spent a good part of his working days devising strategies to deny care.

And Royce was scared — the kind of fear that erupts when a person is sick enough that they think they might die. He opened his mouth to speak, but for the first time in many years, he finally had a clue and was speechless. But, insight could not save him now.

The bright blue sky cradled the central Texas landscape so beautifully that the day could only hold promise. A stage was set-up complete with podium. People milled about everywhere, waiting for the formalities to begin. It was a small community — ranchers mostly. When the administrator of the hospital said he had a big announcement everyone showed up. The news director (and evening disc jockey and sales manager) of the local radio station, as well as the reporter from the regional weekly newspaper, were fussing with microphones at the podium. There was no television station within 100 miles.

Ace Fury smiled conspiratorially with the hospital administrator, a round and sweating man who winked back as he checked in with the Board chairman, a rich rancher named Herb Dawson who had arranged things. He readily accepted Ace's explanation that the doctor's troubles in Virginia was a frame-up by the hospital and the rest of the medical staff, who were resentful of Dr. DeLuca's visions and courage. The rancher chairman got the Texas Medical Board to grant a medical license for the once nationally known physician who was talked about endlessly on all the cable news outlets. She embodied traditional

Texas values he told the Medical Board at a hearing, standing up for local rights in the face of the tyranny of the federal government. He also worked a deal with the local president of the bank to sell them a mansion downtown that was originally built by the rancher's great-grandfather. The former Chief Medical Officer had refinished the mansion to splendid excess, including a walk in sauna, a wine cellar and an indoor swimming pool. The newly married Furys would buy it interest free and pay $450 a month on a 30-year loan.

Ace stretched his legs out and reached over to rub the small of Dr. Fury's back through her white lab coat. The rancher was already half in love with her, Ace could tell. No doubt that would come in handy.

It was no wonder; Denise had truly transformed in a plan to be someone else, at least in appearance. The plastic surgery and liposuction gave her something else to focus on besides the long time burden of being herself. Whatever the reason, the transformation was remarkable. She was tucked in at the waist, protruding high in the front. She had grown her hair out, which she highlighted. But most remarkable was her face: perhaps not beautiful, but with make-up, it was at least striking. The looks she got now were not from people searching for her latest craziness. Now she got "hot, smart, lady doctor" gawks and stares.

Still, none of this made her feel as good as the way things used to be when she was the reigning power in a big hospital ICU. But she was a big dog in a small kennel now, and she planned to make the most of the opportunity. She had not felt good about herself since her rotation on the television talk shows faded out. The dull mask of the painkillers she was now taking helped control her anxiety, but what she needed more than anything was to be back in charge.

The day before, when they had arrived in town, Dr. Fury had gone straight to the hospital where she had assumed the oversight for the care of the three patients in the emergency room. The local family doctor who had been in charge was clearly in over his head. When a nurse had reminded her about gloving-up to stitch a patient, Dr. Fury had used the opportunity to set some boundaries.

"If you want to keep working here, don't you ever correct me again in front of a patient," she had said to the nurse, a 20-year employee, after the patient was discharged. The look in the nurse's eyes was exactly what Dr. Fury needed after nearly a year off from the front line.

The administrator stepped to the microphone and tapped it, which caused everyone in the audience to wince and jerk their heads involuntarily.

"Good morning everyone, I'd like to thank you for taking the time to be here this morning. I have good news to share with you. After a two-year search — and with the intervention of our Board chairman Herb Dawson — I am pleased to announce that Central Texas Plains Hospital has a new Medical Director! And we are not getting just any doctor, we are getting a pulmonary-intensive care specialist and a doctor nationally known for advocating for patient rights in the face of a growing and bloated federal bureaucracy."

The applause to his proven buzzwords was genuine. Many in the crowd rose to their feet; some cheered. It had been some time since the administrator had seemed this pleased with himself.

"But wait — the news gets even better. Our board chairman is so smart, he got us a two-fer!" he joked. There were more cheers and the board chairman removed his white cowboy hat and waved it at the crowd. "It turns out that our new lady doctor has got herself a smart husband who knows a few things about taking care of buildings. He will be joining us as our new Director of Engineering." After more cheers died down, the administrator added a minor footnote. "I want to thank Ronald Myers, who has served as acting Director of Engineering for the past three years. Ronald will transition to the newly created position of Assistant Director of Engineering. Ronald — wave your arm so we can give you a round of applause for a job well done!" A terse looking man in the back row raised his hand slowly. Until right before the ceremony began, he had been unaware that he had been only acting director.

"OK, I'm going to bring our Board chairman up to the microphone now so he can introduce the doctor our community so richly deserves. Let's hear another big round of applause for Herb Dawson!" The crowd dutifully put their hands together. Dawson was the kind of man who would notice any lack of enthusiasm. He was a tall, lanky and confident man in a cowboy hat who knew about horses and cows, and who had recently been elected to his third four-year term on the hospital Board of Directors. He grabbed each side of the podium, pausing for a full ten seconds.

"There's a reason that you and I live here in this part of Texas. We're individuals seeking a community where honest people can speak our minds and live our Christian values without constraint of conventional wisdom." Denise stopped looking around at the crowd and listened intently. These were words that she knew in her heart she deserved to hear.

"For too long we've lacked this kind of conviction in the doctors — and administrators — who we've recruited into this community." The hospital administrator, a local boy who had been selling water softeners a year ago, nodded knowingly. "And ya know — that's on me. You've elected me to this Board for eight years and I've had to learn a thing or two about what kind of people ought to be running this hospital — people who do not get wrapped around the axle of rules and regulations that some liberal in Washington, DC thinks is good for our community."

There were more cheers.

"I stand up before you to tell you — to promise you — that I've got a good feeling about this doctor I'm about to introduce. She shares our values and is just the person to take us to the next level of world-class care. Please join me in welcoming Dr. Denise Fury — although you probably know her better as Dr. Denise DeLuca!"

The doctor strode to the front of the stage, the bright sun lighting up her lab coat pure and brilliant. She stood taking in the applause, a catcall from the back row only making the moment more perfect. She knew now she could get away with anything.

"Thank you the good people of central Texas," Dr. DeLuca began. "Being a cancer survivor helped make me a better doctor. When I was battling cancer, I often found inspiration in the words of Jackie Kennedy, who once said that those who bring sunshine to the lives of others cannot keep it from themselves..."

MAJOR CHARACTER LIST
(in alphabetical order, by setting)

Ascend Medical Center
Camilla Bonfield — Hospital Foundation Director
Stella Cooper — Chief Nursing Officer (CNO)
Denise DeLuca, MD — ICU Medical Director
Harold Fellows — Director of Security
Paul Forrest, MD — Cardiologist
Grace — Royce's Administrative Assistant
Janet Ippolito — ER doctor
Margret Stephenson — ICU Nursing Manager
Virginia "Ginny" Stowe — Media/Public Relations Spokeswoman
Mark Swingle — Patient Relations Representative
Jim Wallace — Board member, CPA
Missy Wallace — Aunt to board members, patient
Robert Wallace — Board member, attorney
Royce Wexler — Chief Executive Officer (CEO)

Valley View General Hospital
Rachael Diller, MD — ER doctor, former Navy doctor
Neil Divinity, MD — Radiologist and Medical Director for outpatient surgery center
Warren Harris — Husband of elderly patient
Flo Johnson — Medical Staff Coordinator
Ethyl Martin — Housekeeper, sister to Mary
Akil Massari, MD - Hospitalist Medical Director and Leo's friend
Mary Martin — Housekeeper, sister to Ethyl
Leo Miller — Chief Executive Officer
Stephanie Mora — Board Chairman
Linda Murphy — House Supervisor
Marianne Quarters — Chief Financial Officer (CFO)
Brittany Sawyer — ER Nurse
Jayne Vargas-Smith — Administrative Assistant
Ben Stall — Chief Nursing Officer (CNO)

Other

Arnie — Owner, Arnie's Bar

Cricket Baynor — So-Sammy's daughter and Dr. Forrest's wife

So-Sammy Baynor — Owen's friend and Cricket's father

Devine Brown — Owen's partner at garage

"Dusty" Chuck Conley — Cameraman

Ace Fury — Dr. DeLuca's boyfriend

Randy Fury — Ace's son

Owen Gregor — Patient, garage owner

Burley Hubiak — EMT, Shades' cousin

"Shades" Raymond Hubiak — EMT

Early Jensen — Flip's father

Flip Jensen — Patient

Myrtle Jensen — Flip's mother

Kenny — CPA, drinking buddy to Luann and Janet

Felicia Monahan — Owen's girlfriend

Harold Rigton — Patient

Marvin Wallace — Investigator for the Wallace cousins

Luann Zahn — TV news reporter

ABOUT THE AUTHOR

J. Willis Mitchell is a retired hospital administrator who has served from sailor to CEO. In 2009, he, along with his senior executive team, was named "Top Leadership Team in Healthcare for Mid-Sized Hospitals" by HealthLeaders Media.

Mitchell holds a BS in mass communications from James Madison University and a MS in communications management from Virginia Commonwealth University. Early in his career he worked briefly as a television news reporter.

He lives and writes on the Western Slope of Colorado where, on most days, his wife Paula loves him more than her horse. Together, they love and enjoy three adult children, spouses, and two granddaughters.

Mitchell can be reached at john@snowpackpr.com